No Moon At Midnight

A Biographical Novel

Gretta Curran Browne

SPI
Seanelle Publications Inc.

With Love
To
My Family

Prologue

~ ~ ~

At his home in Filetto in northern Italy, on this October morning in 1819, Count Ruggero Gamba was surprised to be visited by a priest from Ravenna, Don Gaspare Perelli.

"I have come, Conte, because I think you should know what all Ravenna is saying, what all Venice is saying, and what I cannot believe."

Count Gamba respectfully gestured to an armchair, inviting the priest to sit down, but Don Gaspare declined. "I must return to Ravenna to say Mass at noon. I came only to tell you what they are saying."

"About myself? What can they say about an honourable man such as I?"

"No, Conte, they are saying it about Count Guiccioli, and that is why the young Contessa is no longer in Ravenna."

"Teresa? She is not in Ravenna?" Count Gamba frowned prodigiously. "But she was to return from Venice a month ago. Why has she not returned?"

Don Gaspare lowered his voice to almost a whisper. "They are saying she will never return, because Count Guiccioli has sold her to Mylord Byron for a very large sum of money."

"*Sold* her? That cannot be true. "

Don Gaspare nodded. "I agree. It is hard to believe. Mylord Byron seems too cultivated a young man to enter into such a mercenary bargain. Yet a clerk from the Bologna Bank has confirmed that a large amount of money was transferred to Guiccioli's account."

"How large?"

The priest shrugged. "They are saying one million lira."

"One *million* ... paid to Guiccioli?"

Count Gamba looked like a man on fire. "Go!" he exclaimed furiously, waving his hand in dismissal. "You have said enough! Go and say your Mass. And while you do so – say a prayer for Alessandro Guiccioli that this should not be true."

Don Gaspare Perelli bowed respectfully, but on leaving the palazzo his face wore a slight smile. Only Ruggero Gamba would dare to confront the detestable Count Guiccioli. And if Guiccioli was guilty of the crime, and Count Gamba decided his daughter must be avenged, Don Gaspare was certain that Guiccioli's punishment would be swift.

Ruggero Gamba may be a Count of rank and have the appearance of a genial and respectable gentlemen, which indeed he was, most of the time; but he was also a Carbonaro.

Too vexed and too anxious to ride the fifteen miles to Ravenna, Count Gamba ordered his carriage and directed his driver to go at full speed.

Inside the carriage he fumed. Why had he arranged for Teresina to marry Guiccioli, a man forty years her senior, and twenty years older than himself – why?

Because Guiccioli was suspected of being a traitor to Italy, in league with the Austrian rulers, and he had wanted to place a trusted spy in Guiccioli's house – his daughter, Teresa.

It was something any good Carbonaro would do, but now he realised – bad for a father to do. And what had he got for it in return? Nothing more than confirmation of what he had already suspected.

In the past year of their marriage, all that Teresa had been able to pass on to him was that Guiccioli constantly raged against the Austrian rulers, bellowing for all the household to hear how much he hated them and their government in Rome – protests so loud it was a sure sign that he was one of them, one of their paid spies.

During Napoleon's occupation of Italy, Guiccioli was

known to have been friends with the French; and now he was friends with the Austrians – a man who always went where the smell was sweetest and likely to do him the most good.

And now, it seemed, Guiccioli had focused his greed for money on the young Inglese lord, using Lord Byron's friendship with Teresa to fill his own pockets. But if Guiccioli *had* sold Teresa, he would soon fill his own coffin.

In the garden of his palazzo, Count Guiccioli was enjoying his breakfast on the balcony overlooking the gardens. His table was placed at the side of the long balcony, near to a group of lemon trees below. The citrus fragrance of the lemon trees always awakened him fully, and brought his energy back to life.

He was eating with pleasure, knife and fork in hand, tucking into a plate of roasted chicken strips covered in fried onions, when Count Gamba stepped out to the balcony escorted by a servant.

Guiccioli looked furiously at the servant who had disobeyed his rigid rule – no other person was to be allowed onto the balcony while he was eating his breakfast.

Count Gamba held up his palm. "It is not his fault. I insisted he bring me to you at once."

Guiccioli instantly noticed a certain coolness in Count Gamba's manner, so unlike his usual fake pleasantness whenever they met.

"Ruggero ..." Guiccioli gestured to a vacant chair at the table. "Please join me. Would you like some roasted chicken ... or some coffee?"

"No, nothing, but I will sit."

Count Gamba sat on a chair and then spoke very quietly, for it was normal for servants to be moving about in the gardens below, and they must not hear this.

"Alessandro, do you know what the world is saying about you?"

Alessandro shrugged. "I have always been indifferent

to the opinion of the world."

Count Gamba looked at Guiccioli, his cold blue eyes taking in every detail of Guiccioli's face ... the mottled brown fleshy cheeks, the small eyes the colour of black raisins, but worst of all was the colour of his grey-streaked red hair and the whiskers on his face. Why had he not paid more attention to these features in the past? Was Judas Iscariot not reputed to have had red hair? At least he did so in some of the famous Italian paintings of Christ's *Last Supper* ... Judas the traitor.

"They are saying you have *sold* your wife."

"*Sold?*" Alessandro was so shocked he dropped his knife.

"To the Inglese lord."

"I have not *sold* Teresa to anyone. Who has fabricated this slander?"

"Do you deny that Lord Byron paid you a large sum of money before he took Teresa away?"

"Yes, but it was a *loan*. A loan to be repaid with five-per-cent interest."

"Of one million lira?"

"Of one thousand English pounds. I forget how many lira it came to. But it was only a *loan*?"

If it was a loan, Count Gamba was certain Guiccioli had no intention of ever paying it back; which was a shame, because he liked Lord Byron. He was young and handsome and kind, and he treated Teresa like a princess.

"Why did you allow Teresa to go away with him?"

"Because she begged me, and I with my soft heart *indulged* her, due to her ill health! She said Byron had offered to take her to the lakes at Como where the air was pure and her recovery would be hastened. How could I deny such a request?"

"And yet they are both still in Veneto, nowhere near the lakes of Como. At least, they *were* in Veneto a month ago, in his palazzo at La Mira."

"La Mira? Not Venice?"

Count Gamba could not bear to look at Guiccioli for

one more minute. The man had either not troubled himself to find out anything about Teresa since she had gone, or he was hedging in his answers.

"I do not approve of you allowing my daughter, an inexperienced young woman, to go off alone, and still less, with a young man such as Lord Byron. If you do not go at once to bring her back, I will go and fetch her myself."

Guiccioli had no doubt that Ruggero Gamba would do that.

"No, I will go. I will write to her at Venice and inform her to prepare for my arrival. If she is not at Venice, then someone must be carrying my letters to her at La Mira."

"And if you find she is not there, at La Mira or in Venice, but on a ship to England with Lord Byron; then you know, Alessandro, that Italy will no longer be a big enough country for both of us."

Guiccioli was dumbstruck. He knew what the threat meant. He was also fairly certain that Count Gamba was one of the secret society of the *Carbonari,* and if for some reason he personally could not carry out his threat, it would be done by another Carbonaro in his place.

He affected innocence and ignorance. "Ruggero, we are both Italians, born and bred, so I don't understand why you say this?"

"I say it to make you understand that if you have *sold* my daughter to another man, you will be left with only two choices ... a fast-sailing ship down to the coast of Africa and safety, or the alternative route down to the devil."

PART ONE

Old Friends Come Again

"She (Teresa) was at this time living under the same roof with him at La Mira; and who, with a style of beauty singular in an Italian, being fair-complexioned and delicate, left an impression on my mind during our first meeting, of intelligence and amiableness, and such as all that I have since known or heard of her, has served to confirm."

Thomas Moore

Chapter One

~ ~ ~

Thomas Moore, the Irish poet and long-time friend of Lord Byron, had travelled far; and now he found himself at last outside the gates of Byron's country villa at La Mira.

Opening the front door, Fletcher was astounded to see the Irishman. "Well, by the holy! Is it you, Mr Moore, and here in Italy of all places! Is his lordship expecting you?"

Tom Moore smiled to see Fletcher again, Byron's faithful valet. "No, he is not expecting me, Fletcher."

"Oh no matter, come in, come in. He'll be delighted to see you."

Fletcher found Byron in the garden with Teresa, and he too was astounded. "Moore? He is *here?*"

"Aye. You could have knocked me down with a feather when I saw who it was standing there, but –"

"I have told you about Thomas Moore," Byron said to Teresa. "Come with me, because I would like Moore to meet you."

Tom Moore was somewhat disappointed when Byron entered the drawing-room in the company of a young lady. He had not expected him to have guests. He was, however, still the same Byron whom he had known so well for so long, still smiling with genuine friendship, and still eminently handsome.

Byron shook Moore's hand with delight and a warm welcome; and then introduced him to Teresa. Moore saw that she was very fair and blue-eyed and quite lovely; although she greeted him with some reserve and shyness.

Teresa did her best to make Byron's friend feel very welcome, but their conversation did not go well, due to Moore speaking only English, and Teresa knowing only Italian.

Byron acted as their interpreter, from one to the other, making them both laugh; but it was all very time-consuming. In the end Byron suggested taking Moore over to Venice.

"My little daughter Allegra is out with her nursemaid, so you will have to meet her another time. You have been over to Venice?"

"No, I came here directly from Fusina." Moore smiled. "You were not hard to find, as you are very well known in these parts. Did you know that?"

Byron shrugged. "Everyone is well known in these parts. It's that kind of country."

Teresa was sad that this man, Signor Moore, was now taking Byron away from her – and so soon after she had been rejoicing at the news that Alessandro was allowing her to spend another month here with Byron.

As soon as they had left, she returned to the garden full of despondency and sat down at a table under a tree, her gloom escalating. How hard it was to be in love!

Now Byron would have to spend all his time escorting his friend here and there, showing him places in Venice, in accordance with the tradition of hospitality to visiting friends ... and yet her time left with Byron was so short, only a few more weeks before she would have to return to Ravenna.

Fanny Sylvestrini, her maid and chaperone, came lumbering out to her. "Who is that man, Teresina? Is he English?"

"No, an Irish man, but he has come from England."

"An Irish man? I have seen some other Irish men in Venice. They always wear green cravats."

Fanny plonked herself down in the chair which Byron had vacated, picked a black olive from the bowl on the table, chewed the olive thoughtfully, and then spat out the pit.

"He is not a big man for an Irish man. Most Irish men are big.""

Teresa was not prepared to criticise any of her lover's friends. "He is not tall, but Byron says he has a big heart and is a great poet."

Fanny chewed another olive. "I like men tall like Tita Falceiri, or big and bulky like my Lega Zambelli."

"He is not *your* Lega Zambelli," Teresa countered irritably. "Just because you like him, does not mean he likes you."

"Lega will love me one day," Fanny said with certainty. "I know it, because every night I pray to Saint Jude, the saint who answers all hopeless prayers and makes possible the impossible."

Teresa looked at her with more interest. "Saint Jude? You can ask for anything impossible and he will grant it?"

"*Si*, but only with God's permission. Saint Jude, he was a blood-cousin to Jesus, you know? So why would a father not grant the request of one of His son's favourite relatives?"

"I would like to spend the rest of my life with my Byron," Teresa said wistfully, "but he is married and I am married, and neither of us can get a divorce. My church will not allow it, and his wife will not allow it. So is my dream of spending our lives together possible?"

"Of course." Fanny said. "Everything in life is possible. Why else do we pray?"

~ ~ ~

"She looks very young," Moore said as the gondola cruised over the lagoon.

Byron nodded. "Nineteen. Or maybe she is now twenty, I forget."

"And very fair. It is unusual to meet a blonde Italian."

"Not so much here in northern Italy. They are much fairer than those in the South. But yes, even here, a blonde Italian is not so commonplace."

"And is she the reason why you look better than I have ever seen you look ?"

Byron smiled. "She makes the very air around me feel lighter."

Moore did not smile, foreseeing only complications

and heartbreak for his friend. Byron had a unique talent for always picking the wrong women.

On reaching the Grand Canal, Moore asked if they could stop off at the Hotel Gran Bretagne so that he could book into a room. "Although now it is so late in the season, I'm sure they will have plenty of rooms to spare."

Byron would not hear of it. "You must allow me to accommodate you. There is no need to waste your money at a hotel."

Moore shook his head. "You have your lady with you, and in such a situation, three is a crowd."

"Not at La Mira,. Here in Venice at my palazzo."

Moore stared at him. "You have your own palazzo – here in Venice?"

"On the Grand Canal. You will be able to stand on the balcony and look over Venice and watch all the gondolas cruising up and down – with a view of Saint Mark's Square one way – and the Rialto Bridge the other way. And my Italian servants will not only look after you, they will make a *pet* of you. You won't want to leave."

Tom Moore could not have felt more relieved, for he was in dire financial straits, and not having to pay for a room in an expensive hotel would be a blessing.

They dined at Pellegrino's, out on the terrace; and then sat talking for hours over white wine. Byron had the usual play of humour on his face as they exchanged news, and Moore found himself beginning to laugh at life again.

Finally, Byron became serious. "So Tom, what is it? Something has brought you all the way to Venice, and not just to see me."

"True, my main destination is Rome, but I know no one there, so I was hoping you would come with me?"

Byron was tempted. He had always been so fond of Moore, and loved his dry Irish wit; and, on occasions, his wisdom. Moore was ten years older than he, and in the years gone by, from when he himself was only twenty-four, that wise advice from an older friend had been valuable.

Not that he had always taken the advice – Moore had seriously advised him not marry Annabella Milbanke, considering her "too much of a paragon".

"Rome? No, I could not leave Teresa at La Mira on her own."

"When you were in Switzerland," Tom said. "In my letters to you, did I tell you about Bermuda?"

"Bermuda? No, but I read all your complaints about America, and now America has paid you back and disowned you."

Moore nodded woefully. "I was hoping *Lallah Rook* would sell well there, but the only Indians they are interested in are their own native Indians, not those in India or Persia."

"Also, you have never been to India or Persia to learn their customs and so on. I can only write authentically about those places and people I have seen for myself. Surely it's the only way possible?"

Moore nodded his agreement. "Although I *have* been to Bermuda, and now that place has got me into a devil of a din."

Moore explained his predicament. "You know that any money we may earn from our writing is never a sure thing – well you probably *don't* know because *you* always earn tons – even when the critics slam you."

"Is that my fault?"

"No, but it often makes me boiling jealous. Not of *you,* personally, but of Byron the poet."

"And what has that got to do with Bermuda?"

"A wife and three children," Moore said. "Poetry alone does not provide enough to support them, so I had to look for some other way to earn money. And during drinks one night, I mentioned this to Lord Moira."

"The Irish peer?"

"Yes, and in the way of Irishmen always wishing to help each other, Lord Moira said, 'Oh, I think I can help you there, because I have heard of a munificent post that has just become vacant – Registrar of the Naval Prize Court in Bermuda'."

Moore sipped his wine "He told me that Bermuda has the sweetest climate in the world, but I told him that Bermuda was too damned far away for me. However – 'No, Tommy,' said Moira, 'all you will have to do is go over there for a few weeks, officially take up your position as Registrar of the Naval Prize Court, and then come back. And in return you will earn a handsome yearly sum'."

Byron was frowning, unable to make any sense of it. "How can you officially hold the position and not be there, in Bermuda?"

"By appointing a local deputy to discharge all duties in my place, with the payment of a little bonus of course; and then still collect all the funds accruing to my account in Bermuda, which the bank then sends to England. It's the norm, which former Registrars have been doing for decades."

"It may be the norm, but it's hardly honest. Did you goto Bermuda?"

"Yes, a, beautiful place, but too secluded from the rest of the world for me. So back I came, although I did stay for a few weeks to enjoy the sunshine."

Byron was still puzzled. "I know all employees of the British Government are paid handsomely for doing nothing but spout endless British bull, but what does the Registrar of the Naval Prize Court in Bermuda actually *do?*"

"Very simply, whenever a Navy warship captures an enemy ship – the *prize* taken in the capture – the enemy ship and all its cargo – has to be taken to the nearest Admiralty court, and the Registrar arranges for the ship and its cargo to be sold. He then disburses the profits of the sale between the British Admiralty; the ship's captain and officers; and also the Registrar himself who is entitled to five-per cent of the total."

"No wonder they love war and its profits – racing around trying to catch as many ships as they can."

"It's not as profitable as it sounds, or what I thought," Moore told him, "because *months* can go by without a prize-ship coming in, leaving the Registrar with little to do in his boredom. That is why appointing a local deputy became the norm, and why Registrars went back home and left the deputy to it."

Byron was not impressed. "While collecting a yearly wage from the tax payers?"

"Oh no, didn't I say? – the post carries no salary at all. All money to the Registrar comes from the percentage of the profit from prize-ship sales."

Moore sat back and sighed miserably. "This all happened in 1804, long before I met you. That's probably why I forgot to tell you about it. But now – my Irish luck – the local deputy I left in charge has absconded from Bermuda and run away with all the money. And the Navy are holding *me* to account for it."

"Account? You mean, they are insisting that *you* repay the money?"

"Of course. I'm supposed to be the Registrar, responsible for all proceeds. And if I don't pay it soon, they are threatening criminal charges and placing me in prison."

Byron was shocked at the thought of his friend being locked up in a prison. "How much is due to them?"

"A huge amount – more than I possess – four thousand pounds. It was *six* thousand, but after selling half of our furniture and everything else valuable, I have managed to pay them back two thousand of the total."

"Surely that must have tempered some of their anger?"

"No, it did not satisfy them. They want it all. And now all registrars will be forced to stay in their official locations."

Byron's impulse was to offer some help, but Thomas Moore was not a man to accept anything that hinted of 'charity'. Nevertheless, in an unfortunate circumstance such as this, what were friends for?

"No!" Moore said emphatically. "No, you insult me by

even offering. I did not come to Venice to cadge money from you! I came ..." Moore passed a hand over his tired face, "I came because I needed a break from all the worry, and from Bessy's continual crying. And, well, I always have some cheering-up fun and laughter with you."

He blinked tiredly and looked sorrowfully at Byron. "But that's not going to happen, is it? Because you already have a guest."

"How long do you plan to stay in Venice?"

"A few days, no longer. I'm going to Rome in the hope that I can sell some copyrights of my poetry to an Italian publisher. Do you think that's possible?"

"You'll be lucky. They just pirate all mine without a by-your-leave to me."

Tom's disappointment was crushing. "Then, to quote Shakespeare – 'Write me down as an ass'!"

Byron smiled. "Come, Tom, don't be so hard on yourself. No man can live his life without making mistakes. Am I not proof of that?"

~ ~ ~

Late afternoon brought a letter for Teresa, *post express,* from her husband, Count Guiccioli; informing her to prepare for his arrival in a week to collect her. The journey would take three days, but he had business to do on the way. He had already promised her father that her return to Ravenna was assured. In the meantime, she must leave La Mira and go to the Guiccioli house in Venice and stay there until he arrived.

Teresa went through a maelstrom of emotions before tearfully showing the letter to Fanny Sylvestrini.

Fanny was also devastated, because this would mean the end of her double-pay from both Guiccioli and Byron for her services to Teresa, and neither man knew that the other was also paying.

"Stay here and pretend you did not get his letter," Fanny said. "How can he prove you got it?"

"How can he come in a week when he promised another month in return for the loan?"

"Was the loan from Mylord?"

"Yes."

"And now l'Conte changes the conditions. He has no more honour than a donkey."

"I will have to show the letter to Byron."

"No! No!" Fanny advised. "Mylord is so happy with the coming of his friend from Inghilterra. It would not be fair to give him worries now. We stay at La Mira and say nothing. The letter did not come. You did not receive it – so how can you show it?"

Teresa retired to her bedroom to consider this; finally deciding that she would not show the letter to Byron, not yet ... but she *would* write back to Alessandro, and also to her father, voicing her defiance.

She was tired of being told what to do by those two men – one marrying her off to the other – as if she did not have a mind or heart of her own. Well, she would tell them.

She wrote first to her Papa, and then a similar letter to her husband:

Dear Alessandro ... you will see the letter I wrote to Papa. I am not sorry. I am still at La Mira, a delightful place, where one can very well lead, as I am doing, a retired life, without it being at all tedious. I cannot tell you the attentions of Mylord. He has sent for a pianoforte for me, some music, quantities of books, and then I have his company which is of greater value than them all. If from now onwards I am to compare other men to him, I shall always be very dissatisfied with everyone.

There, now she had told Alessandro the truth, so let him make of it what he will. She was no longer frightened of him.

Chapter Two

~ ~ ~

Stepping from the gondola and walking up the water-steps, Thomas Moore stood on the paved path and stared up at the front of the Palazzo Mocenigo ... it was huge.

"It was originally three large houses turned into one palazzo by a Venetian prince," Byron told him. "You will like it here."

Moore could not help feeling grateful, until he entered the dim marble hall on the ground floor, walking past rooms with open doors where various animals lived like hotel guests and Byron led the way to the grand staircase calling over his shoulder – "Keep clear of the dog"; and a few paces further along, "Take care, or that monkey will fly at you – hoping for a hug."

And on it went, past a menagerie of tame animals no different to all the animals Byron had kept at his home of Newstead Abbey in England.

"This is *their* floor," Byron pointed out, "but they are very amenable to all visitors."

Nevertheless, in his dismay, Moore suggested again that it really might be better for him to stay at the Hotel Gran Bretagne.

"No. I see that you think you will be very uncomfortable here," Byron said, "but you will find that it is not quite so bad as you expect."

Moore followed him up the grand staircase to the apartment destined for him – while throughout Byron was dispatching servants here and there with various orders.

When they reached the door of the apartment on the first floor. it was locked; and the key could not be found. "My keys are at La Mira, and Fletcher holds the others."

"Do the other servants not hold any keys?"

"No, because myself or Fletcher are usually here."

"So what do we do now?"

"The only thing we *can* do," Byron grinned, and then with one of his humorous curses, gave a vicious kick to the door and burst it open.

Thomas Moore walked into an apartment that was like another world. It was not only spacious, elegant and luxurious, it held that aspect of comfort which to the traveller's eye is as welcome as it is rare.

"Oh, this is truly like a palace," Moore said in relief. "And if it were not for that ground floor – "

"These are the rooms I use myself, and in these I mean to establish you. If you want to avoid the animals, harmless and adorable as they are, you can come in and go out through the back way, into the courtyard, and take a gondola from the side canal."

"Oh, that *is* good to know," Moore said with relief, and then wandered through a number of rooms that were luxurious in the extreme – a large library; a dining room; another sitting-room, two bedrooms and two bathrooms, with a small staircase leading up to the next floor which, no doubt, also had more accommodating rooms for visitors.

Returning to the drawing-room, he saw that Byron had opened the doors onto the balcony overlooking the Grand Canal, and Tom wandered out there while Byron was giving instructions in Italian to a group of smiling servants.

Byron joined him on the balcony. "I have sent a note to invite Alexander Scott to come and meet you, so I can put you in his charge when I am not with you. He's a good man, knows Venice well, and he will be happy to have another man who speaks English to gab with."

Tom found it impossible not to feel touched by all this, for in Byron's voice every tone and word spoke kindness and hospitality. Nothing had changed. Byron was still the same as he had always been in England, a true friend.

As he gazed out over Venice, Tom could not help thinking of some lines from his own poem of *Lallah*

Rook –

A friendship that like love is warm;
A love like friendship steady.

The sun was just setting, and it was an evening such as a Romance would have chosen for a first sight of Venice.

Moore's eyes moved up to the pink clouds, saying dreamily. "What strikes me so much about Italian sunsets is that particular rosy hue –"

Byron silenced him in mid-sentence by clapping a hand over his mouth. "Damn it, Tom, don't get *poetical.*"

Three wonderful days in which Thomas Moore was given a complete respite from all his troubles and worries; and every day was spent in the same manner – the mornings with Alexander Scott, devoted to viewing all the treasures of art with which Venice abounds.

The early afternoons, when Byron arrived, were spent riding their horses on the seashore of the island of Lido, when the conversation was such, that Thomas Moore realised he had not laughed so much in years.

But in the evening, after an early dinner, Byron always returned to Teresa at La Mira; leaving Tom to go to the theatre, or the *converzatione* at Madame Benzoni's, with Alexander Scott.

Although in Madame Benzoni's salon it was soon made clear to "Signor Moore" that many people present were very annoyed with both Teresa and Byron. Their liaison had now broken all the rules. A quick fling, a short sexual flirtation, all that was acceptable to the ladies of Venice, but getting hopelessly involved in a *serious* love-affair –

"You really must *scold* your friend Lord Byron," Marina Benzoni said petulantly to Moore. "Until this unfortunate affair with the young Contessa, he had conducted himself so well!"

Tom was puzzled, for Alexander Scott had now told him some of the tales of Byron with Margarita Cogni and other light-hearted flings, so how could that be considered as good conduct in comparison to his relationship with Teresa?

"Because, *this* time," Scott said, "he has committed the Cardinal sin of falling in love with her. That is his main transgression."

"Byron falls in love with all his women," Tom said, "until he falls out of love with them."

"This time it is different," Scott said, "and they all know it. That's why they all *hate* her."

"Hate her? Teresa? Surely that's rather unreasonable. She seemed a perfectly nice young lady to me. So why should they hate her?"

"Because she stole him away from us. Now we rarely see him. And why he would prefer to spend so much time in an old-fashioned town like Ravenna and not here in Venice, is beyond them. They don't wish to blame *him,* so instead they blame her."

For the first time since his arrival, Thomas Moore found himself thinking about Teresa, and feeling quite sorry for her.

"Why do you like him so much?" Teresa asked.

"When I was a boy of sixteen," Byron said, "Thomas Moore was one of my favourite poets. I read every word he wrote, and often wished I could meet him. His *Lallah Rook* may have failed in America, but it was the subject that failed, not the writer. Moore is a great writer. He is Ireland's National Poet, the most famous, and his Irish melodies are sung all over the world."

"When did you meet him?"

"After my book *English Bards* was published, he wrote to me, challenging me to a duel."

"A duel?

Teresa's alarmed expression caused Byron to smile. "Yes, a duel. I was young and angry then, and my book was a satire on all the famous people I wanted to lampoon. Moore thought I had insulted him in the book, and wanted either an apology or a duel to the death."

"Santa Madre!"

"You can't insult the Irish. If you do, they will find some way of killing you in return, either with words or weapons, one way or another."

"Did you fight him?"

"No, when we finally met we instantly liked each other and became the best of friends, and have remained friends ever since. Which reminds me – he is going to Rome in the hope of finding a good Italian publisher. Your brother is in Rome and moves in literary circles. Could you write a letter for Moore to take with him, introducing him to your brother, so he will have someone to contact when he gets there?"

Teresa was glad to do so, and even more glad to learn that Moore was leaving Venice. Time was running out, and she had not yet told Byron about Alessandro's letter.

My dear Pietro, – I wish to introduce you to Signor Thomas Moore. He is on his way to see the wonders of Rome, and I should be gratified and obliged by your acting, as far as you can, as his guide. He is a friend of Lord Byron, and much more accurately acquainted with his history than those who have related it to you. He will accordingly describe to you if you ask him whatever you may please to know about – "that Castle in England where he keeps imprisoned a young and innocent wife, etc." My dear Pietro, whenever you feel inclined to laugh, do send two lines in answer to your sister who loves you, and ever will love you – Teresa.

On this his last evening in Venice, after dinner in the palazzo, Tom Moore was surprised when Byron said he would not be going back to La Mira until later.

"I have something I want to show you ..." Byron said,

going off to the library.

Tom waited, expecting Byron to come back with the rough drafts of his latest epic, asking for his opinion on amendments.

Byron came back carrying in his hand a leather bag, and from it he took out a thick script of foolscap-length paper.

"This," he said, "might be worth something to my publisher, John Murray. Although you, I daresay, would not give sixpence for it."

"What is it?"

"I thought maybe you could sell it to Murray, and then buy it back when that Bermuda business is settled. He could be your pawnbroker in the interim, until you are ready to retrieve it, but in any case, you can have it, it is yours."

Tom asked again, "What is it?"

"My memoirs."

Thomas Moore was dumbstruck. He could only raise his hands in speechless astonishment ... Surely Byron knew that his publisher John Murray would pay thousands for such a document, written in Byron's own hand.

"I spent some time writing these memoirs in Switzerland, so they go up to only 1816, but they do detail the truth of my marriage and its consequences. Mind, there is a condition," he continued. "If you do sell it to Murray for a time or forever, it is thing that cannot be published in my lifetime, and Murray must sign a pledge agreeing to that."

Tom finally found his voice. "I can ... *not* accept this."

"Of course you can. There – it is yours – do whatever you please with it. Now come, the hour is late, and I have something more worthy to show you, something of Venice that you will not have seen before."

Tom was too stunned to go anywhere, but Byron was already heading to the door – "Alexander Scott does not seem to see the things that I instantly see, but I think *you* will, and when you do, keep it in your mind as a memory of Venice."

Thomas Moore was sure the memory of what had just happened – the gift of Byron's own memoirs – could not be surpassed in its wonder and generosity, for he knew this was Byron's way of helping him out of his financial predicament, without any money changing hands.

Byron led him through the dim hall on the ground floor, where all of the animals appeared to be curled up in contented sleep; and then stepping into the gondola, ordered his gondoliers to row them to certain points where Mr Moore could see Venice to its advantage.

The night was hot, so they sat near the prow of the boat, in the open, where Byron smiled and pointed up to the sky.

"The moon is in its fullest splendour," he said, "so this is the very best time to see Venice at night."

The gondola cruised over the water in the silence of the night; and when, some hours later, the gondola returned to the Palazzo Mocenigo to drop Moore off, he went up to the drawing-room and immediately sat down to write in is journal –

Nothing could have been more solemnly beautiful than the whole scene around, and I had, for the first time, the Venice of my dreams before me. All those meaner details which so offend the eye by day were now softened by the moonlight into a sort of visionary indistinctness; and the effect of that silent city of palaces, sleeping as it were, upon the waters, in the bright stillness of the night, was such as could not but affect deeply even the least susceptible imagination.

My companion saw that I was moved by it, and though familiar with the scene himself, seemed to give way, for the moment, to the same strain of feeling. And as we exchanged a few remarks, suggested by that wreck of human glory before us, his voice, habitually so cheerful, sunk into a tone of mournful softness, such as I had rarely before heard from him. This mood, however, was but of the moment; some quick turn of ridicule carried him off into a totally different vein, and at one o'clock in the morning, at the door of his palazzo, we parted, laughing.

Thomas Moore was not laughing now. He stood and walked over to the open doors of the balcony, gazing down at the torch-lit steps at the front of the Palazzo Mocenigo, where Byron had smiled and said farewell – *"for another few years, until we meet again."*

And then he had gone in his gondola, disappearing over the moonlit water into the dark night, back to La Mira and the girl he loved.

Chapter Three

~ ~ ~

It was just after midnight when Byron returned to the house at La Mira.

Teresa was sitting up in her bedroom, waiting for him; rushing to embrace him when he entered her room, so relieved to see him again after such a long day without him. She forgot all about Alessandro's letter, wanting only to know – "Did you think of me even once today?"

"I kissed you a hundred times in my thoughts."

Their initial tenderness sparked into passion as they kissed, and kissed, and kissed.

The white gauze of the mosquito net hung in fine drapes around the bed, the windows open, the smell of starchy-sweet ripe apples coming in from the trees in the garden, the exquisite sensations of love blotting out all thoughts of the future.

The last of the candles had burned out. Moonlight shone into the room through the open curtains that now billowed against a warm breeze as they slept.

It was not until the next morning, after each had bathed and dressed, that Teresa remembered to tell him about the Count's letter.

Byron was not only disappointed, but outraged. "Now that he has cashed the second loan, your time here is suddenly shortened? What kind of a man is he? An unprincipled one, for sure!"

"Then yesterday," Teresa said, "a second letter came from him with a change of instructions. Now I am to go to your Palazzo Mocenigo in Venice and wait for him there. He says he will arrive on the first day of November, and he will stay at your palazzo for two days, if *you* will not mind? And that way, it will show we are all family friends, and this will be the best way to defeat any Venetian gossip."

The first day of November ... in three days? If I had known, I would not have spent so much of my time with Moore. And now, this afternoon, I am obliged to go riding on Lido with Alexander Scott."

"Don't go," Teresa pleaded. "Send him a note saying you are not available."

Byron hesitated, and then shrugged. "No, I must go. He has been looking after Moore every morning, showing him the sights, and taking him to the theatre at night – all just to oblige *me* – so I can't become a snoot with Scott now."

"So ... " Teresa's expression was plaintive, "how long will you be gone?"

"A few hours. I'll make it a short ride and get back as soon as I can."

In the long and sad, restless afternoon, Teresa waited, drifting from the house to the garden and back again, wondering what she could do to prevent being separated from Byron. She would not go back to Ravenna with Alessandro. She would not. To even think of such a thing now was unbearable.

And still the hours dragged by as bleak as her mood. Even the weather had changed now to dark skies and non-stop rain, accompanied by a cold wind. How could anyone ride horses along the seashore in this weather?

On the island of Lido, Byron and Scott had ridden the seven miles away from their gondola when the change in the weather happened suddenly – as if a warm sunny afternoon had abruptly transformed into a Winter's night. The sky had turned black, the rain was torrential, and the winds coming in off the sea were getting rougher and colder by the minute.

They rode at speed back along the shore until they finally reached the gondola, where Byron damned the fact that they had come over from Venice in Scott's gondola instead of his own.

Scott's gondola had no felze – no cabin to shield them

from the wind and rain, and both men were drenched to the skin and freezing cold when they finally disembarked at the Palazzo Mocenigo.

"Look at me," Byron said to his manservant, Tita, "I'm shivering like a girl."

"You cannot go out in it again," Tita advised. "The waves of the Lagoon will be too strong and too dangerous to cross."

"So I cannot get back to La Mira?"

"Not this evening or this night, not until the storm ends."

Strangely, Byron was surprised to realise that he was feeling relieved to be told he could not go out into the storm again. He was feeling hot and shivery one moment and icy cold the next.

"Then tell them to get my bed prepared because I need to lie down under some warm blankets." He looked at Tita, still shivering. "Teresa will be worried."

"No, no," Tita assured him. "She will look at the weather and know why it is impossible for you to return to La Mira. Tomorrow, when the storm is gone and the Lagoon is calm, then we can go."

The following day, Tita arrived alone at La Mira to inform Teresa and Fletcher that Byron was very ill.

"In the night he was so ill," Tita said, "I went for Professor Aglietti – thank God he lives so near on the Canal Grande – he came and said Mylord had a fever ... a *tertian* fever."

"Tertian? You mean it's a form of malaria?" Fletcher said anxiously. "Then he must have been bitten by an infected mosquito sometime in the last few days! Oh, I always feared this would happen. In Greece he got a bad attack of malaria and nearly died from it. They said it could come back again."

Fanny Sylvestrini, who had been listening, burst into tears; and Teresa went off in the same way but less noisy, both females crying. Tita did his best to console them

"The doctor says the tertian it is not so bad as malaria," he said, " not so *maligno,* but he will suffer for some time."

"Aye, aye, but it's something he was told he will always have to be careful of – the malaria," Fletcher said in a fret. "But does he ever heed what he is told? I must go to him. Will you take me back with you, Tita?"

Teresa already had her bonnet on, and so did Fanny Sylvestrini.

"No, not *you,* Fanny," Teresa snapped. "You must stay here and look after Allegrina and her nurse, but don't tell the child that her Papa is sick."

Byron opened his eyes when Fletcher entered the bedroom and, for a ghostly minute, it was his hated mother-in-law he saw, Lady Milbanke. He stretched out his hand to reach for the pistol on his bedside table to shoot her, but his hand was caught halfway and clasped tight by Fletcher.

"It's only me, my lord, only Fletcher. Were you dreaming of you-know-who again? No, no, she'd never come here, not to Venice, her broomstick won't fly this far. So you just rest now, rest and sleep, and we'll soon have you up and about again."

For days Byron was unaware of what was going on around him. Sometimes he thought he saw Teresa sitting by his bed, sometimes Fletcher, and sometimes Dr Aglietti.

Sometimes he thought he heard voices from another floor, raised in argument, and again he thought of his hated mother-in-law. "That damned woman! She's as old as the hills, and still she refuses to shut her mouth and die!"

"She will, one day," Fletcher assured him, clasping his hand again. "She will have to die and stop her trouble-making one day."

"No, no, women like her never die, not even when they are buried. Their malice goes on and on, until finally even the Devil rises up in flames to try and get away from them."

Fletcher grinned. "He's getting better," he said with relief to Professor Aglietti, "and all thanks to your own devoted care, Doctor."

"He is more clear-headed, yes," said Dr Aglietti, "but he is still very weak. Although he is recovering more quickly than I expected, so I am pleased with him. But do not trouble him with anything stressful, not until he is fully recovered."

Which left Fletcher in a stressful quandary of his own, for there were things going on in the palazzo which his lordship had not been told about – mainly the arrival five days ago of Count Guiccioli.

The old Count was in a desperate state, insisting that his wife return to Ravenna with him as soon as possible, and Teresa was stubbornly refusing to go.

On the first day that Byron was up and dressed, and before he had even left his own apartment, Count Guiccioli insisted on seeing him.

Too weak to put up any opposition, Byron said to Fletcher, "Then show him in."

The Count entered the bedroom full of concerned questions about Mylord's health, as courteous as ever in his manner.

"You know, Mylord, that Teresa must now return with me to Ravenna. An obstacle has arisen, and that obstacle is Count Gamba."

"Teresa's father?"

"Yes. Someone told him I had *sold* her to you, and he came to me threatening death or damnation. And Count Gamba is not a man to be put to the test. I beg you to say nothing of his threat to Teresa. Count Gamba has always been well respected in the region, but now I have my suspicions that he is also a Carbonaro."

"A Carbonaro?"

Guiccioli's red-whiskered slight smile was as wily as a fox. "Do you know what that means?"

Byron maintained a blank face. "No."

Guiccioli shrugged. "Suffice it to say then, that a

Carbonaro has many friends, and many friends of friends, so their threats must not be taken lightly."

Byron sat down in a chair by the window. "As I don't know what a Carbonaro is, all I can say is that Count Gamba, once I got to know him, struck me as being one of the best of men."

"He can be so. But you must know, as Teresa's father, he is within his rights to demand that his daughter be returned to her husband, if only to stop all the gossip and the shame it brings upon *him* as well as myself. She refuses to leave you, so you must leave her – give her up. *You* must send her back to Ravenna!"

"I can't do that. She is not happy with you. She has never been happy with you. It was an arranged marriage between you and her father. Her wish is to remain with me. And my own inclination is to take her away to another country."

"No!" The Count's response took Byron completely by surprise – and something close to shock when Guiccioli started crying and clasping his hands together and begging him not to cause any more trouble between the Gamba and Guiccioli families – "You are not Italian, so you do not understand!"

Byron finally agreed to speak with Teresa, which only caused him great sadness of heart, for of all the three men involved, he knew that he was the only one who had no right to her at all.

"Except that I love you."

Teresa was awash with tears. "If I go back to Ravenna, for my father's sake, will you come there soon after? Even if you lodge at the hotel, it means we could still see each other. Will you come, and come soon?"

Byron nodded, promising he would, while knowing it was a promise he would not keep. The situation was beyond solution, so best to end it now.

The following morning Teresa was still weeping as Byron assisted her into the gondola. "You will come soon, my Byron?" she whispered.

He nodded, and then turned to Count Guiccioli who

shook his hand happily, thanking him for taking care of his young wife during her bad health. Then Guiccioli stepped into the gondola and sat himself down beside Teresa.

It was the first time Byron had actually seen them together, side by side; and to his eyes at that moment – and surely to the eyes of any watching stranger – Count Guiccioli looked like an old man sitting beside his young granddaughter.

He stood watching the gondola until it had gone out of sight, then turned and went back into the palazzo.

PART TWO

~

So we'll go no more a-roving
So late into the night,
Though the heart be still as loving,
And the moon be still as bright.

BYRON

Chapter Four

~ ~ ~

The unopened letters had accumulated into a pile: most were from strangers to the poet Lord Byron; and those he gave to his secretary, Lega Zambelli, to answer.

The news from his friends in England passed over his head without interest, only the one from John Hobhouse made him pause ... and then he handed the letter to Fletcher.

"Here, you read this – I can't make head nor tail of what Hobby is saying. What the deuce do I know about vampires?"

Fletcher carefully read through Hobhouse's letter and was appalled. "He's writing about Dr Dori."

"Polidori?"

"Aye, do you remember in Switzerland, when you and the Shelleys were busy writing stories all the time?"

"Yes, Mary wrote her *Frankenstein*, and I wrote ... oh is *that* what he's talking about?"

Fletcher nodded. "Seems like the doctor must have copied down what you wrote, because he brought a book called 'The Vampyre' and tried to sell it to John Murray."

"Ridiculous! First of all, because I wrote down only half of it – the half set in Greece – and the second half, set in London I had not written, so I told the Shelleys how I *intended* to finished it, but I never did finish it."

"And was Polidori in the room when you told them how it ended?"

"Yes, he was always there, always listening."

"What did you do with first half – the half you wrote down?"

"I sent it to John Murray to keep among my papers."

"Then no wonder John Murray sent Polidori packing, he knew it was one of *your* stories. But now Polidori has gone and paid Cawthorne's to print and publish it for him. Why, the brass nerve of the scoundrel! Copying your story and pretending he wrote it."

Byron sat back. "Not that I care. It was a load of nonsense in the first place, and I'm sure Polidori has made a complete hash of it now. His previous efforts at writing were laughable."

"All the same, it is out-and-out robbery! And by a man who was given the hospitality of your house for months because he was supposed to be your *doctor!*"

"He was no good at that either, was he? The only medical condition he knew how to treat was sleepwalking, and we all slept soundly."

"And don't forget that he also turned out to be a drug addict, as well as a liar."

"Poor man, if he makes a few shekels from that absurd story, then good luck to him."

Byron truly didn't care. And the fact that he was so careless about everything now, worried Fletcher.

It was not like his lordship to be so disinterested in everything. He spent most of his time at his desk writing his poetry, as if he had withdrawn from the real world, into a world that was his alone, and of which he had total command. When it came to poetry, no one could write it so quickly or as naturally.

Another letter came from John Hobhouse:

My dear Byron, – I should not sit down to bother you now were it not to tell you that I have been engaged in correspondence with Polidori about you. That cursed and trashy tale, entitled "The Vampyre" was lately advertised by Cawthorne's in your name, and a notice that said you had written it in concert with the Shelleys who produced 'Frankenstein'. The moment I saw this "Vampyre" and knowing your style, swore to the publisher that the whole was a vile imposture and Polidori's sole doing.

And I was right, for he owned it upon my writing

to him. Now, however, he publishes a letter in the papers, stating that though the Vampyre – "in its present form" is not yours – yet the "<u>ground work</u>" is "<u>certainly</u>" yours. To this he puts his damned polysyllabic name.

I think it would be advisable to write to Murray, or if you like, to me, a note to be published in the papers, totally depriving the Doctor of any copyright in "<u>ground works</u>"; or he will continue making use of your name for all and everything. I fear he is a sad scamp.

Ever yours, John Hobhouse.

And still Byron did not care; writing back to Hobhouse without mentioning Polidori's name at all. Instead, as was his habit, he confided in Hobby, the one friend from whom he kept no secrets, telling him he was writing –

... in ill health and worse nerves, and so anxious that I cry for nothing; at least today I found myself in tears all alone by myself, standing over a cistern of swimming goldfish, which are not pathetic enough creatures to make a man weep.

I have no particular cause of griefs, except I have to do with a woman, young and amiable and pretty, only twenty years old and only two years out of a Convent at Faenza.

But I feel – and feel it bitterly – that a man should not consume his life at the side of a woman; that even the recompense, and it is much, is not enough. But I have neither the strength of mind to break my chain, nor the insensibility which would deaden its weight; and yet to what have I conducted myself?

I have luckily, or unluckily, no ambition left; it would be better if I had, it would at least awaken me; whereas at present I merely start in my sleep.

It all came to an end, thus: – Count Guiccioli, discovering that the lady was now completely estranged from him, gave her a choice – him or me – one, but not both. She chose me, and was for leaving him, and eloping or separating; and so should I, for I loved her; but I knew that the event would be for her irreparable, and that of her family – her sisters particularly and father – would be plunged into despair for the reputation of the rest of the girls; so I prevailed on her with great difficulty, to return to Ravenna with her husband, who promised forgetfulness, if she would give me up. He actually came to <u>me</u> crying about it!

After ten days of such things, during which time I had the tertian fever, she agreed to go back with him; but I feel so wretched and low, that I must leave this country; for otherwise, if I formed a new liaison, here in Venice she would cut the figure of a woman discarded, and I never will willingly hurt her.

I can have no other motive for leaving, because here nobody fights duels – and as to assassination, I have risked it many a good time for her at Ravenna, and should hardly shrink now.

But I shall quit Italy. The country has become sad to me; and as I left England on account of my own wife, I will now quit Italy for the sake of the wife of another.

What else can I do? But to sacrifice a woman whom I loved, for life; who had been my pleasure, my pride, and my passion.

At twenty I would have taken her away. At thirty, with the experience of ten such years, I sacrificed myself only.

I shall make my way to Calais, without going through Paris. I return to England with a heavier heart than when I left it, with no prospects of pleasure, and indifferent to everything but that which is my duty to do. I shall bring my little daughter Allegra with me, but I shall not stay in England. I hope to get out to America, if I don't take a much longer voyage, to South America

I think I wrote to you last week, but I really cannot positively recall. Write and believe me – as long as I can keep my sanity – ever yours most truly and affectionately – B.

~~~

In Ravenna, Teresa was faring just as badly, weeping and unable to sleep; but now she had risen to a rage by a *new* set of "Rules" which her husband had sent by a maid to deliver to her.

1. Let her not be late in rising, nor slow over her dressing, nor fussy over lacing and washing, without danger of injuring herself.

2. Let her busy herself at once with household matters, and to do all with method, diligence, and economy.

3. At midday, let her spend the time until dinner with me, in conversation, and reading aloud to me.

4. After dinner, when I rest, let that be her regular time for practising her music.
~~~

5. Let her not do things casually, because a wish or an idea presents itself, but only when this idea has first been referred to her husband, and is seen to be well-advised.

6. Let her accustom herself to prudent economy, and economy in her personal concerns. And let the regret of refusing useless requests be therefore spared me.

7. Let her reflect that only a similarity of habits can render conjugal life agreeable. She can easily change hers which have only lasted for a few years, but I cannot change mine, which have more than forty years of absolute and deliberate practice behind them.

8. Let her receive as few visitors as possible.

9. Let her be completely docile with her husband, and give no one else preference over him.

10. Let her reflect that in so much as she neglects the care of her business and household, so much more shall I neglect her.

11. In so much as she despises practical matters and the aforesaid duties, so much more shall I feel contempt, dislike, and aversion to her, who, while she is served by all, is of service to none. And while greatly increasing my burdens, refuses to bear any part of them herself, exposing me thus to trouble and damage of every kind.

Teresa's fury drove her to run through the palazzo until she found Alessandro outside his room, lunching on his balcony overlooking the garden.

She threw his rules into his face. – "Of service to no one? Exposing you to trouble and damage? What have I been doing since you married me – the *only* reason you wanted to marry me – so you could *use* me to smile at men you wanted to get money from! To pretend even that I might sleep with them if they gave you the business or the money! *That* is why you always insisted that I go with you on business - so you could try and use me as your *prostitute!"*

Alessandro looked at her coldly. "But then you *did* prostitute yourself, didn't you – with Mylord Byron, for which I am very grateful, because in return he has paid me two large sums of money."

"No, the money he gave you was because you asked him for a *loan."*

Guiccioli's foxy red-whiskered smile was back on his face. "Oh, well, those were the words we used, but I'm sure he understood the true business we were transacting. After all, he is a man of the world, and, as he once told me – no fool."

Teresa could only stare at him, not knowing now what to believe. Is that why Byron had persuaded her to go back to Ravenna, so he would not to have to pay more money for her?

She ran back to her room, her rage almost uncontrollable, as she sat down to write a letter to Byron with shaking hands, accusing him of deceit and dishonesty and the worst kind of duplicity imaginable.

But although she hinted, she could not bring herself to state in exactly which way he had deceived her. She sent the letter *post express.*

Her rage had descended into the continual sadness of depression by the time she received a *post express* reply from Byron a few days later.

She saw instantly, from all the dashes it contained, that his answer had been written rapidly and without construct and that he was very angry:

Yes – My Love – I am very "indifferent" to you – my diversions have been so many – yes – you are right in this as in everything.

Think a little – my Treasure – and then I shall challenge anyone to find in my conduct, ever since I have known you, the slightest thing that deserves such a reproach.

A slave is not more humble in the presence of his master than I am in yours – but do not abuse your power. Think only if I deserve the reproaches in your last note – and then forgive <u>yourself</u> if you can.

She shook her head vehemently. Why had she been so foolish as to believe Alessandro? No man could behave so tenderly towards a woman as Byron had with her, not unless he loved her.

And why would he need to *pay* for a woman? – when he could snap his fingers and have his pick of most of the beautiful women in Venice? She was not so beautiful or so special that Byron should single her out like a rare diamond. She was vain about her prettiness, true, but that's *all* she was – pretty.

Now she had spoiled it and he would not come to Ravenna as he had promised. Now she had insulted him beyond forgiveness. Now only a dreary life with that vile old man and his rules lay ahead of her.

His rules? She would show Alessandro what she thought of his stupid rules!

She pulled forward her writing- pad and wrote out her own rules:

1. To get up whenever I like.

2. To spend the time of your rest doing as I please, even if it is only in pulling the donkey's tail.

3. To receive, without discrimination, <u>any</u> visitor who may come.

Her attention was caught by a spider crawling across the desk. She stared at it, wondering how she could cope with living in the same house as Alessandro any longer ... yet she could not go back to her father's house ... that would cause great shame on the Gamba name.

Her only relief was tears, tears, and more tears as she thought of what she had now lost; the beginning and end of her world – *Mio Byron* – Had he ever been real?

Had he truly come here to Italy? Or had he been just a figment of her romantic imagination?

Chapter Five

~ ~ ~

Another calamity at the Palazzo Mocenigo in Venice forced Byron to write to Hobhouse again, and immediately – knowing that Hobby would be running around making preparations for his arrival in London.

There is packing and preparations going on here, but Dr Aglietti has this moment informed me that Allegra has the "terzana doppia,", (a tertian fever form of malaria) which it seems renders my departure from here quite uncertain (as I will not and cannot go without her).

It means the poor child has the fever daily, and her nurse has it too. My own has diminished but is not quite gone. At first it was violent to a degree of temporary delirium, but has subsided in this third week to slightness, but has left my mind very weak and unintellectual.

All these things put together prevent me from entering upon any of my plans; and make me postpone from day to day my departure; for the doctor will say nothing decided of my daughter, and I dare not remove her until her journey is pronounced to be safe.

So here I am in a gloomy Venetian palace, never more alone than when alone; and at the moment when I trusted to set out – taken aback by this indisposition of my child, which, however, thank God, is not dangerous.

All my plans are lulled upon the pillow of a sick infant, but in Italy I will not remain a moment longer than enables me to quit it.

Yours ever and truly, B.

~~~

</div>

With Allegra's nursemaid also being ill and bed-bound, Byron took care of his little daughter himself, sponging her face constantly and doing whatever needed to be done – much to Fletcher's agitation.

"You shouldn't be doing that, my lord, it's too risky."

"Not for me. I've already had the tertian and recovered. *You* should be worrying more about yourself."

"Me? No fear!" Fletcher declared. "No tertian-ridden mosquito will ever get *me* – not a man from Nottinghamshire!"

Byron sniggered. "Do you think the mosquitoes know that and will warn all the others – steer clear of the man from Nottinghamshire?"

"You never know. Insects are strange creatures. How do we know what goes on in their heads?"

"I certainly don't know, because I often find it difficult enough to know what goes on in *your* head."

Fletcher grinned. "A man of mystery, that's me."

Byron smoothed back Allegra's damp hair and stood looking down at her little sleeping face ... "I've decided she should be educated in England, or possibly America. Washington Irving told me there are some good schools in New York."

"Well he should know, coming from there, New York. Is he back there now?"

Byron shrugged. "Probably. I have not heard from him since I left England."

"Only a mad American would write a story like *The Legend of Sleepy Hollow*. Frightened the life out of me the night I read it. But then, in the daytime, I kept
~~~

thinking to myself – how could a headless man ride a horse? How could he *see* where he was going?"

Byron was tired of Fletcher's prattle. "Pray do me a favour, Fletcher."

"You say it, my lord, and it will be done."

"Scram."

"What? You want me to go?"

Byron turned up his eyes. "Irving must have already met you when he came up with the idea of a headless man."

The door quietly opened and Fanny Sylvestrini popped in her head. "How now is Allegrina?"

"And now comes one of the witches from *Macbeth*," Byron muttered. "I'm off."

Fanny dipped a quick curtsy as Byron passed her, and then tiptoed over to the bed, whispering to Fletcher, "He is still in a bad mood because the Count took Teresina away, he is, eh?"

"No, that's not why," Fletcher argued. "He's in a bad mood because he can't make his way out of Italy, not until the child is better."

Byron allowed his bad mood to be vented in full flow while writing a long letter to John Murray. He had lost his natural instinct to be polite to his publisher, because really the man was getting too careless and slip-shod, and had to be told so.

Consequently, a week or so later, in his office in Mayfair, John Murray was surprised by the blunt anger and personal rebukes fired at him in this letter from his favourite author.

Dear Mr Murray – In the name of all the devils in the printing office, why don't you acknowledge receipt of the first, second, and third packets I sent you? You forget that you keep me in hot water until I know whether they have arrived, or I must have the boredom of re-copying.

I have sent you a warehouse of poetry within the last months, and you have no sort of feeling about you. A pastry-cook would have had twice the gratitude, and thanked me at least for the <u>quantity</u> I sent.

As for Don Juan, I have received no proofs, not by the last post, and I shall probably have quitted Venice by the next ...

John Murray read on, feeling duly chastised, and even more so by the last paragraph in which Byron attempted to be more forgiving and conciliatory:

Don't suppose I want to put you out of humour. I have great respect for your gentlemanly qualities, and return your personal friendship to me. Although I think you have become a little spoilt by your success and your – persons of honour, man about town, authors, and fashionables, together with your – "I am just going to call on the Prince Regent at Carlton House, are you walking that way?"

Notwithstanding all that, you deserve the esteem of those whose esteem is worth having – and none more (however useless it may be) than yours truly.

John Murray was frowning; knowing this was one letter from Lord Byron that he would *not* be showing around his four-o'clock parlour gatherings, where and when friends would be eagerly seeking fresh news from Italy.

Had he really become so grand and affected in his behaviour? It was something he would have to think about and consider ... That was the devilish thing about Byron; although he may say nothing at the time, he could spot pretensions instantly.

Well, if he really *had* said those words in that way,

then he had probably been going to Carlton House merely because the Prince Regent's secretary had sent a note requesting a copy of Lord Byron's latest book to be brought to him – Byron and Sir Walter Scott – they were the only two authors that interested the prince.

Well, he would have to smooth the rankles and remedy this situation by writing Byron a nice long letter, full of chatty news from England, along with a pile of proofs for him to edit and alter.

A few days later, Murray had his letter written and his parcel of proofs all packed up ready to send to Venice, when another letter arrived from Byron.

Murray looked at the Venice stamp and smiled smugly at his editor, William Gifford.

"No doubt *this* letter will be full of apologies with the explanation that he had consumed too much wine, or some other reason. I do hope so, because I would hate for him to fall out with us."

Murray was sorely disappointed when he opened and read the two-line note:

Still no reply. Well, have it your own way. If you can't be bothered, then neither can I.

William Gifford read the note with puzzlement. "This is so *unlike* Byron. He usually dreads receiving our proofs with requests to alter or amend."

Murray nodded. "True."

"And it's a long time since he was last so rude to you. Not since he threatened to borrow the giant staff from St Dunstan's church and *immolate* you with it."

Murray smiled weakly. "Yes but he was very young then, just returned from the wilds of Albania."

"So how do you explain it? This sudden and complete change of tone in his letters?"

Murray shrugged. "I don't know ... it can't be the delay in hearing from me, that has never troubled him in the past ... yet *something* has made him very cross and agitated."

In Venice, Byron stood on his balcony in the darkness, gazing down on the golden glare of the torch-lights along the Grand Canal, illuminating the beauty of the city built on water. Yet his eyes were blind to the sights before him, seeing in his mind only a blue-eyed Italian girl.

His constant irritation and short bouts of anger concealed a consuming inner anguish, yet even as a poet he could not speak, nor write about it. No more than a deaf mute could hear an opera or sing out its story.

He loved, and yet the loss of that love he mourned. A self-inflicted pain, because he had known from the beginning the difficulties; and at the end it was *he* who had sent her away.

What else could he do, when her legal husband had stood before him weeping tears, begging for the peace and unity of the two families in Romagna.

And yet he still loved.

He loved, but was no longer able to caress, to kiss, to lay with her in the softness of a moonlit room and drown in ecstasy.

And yet it was the small things he missed, nothing to do with love, and everything to do with love. The way she played with Allegra; or played soft tunes on the piano. The seriousness of her face when she quoted Dante to him; and the sunshine in her eyes when she laughed at something funny. Or when they had sat on the garden-bench in the evenings at La Mira, and she rested her head against his shoulder while both watched the changing colours of the darkening sky.

He longed to be free of such memories. So after a short stay in England, he would seek deliverance by sailing across the Atlantic to America, and there he would be saved. A whole new world was opening up for men of talent and ambition in America, and he had friends there. Bedamned to England and Italy. He and Allegra would become Americans.

Chapter Six

~ ~ ~

Count Ruggero Gamba was a man of past sorrows that still besieged him. The recent death of his wife through a quick and sudden illness, and also the death of his eighteen-year-old daughter in her first childbirth, still caused him much grief.

And now he had the added worry of Teresa, who had always been a delicate child, but now her illness seemed to be more of the mind than the body.

To also lose Teresa now would be a devastation to him. She was his fairest and his favourite, but the tales that were being brought back to Filetto by her sisters, whenever they visited her in Ravenna, were enough to make any father concerned.

Odd tales, about her odd behaviour. She had lost all interest in food and drink, and she never went outside to the garden or the town, preferring to sit all day in the silence of her room with the curtains drawn. Was that not odd? And so unlike Teresa who loved to laugh and talk and have lots of company.

When his carriage arrived at the Palazzo Guiccioli and he entered the house, he was relieved to be told that Count Guiccioli was not at home.

"Take me to my daughter," he told the maid.

"But, Conte ..." the maid became flustered, "she is not allowed any *man* visitors."

Count Gamba looked at the girl. "Not even her own father?"

"I don't know ... she is sick ... the doctor says she is suffering from the consumption."

Count Gamba strode on down the hall to Teresa's apartment. He paused outside the door and gestured for the flustered maid to go inside. "Tell her Papa is here."

The maid went inside, and swiftly the door was opened again by Teresa herself – flinging her arms around his waist and hugging him so tightly and strongly he knew she could not be suffering from consumption. "So, Teresina, what are these strange things I hear of you?"

Just as she had often done when she was a child, Teresa took his hand to lead him into her sitting-room where the curtains were drawn, but he held back and refused. "No, I wish to sit with you in the garden."

Teresa shook her head. "No, the summer is gone and it is feeling cold now."

"Then I will keep my coat on, and you must wrap up warm, and we will sit on your balcony. It is not good for you to hide away in shadows."

After a pause, Teresa nodded, and went to her dressing-room to get a warm cloak; while Count Gamba walked around the sitting-room opening all the curtains before stepping out to her balcony where it did indeed feel slightly cold.

He sat down on one of the balcony chairs by the small table and waited.

Teresa joined him, wrapped in a dark blue cloak. Only then, in the brightness of the daylight, did he see how pale her face was, how dull her blue eyes.

"So, what is this talk of consumption?"

Teresa half-smiled. "The Count's doctor, he is a fool. I do not like him coming to me, so one day I coughed a little, and told him I had spit up blood, and he jumped back with fright, saying I had consumption. He has not been back since."

"And you thought that was clever?"

"No. I thought it was necessary."

Count Gamba sighed. "I will send my own doctor to you."

Teresa lowered her head to look down at her clasped hands in her lap.

"If not consumption," Count Gamba said, "then *something* is very wrong with you. Your sisters are certain of it. Will you not tell Papa?"

Teresa slowly lifted her head, and he saw the tears of

sorrow streaming down her face; a sight that upset him.

"Ah, *mia cara* ..." He reached out to hold her hand in his own, and they sat talking for some time. She told him everything; her love for Byron, her heartbreak now; and he understood, but he was not prepared to agree.

His words were full of compassion, and his eyes soft with his natural love for her as he said: "I pity your state, and I know by experience that love is something that is felt and not commanded. But you must never forget that you are a wife, and your duty is to your husband."

"My duty?"

"As he has a duty to you. To take care of you and protect you."

Teresa's anger was rising. "Protect me from what, Papa?"

"From all harm, all poverty, and from seductive young men like Lord Byron."

"Papa, you have no idea how *good* Byron is, and ... why I idolise his very name!"

"If that is your sickness then you *do* need a doctor," her father replied sternly. "A doctor of the mind! If your mother was alive to hear you now, she would make you go before God and repent the breaking of your wifely duty."

Teresa could not restrain herself, quickly rising to her feet to stand and stare accusingly at her father. "My duty to a husband who must take care of me and protect me?"

"Yes! That is his duty – the marital obligations are on both sides."

Teresa's eyes were no longer dull, but blazing. "Will I tell you how Guiccioli does his duty to take care and protect me, Papa? If you knew, you would not say such bad things about my Byron."

What should I know?"

"From the first days after the marriage, when we went to Venice ... " She then told him of all the business trips where she was instructed by Guiccioli to flirt with men and give them false hopes and expectations of sex with her, so that the Count could get their money or business.

"He tried to *prostitute* you for his advantage? My own daughter! Is the man so insane that he thinks we are still living in the times of the *Borgias!* Is all this true, Teresa?"

"All is true, Papa – on Mama's soul I swear it. Even in Venice, at Contessa Benzoni's salon, he made me wait in the hall because he intended to bring me in later to introduce me to Count Rangone in private. But it did not happen, because the Contessa had taken me into the salon and introduced me to Lord Byron."

Count Gamba's blue eyes were zero-cold.

"And when Alessandro saw this," Teresa continued, "that his plan for me to flirt with Rangone was spoiled, in the gondola going home he told me that Lord Byron was said to be very rich, and rich men were good to know – that was his way of telling me what he wanted without saying so. And then, all the time in Venice, he left me unattended all day, free to meet Lord Byron whenever I wished – "

"He *encouraged* you to liase with Lord Byron?"

"Yes, but not by directly saying so. And since then, Alessandro has cheated Byron out of two large sums of money, pretending he was asking for loans. I did not know about the first loan, but for the second one, he wrote a letter wanting *me* to ask Byron for a loan, which would allow me to stay longer with Byron at La Mira. But now ... now Alessandro tells me the loans will never be repaid."

Count Gamba realised that the gossip which Don Gaspare Pirelli had brought to him in Filetto was true; for in his own way, Guiccioli was indeed in the business of *selling* his young wife to other men.

"Are you sure Lord Byron was innocent in all this?"

"Yes! Yes! If he knew, he would believe *I* was the one who used *him,* to get money from him for Alessandro. Do you understand now, Papa, why I am so sick in my mind, and so heartbroken?"

"And the other men? The *business* men? Where and when?"

"In Bologna and Ferrara," Teresa said, "but all I did was smile at them and be nice and polite, nothing else, nothing bad. When they came too close and touched me, I pretended to sneeze and cough, which annoyed Alessandro."

Count Gamba was silent, swamped in his own guilt for allowing Guiccioli to marry Teresa. To kill Guiccioli would be too easy. To make him suffer first would be more preferable. And to make a man suffer, one must know his personal weaknesses. Guiccioli was a sly and wily fox, so to defeat and torment him one must use the methods of the snake.

He looked at Teresa who was still standing and looking at him nervously. "Sit down."

She obediently sat down.

"Is there no cure for these feelings you have for Mylord Byron?"

She shook her head.

"And are you certain his feelings for you are true?"

She nodded.

He patted her hand. "Then leave it to Papa."

Teresa was suddenly hopeful. "What are you going to do?"

"Nothing much, but you are unwell, so you must confine yourself to your own apartment and have nothing more to do with Guiccioli. Lay in your bed, read books, and I will send my own doctor to you. He will advise me that you are very ill with consumption. Did Guiccioli's own fool of a doctor not say so?"

"Yes."

He stood up. "Now I must go, but in the meantime, do not let Guiccioli know that you have told any of this to me."

Chapter Seven

~ ~ ~

Allegra was at last recovering, stretching out her little arms to *"Buon Papa"*, and when she was lifted, smiling and rubbing noses with him.

"Is she well enough to travel as far as England?" Byron asked Dr Aglietti.

"Yes, as long as she is kept warm and in the care of a good nursemaid. However, I would not recommend her present nurse, who is thankfully recovering from the tertian, but she has some other small disorders that keep her weak. You must find a strong and healthy nurse to accompany the child as far as England."

As usual, Byron sought the assistance of the British Consul in finding a new nursemaid for Allegra, arriving at the Consulate only to discover that both the Hoppners were away in Switzerland, visiting Mrs Hoppner's family.

"They will be back in time for Christmas," a clerk told him. "Is it urgent, my lord? Do you wish me to send a letter to Mr Hoppner, post express."

"No, I will have to solve the problem myself." Byron's eyes were caught by an edition of the English *Times* newspaper lying on a table.

He picked it up. "May I borrow this? I will send it back as soon as I have read it."

"Oh no, my lord, pray keep it – it is at least three weeks old."

"Thank you." Byron made his way out of the Consulate, still glancing over the headlines in the *Times* when he bumped into a gentleman outside the front door, on his way in.

Both men apologised.

"Ah, another Englishman in Venice! Have you been here long?"

"No," Byron replied, "not too long."

"Is the weather always so chilly?"

Byron smiled. "Well, we *are* on the doorstep of December."

"Yes, but the reason why I have come here out of season is to avoid those crowds of ragamuffin tourists. A damned nuisance, I say, and unbearable in Rome."

The man had an overblown top-drawer accent with a slight Northern twang, probably the owner of an industrial mill or a coal mine or something like that.

"I was advised to come here by Lord Byron. Do you know him?"

"No." Byron blinked. "Do you?"

"Oh yes. Know him well. I've just spent a few days with him down in Naples, but due to my detour to Rome, he is probably back in Venice now. Are you sure you don't know him? I'm told everyone in Venice knows him."

"Sorry, no," Byron said, deciding it was not a lie, as no man really knows himself.

"Well, he invited me to call in on him whenever I am in Venice, but drat me for losing his address. I'm hoping the British Consul will give it to me."

Byron half-smiled, knowing his address was never given out to anyone now, not without Hoppner incurring his wrath.

Yet he could not resist a bit of fun. "Byron, did you say? Is that his surname?"

"Yes, and it is *Lord* Byron if you please. He dislikes it if anyone refers to him without his noble title."

"My apologies again, but it is not a common name, so can you tell me –" Byron took out a card from his inner breast pocket and showed it to the liar – "does your friend spell his name in *that* way?"

The man looked down at the name on the card, *The Honourable George Gordon Lord Byron,* and then at the Byron Crest and Coat of Arms above the name; his face flushing a deep red with astonished embarrassment.

Byron was still grinning when he returned to the

Palazzo Mocenigo and told Fletcher about the overblown toss-pot. "Either he met an impostor in Naples who bamboozled him; or else he needs to grow whiskers to cover up all the lies coming out of his mouth. And when you think, Fletcher, there are many *more* liars like him in England – dare I go?"

"Did you make any headway in finding a new nurse for Allegra?"

"No. Hoppner has gone over the Alps."

Fanny Sylvestrini, who was sitting on the drawing-room carpet playing with Allegra, suddenly piped up: "If you like, Mylord, I will come with you as far as England. I could be Allegrina's nurse for you?"

Byron hesitated. ""No, Fanny, that would be impossible."

"Why?"

"Because you do not speak English."

"Allegrina also does not speak English, so she will feel more comfortable with an Italian? She will, eh?"

"I will not be *remaining* in England, Fanny. Most likely I will go on to America."

"You are taking Lega, so why not take me? They say there are many Italians in America. If you take me, Mylord, I will fulfil to Allegrina, all the duties of a mother."

"By the holy!" said Fletcher, who had been flicking through the *Times*. "There is an article about *you* in here, my lord, and you should read what they say!"

Byron closed his eyes and shook his head. "I dare not, because it's bound to be lies, lies, and more lies. You can give me the drift of it, Fletcher."

"Drift is right – it says here that a few weeks ago you were *'reported by an English traveller to be in the Borromean Islands, in a pleasant rural retreat, staying in a country house with your friend the Princess of Wales, and both of you looked to be very intimate in your friendship."*

Byron glanced at Allegra playing on the carpet. "A child could make up better stories than some of those liars who sell their fictional tittle-tattle to newspapers."

Byron stood up and pulled on his cloak to go out again. "I think I will call on Dr Aglietti to see if he can recommend a travelling nursemaid for Allegra."

While he was out, a letter was delivered for Fanny Sylvestrini from Teresa, begging her for some news of Byron, and to write back without delay.

As Allegra was now sleeping, Fanny rushed into the library and immediately wrote back, in her usual dramatic way:

My dear Teresina – Mylord is leaving Venice, is abandoning Italy, is crossing the mountains and the sea in such a bitter season, is going to England, for you, only for you.

He however assures me, and charges me to assure you in his name, that if you continue to feel the same sentiment for him, he is prepared to return here from London, only to see you, as he is leaving for your sake.

And so certain was Fanny that she would finally persuade Mylord to take her with him to England as Allegrina's nurse, she continued –

Do not doubt Teresina, that you will have news of Mylord by every post, so far as I can gather it during his journey. Calm yourself, for pity's sake. Think of your health, which is dear to Mylord, I vow it. Do not believe you have been deceived, he would not be capable of deceiving you, he has always been swayed by your will. But after all, what use is it going over the past? Do not heed the present too much, but give a great deal of thought to the future. I am writing from my heart, and no one can be a better friend to you than I.

Mylord is taking the cook, Valeriano, with him, as well as many of his other servants, and when he gets to Calais, he will send Valeriano back. From him you will be able to hear about the journey. I will close, impatient to know that you are a little calmer. My friend, farewell again – Fanny.

Reading the letter, and now certain that she would never see her beloved Byron again, Teresa had a serious and genuine relapse, from hope to despair.

It was too late for her Papa to do anything, even though he was now here in the house – having brought his own doctor who claimed to have "examined her thoroughly" – but had merely sat by her bed for a long time, pretending to feel her pulse while dropping off into a short nap. His diagnosis of consumption had already been written before he arrived.

In his drawing-room, Alessandro Guiccioli flinched as Ruggero Gamba stood there looking at him. Count Gamba's bearing was as dignified as ever, but the scorn and the hatred he felt for Guiccioli was now clear to see.

"My daughter's health is failing," he said. "You have failed her."

Alessandro said with an attempt at reasonableness, "Ruggero, I have done everything possible to make your daughter's life as tranquil and happy as possible. What more can I do?"

"You can stop sending her pages of your rules and treating her like a slave. She is imprisoned here, allowed no visitors, and now this – "

Count Gamba lifted the pages in his hand containing the "Rules" which Teresa had thrown at Guiccioli and which he had sent back by a maid to re-deliver to her. To Guiccioli he read out the last rule:

"Let her reflect that so much as she neglects the care of her business and the house, so much will I neglect her. In so much as she despises practical matters and the aforesaid duties, so much and more shall I feel contempt, dislike, and aversion to her..."

Count Gamba's eyes were blazing now. "You speak like this to my daughter?"

Guiccioli's flinty smile was trembling with apprehension. "No, Ruggero, that is all irrelevant, a silly jest we shared. She knew I was not serious."

Count Gamba burst out furiously — "Were you serious when you tried to *prostitute* her to your business friends? You think you can treat my daughter in such a disrespectful way and not hear from me? Do you think I will suffer such disrespect? "

"No, Ruggero, *no!* Those are lies! Malicious lies! Where did you hear such a thing?"

Teresa's father drew in his breath. "I feel too much disgust for you to speak of this any further, not now, not while my daughter is so distressed, but in the future you will be called to answer for it."

Guiccioli spread wide his arms. "Ruggero, I do not understand what you are talking about."

"Then you will understand what I have to say now, because it is simple," Count Gamba said. "My doctor states that Teresa is very ill. She needs care and consolation. This cannot be given by you, because you care for no one but yourself. So I have sent for her English friend in Venice to come to her. If he comes, and when he comes, you will allow him to see Teresa whenever he wants. If you refuse, all your crimes will be made known to the world, and you will be hissed out of Ravenna. And if you refuse and do not leave Ravenna, you will be shot dead by either myself or one of my compatriots."

Count Gamba turned to go. At the door he paused and looked back at Guiccioli with great regret in his eyes. "It is my own heavy cross to bear, that I allowed my daughter to marry a man like you."

Chapter Eight

~ ~ ~

"It is dark, and I love the light ..."

Byron was standing on the balcony of his drawing-room in the darkness of the night, taking his last sad look at Venice before his departure in the morning. It was not the darkness of the night that troubled him, but the darkness of his thoughts.

He had loved Venice, but Venice was no longer a great Republic, and it was hard to see her degraded in every way by Austria's hated yoke which had diminished her in her wealth and her population. Now Venice was like an empty shell without its pearl.

The sound of voices in the room behind made him turn his head to see two of his friends rushing towards him – Alexander Scott, assistant to the British Consul, tall and thin and Scottish; and Angelo Mengaldo, short and stocky and Italian.

Both men came out to join him on the balcony, in a rush to counsel him against such a rash decision.

Scott said: "I believe I have the answer to your situation. You told me that you had promised the Contessa if you did not go to see her in Ravenna, it would be because you had left Italy."

Byron nodded. "Yes."

"But it is a promise you need not keep, and therefore need not leave Italy and return to England. This afternoon I was reading a chapter by Machiavelli, entitled, *'In che modo i Principi debbono osservare la fede'* – and though I am a Scotsman with a religious education and very well disposed to keeping my promises, I confess I was rather shocked at the idea of you starting out on a long journey in the cold winter, solely to keep your promise."

"What has that got to do with Machiavelli?"

"In that chapter, discussing the qualities of the lion

and the fox and the mix of which ought to decide the character of a prince, Machiavelli counsels that a prudent prince should not keep his word, when to keep it is against his own interests ... and surely going back to England is against your own interests?"

"England will be just a short stop on my way to America. I have friends in New York; Washington Irving, George Ticknor, and some others."

Angelo Mengaldo, a former soldier who had loved no man but Napoleon until he met Mylord Byron, now spoke up in fury – "What about the adoration of the Venetians? Do you not care about them? What have they done to make you dislike them?"

"I know nothing about the adoration of anyone, and I don't dislike the Venetians. None have ever harmed me, and I have done nothing to harm any of them, at least not intentionally."

"So why leave? Are you tired of Venice?"

"No." Byron sighed and looked down over the Grand Canal. "For me, all of Venice's disadvantages are compensated by the sight of a single gondola."

"So," Mengaldo demanded, "is it the whole country of Italy you are tired of now?"

"No, I am not tired of Italy, but the ways here are strange to me – I like women – God he knows – but the more their system here develops upon me, the worse it seems, and after Turkey too. Here the *polygamy* is all on the female side."

Scott laughed, but Mengaldo sighed, knowing this Englishman could never be dominated by a woman – so why did everyone in Venice say the young Contessa had him completely in her power?

It was true, Teresa filled his thoughts day and night, but their situation was insoluble, and that is why he had to leave Italy and find a new country and a new life. He would leave with a deeply wounded heart, but to stay in Italy, so far from her and yet still so near, was beyond him. His only alternative was to go somewhere *very far away*. And nothing that Scott nor Mengaldo nor anyone else in Venice could say to him now would change that.

~~~

By noon the following day, most of the luggage had been loaded into the gondola. Byron was dressed and ready to go, his cloak and hat and gloves on, waiting only for the last of the boxes to be brought from upstairs and placed in the gondola.

Fanny Sylvestrini was weeping, for she had not been chosen to go to England and America. A new nursemaid had been provided by Professor Aglietti: a widow of forty-five who had brought up her own children and occasionally worked for the professor as a nurse.

"If you don't take me with you, then I don't want you to go," Fanny wept. "What is Venice without you?"

Byron ignored her, too lost in his own silent determination – until Lega Zambelli brought him a letter which had been delivered by courier.

The postmark was Ravenna ... but Byron could see that the seal in the red wax was not that of Teresa or Count Guiccioli. He opened it and looked down at the signature – *Il Conte Ruggero Gamba Ghiselli.*

Teresa's father!

The opening of the letter was surprising in its modesty – "*How, indeed, could I, Count Ruggero Gamba, claim to restrict the freedom of a man like Lord Byron.*"

He then went on to say that his daughter, Teresa, was very ill, although the greatest malady lay in her soul, and he now begged Lord Byron to come and see her.

"*Life readily flows afresh through the veins of young people who are sick at heart, once the cause of the sickness is removed.*"

Count Gamba also then reminded Byron of the promise Mylord had made to *him* back in the summer, to return to Ravenna in winter to go out riding with him.

"*So come, Mylord, and spend the winter here in*
~~~

Ravenna, as you promised, to be close to the sea and the Pine forests which you liked so much. If you do, believe me, my dear Lord Byron, you will have my gratitude.

The letter had a short P.S:

Count Guiccioli has acquiesced to your visit, in consequence of her relapse."

Byron did not know what to do. He longed to stay and go to Teresa, but he knew that he really *should* leave her and Italy to avoid any further complications in her marriage.

The heart said one thing, the mind said another. Torn between confusion and love and anxiety; and at a loss to know the *right* thing to do ... he finally resorted to an old superstitious trick often used by his Scottish mother, looking up at the clock on the wall.

"If the clock strikes one o'clock before the final trunk is brought down and loaded into the gondola, I will take it as a sign that I am *not* to leave Italy."

Fanny Sylvestrini looked up at the clock – less than ten minutes to one o'clock – she quickly slipped away, lumbering up the stairs and into the drawing-room where the final trunk of books was already strapped up and ready to be lifted.

"Is that the last one?" she asked the two male servants.

One of the men nodded. "*Si.*"

"*Si?* Let me see!" Fanny waved them aside as if inspecting the outside of the trunk, and then sat her big bulk on top of it, ignoring the men's arguments and refusing to budge – not until she heard the clock downstairs striking out the hour of one o'clock.

"*Si!*" she said to the men, folding her arms, "now you may thank Fanny."

"For what?" asked one of the men.

"For saving your good jobs here at Mocenigo! Unless you want to go back to slavery and earning no more than a few sequins in some other house?"

Chapter Nine

~ ~ ~

In his room at the Hotel del Pellegrino in Bologna; knowing that Fanny had rapidly written a letter and sent it post-haste by courier to Ravenna, Byron finally wrote to Teresa:

Fanny will have told you that Love has won. I have not been able to find enough resolution to leave the country where you are, without seeing you at least once more. You should know, by now, what is more conducive to your welfare, my presence or my absence.

I am a citizen of the world – all countries are alike to me. I believed that the best course, both for your peace, and for that of your family, was for me to leave and to go very far away; for to remain near and not approach you again would have been impossible for me. But you have decided that I am to return to Ravenna – and do – and be – what you wish. I cannot say more. I have brought my little Allegra with me. She too will be happy to see you again.

Arriving at his former lodgings in Ravenna, at the Hotel Imperial, he was welcomed heartily and warmly like a friend who has come home again.

He had scarcely arrived when the news spread, followed by invitations to festive gatherings pouring into the hotel from Ravenna's elite, all confessing their pleasure at hearing of his return to them.

The only invitation to which he gave any serious

attention, was from Count Ruggero Gamba, inviting him to attend a festive Gamba family gathering the following evening, on Christmas Eve.

It was the custom in Ravenna that each of the leading families, in turn, during Christmas, Advent and Easter, held the first party in their house. And this year it was the turn of the Marquis Cavalli, Teresa's uncle.

Every friend and relative of the Gambas was there, and when Byron entered he was welcomed like the guest of honour; all so warm and joyful in their greetings; including Teresa, who devoured him with love in her eyes, and was a portrait of smiling happiness – and looking as healthy as a girl who had not suffered a day's sickness in her life.

She joined him without hesitation; as did her father, who took Byron's hand in his own, and then told him that from now on, he must consider himself as one of the Gamba-Ghiselli family.

"Here, and throughout Romagna," Count Gamba said, "you shall be known as an honoured friend and intimate of the Gamba-Ghiselli household, and every door of every relative shall be opened to you – as one of our family."

Byron's heart was full at being welcomed in such a way by a man like Count Gamba; but later, when his feelings were more balanced, he asked Teresa: "In his signature, and earlier when speaking, why did your father add the word 'Ghiselli' to the Gamba name?"

"Ghiselli was his mother's name. It is the custom for all Italian males to add their mother's maiden name to that of their father's name," she told him. "In that way her name lives on, as does *her* father's name live on, as does their blood which runs through the veins of all their descendants."

She smiled. "Now you know why we Italians have such *large* families with hundreds of relatives with different names. And now hundreds of doors will be opened in welcome to you throughout Romagna."

Minutes later, Byron was welcomed by a tall young

man who pushed his way through the crowded room and held out his hand in welcome. "Lord Byron, may I also welcome you?"

Byron shook his hand. "And you are, pray?"

"Count Pietro Gamba."

Byron was slightly puzzled until Teresa laughed, "Byron, here now is my beloved brother Pietro, who has come home from his university in Rome, and who once truly believed you had locked up a virtuous young woman in your Castle in England."

Pietro smiled with some embarrassment. "I was a fool, Mylord, but your friend, Signor Moore, he has educated me."

Byron was surprised by the honest good-humour of that handsome face. He had expected Pietro to be suspicious and spiteful.

"I can only offer you my sincere apology," Pietro said. "I now believe that those tales and gossips about you in Rome are all based on ... jealousy."

Byron had to laugh at the contemptuous slow drawl in Pietro's voice when he said the word ... *"gelosia"*.

~~~

Count Alessandro Guiccioli was not at the party, because he had not been invited. Yet he knew that Count Alborghetti, Francesco Rangone, Guilo Rasponi, and all the others were there.

Teresa was there too – he had sent a servant to spy on her – and now he knew that Lord Byron had returned to Ravenna and was also at the party – welcomed with open arms and a kiss on both cheeks by Count Ruggero Gamba – *sanctioning* the lover in front of everybody, while the husband had been ignored and left at home.

This was outrageous! This would make him the laughing-stock of the town, open to ridicule as the older man cuckolded by the young lover ... unless he could find a way to circumvent it, and save face.

After some angry thoughts, he decided he would
~~~

attempt to save face during the next few days of the Christmas holiday. But tonight, he would make some mischief for the English lover, by visiting some important friends.

Although it would have been hard for a visitor travelling through Ravenna to see or know, Ravenna was a place ruled by two different sets – the Nobility who were devoted heart and soul to their country of Italy – and the religious Clerics devoted only to Rome.

For the previous five years, since the departure of the French and the restoration of Papal Rule, enforced by the Austrians, the Clerics held all the power and received most of the people's taxes directly into their own pockets. In this way, the Austrians could be certain of the Clerics' loyalty.

Guiccioli drove in a closed carriage to Cathedral Square, for there lived the Cardinal Legate, the Pope's representative in Ravenna.

Once inside, Count Guiccioli was greeted in the same way as any respected parishioner, and in a private room he voiced his concerns to the Legate, Cardinal Malvasia.

"Your Eminence, the unrest in Ravenna continues to grow, and the Church must suspect men like Count Ruggero Gamba who is not only a traitor to his divine religion, but also to his class."

Cardinal Malvasia appeared dubious. "I do not believe Count Gamba is a traitor to his religion. I know him to be devout. As to his noble *class*, well you are all scoundrels, aren't you?"

Guiccioli sighed, knowing the Cardinal was too clever to reveal his hand; and so the pretence of no collaboration must go on, as always.

"Pray continue," invited the Cardinal.

"Count Gamba, in particular, has been heard to speak of the incompetence of Rome, and the injustice of the Austrians. He and his friends speak passionately of an independent Italy – free of Austria – and free of Papal rule. Everywhere in the country secret societies are growing, and now comes Lord Byron to Ravenna."

"Lord Byron of Venice?"

"Of England, but now of Ravenna. They say he has come here to stay."

"To stay? So he finds Ravenna more delightful than Venice? How gratifying."

"Your Eminence, you must know of his reputation in England?"

Cardinal Malvasia pretended innocence. "As a poet?"

"No, as a dangerous liberal and free-thinker. As a lord in their House of Parliament he is known to have stood up and abused their King, their Prince-Regent and their Conservative politicians with damning words of ridicule."

The Cardinal remained unmoved. "I also read the Italian and English newspapers, Conte, and their reports stated that he spoke very strongly of behalf of equal rights for the *Catholics*."

"And also the lower classes, the *peasants!* He is not to be trusted, Your Eminence, because I believe both he and Count Gamba are Carbonaros from different lodges."

The Cardinal sighed impatiently. "All this talk of Carbonaros – like fairies in the forest, or ghosts in the night – and all of it just gossip to keep the people occupied and amused. The citizens of all Italy love their Pope, and all respect the Austrians."

"And Lord Byron?"

"Oh, the new Robin Hood now in Italy! Really, Conte, you are too old to believe such fables."

Cardinal Malvasia rose from his chair. "Now, forgive me, but I must retire and prepare for Christmas Mass in the morning. I will personally see you out."

At the lighted open doorway, Guiccioli stepped out into the darkness, and Cardinal Malvasia also took a few steps out into the dark square; and there, in a low whisper, he finally spoke his first words of truth: "*Grazie,* my friend, *grazie.* As to Lord Byron, you must keep him very close to your eye."

In his carriage, as it moved off, Guiccioli sat back, satisfied. Cardinal Malvasia had played his usual innocent game, but every word of the conversation would be sent to Rome.

As to the Cardinal's command to keep Lord Byron close; well, he had every intention of keeping Lord Byron *very* close; not for the Cardinal's purposes – but for reasons of his own.

There was still quite a lot of money to be got from that very rich young Englishman ... and some friendly favours to be got from him too ... *favours* that Guiccioli knew he might need in the unpredictable future.

Chapter Ten

~ ~ ~

On the day after Christmas, the national holiday of *San Stefano,* Byron was helping Allegra to play with her new doll and other toys when the manager of the hotel informed him he had a visitor.

"Il Conte Guiccioli has come to see you, Mylord."

"Count Guiccioli?"

"He gave me this to hand to you with his greetings." The manager held out a large basket of assorted fresh fruits; oranges and pomegranates; as well as jars of candied dried fruit, nuts, and dates.

Byron took the basket in amazement. "Is he still here, or has he gone?"

"He awaits you downstairs."

Byron handed the basket to Allegra's nurse and then followed the manager downstairs to the lobby, where Count Guiccioli greeted him with a smile. "Mylord, only this morning did I hear that you had returned to us."

They shook hands, and Byron prepared himself to play out a part in something similar to one of Congreve's farcical comedies.

"Thank you for the basket, Count Guiccioli, but – "

"You must call me Alessandro, please! Are we not old friends? The basket is for your little girl, *un bel bambino,* especially the candied fruit and almonds."

"Thank you, but she is not yet three years old; so is she not too young for candied nuts?"

"Oh, these things I forget. My last child is now ten years old and I cannot remember. You must forgive an old man."

Guiccioli paused as if waiting for Byron to refute that he was old, but received no response as the younger man looked towards the small dining room. "May I offer you some coffee, sir?"

Guiccioli sighed. "Coffee would be nice, but I have not time for such refreshments. I have come to ask you a favour. A very small favour, which I am sure you will not refuse. Perhaps you will agree to take a short drive with me in my carriage? The air outside is as fresh and as crisp as October apples."

Byron looked at him shrewdly. "Why not ask me the favour here and now?"

" I *have* asked you," Guiccioli said. "To come for a short drive in my carriage. That is the favour."

Byron was baffled. "Why? For what purpose?"

Count Guiccioli said smoothly, "My dear young English Mylord, I am fond of you, because you have been so kind to me, but I think, in the circumstances, that it is of the utmost importance for the people to see you and I together, as friends, if only to defeat any unnecessary gossip. It is the only way I can allow you to see Teresa ... as a family friend."

'A friend of yet *another* family? It surely must be Christmas!' Byron thought cynically; but he understood the sense of Guiccioli's reasoning; although he was not fooled by the Count's sugary politeness.

"It is my misfortune that I have to ask this favour of you at all," Guiccioli continued, "but I am not a jealous husband – a foolish thing to be in Italy. However, as a matter of honour, I do *insist* on maintaining the traditional form of keeping up appearances, and so the need for our carriage drive together."

Byron nodded. "I will get my coat."

In his room he strapped on the shoulder-brace of two loaded pistols which he always wore under his coat when venturing out alone, even in Venice; and then he returned downstairs and joined Guiccioli in his open-topped carriage.

"Are you sure it is warm enough to have the top down?"

Guiccioli's smile was more like a sneer. "How else are they to see us together?"

He then instructed his driver to go very slowly, and the horses moved off at a clip-clop pace.

From then on Guiccioli kept him talking, while often

laughing loudly at his own jokes whenever he saw people passing on the street and staring at them, causing Byron to smile at the farce of it all.

"How long do you intend to stay in Ravenna?" asked Guiccioli.

Byron shrugged. "A few days, weeks, months, years, I have no idea."

"At the Imperial? To stay there long would certainly be very uncomfortable for you. The rooms are on the small side."

"Yes, it already feels too cramped for myself, my daughter and my family of servants. If I stay in Ravenna, I will look for a suitable villa to rent."

Here and there along the streets people were walking and talking together. Byron could see their looks of astonishment as they caught sight of the two men in the open carriage.

Guiccioli saw them too, and it gave him an idea for a way to not only save face and keep up appearances, but also to rake in some more money from the English Mylord.

"Mio Dio!" He pretended surprise as if a blast of a brainwave had suddenly hit him. "My dear Mylord Byron, such a good scheme to help you has now come into my head! As a replacement for you coming to visit Teresa at our palazzo every day, why not come and live with us? We could grant you some very good accommodation."

Byron sat looking at Guiccioli's face with puzzled scrutiny, wondering if the Count was totally mad, or just hovering on the verge of insanity.

"You do know why I am here in Ravenna? I'm in love with your wife who is forty years younger than you, and she is in love with me. I know it, and you know it, so should you not be offering me a duel to the death, instead of accommodation?"

"Yes, it came into my head like a bolt of lightning," Guiccioli said, as if Byron had not spoken. "We reside on the ground floor, but the whole of the top floor of the palazzo stands vacant, and such a waste. I was considering the possibility of renting it to someone of high respectability and credentials; but *who* could have higher credentials than you, Mylord?"

Byron hesitated, unable to make out this Italian. Was he truly so generous and accommodating? Or did he have other devious motives?"

"And the *expense* of a hotel even for weeks!" Guiccioli continued. "A great expense. As for an empty villa to rent, I don't believe you will find such a thing here in Ravenna. All houses are lived in. So, Mylord, is my invitation to you not a good one?"

Byron could see the advantages and disadvantages of the proposition, but he needed to think about it and discuss it with Teresa. For now, he was completely flummoxed.

"It is not a decision to be made lightly," he said, "so I will need to think about it."

"It would be good for us both," Guiccioli urged, "if only to stop the gossip of the people and the frowns and questions of the priests. You are a family friend who has come to stay with us for a time – how normal and regular is that?"

Byron's mind drifted back to the three or four weeks he had spent at Aston Hall in Sheffield with the Wedderburn-Websters in 1814. During that time a friend of the Websters, Lord Petersham, was there, and had been staying there with the Websters for months, as a friend of the family; and yet he had seen nothing odd or unusual about it. In England, at least in the upper classes, it was quite usual to have friends come to stay for as long as they liked; and the more the merrier.

A few days later Byron rode out to Filetto and sought the guidance of Teresa's father, Count Gamba.

Inwardly, Ruggero was shocked by Guiccioli's offer of accommodation to Lord Byron; but then, shrewdly, he realised that this was Guiccioli's way of avoiding the humiliation and ridicule that Ruggero had hoped he would be forced to suffer at the return of the young Englishman.

The sly old fox had cleverly averted all that. So now, Ruggero realised, he must look at this more objectively. And as he did so, he, too, saw the advantages and disadvantages of Guiccioli's proposition.

On the one hand, it would be a relief to himself to know that Teresa would not be alone in the palazzo with Guiccioli and at the mercy of his bullying and preposterous *rules*. She would have Mylord there to protect her. On the other hand, Count Guiccioli never did anything that was not to *his* own advantage.

"Whatever he does, he always makes sure to come out of it with a good profit for himself," Ruggero said to Byron. "Money is his obsession. He cares for nothing else. Teresa told me of the loans you made to him. You will never see that money returned to you. He will make every excuse to delay payment until doomsday. He is full of tricks in that way."

Byron grinned. "Don't worry, I get wiser with each day I get older, and I am quite capable of pulling off a few tricks myself."

Teresa was both terrified and excited when Byron arrived to view the apartment of rooms on the first floor of the Palazzo Guiccioli. Terrified that Byron would not like the apartment and refuse it; and over-excited at the romantic idea that he might really be coming to live in the same house as her – just one staircase apart.

She was not allowed to go upstairs with the two men, so she waited while her apprehension and pulse increased by the minute.

Byron was pleasantly surprised when Count Guiccioli showed him the apartment of rooms, spread over the entire first floor of the palazzo – it was a splendid and spacious apartment, with rooms enough for Allegra, Fletcher and Tita, as well as a drawing-room, library and private dining-room for himself. His other servants he would leave housed in the smaller rooms at the hotel, which was only a short walk away.

Finally, he said to Guiccioli, "In the belief that I may eventually rent a villa here in Ravenna, I have brought my own cook with me, Valeriano. He would not wish me to dismiss him and send him back to Venice, so would he have access to a kitchen here?"

"*Si*. There are two large kitchens downstairs, but only one is used. He may take the spare kitchen and make it his own." Guiccioli paused for a moment, and then went on curiously, "Do you have many servants?"

"A groom, a few domestics."

"We have domestics here."

"I prefer my own. All are vetted by Mr Fletcher and Signor Falceiri, and all are very trustworthy. Most have been with me since a few months after I arrived in Venice. It would be one of my strict conditions that no other servants but my own, should be allowed, for any reason, to enter my apartments if I choose to live here. And to satisfy myself in that respect, would I be allowed to change the locks?"

Guiccioli had not expected this. It opened his eyes and his mind to the fact this young nobleman actually came from the British *aristocracy,* was reared and educated by them – the British – who thought they ruled the world, and for the most part *did* rule it.

"Certainly you may change the locks to those of your own," Guiccioli said, deciding to raise the rent to an even higher figure. "But may I ask, exactly how many servants *do* you have, Mylord?"

"I have no idea. You would have to ask Mr Fletcher. Too many, I suppose. But the fault is mine. Once they come into my service, few like to leave, and I usually become so fond of them that we all become more like one big family."

Guiccioli frowned. "A family of servants?"

"Quite so. Whether to serve, or be served, all our interests are satisfied and united in the maxim of – all for one and one for all."

Dio! – he was even more British than Guiccioli had

ever realised, which was good, very good – it would allow him to put the rent up even higher. A man who did not even know how many servants he had, was surely a hopeless fool when it came to the business of money.

Byron wandered from room to room, half-smiling to himself ... he knew exactly how many servants he had, and exactly the amount each were paid.

Returning to the drawing-room he said to Guiccioli, "This indeed would be much more comfortable for me than the Imperial Hotel."

"Then all we need to discuss is the rent ..." Guiccioli said.

Byron gave him his full attention, glancing away as he heard a monthly figure that was at least three times higher than the rent of his Palazzo Mocenigo in Venice, and certainly much higher than any villa or hotel in Ravenna.

"I am agreeable to that monthly amount."

"You are?"

"Most definitely."

Guiccioli could not believe his luck, smiling at his good fortune ... he should have made the rent even higher.

"May I move in immediately?" Byron asked.

"As soon as you wish. And you will know, I am sure, that the rent will begin from the day you move in."

"Of course." Byron nodded. "Well, I suppose I should go back to the Imperial and arrange the packing. Most of it remains unpacked, so hopefully we should be able to move in before nightfall."

Guiccioli was now in such a good humour, he said mildly, "You must inform the gentlemen of Ravenna that your new address in future will be at the pleasure of Il Conte Guiccioli here at his palazzo. Otherwise, after tomorrow, all their invitations to you will be sent to the Imperial."

Byron was already at the door. "I will do that *after* I have moved in."

"Tonight I am invited to a *conversazioni* at Count Alborghetti's." Guiccioli went on. "It is for gentlemen only. May I take you along with me?"

Byron hesitated. "Have you accepted his invitation?"

"*Si*, and now it would be rude of me not to go. Count Alborghetti is very insistent in this respect."

"Then I will be delighted to go with you," Byron said; and his smile almost melted Guiccioli's heart ... such a fine young Englishman. Those people may dominate the world, but who could compare to them when it came to such exquisite politeness and fine manners and generosity?

By late evening all the boxes and unopened trunks had been carried up to the first floor of the palazzo, and Byron's own sheets unpacked by his servants and the beds made.

The dusted furniture was all now being re-dusted by the domestics and Fletcher was now carefully hanging up his lordship's clothes in the huge mahogany wardrobes in the dressing-room.

In the drawing-room, Lega Zambelli was sitting at the desk with an accounts ledger opened in front of him, while Byron leaned over his shoulder looking at the monthly-rent figures which Lega was writing down, each one under the other, attempting to reach a final total.

A knock on the door was followed by Count Guiccioli, dressed in all his finery as if going to the opera, and now being shown into the room by Byron's bodyguard, Tita Falceiri.

"Il Conte, Mylord."

For a moment, Guiccioli felt like a visitor in his own palazzo; and was also disappointed to see Mylord still wearing his day clothes.

"You are not ready and dressed to go to Count Alborghetti's *conversazione*?"

Byron looked at him in puzzlement. "Oh goodness, with all the moving from one place to another, I had forgotten all about it, and now I am much too tired to go anywhere. Pray will you excuse me?"

Guiccioli was not pleased. This was to be his major opportunity to show all the gentlemen of the town that Lord Byron was *his* friend, *his* guest, and so now all gossip to the contrary should cease.

"You do not want to go?"

"I would love to go," Byron said, "but I really do not have the energy. It has been a very tiring day. Another time, perhaps?"

Guiccioli felt extremely discommoded, verging on furious; but then he remembered the great financial compensation that came with this new tenant, and he asked: "May I speak with you in private?"

"Of course." Byron gestured for Lega to leave the room, while he remained standing behind the desk.

When Lega had gone, Guiccioli said: "You will recall that I did mention to you today, Mylord, that the rent begins from the first day?"

"Yes, I recall."

"And did I say that each month's rent must be paid in advance?"

"No, you did not say that, but no matter." Byron looked down at the open page of the ledger containing Lega's figures.

"I am sure *you* will recall, sir, that you are a man very much indebted to me. Specifically, one loan for a very large sum of money; and a second for a smaller amount, yet still a great deal of money."

Guiccioli shrugged, attempting to be blithe. "I told you I would repay those loans at five-per-cent interest."

Byron looked down at the ledger as if scrutinising the figures. "Yes, I see that is the amount of interest which my secretary has added to each monthly payment ... five-per-cent."

Guiccioli was caught off-guard, "But I have not yet made any monthly repayments, so why should interest be added now."

"He is merely doing what any banker would do.

Divide the total sum into yearly payments, divide by twelve, and add the monthly interest thereon."

Byron looked at Guiccioli. "Can you repay those loans to me? It has been four months, and yet not one mention of any repayment has been made by you. I, on the other hand, would like repayment of the total amounts within the next three months – at the latest."

Guiccioli was so staggered by the shock and impertinence of this, he almost cursed aloud. But that was these *British* all over – they smiled and politely shook your hand and made you believe they were a fool, while all the time they were politely preparing to ruin you.

"I made no time limit on the loans. No definite time limit was stated or agreed."

Byron looked at him with wide-eyed disbelief. "But that could mean until the end of time, or never at all. No, sir, that is not only unacceptable, but unconscionable. As you know, with my daughter and my family of servants to maintain, I have great expenses of my own. Can you repay the total of the two loans within the next three months?"

Guiccioli knew he had only one answer. "No. It is not possible for me to repay in such a time. My own expenses are – "

"Then what are we to do?" Byron asked. "I would be very reluctant to bring your debts to me before the judgement of a Ravenna court. Especially as you have been so kind as to offer me the residence of these apartments in your palazzo. So I can only think of one possible solution ... in the interim, at least."

Guiccioli was speechless, realising he did not know this man at all.

"For your benefit, and *your* benefit only," Byron said, "I suggest that instead of paying you any rent while I reside here, each month the due rent is deducted from the total of the amount you owe to me, as listed in this ledger, decreasing the balance owed, month by month. Would that be agreeable to you?"

Guiccioli sniffed and looked around him while attempting to control his rage. "And if I were to terminate your residence here."

"Oh, then I would have to return to the hotel or look for a villa, and you would have to make full repayment on the day I leave, or meet me a few days later in the Ravenna court. However disagreeable that would be to both of us, that choice must be yours."

Guiccioli was feeling breathless, a tightness in his throat and chest – he had never in his life encountered such impudent trickery, but that was the British – the damned *British* – not even Napoleon could beat them.

"I will be late for Count Alborghetti's *conversazione*." he said, turning to the door and eager to be gone. "You may set your rent off against the loans, until I can repay you."

And then he was gone.

Byron was grinning – when it came to fools – there was no fool like an old fool.

As soon as Tita gave him the news that Count Guiccioli had gone off in his carriage, Byron hurried down to Teresa's apartment.

Opening the door she was shocked to see him, delight moving on her face. "Byron! I thought you had gone in the carriage with Alessandro."

"No."

"You did not want to go to the *conversazione*?"

He turned and locked the door behind him, smiling as he caught her in an embrace. "I prefer more to make love in private, than conversation in public."

Chapter Eleven

~~~

During the following weeks, Count Guiccioli had studiously considered his situation, and made a decision.

When you are in financial debt to a man, a great deal of financial debt, with the possibility of an expensive and shame-filled court case hanging over you – the wisest thing to do is to keep on that man's good side, and make a friend of him.

And this Alessandro did; occasionally and cheerfully inviting Lord Byron to play chess with him in the afternoons; expressing great interest in his daughter, his poetry, and his dogs; and turning a blind eye to his love affair with Teresa.

They lovers were very circumspect, of course, out of respect to him personally; and if one did not know, one would hardly suspect, due to their perfectly respectable behaviour towards each other in public.

Apart from the absolute necessity of their affair being kept secret from Ravenna's public opinion, and causing no shame to him personally, Alessandro did not care one iota about their romance. To him, one woman was as good as another, and Teresa had always been too timid and shy for his taste, treating the entire thing like a insufferable marital duty instead of a delight, her eyes squeezed shut as if repulsed.

No wonder he had lost interest in her so early on in the marriage, deciding she was just too young, and too purely *Convent-bred* for him.

He preferred women who sinned with their eyes wide open, without any guilt or disgust, and usually he found that with one of his maids. But his latest maid, who had been his bed-companion for almost a year ... he had now become rather tired of her.

Somehow, with all the secret romantic glances
~~~

between Byron and Teresa, he had started to feel that he was missing out on something; so he had dismissed his regular bed-maid and hired a new one – a pretty young woman of peasant stock who appeared to think it a special honour to be invited into her master's bed.

Only one thing was imperative, *essential* to his pride and peace of mind, and it was that no one in Ravenna would suspect what was truly going on in the Palazzo Guiccioli – that *he* was forced to sleep with his maids – while his young wife was besotted with another man.

Well, there was always the last resort of the poisoned wine chalice, and one day he would probably kill them both; but for now he would carry on smiling ... if only to silence the gossips of Ravenna.

~~~

In Venice the Palazzos of the gossips were in full buzz, unable to believe that their favourite and most famous Englishman had gone back to that little country town where nothing exciting ever happened except an occasional murder now and then.

How could a man who had lived for three years in glorious Venice endure such a quiet place? No hotels, no Casinos, no Ridottos, no courtesans in their luxurious bordellos, so what could a young man do for pleasure or excitement in a place like that?

Of all the inhabitants of Venice, not one was more furious than the British Consul, Richard Hoppner, who had returned from a trip to Switzerland to find Byron had gone again. The discovery maddened him, because he had always viewed Lord Byron as one of Venice's main attractions to *English* tourists. All other nationalities could go to blazes.

If Lord Byron was here, the rich English would come, such was their fascination with him. And then he, their Consul, would have some English people to talk English with occasionally and hear all their news from back home.
~~~

And that was not the only benefit of having Lord Byron here in Venice. For the past three years he had proved an absolute *boon* to Venice's economy, bringing the British sightseers here in droves, boosting the takings of hotels and restaurants and gondoliers, making it a much happier place to live.

Since the occupation of Napoleon's French army, few people had come to the island of Venice, turning it into an impoverished outpost of bankrupt hotels and starving beggars.

After Napoleon's defeat, the British had thanked the Austrians for their assistance in defeating the French at Waterloo by giving them the country of Italy as a gift. And so the Austrians had taken over the occupation of Italy – a bullying bunch of blackguards who treated the citizens like dirt and forced all hotels and businesses to pay 60% tax on all their earnings.

Venice had become one of the worst places for a British civil servant to be sent – a damned impoverished outpost where the people gabbled only Italian, and made no effort whatsoever to learn English.

He had written letter after letter to London requesting a posting to elsewhere, but his letters had always been ignored.

Then Lord Byron had arrived, and within months Venice had become a "*romantic*" island, especially to the English who had been reading all his inspirational poetry about the place – "*I stood in Venice on the Bridge of Sighs*" – "*Venice, O Venice! – "And silent rows the songless gondolier.*"

Within a year Venice was seeing the arrival of rich English visitors every week – visitors who spoke English and spent lots of lovely money – and some of that lovely money was spent on *him* personally, by those who wished to entertain his company with good wine and good food while quizzing him on all he knew about that errant young man, Lord Byron. Was he as romantically *scandalous* as ever? At what address could one call on him and make his acquaintance?

But now Byron had abandoned Venice to go and live in Ravenna! On the mainland. Nearer to Rome! The English *always* visited Rome when in Italy. Oh, such lack of loyalty and consideration by Lord Byron for his friends stuck out here on the island of Venice was just too much to tolerate!

His fury became even more inflamed when he received a letter from Byron, hoping he had enjoyed his holiday in Switzerland; and telling him that the Ravenna Carnival was in full swing, and Allegra was to drive with Teresa down the Corso in her coach and six, preceded by outriders with blue and white feathers in their caps as part of the cavalcade.

"There is – to a foreigner – a mixture of mystery and hilarity in the general burst from everyday cares, that render a Carnival peculiarly attractive. Old and young, handsome and those who may be called so by courtesy, are all abroad, laughing, flirting, pleasant and sometimes pleasing. It is at this periodical Saturnalia that all ranks are jostled, and mingled and delighted, and all this without fear, observance or offence. Curiosity is always excited. Life becomes for the moment a drama without the fiction.

Hoppner shrugged, wondering why Byron appeared to find it all so delightful, when he had attended numerous Carnivals here in Venice, and surely much better Carnivals than anything Ravenna could produce.

Yet it seemed that Byron was enjoying every aspect of his life in Ravenna, from the card games to the theatre and the opera, besides the fine weather of nature's giving, and the rides in the Forest of Pines – but it was the next line that made Hopper lose his temper completely – *"Conversazioni, and much better than any at Venice."*

"I thought he was my *friend,*" Hoppner fumed to his

wife. "I *believed* we were the very best of friends, but obviously not. Now who am I going to speak English with and have all the English visitors courting my company in the hope of meeting him."

Mrs Hoppner, while continuing her knitting, had been considering the situation from a woman's perspective, and shrewdly so. "Of course, you know *why* he has gone to Ravenna, and to whom?"

"All Venice must know by now."

"And we also know," she said slowly, "that Lord Byron is a very *proud* young man. So perhaps ... perhaps if you were to write to him and hint – merely *hint* – some unfavourable criticisms about his lady-love, it might dent his vanity and dampen his ardour for her somewhat."

Hoppner stared at his wife. "Hint? I know nothing about her, so what the deuce could I *hint*?"

"You could hint that all Venice is laughing at him, running after her like that."

"And are they ... laughing at him?"

"Not as I know, but how is *he* to know one way or the other, down there in Ravenna? It's certainly worth a try."

After a long silence, Hoppner nodded. "Yes, it's clear he has now become hopelessly involved with that young Romagnola woman, and despite her being married she has caught him in her net. Now he will be at the mercy of all those barbaric Romagnoles. So, as I am the British Consul and he is a British Peer of the Realm, it will be my duty to save him and lure him back to Venice for his own good."

A maid interrupted, informing the Consul that one of Lord Byron's servants, a female, was downstairs in the hall, requesting to speak to him on Lord Byron's business.

"To me? To speak to *me*?" Hoppner was outraged. "I doubt she has come from his lordship who must know by now that I *never* speak to servants. Tell whoever she is to shoo!"

A few minutes later the maid returned to the drawing-room. "She won't shoo, Signore. She says she must speak to you on Lord Byron's business and will wait."

"Then let her wait – in the hall."

When the maid had quitted the room, Hoppner said to his wife. "This, if nothing else, will show Lord Byron how angry I am with him. I have been his humble servant long enough, but I shall not be so again – not unless he returns to Venice."

In the hall, Fanny Sylvestrini stood looking around her - there was not a chair to sit on, and the hall was freezing cold.

After standing for half an hour, Fanny was feeling irritable. Surely the British Consul was not so busy that he could leave her waiting for so long?

Still, she would have to endure it. Lord Byron had entrusted her with the task of arranging with the British Consul for some of his furniture in the Palazzo Mocenigo to be sent down to his new lodgings in Ravenna. And as Mylord always paid her well for any task that she did for him, she would have to wait for as long as necessary.

Fanny was still waiting in the hall at the end of the day, almost collapsing with the fatigue of standing for hours without a chair to sit on. Only the English could be so rude as to leave someone waiting for so long; and only for Mylord Byron would she suffer this!

The maid finally reappeared again, stating that Signore Hoppner had been too busy to see her today.

Only because she had come as an emissary of His Excellency, Mylord Byron, was Fanny able to maintain her dignity.

"I have been trusted with a task for His Excellency Mylord Byron, and I will not let him down, so you may tell the Consul that I will return in the morning, *before* he becomes too busy."

Once outside on the cold winter street, and frozen to the bone, Fanny lost all her dignity and gave way to her rage – pulling the lace veil from her head and furiously tearing it into remnants.

She had just flung the torn pieces of lace aside when the maid caught up with her. "Signora, he says you are not to come again in the morning *too* early. You may come at eleven. He will see you then for five minutes only."

~ ~ ~

In Ravenna some days later, Byron was quite shocked when he read Fanny's letter about the unpleasant behaviour of Richard Hoppner.

"If I could have believed that he would be so uncivil to me, I should have spared myself the trouble of waiting in a very cold waiting-room on the ground floor, and without a chair, in icy cold, tired from the long wait.

I returned the next day at the time he humiliated himself to see me, and he received me standing, in the same waiting-room or hall, without greeting me either when I came or when I went, and hardly condescended to tell me that he would see to everything, but I assure you Mylord, he did so with an air and voice that you, Mylord, would not have used with the least of your servants.

I cannot see the reason for such behaviour to me. You, who have always shown such goodness to me, came into my mind, and the comparison made odious to me the presence of the rude Mr Opner."

Byron found it hard to believe – Hoppner, who had always been so solicitous to him – was he truly capable of behaving in such a way? Did he even believe Fanny?

Was she exaggerating her treatment and misery in order to get extra pay?

Any doubt as to *who* had behaved badly was soon wiped out when another letter arrived on the afternoon post, from Richard Hoppner himself, and the tone and words of the letter were somewhat odd.

It is a thousand pities for your sake as well as my own, that I dare not always speak to you as I think, because if I tell you something for your own advantage, which concerns another person, you directly tell that other person from where you got the information, and then what was intended for your good alone, becomes a means of making me hated by others. You will not be surprised at the above remark, however puzzled you may be to guess at its meaning. And puzzled you must remain, and to your own cost.

The following day another letter arrived from the British Consul; and this time Hoppner's tone and words were rather menacing.

I am glad you are amusing yourself so well in Ravenna, but I would have you take care and heed my warning of their use of the knife. A blow in the dark costs little to people who are accustomed to making their passions stifle any appeal to their conscience.

And the letters kept coming, day after day, all odd and incomprehensible; as if Hoppner was playing some tortuous letter-game with him.

Byron was so baffled he showed some of the letters to Teresa, who could not help laughing a little. "He is jealous!"

"Of you?"

"No, of Ravenna. Now you are not in Venice he cannot boast of you. In Venice, Madame Benzoni told me how Signor Hoppner loves to go to her conversaziones and also Madame Albrizzi's only to talk to strangers of how well he knows you, and how good friends you are. He is writing these letters hoping you will go back to Venice, that is why he keeps asking when you will return."

Byron thought it all rather impudent and childish and wrote back a sharp note to Hoppner, ending with the assertion – "*I can fix no time for my return to Venice – it may be soon or late or not at all – it all depends on my dama.*"

In Venice, Hoppner's blood pressure was racing to his head as he showed the note to his wife. "Do you see what he says – it all depends on his *lady.*"

"Why, the audacity! She is not *his* lady. She belongs to that old gentleman who is legally her husband."

"Yes, another damned Romagnole! And *he* looks the very type to plunge a knife into Byron's back one dark night. It's no use, Isabelle, I will have to come straight out and tell him the truth, for his own good."

My dear Lord Byron – I am very sorry for the distress you feel on the Contessa's account, not only because I think they are good feelings thrown away on an unworthy object; but because I have reason to think it is particularly so in the present instance.

Human nature is such that our greatest pleasures derive from, and depend upon illusion: but I really cannot with patience see you throw yourself away on such people.

While it is merely for your amusement, I would never interfere with your pleasures: but to hear you talking of a serious attachment to a woman who, under her circumstances, would be unworthy of it, and who is reported to have entangled you in her nets merely from vanity, is what the friendship you have honoured me with, does not allow me to witness without a remonstrance.

Perhaps you will think I am taking an unwarrantable liberty with you. But I see you overwhelmed in a passion which is unworthy of you, and for one who, when she thinks herself sure of you, will leave you in the lurch, and make a boast of betraying you.

Should her present illness prove fatal, what I have said will appear offensive,, as there will be no time to prove the truth of it. If she recovers, which I hope she may do, you will have the leisure and opportunity to discover if I am not right in my opinion.

Your most humble and obedient servant,
R. B. Hoppner.

After which, the British Consul waited; certain his letter would cause a final and permanent breach in the relationship, and bring Byron back to his friends in Venice.

But as January stretched into February and then the month of March arrived, it finally dawned on Hoppner that Byron had no intention of giving his letter the respect or even the courtesy of a reply.

Instead, Byron was happily writing a letter to his friend John Hobhouse in London.

The other day, February 25th, we picked violets by the wayside here, at Ravenna; and now, March 3rd, it is snowing for all the world!

Chapter Twelve

~ ~ ~

By mid-March, when the snow had melted away under the warm sunshine, making deliveries of the post more reliable, Byron was astounded to receive a letter from his publisher, informing him that his friend John Hobhouse had been up to all sorts of bad behaviour in London.

Hobhouse had abandoned the Whigs and joined the *Reformers*, and then had written and published a pamphlet damning all the politicians in the House of Commons – for which offence the House of Commons had voted for him to be sentenced to five weeks in Newgate Jail – a term which Hobhouse had served without complaint for the past five weeks and was now due to come out again.

"So that's why I have not heard from him." Byron showed the letter to Fletcher: "Can you believe it – our *Hobby* – in prison, jailed for being a political dissident!"

"Now, if it was *you*, or even Mr Shelley, locked up for politics, my lord, I would not be at all surprised, but Mr Hobhouse ... I always thought he was so *sensible.*"

"I always knew he had grit," Byron said. "He is determined to one day become a politician and abolish child labour, but getting himself thrown into jail ... Of course, now that he has martyred himself into a prison cell on their behalf, the mob will love him."

Byron could not restrain the impulse to dash off a ballad about it, which he enclosed in the letter he had just written to John Murray, asking him to give it to Hobhouse.

My boy Hobby-O

Why did the House make this call
My boy Hobby-O?
They voted me to Newgate all,

Which is an awkward Jobby-O

How came you in Mob's pound to cool,
My boy, Hobby-O?
Because I bade the people pull
The House into the Lobby-O

You hate the House – why canvas, then?
My boy Hobby-O?
Because I would reform the den
As a member for the Mobby-O

The verses went on, silly and buffoonish, reminiscent of their college days at Cambridge. Byron even signed it as written by *"Infidus Scurra"* a name which Hobby would remember well.

Byron had not expected Hobby to take offence, but offence he took – writing back in fury to accuse Byron of laughing at his prison sentence.

Byron immediately wrote back:

Laugh at you? "Did I ever – no I never." The ballad was buffoonery, and this, you know, has all along been our mutual privilege. However, if this is but a prologue to a seat for you in Westminster, I shall less regret your previous ordeal; but I am glad now that I did not come back to England, for it would not have pleased me to find on my return my best friend in Newgate.

Still, I admire your gallantry, and think you could not do otherwise, having written the pamphlet, "but why bitch Mr Wild?" Why write it? Death and fiends! You used to be thought a prudent man, at least by me, whom you favoured with such good counsel. However, the king is dead, so get out of Mr Burn's apartments and get into the House of Commons, and then you can abuse it as much as you please, and I'll come over and hear you. Seriously; I did not "laugh" as you supposed I did; no more did Fletcher; but we both looked as grave as if we had been told we were to have been your bail.

And being truly serious, certain that Hobhouse's five weeks' imprisonment in Newgate would serve him better than years of political canvassing and electioneering around the country, Byron ended his letter to Hobhouse with yet another verse:

Would you go to the House by the true gate
Much faster than ever a Whig went
Let Parliament send you to Newgate
And Newgate will send you to Parliament.

In London, Hobhouse liked this last verse from Byron much better than all that Hobby-O nonsense; and later cherished it as being not only wise, but "*prophetic*".

A month later, on 14th April 1820, in Britain's General Election, John Cam Hobhouse won the peoples' vote and was elected to Parliament as the Member for Westminster.

On the platform, Hobhouse's acceptance speech was short, and sincere: "*I am a man chosen by the people, for the people, and I will do no other business but that of the people.*"

Stepping down from the platform, Scrope Davies embraced him with a smile. "Well done, Hobby. That speech of yours was short but true. If Byron was here, he would be very proud of you."

In Italy, having received a letter from him, Byron was not feeling proud of Hobby, but anxious, very anxious. The low of his imprisonment, followed by the high of his unexpected election victory, had suddenly smashed together to render poor Hobby depressed and panicky.

My difficulty is a sort of nervous sensibility about reputation, which may go far to preventing my having a reputation. I cannot conceal from myself that one of the causes is that I am not qualified for making ... 'a figure' ... in the House of Commons. I am too afraid of failing ever to succeed. My time in prison has certainly damaged my health ...

Byron was one of the very few people who knew that although John Hobhouse always appeared outwardly confident, he regularly suffered from severe self-doubt, and was too inclined to an unhealthy introspection on his own abilities.

He also knew that Hobhouse could be one of the finest politicians in the British Parliament, and wrote back telling him so.

"Take your fortune, Hobby – take it at the "flood" Now is your time, – & remember that in your very <u>Start</u> you have overtaken all whom you thought were better and before you.

Above all don't be diffident in yourself – nor be nervous about your health – leave that to poets & such fellows – & don't be afraid of your own talents. You have great talents – I tell you as I have told others – that you think too humbly of them. You have already shown yourself fit for very great things – & once in the House of Commons – I hope to hear of you being the best heard in it. Above all, recollect that it is all Luck in this world, and that all men have their time offered – and this is your time, Hobby – seize it."

Hobby replied by return of post. Knowing how Byron

had always hated any kind of hypocrisy or false flattery and would never deal in it, his letter had given a major boost to Hobhouse's confidence in himself, and now all his inner doubts were erased.

Yet Byron could not help smiling at the typical *modesty* of Hobby's reply, ignoring all comments about his "great talents".

> *"However, an honest man in Parliament I can be. And, I may add, I will be."*

PART THREE

Love and Separation

"Life is made up, not of great sacrifices or duties, but of little things, in which smiles and kindness, and small tendernesses given habitually, are what preserve the heart and secure comfort".

Sir Humphry Davy.

Chapter Thirteen

~ ~ ~

The hot Italian sun tinged the landscape of the gardens with a golden gleam as Byron and Teresa wandered through the fragrant, flowered air.

They confined themselves to the section of the gardens which the Count's balcony did *not* overlook, nor any of his windows, even though he caused them no difficulties or disturbance and seemed resigned to the situation.

So much so, that in her heart Teresa had forgiven the Count for every bad thing he had ever done or said to her, now feeling only gratitude for his generous act of inviting Lord Byron to lodge in his palazzo, which allowed her the happiness of being able to see Byron constantly.

In the garden as they strolled through the flowers and lemon trees, Allegra skipped beside them, declaring every flower she touched to be beautiful, continually turning her head to look up at her papa to see if he agreed ... *"Bel fiore, Papa?"*

"Bel fiore," Byron always agreed, even when she pointed to a small yellow-flowered weed. He felt great pride in his daughter, for she was a lovely little thing, although she could be a stubborn handful when it suited her.

The previous evening he had written to his sister Augusta, informing her of the progress of her niece:

"Allegra continues to develop as healthily as a pomegranate blossom, but is as obstinate as a mule. She thinks herself handsome, and so will do as she pleases. Is that not a true Byron?"

In Teresa he could find no fault at all. She was still as

lovely as she had always been, She had confided to him that her feelings for her husband had always been *filial*, like that of a granddaughter, due to the difference in their ages — "How else could it be?" she said. "You know he is older than my father?"

Byron knew, because during his visits to Count Ruggero Gamba's villa at Filetto, he had been introduced to Teresa's *real* grandfather, who was only ten or so years older than Guiccioli; a dear old man, whom all the girls called "*Nonno.*"

Byron had instantly liked the old Count Gamba Senior, who, despite his increasing age and infirmities, still bore himself with all the dignity of a nobleman of former times. He, too, yearned for the freedom of Italy, he told Byron, "but not for riches, no – only for the return of Italy's honour."

Byron watched Teresa with her grandfather, and saw how she treated the old man in the same way she generally treated Guiccioli, with patience and timidity and duty.

So different to the passionate and loving woman she was with him.

He truly loved her; although he could not help noticing that she, too – like Allegra – had her childish oddities, which secretly amused him.

An old acquaintance, Sir Humphry Davy, not finding Byron in Venice, had come to Ravenna and found him at the Palazzo Guiccioli.

Byron greeted him with pleasure "It is always good to see old friends again."

Humphry Davy laughed; "And that is why I have come all the way here to see *you*. How are you, dear boy?"

Teresa liked the look of Sir Humphry, a man of forty-two; and she helped Byron to entertain his guest in his first-floor drawing-room. Byron had told her that Sir Humphry Davy was "a famous scientist" and so she listened intently to their conversation, which did not seem to be about science at all, but the importance of knowledge.

"Learning, naturally, is a true pleasure," Sir Humphrey said, "so how sad it is, that in most schools it is made a pain?"

Byron agreed. "As in my days at Harrow – being forced to read *Prometheus* three times a year. I soon began to detest that book."

Byron poured more wine. "So, you are spending the summer in Rome? Have you been yet to Paris?"

"Yes, but do not ask me about Napoleon and his legacy, Byron, because on that man you and I will always differ."

"I was thinking more of John Hobhouse. When he came back from Paris he raved about all the art."

And on that Sir Humphry also differed, speaking of his time in Paris and his regret that he possessed no mental facility whatsoever for appreciating art.

"Did you go to all the art galleries?" asked Teresa.

"Oh yes," Sir Humphry sighed. "I toured all the galleries which had some of the finest frames I ever saw, but I can't remember what pictures were inside."

Byron smiled, knowing Davy was not joking. Such was the difference in the views of men – some admired the paintings, he admired the frames.

Yet Davy was a genius in his own field of electrochemistry; a man who came from Cornwall, and, together with his friend Gregory Watt, had invented the first 'incandescent light bulb' by passing an electric current through a thin strip of platinum. He had also discovered Potassium, and used the same method to isolate sodium.

All very clever, but none so funny as his experiments with some nitrous oxide mixed with air, which resulted in a strange kind of gas.

"Pray tell Teresa about your strange new gas," Byron urged him.

"I don't think it is strange at all. In fact, I believe it has great potential for relieving pain during surgery."

"Yes, but its *name* – pray tell her its name and how it

came about?"

Humphry looked sheepishly at Teresa, who nodded. "Please do, Signore."

"Well, as Lord Byron said, I was experimenting with nitrous oxide, and was astonished when it made me start laughing, and keep on laughing, and I began to feel very euphoric, so I nicknamed it 'Laughing Gas'.

Byron was grinning. "You don't happen to have any of it in your bag now, do you?"

"Of course not, it's too addictive, and so remains in my laboratory. But seriously, I *do* believe that once modified to induce only a feeling of pleasant calmness, and used through a tube, it could prove a great relief to patients during surgery."

Teresa decided that the Cornishman was a wonder-worker, capable of inventing anything, and later that evening she asked Byron how long Signor Davy was to stay with them.

"A few days."

"So, as he is your friend, will you ask him to invent something for *me?*"

"For you?"

"Pray beg him to make me something to dye my eyebrows dark – I have tried a thousand things but the colour *will* come off."

"All this she said with the greatest earnestness," Byron wrote with amusement to Hobby, *"and what will surprise you, is that she is neither ignorant nor a fool, but well educated and clever. But they speak like children, when first out of their convents; and after all, this is better than an English blue-stocking."*

~~~

Other English friends and acquaintances had called in on Byron at Ravenna, although small in number compared to those who had visited him in Venice; and
~~~

these many visitors had roused the suspicions of the Austrian police.

Why was Lord Byron so popular a man? Why were so many fascinated with him that they would travel so far to see him? And why did so many openly refer to him as *"One of the leaders of the Romantic Movement."* Surely they knew that in Italy the word *Romantic* meant "liberal" and all those who opposed the present Government.

The Austrian police finally came up with the only possible reason for so many Englishmen coming to visit Lord Byron; and reported to their superiors in Rome:

> *By the most careful supervision, it has been discovered that his secretary, Lega Zambelli, is chiefly occupied in writing in various cyphers. But it is not known in what way these writings are despatched, for they are certainly not sent through the post. There is reason to believe that these English travellers, many of whom have introductions to Mylord, are charged with these despatches to hand to Carbonari in other parts of Italy.*

The next letter written and sent through the post by Lega Zambelli was opened and scrutinised; but the hidden cyphers which the police believed it contained, were too difficult to understand ... and so they reported to Rome that the letter to Milan *"contains an extract from a very curious and rare work on Jesuitical Masonry."*

The fact that Lega Zambelli had, in his younger days, been a Catholic priest, was obviously unknown to the Austrian police.

The hint of "Masonry" had an inspirational effect on one of the spies – an Italian double-spy named Giusseppe Valtancoli – who reported to the Austrians, who in turn reported to Rome:

"His Lordship wears on his watch-chain a triangular (or pyramidal) seal, on the face of which are engraved three small stars. And on the seal are cut the letters F.S.Y. This is the new signal adopted some months ago by the Guelph Society of Freemasonry Carbonari, and Romantici.

The Romantici form a band that aims at the destruction of our literature, our politics, our country. Lord Byron is certainly its champion, and you deceive yourself if you believe that in Ravenna he is only occupied in making a cuckold of Guiccioli.

In Rome, the Director of Police was beginning to have suspicions about all these reports sent to him about Lord Byron, especially those from Giusseppe Valtancoli. Could a *double-spy* ever be truly trusted?

If all the reports were true, then Lord Byron must do nothing else in life but travel. In one report he is in Bologna, solely to head a branch of the *Società Romantica*, accompanied by the Irish writer Lady Morgan, and also his friend Lord Kinnaird. The next day he is reported to be in the Borromean Islands, and the next day in Naples. All impossible.

The Director sat back and mused ... So what *did* Rome know about Lord Byron for certain and true? That he was a poet whose fame had now spread all over Europe. That in France he was known as *"The Napoleon of Poetry."* That in Germany he was adored by the *literati* and idolised by the famous German poet, Johann Wolfgang von Goethe.

So ... perhaps it was Byron's *poetry* that needed to be studied, and not the man? Perhaps all the cyphers and hidden messages to the Carbonari were to be found in his poetry? That would explain why so many pirated editions of his writings were printed and distributed all over Italy by unknown people.

The Director finally shrugged tiredly at the futility of

it all.

Even if it were so – even if the Englishman was sympathetic to the Carbonari, and even if he was one of their so-called "Good Cousins" – he was also a *Peer of the British Realm,* a member of the British House of Lords – and so they dare not touch him.

The British were very proud in that way. They would allow you to assist them in destroying the French. But they would never allow you to interfere with one of their own.

And yet, were *any* of these conflicting reports and dark rumours from spies about Lord Byron true? The Director of Police was seriously beginning to have his doubts.

Chapter Fourteen

~ ~ ~

One of the reasons why Byron liked life in Ravenna so much, was his great friendship with Teresa's father, Count Ruggero Gamba. Their affection for each other was as true as it was mutual; and in Byron, Teresa's father saw the son-in-law he should have had, and *could* have had, if only he had waited.

They talked often about Italian politics, and now Ruggero informed Byron that Ravenna had a new Cardinal Legate.

"He is one of us, from Romagna, so not so much in the pocket of the Austrians. You may like him – unlike the last Cardinal who was a secret friend of Guiccioli."

"A *secret* friend?"

Ruggero nodded. "I told you, Guiccioli always secretly keeps on good terms and holds hands with *both* sides. In that way, whoever triumphs, he thinks he cannot fail to be on the side of the victors. He thinks only of himself, and the *position* of himself. Even in the oppression of Italy by the Austrians."

This made Byron confide to Ruggero something that had been troubling him lately about Count Guiccioli.

"When Teresa and I are together, he does not appear critical in any way. He remains aloof and polite, as if it has nothing to do with him. But, of late, he actually seems to be *conniving* at our relationship, and pushing us together even more. Why do you think that is?"

Ruggero knew instantly. "He wants something from you, something important. And again he is using Teresa to get what he wants."

"It can't be money," Byron said. "He is already in too much debt to me, with the threat of court proceedings hanging over him if he defaults. So what else is there?"

"With Guiccioli, who knows?" Ruggero replied. "But sooner or later, for certain, he will make it known to you."

~~~

Byron wondered if the time to discover the intentions of Guiccioli's conniving had come, when another huge basket of fruits and candied nuts was delivered to his drawing-room by one of the Count's servants.

The basket contained no note, and the servant had not been given a reason.

A few minutes later a second servant arrived, delivering a basket containing a selection of bottled wines from Guiccioli's own vineyard.

Again there was no note, and the servant had been given no reason.

This kind of behaviour in sending gift after gift, was how a rich man courted a woman; so what was Guiccioli up to?

Byron came to the conclusion that the Count was either a touch mad, or a complete eccentric. How else to explain all his strange ways?

As for the wine – with the rumours of Guiccioli having poisoned two wives and a priest in the past with glasses of his wine – not a drop of this new delivery would be drank. As soon as darkness came, he would get Fletcher to empty the bottles out into the soil somewhere at the back of the gardens.

The Count arrived next, in person, a sheepish smile on his face. "We had a small disagreement yesterday," he said. "So this is my way of apologising."

Byron was slightly baffled, unable to recall any disagreement the day before; and it was hardly possible as he had been out all day with Teresa at her father's palazzo in Filetto.

"Do I have your forgiveness?" the Count asked.

"There is nothing to forgive."

"Good. Then we will drink some wine together in friendship."

The Count sat himself down and looked around the drawing-room, surprise and curiosity on his face.
~~~

"Where is the furniture that was in here? You have replaced it all with *new* furniture?"

Byron nodded as he opened a bottle of wine and began to pour some into a glass. "It's an oddity of mine. Wherever I live, I prefer my own furniture. Some of this new furniture came from my palazzo in Venice, and the rest I purchased in Bologna."

"Why did I not see it being delivered?"

Byron smiled. "It must have come during the time of one of your one afternoon naps."

"And where is the old furniture?"

"It is quite safe. All neatly put away in one of the empty rooms."

"Well, I'm glad to know you did not discard any. Some of those pieces are family heirlooms."

Which was exactly why Byron had replaced them. How did he know if one of the wives, or even the priest, had been sitting in one of those chairs or sofas on the night they were poisoned?

Guiccioli stared as he saw Byron filling his own glass from the jug of soda-water. "You are not drinking any wine?"

"No, my stomach feels a little bilious today, so I must confine myself to simple soda-water."

The Count drank his own wine rather quickly. "Bologna? Do you often go to Bologna?"

"No, not often."

"We have a new Cardinal Legate. He is from Bologna. Have you heard anything about him?"

Byron sat down. "No. Why should I?"

"There is a rumour that he has great sympathy for the Carbonari, unlike the last Cardinal who cared only for Rome and the Austrians. It is very worrying."

"Why so?"

The Count paused, wondering if Lord Byron was as innocent as he looked. "Do you not know that there is great trouble brewing in Italy?"

"What kind of trouble?"

"The Carbonari want to throw out the Austrians and

gain the freedom of Italy and the freedom from Papal rule, but the Austrians and Rome are determined they shall not get it. For myself, personally, I take *no sides*. Not one or the other. I have a great hatred of any kind of violence, and I detest all politics. All I wish is to live a quiet life with no disturbance.

"If you take no side, then why need you worry? If there is going to be trouble, you would not be involved."

"No, I would not be involved," the Count agreed, "but some might *make* me so. You do not know the people of Romagna as I do. Some might say I am friendly with the Carbonari, which I am not. But if the Austrians win, I could be arrested and imprisoned. There were a number of arrests in Milan a few days ago. Arrests of men of high Italian rank. No one is safe."

"Milan?" Byron caught his breath. "Do you know their names? The men arrested?"

The Count shrugged. "Their names are in the newspaper. I remember the name of only one, because he is well-known in Italy as a poet ... Silvio Pellico."

Byron feigned indifference, managing a slight shrug. "A poet? I have never heard of him. Why did they arrest him?"

"Because Milan is a hot-bed of intellectual revolutionaries who want to unify Italy and remove the Austrians, even worse than Naples and Bologna. Which reminds me ... this new Cardinal from Bologna, I do not trust him."

Byron did not give a damn if Guiccioli trusted the new Cardinal or not, he was inwardly too distressed about the arrest of Silvio Pellico. All he hoped now was that his friends in Milan, Ludovico di Brême and men such as Monti, had not been arrested also.

He had first met Ludovico di Brême at the Swiss home of the former French revolutionary, Madame de Staël. Some months later, arriving with Hobhouse in Milan, they had been met and been looked after for three full weeks by Ludovico di Brême, who introduced them to more Milanese Carbonari, including Silvio

Pellico. He and Hobhouse had spent all of their time in the company of these good men. Now Silvio Pellico had been arrested. What of the others?

He was so lost in his thoughts he did not realise that Guiccioli had been speaking to him, until the Count stood up to pour himself more wine saying – "Tea is good for the stomach. If you drink some tea it will make you feel better and look less pale."

Byron affected an amused smile. "I thought my years in Italy had *bronzed* me."

"Yes, yes, but it is a *British* kind of bronze, which to us looks pale."

The Count sat down again with his refilled glass, an uneasy look on his face. "As I said, Mylord, I take *no sides*, but in the event of trouble I need to protect myself. And so I would ask you to try to grant me some accommodation?"

"Accommodation?" Byron had no idea what the man was talking about. "Is it not you that has granted *me* accommodation?"

"As a way of paying off my loan, yes, but you know that is not what I am talking about."

"No, I have no idea what you are talking about," Byron responded with some impatience. "To me accommodation is accommodation ... a place to live."

The Count sighed, and then said cajolingly. "It would do no harm to you. But it would provide great safety for me. And if you helped me in this way, I would be forever grateful to you. Surely you can do something? You are, after all, a British Nobleman."

The man was becoming tiresome. Byron held up his palm. "Alessandro, pray come to the point and state what this favour may be, but speak plainly, as my Italian is not as fluent as yours."

Guiccioli said: "Perhaps you do not understand how powerful the word *'British'* is here in Italy. Even the Austrians respect and fear the British. And as you are of the British House of Lords, you are *untouchable* to both the Austrians and Rome. And in that way you can help me."

Byron still did not understand how.

So Guiccioli explained on. He took *no sides,* but the Austrians and the Papal Government were now on very bad terms with him. He had suspected it when they intervened against him in his recent lawsuit in Bologna, ensuring that the other side won their case unfairly. And now his friend, the former Cardinal, had left Ravenna and this new one from Bologna was in his place.

Now Byron was certain that the old man was a paranoid eccentric, suspiciously convincing himself that the Papal Government would intervene in a small Bologna lawsuit. He even seemed to think that the new Cardinal had been sent from Bologna for the sole purpose of making life difficult for him.

And then, at last, came the favour; which was as ridiculous as its petitioner.

What Guiccioli wanted, was for "Mylord Byron", as a British Peer, to write to the correct authorities in the Foreign Office in England, requiring them to give Count Alessandro Guiccioli, the post of the British Vice-Consul at Ravenna.

"To a request from *you,* they will agree," Guiccioli said. "And if I am given the post of Consul to a great foreign nation such as Great Britain, it will protect me against the Austrians and the Papal Government. It will also enable me to obtain a lot of privileges."

Byron did his best not to laugh, but just as quickly he saw a number of possibilities in this for himself. It would be yet another way of keeping Guiccioli indebted to him, which would keep him in order while he strung him along waiting for an official reply from England.

"I could write and make the request, yes."

"And they would not refuse their most famous Lord," Guiccioli said with certainty.

"I can make no promises," Byron said. "All I can do is write and make my request for you to be given the post."

"Write now," Guiccioli said eagerly. "Who knows when Italy will blow into turmoil, so I beg you to write now."

Byron could not refuse, yet he had no intention of writing to the Foreign Office. If Britain was to have a Consul at Ravenna, he would want someone more competent and less money-grabbing than this eccentric, Guiccioli.

The Count had risen and was already standing over by the desk, as if looking for the pen and ink.

Byron joined him and quickly moved him aside as if he was treading into a private and sacred space. "Do not touch anything. Not even my servants are allowed to touch my desk."

The Count smiled meekly. "Forgive me. I sometimes forget that you are a poet. In comparison to you I am illiterate, but I take pride in having proved myself a great man in business. Even my lawsuit in Bologna would not have failed, but for the intervention of the Austrian and Papal Government."

Byron sat down, dipped his pen in the ink, and paused. "If there *is* trouble in Italy, you appear to be very confident that it is the Austrians who will win."

The Count shrugged. "Already they have arrested some of the Carbonari ringleaders in Milan, so who would wager against the Austrians holding the field. They did at Waterloo, alongside the British."

Byron lifted out a sheet of his writing paper, causing Guiccioli's eyes to glow at the sight of the Byron Crest with the coronet above it.

"Do you know to whom you write?" he asked.

"To one of the most influential men in London."

"And you know him well?"

Byron nodded. "He is like a father to me."

"Good, good ... will there be much pay with the post of Consul."

"That I could not say. We British consider it very bad form to talk socially about money."

"The amount is of no consequence, because I know the British pay well. But more than that, it is the protection of the British post that I seek."

Byron had fidgeted for long enough, cleaning the nib of his pen with a cloth, but with the Count looking over his shoulder, he began to write.

... Count Guiccioli is a man of large property, but he wishes to have a British protection, in case of changes here in Italy, so that his office of Consul would be useful; so I would be obliged if you would use of your connection with the Prince Regent to make this request of mine to the Foreign Office on behalf of Count Alessandro Guiccioli.

When the full letter was completed, Guiccioli asked that it be read to him In Italian. Byron did so, and Guiccioli appeared elated.

"Now if you will address the cover and seal it, Mylord, I will have it sent to the post immediately.

Byron addressed the letter to *The Honourable John Murray, Albermarle Street, London.*

And then the Count was gone, letter in hand; and Byron could not help smiling as he thought of the reaction of his publisher when he received the letter – probably declaring to his editor William Gifford in amazement – *"Why the deuce has Byron written this nonsense to me? What do I know about Foreign posts for Consuls?"*

Chapter Fifteen

~ ~ ~

Now that the letter requesting the post of British Consul at Ravenna had been sent; a post which Guiccioli was certain would be given to him; the Count's strange behaviour increased, and his attitude became malicious and spiteful – not to Lord Byron, whom he now claimed to love like a son – but to Teresa, who had not only deserted him in every way, but took up all Mylord's time and kept him all to herself.

This new jealous hatred he felt for Teresa was something he showed only to her, and only when he could speak to her alone and in private. She strove to soothe and pacify him, but his heated words became harsh and distasteful and cutting.

Day after day he made all kinds of quietly-spoken threats to her, and she began to fear for her life. He threatened to make her infidelity known to the Pope in Rome – and to the Pope he intended to provide *proof*. If that did not work, he would find some other way.

Teresa became so frightened, she, too, refused to drink any glass of wine that had been poured by her husband, nor eat any food that had been prepared by his cook.

Nor did she make any mention of the Count's threats to Byron, who might decide to be very English and do the decent thing by removing himself – the cause of all the problems – from her and Ravenna; and that would break her heart.

Byron had his own sadness to deal with. A letter from Hobhouse had told him that their dear friend since Cambridge, Scrope Davies, an inveterate gambler, had been cheated in some way and had lost all his money, a very large amount, and so he had gone the way of Beau Brummell – ruined by gambling and had escaped to the Continent – never to see England again, not unless he wished to reside for years in a Debtor's Prison.

So Scrope is gone – down-diddled – and fled to Bruges? What has become of him? Does nobody know? He could hardly remain at Bruges. Am I to never hear his jokes again? What fools we were to let him go back in 1816, from Switzerland. He would at least have saved his credit and his money, and now, <u>what</u> is he to do? He can't play, and without play he is wretched.

Hobhouse replied by return of post, still upset about the disappearance of Scrope Davies, and now beginning to fear the disappearance of Byron. Hobhouse's prejudices against the people of the Romagna region, and his fear of their hot-tempered violence, had not abated.

"He worries like a woman," Byron said to Fletcher; and then, half-grinning, wrote back to reassure Hobby that he was quite safe in Romagna, and there was nothing to worry about.

The last person to have been assassinated here was the Commissary of Police, three months ago; they <u>kilt</u> him from an alley one evening, but he is now recovering from the slugs with which they sprinkled him – from an "Archibugia" that shot him from round a corner, like the Irishman's gun.

It is the custom of the country, and not much worse than all the duelling in England. They killed a carabineer the other day, and wounded another – that is, some annoyed country gentlemen did, because they had been shut out of the theatre, due to arriving late.

We have sad windy weather here at present, and no very bright political horizon. But on that I shall say nothing, as I <u>know</u> the police have spies upon me, *because I sometimes shoot with a rifle! They are in such a state of suspicion as to dread everything and everybody. They know why I came here, yet they don't think a woman a sufficing reason for so long a residence. As for the Austrians, they are bullying Milan and Lombardy as usual.*

~~~

Now that Count Guiccioli had passed on his duties as Teresa's escort to Lord Byron, he accepted an invitation to spend the evening in the parlour of a priest, a minor prelate to the Cardinal Legate. The prelate longed to become a Cardinal Legate himself one day, and so was a slave to Rome and the Austrians.

The prelates fierce ambition had corrupted him, and so he was more loyal to the previous Cardinal Malvasia, than this new Cardinal Rusconi from Bologna, who was too soft on the people and too dismissive of orders from the Austrians.

In the absence of Cardinal Rusconi in Rome, the prelate was at his most cheerful, eager to glean information about Lord Byron from the Count's consumption of too much brandy, which would surely lead to indiscretions, and so he kept topping-up the old man's glass.

Politics were discussed.

Guiccioli knew the prelate was on the side of the Austrians, and so he praised the Austrians.

"This new Cardinal from Bologna," said Guiccioli warily, "he does not think or feel the same as you."

The prelate shrugged in disgust. "He is an old man who for forty years has kept the same woman as his housekeeper and comforter. He lives by the *old* Italian ways."

"Last week," Guiccioli said, "before he left for Rome, this new Cardinal from Bologna invited Mylord
~~~

Byron to dine with him."

The prelate sat up. "And did he attend?"

"Yes, and when Mylord returned that night, he referred to the new Cardinal as 'a fine old boy'."

"I'm sure His Catholic Holiness in Rome would not approve of Cardinal Rusconi inviting a Protestant heretic to dine with him," said the prelate with more disgust; and then he sat and sulked ... His order from the Austrian police in Ravenna was to somehow find a way to get Lord Byron to leave Romagna. And the Austrians had ordered this, because they knew the priests held more power over the people than the police.

He topped up Guiccioli's glass with more brandy, and then said with exquisite softness and subtlety:

"My dear Conte, you will forgive me for asking, but why have you provided lodging in your house for a man as fascinating as Lord Byron?"

The Count did not immediately answer, unwilling to reveal his indebtedness and all the money he owed to Byron.

"Mylord is, as you say, fascinating."

"Especially to your wife. They say she idolises him. Do you think it wise for you to tolerate his intimacy with the Contessa?"

"He is her friend, nothing more. He is my friend also. A *family* friend."

The prelate ignored such ridiculousness. "You know, Conte, in the town, the tongues are wagging. They are saying that, by allowing him to live in your home and consort with your wife, under your eyes, and with your approval, you have made him the master of your house – and you have become *his* tenant. Is that satisfactory to you? To your pride?"

"Nonsense!" Guiccioli was fuming. "He is our friend and honoured guest, and the people in the town are jealous."

Seeing him enraged and therefore off-guard, the prelate persisted: "Does he ever speak to you of Italian politics?"

"No, never."

"Never makes an unpleasant comment about the Austrians?"

"No. I am sure that, like myself, he admires the Austrians and the manner in which they keep the people in order."

"Nevertheless ... perhaps it would bring peace all round if you were to suggest that he return to England? He must have duties there. After all, there is soon to be the crowning of their new king, and as a lord of the English realm, his attendance at the Coronation will be expected."

"That is his business. I know nothing about it."

"Maybe Mylord does not know either, due to being so involved with your Contessa. Perhaps *you* should inform him of his new king's coronation and his duty to attend?"

Returning home in his carriage, Count Guiccioli was white-faced with rage. How dare that arrogant young prelate tell him what to do? How dare he say who should live in his house or not? Oh, such disrespect!

The more he thought of it, the more he fumed; and then he decided that it was all Teresa's fault. She was the one to blame. That young *squaldrinetta* had now brought his household and his noble guest under the watch of the priests. He would have to make changes.

Byron had already received his invitation to the Coronation of the Prince of Wales, forwarded on to him in the post by Hobhouse.

He wrote back to Hobby saying he could not go, because –

"My spouse and I could not walk together at it. So I will leave 'dearest duck' to waddle down the aisle on her own. She will glory in it; and I have no great inclination to attend."

~~~

Count Guiccioli's behaviour towards Teresa became even worse; no longer harsh and sharp, but sly and evil, quietly accusing her of plotting treachery against him.

Again she did her best to soothe and mollify him, reading to him from the French newspapers while he sat back and listened, translating to him after every paragraph, answering his questions.

Then he asked her to do what he had never done before – demand that she read a book to him while he ate his lunch and dinner, chewing and slurping while she quietly read, and leaving her no time at all to see Byron during the day.

At the end of these various duties, he never thanked her, but always finished by putting his finger to his eye in silent warning, reminding her of his threats against her.

Byron had no idea of the turmoil Teresa was going through, nor of the threats she was daily suffering. He had noticed, with some puzzlement, that she now always seemed to be very busy with Guiccioli during the day, unable to go walking in the gardens or riding in the forest with him.

Only in the evenings, when the Count went out to the theatre or a conversazione, was he able to see her in private and be alone with her.

Teresa's only explanation was that the Count was "depressed in his mind and ailing in his body" so it was her duty to attend upon him.

Yet whenever the Count ventured upstairs to call on Byron, he looked as fit as always – a little too wide around the girth, perhaps, and a little red in the face after climbing the stairs – but his manner was always friendly and cheerful.

So he was very surprised when, going downstairs one evening to call on Teresa, he was halted at the foot of
~~~

the staircase by Count Guiccioli in a jealous rage, informing him he could no longer allow him to visit Teresa.

"This is a change in your attitude," Byron said.

"I can no longer allow your friendship with the Contessa to continue. The tongues in the town are wagging, causing not only damage to *my* reputation, but also to *yours*, Mylord. They are saying you are now, with my approval, her *cavalier servente,* her official lover. Do you wish people to speak that way of you? I can no longer allow it!"

Byron could only stare at Guiccioli in disbelief. He had actively been *encouraging* the relationship, so why the change now?

"They are saying I am no longer master of my own house!" fumed Guiccioli. "I do not blame you because I know it is the Contessa who is to blame. Like all women she cares nothing for rules and regulations. To be allowed to be with you she has threatened and harassed me and – "

Byron held up his palm, refusing to hear a word against Teresa, saying coldly: "She is incapable of such behaviour, but with respect to both your age and your house, I will not quarrel with you."

"Your visits to her apartments are now displeasing to me," Count Guiccioli went on. "I wish them to stop!"

Byron did not answer. He had turned on his last word, and was already walking up the stairs back to his own apartments.

Ten minutes later he descended the stone stairs from his drawing-room down into the grounds of the rear garden, and then walked around to the French doors of Teresa's bedroom and lightly gave three *rata-rap-tap*'s in their familiar signal on the glass of one of the doors.

She rushed to open the door in fright; she had been listening at her apartment door, down the hall from the stairs, and had heard it all.

"We have to be careful," she said. "Some of his servants are loyal to him because they fear him, and fear losing their employment."

She then explained how difficult Alessandro had been of late, but did not mention the threats. Also, she had not heard Byron's quietly-spoken words at the end, and asked him, "Did he insult you?"

"Only in that he referred to me as your *cavalier servente,* which I do find rather insulting. The *cavalier* I do not object to, but the *servente* part does not sit well with me at all. I don't possess the right personality or temperament for *serventisimo* to anyone.."

Teresa sat down in a chair, foreseeing great trouble and unhappiness ahead. She was certain of only one thing – she would give up her life before she would give up Byron.

Chapter Sixteen

~~~

Count Ruggero Gamba had rarely seen Teresa's face looking so pale, not since the day he had visited her in Ravenna in her curtained room, before he had written to Mylord Byron requesting him to return.

"Teresina ... why do you come to Filetto so early in the morning? What is wrong?"

"I was awake all night, Papa. I could not sleep ... and now I have made my decision. I want to leave Alessandro and his house, and leave them *forever*. I have long endured his warped morals to get money, his violent behaviour, his offensive and vicious remarks. And now he has become evil, making all sorts of threats to me."

"Threats?" Count Gamba made his daughter sit down and calm down, and tell him about all these threats from Guiccioli.

So Teresa told him, trembling as she did so, for since the threats she could not stop herself thinking of Alessandro's two former wives who had died suddenly and without warning, and rumoured to have died by his sly hand.

"And now – after all he has said to me – I am afraid of the very air I breathe!"

Count Gamba managed to control his rage. "What does Mylord Byron say?"

"About the threats? I did not tell him. He would blame it all on himself, and go back to Venice. And if he goes from Ravenna, I will go with him."

"You *must* leave Guiccioli, yes, but you cannot leave Ravenna or the Palazzo Guiccioli – not yet. We must do this right, so *you* are not placed in the wrong by running away from your husband. *Your* name and reputation, must be protected."

Teresa stared at her father in confusion. "How can
~~~

that be done?"

"Leave it to Papa." He patted her hand to reassure her that everything would be all right; his mind rapidly working it all out.

"We will do it the right way – God's way." He stood up. "Now I will go to my study and write a letter for you to give to Mylord Byron, to apprise him of the true situation, and to ensure his protection of you. In the meantime, until this matter is resolved, I want you to go back to the Palazzo Guiccioli and behave as if you have forgiven Alessandro. Read to him from the French newspapers whenever he wishes, and also his books. Do not refuse, and do not make him suspicious of anything out of the ordinary."

"Papa, what are you going to do?"

He told her, and slowly she smiled, standing up to hug him. "You will do this for me?"

A look of great sadness came onto her fathers face. "*Mia cara*, you would not be in this situation at all, if it were not for me. I should have chosen better for you."

As soon as Teresa had left, Count Gamba dismissed all other personal emotions, all other solutions aside; feeling only the urgency to rescue his daughter from such a terrible marriage; and in his own name, he addressed a Petition to the Sovereign Pontiff in Rome, Pope Pius VII.

When it was written and signed, he took the Petition into town, and showed it to the Cardinal Legate – Cardinal Antonio Rusconi – who had just returned from Rome.

They were old friends, and Cardinal Rusconi was not surprised at the document placed before him. He knew Guiccioli, and thought him a very strange man. He read the Petition carefully, and then picked up his pen and endorsed it with his signature.

Ruggero knew he could ask Cardinal Rusconi to send the Petition to Rome for him, on his behalf; but he did not ask, because he knew he had an even better emissary to the Pope than the Cardinal – Countess Cecilia Machirelli Giordani.

Countess Cecilia was a German lady, of the highest merit, the sister of Count von Cobentzel. She was related to the leading houses in Germany, and the Pope had the warmest regard for her.

She was also the mother of Ruggero's late wife, and Teresa's maternal grandmother.

Pope Pius VII, when he had been a mere priest and then a Cardinal in Bologna, had been a close friend of that German aristocratic family, and he himself had officiated at the wedding of Ruggero to Countess Cecilia's daughter, in the chapel of their summer residence near Bologna.

Now Ruggero sent the Petition by courier to his mother-in-law, in Pesaro, with a note requesting her to do what needed to be done. It was imperative now, that Teresa be granted a Decree of Separation from Count Alessandro Guiccioli, who, in the short time they had been married, had attempted on numerous occasions to *prostitute* Teresa for his own financial gain.

Countess Cecilia did not hesitate; and a few days later, within the Vatican, Ruggero's petition reached the Pope's hands.

As Pope Pius read the Petition, he was heard observing to his secretary, "A courteous request made by Count Gamba on his daughter's behalf, and recommended by Countess Cecilia, cannot fail to be a just request."

Still, as a precaution, and for the sake of fairness, it was decided that Cardinal Rusconi, the Legate in Ravenna, who knew both parties in the marriage, be called upon to write and send his own detailed opinion to the Pope, before the decree could be signed.

~ ~ ~

In Ravenna, although only a short time – the waiting for a definite reply from the Pope seemed endless to Teresa.

And yet again Byron was writing to his sister Augusta, asking her to beg his wife to agree to a divorce – and if not – *"Is there no way it could be got in Scotland? Cannot it be done there by the husband solely?"*

In replies to his previous letters with this same question, Augusta had made no reference to his request for a divorce. Nor did she this time – except *this* time – she enclosed with her short note in reply, a *Prayer Book*.

"Now I *know* for certain that she has been commandeered by my wife and is under her rule. Poor Augusta, little does she know the true mind of the viper who gives her prayer books to send to me."

Teresa could not comprehend his rage. "But, *mio Byron*, surely you understand, even if she were to grant you a divorce, and even if the Pope was to grant me a Decree of Separation, under the laws of my Church, I still could not *marry* you."

"If Alessandro died, you could marry again. And is he to live forever?"

In the meantime, Alessandro was acting very oddly, giving himself up to a host of shifts in his behaviour. The oddest of all was his pleading every day for discussions with Byron.

Byron thought all this very peculiar, and was on his guard; refusing, by pretending to be ill or any other excuse he could think of.

Not strictly following her father's instructions, when the Count was around, Teresa confined herself to the seclusion of her own apartments where she read new books, filling her mind with knowledge, so that she would be more equal to Byron when they had conversations on literature.

Occasionally she did force herself to read from the French newspapers to Alessandro, translating for him; and also, occasionally, some pages from a book or two. Why he needed *a wife* to read for him, and not his own eyes, annoyed her.

"I have a problem with my cataracts," he told her.

This was the first she had heard of any problem with his eyes.

"Then should you not go to an eye doctor?"

"No, they are too expensive. And why should I – when I have you to read to me?"

~~~

Cardinal Antonio Rusconi was an honest man, and so he was having some difficulty in writing his own personal opinion for the Pope; and told this, with regret, to Count Gamba.

"You must understand, Ruggero, that I cannot, in God's name, lie to His Holiness. And although I know you and your family very well, I know l'Conte Guiccioli hardly at all. In Bologna I heard many bad rumours about him, but I cannot base my written opinion on rumours."

"Do you not believe my words?" Ruggero was angry.

"I *do* believe your words."

"And yet you still cannot write your opinion?"

"I have prayed about this, Ruggero, and now I believe it is *your* honest words that should be read by Pope Pius. Your Petition to him is very courteous, but it does not go into the detail of all the unpalatable facts."

"So what am I to do?"

Cardinal Rusconi put the fingertips of both his hands together as if in prayer.

"What I am going to ask you to do, Ruggero, is to write to me, giving me all the facts of the marriage, as you know them; and also your opinion on the marriage, as Teresa's father. If you do that, I can then send *your* written words to the Pope, with a short note of confirmation from me, because I have known you for so long, I know you will not write an untruth."

Upon his return to Filetto, sitting in the quiet of his study, Count Gamba began to write his letter to the Papal Legate in Ravenna, His Eminence, Cardinal
~~~

Rusconi, which would be forwarded to the Pope; and as he did so, Ruggero's rage against Guiccioli made his hand shake as he wrote furiously — stating to the Cardinal that his daughter should be granted a decree of separation from Alessandro Guiccioli, on the grounds that —

In the short space of one year of marriage he has behaved so strangely and heaped so many insults on his unhappy bride, that it has become wholly impossible for her to live any longer with so exacting and despotic a husband. And she is obliged, in the opinion of the whole city, to seek a complete separation.

And by this behaviour, does Count Guiccioli not admit himself to be the blackguard which the world considers him? I hope that Your Eminence will recognize him to be one — and that will suffice me. For if I wished, by words, deeds or writings, to prove how he attempted, for vile financial considerations, to prostitute, or sell, and disgrace my daughter and make her unhappy, I could show it with the greatest clearness; but the extremely delicate nature of the subject obliges me to keep silent, avoiding the scandal of public controversy; so that, satisfied by public opinion, who feel the same as I do about Count Guiccioli, I am willing to trust myself and my Petition to the conscience and justice of my superiors.

~~~

In the Vatican, reading Count Gamba's words, Pope Pius had no hesitation in granting the Papal Decree of Separation, adding that a suitable yearly allowance was to be made by Count Guiccioli to the Contessa, *"in order*
~~~

that she may live suitably and in comfort, as befits her noble birth and position. By the grace, etc., etc.

The Pope's secretary then took the Rescript to one of the Cardinals, who would decide the amount for a suitable allowance, and instruct the secretary in the details of the document to be drawn up.

The Cardinal to whom the secretary solicited for assistance with the Rescript, was Cardinal Alessandro Malvasia, the previous Cardinal Legate of Ravenna, now in Rome.

Cardinal Malvasia personally disliked Count Guiccioli, but he had been a good informer for the Austrians when it was needed, And Count Ruggero Gamba – that Carbonaro – along with his friend Lord Byron, should not be the victors in this. No, they should not ... yet, as always, it would be the woman who would have to pay, and deservedly so.

He said to the secretary: "I will draw up all the details of the Guiccioli Decree of Separation. When it is completed I will take it to His Holiness for his signature."

The secretary bowed, and then returned to the office of Pope Pius, who reminded him to send a letter to His Eminence, Cardinal Legate Rusconi in Ravenna, informing him of the Papal decision in favour of Count Ruggero Gamba's petition.

Cardinal Malvasia worded the Separation document very carefully, inserting within the details, his own small clause. His Holiness, he knew, would expect the document to be drawn up in accordance with his instructions, and so would merely sign it and stamp it with the Papal crest. And after that, who would dare to question the Papal office about it? Certainly not the Very Reverend Cardinal Rusconi in Ravenna.

Three days later in Ravenna, upon reading the secretary's letter informing him of the Pope's decision,

Cardinal Rusconi was so happy, he ordered his carriage and travelled out to Filetto to personally give the news to Count Gamba.

As soon as the horses halted outside Casa Gamba, Ruggero came out slowly and warily to greet him.

The Cardinal gave a sympathetic sigh. Teresina's father had the face of a man who had been suffering the dreaded arrival of bad news.

Cardinal Rusconi smiled and said brightly, "Ruggero, the news is good! His Holiness has consented to your petition. The Decree of Separation will arrive in the next few days."

Count Gamba almost wept. "I kiss your hand in gratitude," he said. "You are a true friend who has rendered me a great service."

Later, as they sat in two comfortable chairs in the cool drawing-room drinking wine in celebration, a strange and bewildered look suddenly came onto Cardinal Rusconi's face.

"What is it?" Ruggero asked.

"Il Conte Guiccioli ... I have spoken to many people about him of late. Not so inquisitively as to be obvious, but merely as a shepherd interested in *all* his flock. Sadly, I found not one who was ready to speak well of him. All said he cared only for money, was avaricious for money, and valued nothing more than money."

"I told you that also."

"Yes, and that is why I feel so sad for him. He must surely at times feel very lonely. A man who has learned so well the value of money, but has still not yet learned the value of *friends*."

Chapter Seventeen

~ ~ ~

The following afternoon, Teresa's sister, Giulia Gamba, made her weekly call at the Palazzo Guiccioli, a day earlier than usual.

Teresa's surprise was evident. "Giulia – why do you not come tomorrow?"

"Because you will not be here tomorrow. Today I must take you home to Filetto."

Giulia told her the news of the Pope's consent to the separation, and then did her best to calm her sister with words and embraces while Teresa cried and laughed at the same time.

"Is it true? Have I been given my freedom?"

"Not yet. Papa fears Guiccioli's retaliation against you when he is informed. He wants you to leave this palazzo today and come home to safety. You know in such a serious matter, you cannot disobey Papa."

"No, but I must tell Byron."

Count Gamba had timed Giulia's arrival to take place during Count Guiccioli's ritual afternoon-rest period, which also allowed Teresa to slip upstairs unobserved to see Byron ... and he was not there ... Lega Zambelli said he had gone riding in the pine forest with his dogs, accompanied by Tita and her brother Pietro .

She told Lega what had happened, and then said to him: "My Byron is not here for me to tell him, so what will I do?"

"Whatever you must, and when he returns I will tell him all that you have told me."

"And you will tell him how much I love him?"

Lega silently inclined his head .

"And you will tell him that I will send a letter to him tonight?"

"I will."

She returned downstairs to her own apartments

somewhat deflated, not wishing to go; not until she had spoken to Byron.

"We must stick to Papa's arrangements," Giulia said. "We must leave here by four o'clock, before Count Guiccioli awakes."

"*Si, si ...*" Teresa knew that Byron's absence was not his fault. When he had gone out riding he had known no more than she had known. She consoled herself thinking of all the time they would have together in the future.

"Now I must see little Allegrina – how do I tell her?"

Giulia shrugged. "Children believe anything you tell them."

"I don't want to lie to her, and then confuse her."

Teresa finally located Allegra in the far end of one of the gardens with her nursemaid, playing with the flowers again.

"Allegrina!"

The child turned her head to look, and let out a shriek of delight, "*Mammina!*"

Teresa could feel her own sadness as Allegra ran to her on her little legs, because although she had been told the truth many times, the child was convinced that Teresa was her mamma.

"*Mia cara ...*"Teresa scooped her up into her arms in a tight hug, ready to explain to the child that she would be gone for a while, a little while – Allegrina nodded, unperturbed, more interested on the string of white pearls around Teresa's neck.

Teresa knew the child probably thought she was going no further than into Ravenna's town for an hour or two – but how to tell her the truth?

Instead she kissed her and hugged her and gave her the string of white pearls to play with.

Some minutes before four o'clock, the usual time when Giulia left for home after her visit, Teresa strolled with her sister some way down the path, as she often did; but today, instead of saying farewell at the turn-off, they kept on walking until they reached a carriage that was waiting further down, out of sight of the palazzo windows.

The two sisters quickly climbed inside, and the carriage drove off.

At Filetto, it was not until he saw Teresa stepping down from the carriage, and knew that his daughter was now safe from all possible harm, did Count Gamba finally exhale a sigh of utter relief.

Riding together in the forest, Byron could not help smiling at Teresa's brother who was more hot-headed than was good for him. Pietro had finished his time at the university in Rome, and now was full of talk of Italy's freedom and the necessity for revolution.

"You have mixed for too long with your intellectual liberals in Rome," Byron told him.

"No, the liberals are not the problem," Pietro replied. "Italy is ready now to take her freedom and rule herself. The Austrians are the only problem."

The kept their horses at a steady walking pace.

"I don't believe that the Italians *are* ready," Byron said. "They lack unity and organisation. One province does not know what other provinces are doing, or how ready and willing they truly are."

Pietro grinned smugly. "Then, Mylord, we will show you our unity. If the South rises first – as soon as the Southern flare is raised – the North will rise also. Bologna will be the first to rise in the North."

Byron was not so sure. The liberals and intellectuals of the Carbonari in Bologna seemed to more enjoy *talking* about an Italian revolution than practically organising for it.

Nothing could dissuade Pietro or dampen his ardour. "You will see – when the five-pointed white star of the new Italian Republic is raised – *all* Italy will be a part of it and will cheer and fire their guns in victory. Is that not true, Tita?"

Tita Falceiri had already raised his rifle and fired into

the sky – not in victory, but at a fierce-looking falcon flying overhead.

"You missed!" Byron said, pleased. "And why shoot at birds who do no harm to you?"

"Falcons are savage," Tita said. "They swarm over Italy as if they rule it. But, *si,* that one was too swift for me."

Arriving back at the palazzo and entering the hall, Count Guiccioli came out, his eyes piercing over the tall young man who stood beside Tita Falcieri. "Who is this?"

"Count Pietro Gamba," Byron told him – in Italy all first sons of Counts were also Counts from their birth – "Teresa's brother," he added.

"Teresa is not here," said Guiccioli, looking at Pietro. "They say she has gone to visit her father. When you return to Filetto you must give her my order to return."

Pietro silently bowed in a sarcastic way, and then followed Byron and Tita up the staircase.

On entering the drawing-room, Lega gave Byron the news. "The Pope has consented to Teresa's separation from Guiccioli."

Byron and Pietro Gamba smiled and looked at each other, and then laughed with delight as they lightly embraced in the joy of the victory. "Soon you will become my brother!" Pietro said.

"If and when my estranged wife gives me a divorce, and *when* Guiccioli dies," Byron agreed.

Tita was also gleeful, because he hated that human *falcon,* Guiccioli.

"Lega – champagne from the cellar!" Byron ordered. "Send someone down for it."

When it came and was poured, the French champagne from the cool and dark cellar was like nectar on the tongue.

Byron wrote a note to Teresa and gave it to her brother to take back to her.

Returning home, Pietro gave Byron's note to Teresa who grabbed it and ran to her bedroom

As soon as Pietro had eaten his dinner, she gave him a letter to take back straight away to Byron.

"Am I to sit on a horse all day?" he asked her.

"Yes," said his father, "because I too have written a letter for you to take to Count Guiccioli. It is time he learned the truth."

Arriving back at the palazzo in Ravenna, Pietro handed his father's letter to Count Guiccioli's manservant; and then took Teresa's letter up to Lord Byron.

Byron also took his letter away, and some ten minutes later came back to the drawing-room with a reply for Pietro to give to Teresa.

Once back at Filetto, Pietro Gamba handed over the letter with a warning to Teresa. "I will *not* be going back again this night, so write no more love-letters for me to take!"

In her bedroom, Teresa almost cried when she read Byron's letter, removing all her fears and doubts.

My Love – your letter was brought to me by Pietro. He is leaving almost at once – so I have only a few minutes in which to answer you: but you will forgive me. In answer to your question, for my part, we will live together (if you will) and send A. to the . . . .

You are afraid for me while out riding – I don't know why – but what can I do about it? What will be, will be – and one place is not safer than another. Look after yourself well – this means much more to me than myself. Papa will keep you informed about the gossip (if there is any) but remember, whether it is good or bad, it will be over in a month.

Farewell, my Teresa. Be calm, and believe me your most faithful friend and lover – and one day your husband xxx Byron.

~~~

Alessandro was shocked and furious at the news from Filetto informing him of the Papal Decree Of Separation; but furious only in that he had been outwitted by Ruggero Gamba.

As for the loss of Teresa, he did not care. She was no longer of any use to him in business; and with her lack of obedience and respect towards him, she had become a trouble he would not miss.

But what of Mylord? Was he to lose him too? If Mylord left the palazzo he would want repayment of his loan, and that would not do. And what of his post as British Consul at Ravenna? Would he still be given that? He would have to find out what Mylord Byron's plans were now?

But first, he would have to go into town and show all the people how little he cared.

He called first on Count Alborghetti, and asked him if he had heard anything about his marriage?

As the Gambas were not saying anything to anyone until the actual Decree arrived, Count Alborghetti replied with some puzzlement, "No, what should I have heard? Is all not good at the Casa Guiccioli?"

"No, not good. I have decided to discard her and send her back to her father's care. She has always been more trouble than she is worth. And at my age..." Alessandro shrugged up his shoulders, "life is too short to live it in misery."

"*Gesù!*" Alborghetti was truly shocked at such words and careless attitude; and Alessandro knew that before nightfall, the dear man would have told everyone in Ravenna that Count Guiccioli had dismissed his wife and sent her back to Filetto.

Count Alborghetti did tell everyone who called at his home, but not in the way Guiccioli expected, saying to all – "The young Contessa has finally left him."

Within days of Guiccioli's visit to Count Alborghetti,
~~~

Byron began to receive discreet notes and letters of warning from anxious well-wishers and friends in Ravenna. All dreaded the worst, and all feared for him.

Byron, in his English way, thought such warnings were over-dramatic, and refused to be intimidated; writing of it in a flippant way to his friends in England:

Guiccioli is suspected of two assassinations and in consequence I have been warned. They say he will have me taken off, it is the custom here. They pop at you from behind trees, or put a knife into your back in company, or in turning a corner. Guiccioli may do as he pleases, I only recommend him not to miss, for if such a thing is attempted, and fails, he shan't have another opportunity. I have taken no precaution (which indeed would be useless) except taking my pistols when I ride out every evening. A man's life is not worth holding on such a tenure as the fear of such fellows.

~~~

The official Papal Rescript was sent from the Vatican to the Cardinal Legate Rusconi in Ravenna; who then sent it by express messenger to Ruggero at Filetto.

Sitting in his study with Teresa, Ruggero read to his daughter from the document:

"After the depositions had been heard and the pertinent information received, His Holiness, considering it evident that Teresa Gamba, the daughter of the petitioner, had come to a state where she could scarcely live safely and peacefully with her husband, graciously grants all the necessary and appropriate powers of the Separation to the Most
~~~

Eminent Cardinal Legate of Ravenna, so that she may leave her husband and return to her paternal house ..."

"The Holy Father desires that one hundred Scudi per month is to be provided to you by your husband," Ruggero continued, still reading, "so that you may live in a commendable manner that befits a noble woman separated from her husband."

Teresa was happy to hear it. Throughout their marriage Alessandro had *never* allowed her to have any money of her own – not even one *soldi*. Nor was she dismayed when the Writ stated that any gifts she had received from her husband during the marriage must be returned. "I will return the ring he gave to me."

But then came the shock ... even Ruggero could not believe it when he stared at the small and unexpected clause.

Alarmed by the disbelief on her father's face, Teresa asked, "What is it, Papa?"

"Until Guiccioli's death, if you do not agree to confine yourself to live solely under your father's roof and no other; then, under the conditions of the decree of separation, you must retire and confine yourself to a religious life in a Convent."

Teresa could hardly get the words out, "So I must live nowhere but Filetto, or be locked up in a Convent...?"

Count Gamba was shaking his head. "It is an unusual and harsh condition, when the Holy Father's first words were so kind ..."

Chapter Eighteen

~ ~ ~

"Day or night – he is invisible!"

Alessandro Guiccioli could not comprehend how the young Inglese who lived on the floor above him, could go in and out of the palazzo and yet never physically be seen.

"Can he *make* himself invisible? Like a ghost?"

Alessandro realised that even to ask himself that question was a sure sign that he was losing his clearness of mind and his patience.

He could not know that after years of being so famous, Byron had become very skilled in ways of evading the eyes of curious strangers. If he did not wish to be seen, he was not seen.

Of course, Guiccioli realised, there were many doors out of the palazzo, and all could not be continually watched; nor the gates from the gardens to the vineyards, nor the paths out to the woods.

Since the news of the Pope's decree, Alessandro did not know his future, and yet all attempts to see Mylord had failed; even his notes and the servants sent up to him requesting a meeting had failed: Mylord was either out, or in bed asleep, or writing and could not be disturbed.

And now it was he, Alessandro, who was the most disturbed. Like all misers, it pained him to have to pay back money he had borrowed or swindled. If he had married another miser instead of a fickle and wasteful girl, he would now be living in true affection and matrimonial harmony. But now he might be facing another embarrassing court case, and like the last one in Bologna, it would be a court case he would lose.

He poured himself a glass of brandy and drank it quickly, while silently cursing Teresa and all the trouble she had caused him by running away.

A knock on the study door was followed by a manservant excitedly popping his head around the door.

"Conte, Conte ... they have come from their riding in the forest, Mylord and Signor Falceiri. They have now gone up to Mylord's apartments."

Guiccioli frowned. "I heard no footsteps in the hall."

"They went up to the apartment from the stairs in the rear garden – it is a quicker way from the stables."

Alessandro stood up quickly. "Then you go up *now* and tell Mylord that I wish to speak to him, that it is very *important* that I speak to him, of the utmost importance!"

"*Si, Conte, si!*" The servant disappeared.

Alessandro poured himself more brandy to steady his resolve and determination to persuade Mylord to remain in this palazzo with him, and not go back to Venice with that traitorous Teresa. To stay here would mean he would not need his loan back.

The servant returned. "Mylord says he will be very happy to see you, Conte, if you go upstairs."

For a moment, Alessandro was indignant. "So he is not coming down to me?"

"No. Mylord requests that you attend upon him upstairs."

Alessandro was about to refuse, and then realised that Mylord may *not* have intended to insult him. After all, he was *British*, and the British always acted as if they were the masters of the world.

"Inform him that I will come up at my own convenience," Alessandro said airily.

Five minutes later he knocked on the door of Byron's apartments, surprised when it was opened by Mylord himself, a smile on his face. His greeting was pleasant and polite and his manner no different to how it had always been.

In fact, Mylord was so polite and friendly, it made Guiccioli suspicious. The British, in their exquisite politeness, knew how to insult a man without him even knowing it – the insult usually being hid under some sentences of what *they* called "dry wit".

Yet as he entered the apartment, he could detect nothing of scorn or the dry wit in anything Mylord said, nothing out of the normal. As always, there was something very pleasing in his smile and his way of speaking, something that made him immediately likable to both women and men.

Lega Zambelli and Tita Falceiri were in the drawing-room. Mylord gestured for them to leave, and then turned to Alessandro. "May I offer you some wine, or coffee?"

Alessandro nodded. "*Grazie,* I will take some wine."

Sitting down on the sofa, Alessandro sat back and keenly watched as Mylord walked to the black mahogany sideboard on which were placed all the drinks; and there he poured some red wine from a crystal decanter into two glasses. He was dressed in a white silk shirt, and tan breeches tucked into dark-brown riding boots.

Alessandro was both dismayed and disarmed by this reminder of how young and handsome Mylord was. Such a man to have as a rival was not good. Better to keep him as a friend.

"You have been told all by the Contessa?" he said flatly.

Byron nodded. "As much as I needed to know."

Alessandro took the glass in his hand and sat forward. "And now what are your plans?"

"My plans?" Byron sat down in an armchair opposite the Count. "I have no plans, which is rather a good thing, because I am told I am likely to be assassinated."

"By whom?"

"By you."

The Count shrugged his disgust. "These Italians who are your friends and give you such advice – most are descended from primitive peasants. And despite their noble titles they still have the mentality of peasants. This is Ravenna, not Naples or Sicily. You have been my friend and benefactor, so why would I seek to harm you?"

"I don't know, because it was *you*, in the first place, who asked me to come here to Ravenna. *You* who invited me to live here in your palazzo. *You* who asked me to escort Teresa to the theatre and conversazioni and everywhere else. In all things I was openly given your blessing. So why would you now seek to assassinate me for obligingly doing all you asked?"

"Yes, yes ..." said the Count, "I am grateful to you."

Byron sipped his wine, enjoying the game they were both playing, but aware of Guiccioli's small black eyes studying him.

"So, Mylord, you have no plans to leave my palazzo and go back to Venice or England?"

"I told you – no plans at all."

The Count sighed and drank from his glass, relief flooding through him.

"And my post as the British Consul, I still may expect it?"

"Of course. As a peer of the realm I have requested it, but these things take time, and the post from England is so slow."

The Count nodded, his eyes thoughtful. Finally he said: "I think you should stay here under my protection, Mylord. Because here you will be safe from the Italian police and the Austrians. It is *they* who wish to harm you, not I."

"I can't think why. Is an Englishman not allowed to reside in Italy?"

"The Italian police and the people here in Romagna are very suspicious of all foreigners," Guiccioli said, as if he was not a Romagnole himself. "But I am your friend, and now you are *my* only friend here in Ravenna. So it would give me great consolation, Mylord, if you were to stay here in the Palazzo Guiccioli. And perhaps in the future we could meet for conversations and occasionally share dinner together. I have always been very interested in English literature."

Byron smiled. "You have not mentioned that before."

"No, because *she* was always in the way. But now she is gone and I don't care. Like you, Mylord, I am a man happily separated from his wife; and your role as her *cavalier servente* is now over."

Byron restrained the urge to stand up and smack his face. "I was never her *cavalier servente.*"

Guiccioli sighed. "Yes, yes, forgive me, you were only her friend ... her *friend* ... But from now on, here in Romagna and even in Venice, not even that friendship will be allowed to you."

Byron was surprised. "Not even as a friend? Why so?"

"Because ..." the Count informed him, masking his glee with an expression of sorrowful regret, "it is only a *married* woman who is allowed to have a *cavalier servente*, with the permission of her husband. But a single or separated woman is not allowed to associate on even a friendship basis with *any* man, and not without a watchful chaperone always being present. That is the law here in Italy, or at least, the *social* law."

Guiccioli drank some more wine. "If a separated woman went against this, she would have to flee to hide in Africa or some other place to escape all the *disgrazia* heaped upon her name."

Byron remained silent, not sure if Guiccioli was lying.

"That is why," Guiccioli continued, "so many separated women eventually retreat into Convents. No Italian man will dare speak to them beyond a greeting and farewell; and all Italian wives drift away from friendship with separated women, because they fear them as a rival who may become a secret mistress of her own husband. It is not a good way to live, so I don't know why Teresa acted so foolishly."

~

In Filetto, Teresa was suffering, still in shock at the realisation that her new freedom had turned out to be an illusion. She was now more restricted than ever; yet even this was preferable to living with Alessandro

She wept for herself, and she wept for Byron. Had he, too, now learned that all rays of happiness also had their shadows?

Her sole consolation was in writing to him, long letters that continued to warn him not to trust Alessandro, and to be very careful.

His replies did little to pacify her.

"My love: I do not fear him nor regard him. He may do as he pleases..."

His nonchalance made her angry. Was he not suffering as she was? Her fear of losing him now, and his possible return to Venice, caused her to write bitter and accusing words; leaving her full of regret when he immediately replied:

"Of what can you accuse me? I have come, I have gone, I have come back – I have remained. It is more than a year that I have done nothing but obey your wishes in every respect. You accuse me – I do not deserve it – and you know it."

She cried and hated herself for being so cruel; and then wrote back to him full of sincere apologies and love, and wishing only to be able to *see* him. Would he dare to come to Filetto?

"My Love + I will come – but when and how? – If you do not fear for yourself, we must think of your family – for it is really against them that these things are directed – Against myself (apart from what I feel for you) they cannot do anything – but it would not be very heroic of me to compromise you all without sharing in the danger. So I would like to be instructed beforehand – how to behave – and for this purpose I should like to speak to Papa."

As his personal friend, it was quite acceptable for Lord Byron to visit Count Gamba at Filetto; and there Ruggero smilingly welcomed him with open arms and a kiss on both cheeks as if greeting a beloved son. They spoke for some time in private.

"Again, I must wonder if I did the wrong thing," Ruggero said quietly. "First to marry her to him, and then to request the separation."

"There is something in this that I don't understand," Byron said. "Something not quite right. But what is done is done, and all we can do now is find the best way through it or around it."

Later he was permitted to walk and talk with Teresa in the Gamba's olive grove, shielded from all eyes.

"It is Sunday, so there are no workers about," Ruggero said. "And we do not harvest the olives until late October. But I beg you, no more than a few minutes? I do not wish to show bad behaviour to my other daughters."

Byron smiled. "Is just walking and talking bad behaviour?"

"Now – for Teresa, who must appear as pure as Caesar's wife – yes."

In the olive grove, under the sun, they walked a respectable distance apart, but as soon as they were sure they were out of all sight, they embraced and kissed.

Yet Byron was not happy. "Allegra is sick again with one of those swamp fevers they have here. I need to move her to some place more inland."

And then Teresa was surprised to learn he had not been idle either. "I have found and rented a villa a few miles from here – for my two girls – Allegra and you."

Teresa looked at him wide-eyed, not sure if she understood.

"The name is the *Villa Bacinetti*. Allegra and her nursemaids and a few male servants will move into the villa, but I will continue to lodge at Guiccioli's palazzo in Ravenna for the sake of propriety. The villa is near enough for you to wander over and visit the child."

"And sometimes, I can visit the villa at the same time as *you* visit your daughter?" Teresa laughed as she finally understood.

Byron grinned. "I shall visit Allegra daily. Why would I not?"

Teresa's face straightened. "But little Allegrina, is it true? Has she the fever?"

"Yes. She seems to have a weakness for them, so she will recover more quickly in the cool of the villa and the quietness of the location."

"But who will guard them all when you are not there to protect them?"

"Two of my guard dogs, Only a madman would try to get past them."

"And the servants, can *they* be trusted?"

"All my servants can be trusted, and the male servants will have guns."

Teresa hesitated to ask. "The ones with guns, are they Carbonari?"

Byron pretended innocence. "How would I know? I am merely a poet living in Italy because I love the sun."

Teresa sighed, an idea coming into her mind as they strolled. "But in the villa," she said, "as well as the nursemaids and servants, I think you will need a housekeeper also. Someone to keep all in control and command when you are not there."

"Perhaps. I did not think of that."

"A housekeeper you can trust," Teresa said. "Someone who will always put *your* interests and the care of Allegrina above everything

"Easy to say. And where would I find such a person at short notice?"

"I know of such a good and reliable person who is twiddling her thumbs in discontent up in Venice. And she is also very annoyed with *you* for not answering any of her letters."

"No." Byron stared at her. "Not Fanny Sylvestrini?"

"Who better?" Teresa said cajolingly "And she could also double as my *chaperone* when we want to go walking together. And as before, Fanny would be our obliging *confidante*."

"No. Fanny in her letters is bad enough. Fanny in person would be *death* – hell in this weather. Even now I can hear all her constant complaints about the summer heat – as if she had not lived in Italy all her life!"

"She is very distressed about our terrible situation. She wishes to come and help us, like the nurse in *Romeo e Giulietta*. I have already wrote and asked her to come. So when she does, may she stay at your villa as your housekeeper?"

"She is coming? No – write to her and stop her and deliver me – otherwise I don't know what will become of me if she finally succeeds in driving me mad – I foresaw you would do this – and now you say she is coming – and now you want her to live and rule the roost in *my* villa?"

Teresa was laughing. "*Mio Byron,* you cannot fool me, because I *know* you are fond of her."

"Fond of Fanny Sylvestrini? That woman is every man's nightmare! Lega – Tita – myself. If she comes, I shall turn monk at once, and the Church will gain, not you. Pray write and tell her you have made a mistake."

From a high window in a top room, Ruggero watched as Byron and Teresa walked back towards the gardens hand in hand.

He grimaced to see they had defied his instructions by their intimacy in holding hands, but there was nothing to be said or done about it. They were not children.

Chapter Nineteen

~~~

The Pope's Legate in Ravenna, Cardinal Antonio Rusconi, had created numerous necessary delays in taking to Count Guiccioli his copy of the Papal Decree of Separation, so much did he dislike and dread the man, certain he was a little insane.

He had become certain of it on the night he had gone to the opera, and there he had seen with his own eyes, Count Alessandro Guiccioli laughing and enjoying the comical performance on the stage, even though his second wife, Angelica, had died only a few hours earlier.

A man whose love for money had reached the point of mania. A man of rapacity whose love of money was only equalled by his lust for power. A man who loved to dominate by threats and menaces and terror.

Even he himself, the Cardinal had to admit, was secretly terrified of him, as were most people in Ravenna. Only the Austrians did not fear him, describing him in a report as "*a sordid, miserly man.*"

Upon entering the palazzo, the Cardinal was greeted with bows and great deference by all the servants; but the Count merely smiled patiently as he waited for Rusconi to take out the Deed from his bag and hand it to him.

"I knew God would not let me down," Guiccioli said jovially. "I prayed He would somehow free me from her, and my prayer was answered. Now I have only her *mascalzone* to deal with."

Cardinal Rusconi paused. "Lord Byron? *Is* he a scoundrel? I did not know that."

"Scoundrel, rascal, rogue and heretic, he is all those things. But are we not Christians, and so must always pity the sinner?"

"He did not strike me as a man to be pitied."

Guiccioli leaned closer and lowered his voice almost
~~~

to a whisper. "I believe he is a Carbonaro."

"Oh, surely not!" said Rusconi, who secretly sympathised with the Carbonari. "He is a Lord of England, and one of their most famous sons. Why would he involve himself with Carbonari?"

"Because he is a little ..." Guiccioli pointed a finger to his head and twirled it. "Like all the English – even their King George. It runs in their English blood, so they cannot help it."

Cardinal Rusconi sighed. Here was yet another example of a madman who thought everyone else was mad, but not himself.

He handed over the document, and turned to leave; but Guiccioli stopped him. "No, Your Eminence, pray be kind enough to stay."

The Cardinal looked at him. "Why?"

"In case there is anything I do not understand ... these Papal documents can be ..."

Guiccioli's eyes had been running down the short document as he spoke ... and now something in his brain seemed to snap and he let out a roar of rage – *"One hundred Scudi every month?"*

The Cardinal had not read the document, and now thought that figure quite a fair amount of contribution to a wife who had been forced to leave her home due to her husband's unreasonable behaviour.

"You must remember, Conte, that your estranged wife, as young as she is, will not be able to marry again, not until your own decease."

Guiccioli could not take it in – one hundred Scudi a month – 1200 Scudi a year! That yearly sum was almost as much as the first one thousand English pounds he had borrowed from Mylord Byron. And it would have to be paid *every* month of *every* year, until he died.

"*Bestia!* That pope is an animal! Does he think we all get our money from the collection boxes as he does! Does he think we all rob the poor as he does?"

He was still ranting when Cardinal Rusconi hurried out, telling his driver to go at speed and then huddling inside his carriage muttering in a distressed tone, "*Mio Dio, miserabile, miserabile ...* " Guiccioli was even more miserable about money than he had been led to believe. But to insult the Pope? "*Un Disgrazia!*"

~~~

In the days following, for some strange reason, Guiccioli continually chose to seek out the heretic Mylord Byron to complain about the Pope and all Catholics, certain he would agree.

"And one hundred Scudi *every month!* Does that fool dressed in purple robes think we are all as rich as he is in his Vatican in Rome? How dare he grant Ruggero Gamba a separation – *I* did not request a separation! Oh, Mylord Byron, Mylord ... they have put me on the Cross! They have nailed me down. And all to get *one hundred Scudi* for the Gambas every month."

Byron pretended to listen, making the occasional sympathetic comment, while stemming his laughter and finding it all hilarious.

So much so that he began writing a running commentary on the farce which he found himself in the midst of, for the amusement of some of his close friends in England.

"*He does not want to have to pay alimony, so now he does not want a separation, and intends to object to the decree. It was* <u>*she*</u> *and her father who demanded it, on the grounds of her husband's extraordinary usage. The Pope granted the decree; and now the Count says it came from Babylon, not Rome. He insisted on her giving me up, and then he would forgive everything, even the adultery, which he swears that he can prove by "witnesses". But in this country, the very courts hold such proofs in abhorrence, the Italians being much more delicate in public than the English, as they are*
~~~

more passionate in private.

The friends and relatives of the Gambas, who are numerous and powerful, reply to him – "You, yourself, are either fool or knave, – fool, if you did not see the consequences of the approximation of these two young people – knave, if you connived at it."

They say to him: "Take your choice, – fool or knave, but don't break out, after twelve months of the closest intimacy, under your own eyes and positive sanction – with a scandal that can only make you ridiculous and her unhappy.

He swore that he thought our relationship was purely amicable, and that I was more partial to him than to her, till melancholy testimony proved the contrary. To this they answer, that I was not an unknown person; – and that her <u>brother</u> a year ago wrote to warn him that his wife would infallibly be led astray by this "Will of the Wisp" unless he took proper measures to prevent it, all of which he neglected to take, etc., etc.

Now he says he encouraged my return to Ravenna, only to see "in quanti piedi d'acqua siamo" (how many feet of water is the depth of our relationship – mine and Teresa's) and he has found enough depth to drown himself in."

When Teresa read Byron's copy of the letter a few days later, she thought the word "adultery" was *cruel*.

"It is *love*, true *love*, and the separation was caused by the ill-conduct of the Count, not by you. It would have happened sooner or later, even if you had not come into our lives."

Byron apologised sincerely for his crude use of such a word; yet kept on writing his honest and amusing running commentaries on the Count's rages to his friends; but now he was wise enough not to mention or show any more of his letters to Teresa.

"He has written his objection to the Separation to the Pope in Rome, but what will be the decision of His Sanctity, no one can predicate. She lives in her father's house, and I can only see her under great restrictions. The relatives are all on my side."

One person who was no longer on Byron's side was Count Guiccioli. He was now certain that Mylord had taken part in the trick that had been played upon him to extract one hundred Scudi a month from him.

Alessandro was now, once again, seriously considering having Mylord Byron assassinated for such treachery against him. His favourite choice of weapons were the poisoned glass, or the stiletto or dagger in the hand of a hired assailant – silent weapons. He did not like guns, they made too much noise and drew attention.

But, alas, he realised that no matter which weapon or way, everyone would suspect him of the deadly deed, or his order behind it. Under *social* law, of course, he would be justified; the husband ordering the death of his wife's lover.

But then, Ruggero Gamba, and Holy men like the Cardinal Legate Rusconi would make sure he stood before a court charged with ordering the assassination. If they only *suspected* him of murder before, they would be certain now.

Later that day he was somewhat mollified when his friend, the Prelate Marini – no friend of Cardinal Legate Rusconi – called in on him at the palazzo bringing good wishes and some advice.

"Alessandro, why do you have this heretic foreigner living in your house?"

"To feed off his money you fool," Alessandro wanted

to say, but instead he bowed his head. "I am too kind, too generous of heart."

"There are wolves gathering in the forest," Monsignor Marini said. "So we must get this dangerous foreigner out of our city."

Alessandro raised his head and stared at the Pope's prelate, convinced all these religious clerics were mad. "Wolves in the forest? What are you talking about?"

"Carbonari."

"And the foreigner is dangerous in what way?"

"The Austrians suspect he is associated with them, but they can find no proof, because the liberals have been very good at protecting him."

"No liberals have come here, not as I have seen, not in *my* house. Some Englishmen have called, but all were very respectable, all on their way to see Florence and Rome."

"This is what we suspect, that these English callers are the messengers who carry his letters and orders to other Carbonari in Florence and Rome."

"No, I would not allow a Carbonari sympathiser into my house. Mylord is a rascal, a rogue, a heretic, and an impudent seducer, but he is not Carbonaro. And why would he be – he is *British!*"

Monsignor Marini smiled patiently. "Perhaps you are right. Is it true he rides every day in the forest?"

"He rides – God knows where. All I know is he and his bodyguard Falceiri go off on their horses every day."

"Battista Falceiri ... he is from Venice ... a sinful place full of Carbonari. Is he the only one who accompanies Lord Byron when he goes riding?"

"No, he is also always accompanied by Elisei, his groom, and sometimes the younger Count Gamba."

"Never alone?"

"How would I know? He is merely a tenant in my palazzo. I don't keep watch on him coming in and going out. Why do you ask *me* all these questions?"

"Because I know you are loyal to the Austrians and wish Romagna to remain a Papal State. And you are a wise man to be so loyal. The Carbonari will be destroyed."

"*Bestia!*" hissed Guiccioli as he watched the Prelate Marini's carriage drive off. "Why would I do anything now to help Rome?"

The Austrians, on the other hand ... paid well.

Chapter Twenty

~ ~ ~

In his study, sitting in the armchair by the window, Guiccioli came out of his thoughts and sat up more alert as he saw a carriage approaching towards his front door.

Who was this now? He was not in the mood for visitors.

A young man stepped down from the carriage, a stranger ... he was tall, and his face was boyish. He was dressed well but his clothes were untidy, as was his fair-coloured hair, which was long and a bit wild as if he had been pushing it back and forth during his journey.

A Carbonaro?

As he disappeared from sight, Guiccioli strained his ear against the window-glass and listened as the front door was opened ... hearing the voice of the stranger speaking in bad Italian.

An Englishman! *Mio Dio!* Another of those damned *British!*

He could hear the footsteps on the marble floor of the hall and then going upwards as a servant took him up the staircase to Mylord Byron's floor above.

Who was he? Was he one of those "messengers" that Monsignor Marini had spoken about? Too late now to interrogate him. He would have to wait and watch for his chance.

On the floor above, the door was opened by Tita Falceiri, who looked and listened to the stranger, and then bowed, inviting him in.

Byron was sitting at his desk writing a letter, looking up to see the visitor, an expression of pure delight coming on his face – "*Shelley!*"

Shelley was smiling. "I gave up any hope of you coming to visit us at Pisa, so here I am, the mountain coming to Mahomet."

Byron was on his feet, shaking Shelley's hand and

grinning. "For how long?"

"A few days."

Shelley had known he could be sure of a good welcome from Byron; but his visit turned out to be so good, so accommodating of every necessity, and so entertaining, that he stayed longer than he had planned.

Shelley wrote to his wife, Mary, explaining his delay, and telling her – *"Byron has the most splendid suite of apartments here in Ravenna."* He also told her about Byron's very serious attachment to Teresa – *"but don't mention that to Claire."*

Byron took Shelley everywhere, even out to Filetto. Teresa was not there, out visiting Allegra at the Villa Bacinetti, so he introduced him to Count Gamba and Pietro declaring Shelley would be "a very famous poet one day."

This intrigued Pietro, who asked, "Are all of your English friends poets? Signor Thomas Moore, he was a poet too."

"And a good one, but nowhere near to the level of Shelley."

Pietro looked curiously at Shelley, liking him. "And is it your biggest dream to be famous?"

"No," Shelley said mildly. "My biggest dream is to one day go back to England and stir up the oppressed into a revolution against the ruling class."

"Oh, young blood! Young blood!" laughed Count Gamba, and then pulled Byron aside, knowing he was involved with an underground group called *Young Italy*; leaving Shelley to be entertained by Pietro.

Ruggero spoke quietly. "They say Naples is ready."

"So that's the South. What of the North?"

"If the South goes, the North will follow. In the North, Bologna will be the first to go."

"And His Holiness?"

Ruggero shook his head. "They will not touch him. He will be protected on all sides by his own guards *and* the Carbonari. He is still our Holy Father."

"That's good to know. It is the Austrians that must be

cleared out of Italy, not God's men."

Ruggero sighed. "I wish they *were* all God's men. Some are as devious as the devil."

Riding back to Ravenna, and coming to a small village where its occupants were sitting on chairs outside their front doors, enjoying the sun in the Italian way; they slowed their horses to a walking pace as they rode down the street – until Shelley was surprised when Byron suddenly halted his horse and stared at an old gentleman sitting outside his house, speaking down to him in Greek.

The old man seemed to come alive, jumping up from his chair and talking back excitedly to Byron in Greek; a language which Shelley had studied at Eton and Oxford, but not well enough to understand when it was spoken at this rapid pace.

Shelley waited as their conversation rattled on, both men laughing as if recounting old times and places. And now all the other villagers were watching curiously, some of the women moving closer.

Finally Byron gathered his reins to move on, wishing the old man good health, "*Kalí ygeía.*"

"Eh? Eh?" said one of the Italian women who had moved closer, wanting to know who the stranger was.

The old man pointed up excitedly, "*Lórdo Vyronos! Lórdo Vyronos ... Inglese!*"

On that Byron was off, no longer at a walking pace, but cantering until they were well clear of the village.

"How did you know he was Greek?" asked Shelley. "Did you know him in Greece?"

"No, but I suspected he was Greek because his cottage was painted blue. In Spain, they paint their houses white. In Italy, yellow, and in Greece, blue. And did you notice – his was the only blue house on the street?"

Shelley grinned. "I never notice the odd things that you notice. Poor man, though, he must often feel lonely if he's the only Greek on the street."

"Oh, I'm sure he speaks Italian as good as the others, and if he don't, they will know enough Greek to be able to understand him."

Shelley was puzzled. "How can you be so sure of that?"

Byron looked at him. "There is a strain of Greek blood in most Italians. It was the *Greeks* who first cultivated this land. Well, the southern end. Have you ever been to the south?"

Shelley had not. No further than northern Naples.

"If you ever go down south you will see many Greek ruins, especially in Castelvetrano on the island of Sicily. Ruins of once-magnificent Greek buildings that were built a thousand years before Christ was born."

Byron flicked his reins, as if angry. "And now the greatness of the Greeks is forgotten, and the Greek people are treated like serfs in their own country by the ruling Turks."

Shelley, who had never been to Greece, so had not lived there for two years as Byron had, could not be as fond of that poor country as his friend. He changed the subject to Claire Clairmont – Allegra's mother.

"In your last letter," Shelley said, "I wish you had not expressed yourself so harshly about Claire, because she always insists on reading your letters to me."

"She wanted to come to Ravenna – not to take Allegra back – but to *'see us both'*. I will not have it. She gave Allegra away when she was a baby, and for what – to go gallivanting with you and Mary. If she really cared for the child, she would never have deposited her on me. And little Allegra has been ill, so I won't allow her to become confused and discommoded by Claire."

Shelley said: "You are mistaken in thinking that Claire has any desire to thwart your plans regarding Allegra. What letters she writes to you, I know not; perhaps they are very provoking, but in all events it is better to forgive the weak."

"Claire – weak? That girl has done more damage to myself, and to your Mary, and to everyone else she has come into contact with – more damage than the last earthquake in Selinus."

"I do not say – I do not think – that your resolutions are unwise, only next time you write to me, express them more mildly – and pray *don't quote me."*

Byron smiled. "Did I get you into trouble?"

Shelley shrugged. "I just hope you know what my feelings and those of Mary have ever been about Allegra. And whatever plans you and Claire agree upon, about her future life, remember that *we* as friends to all parties, would be always happy to help."

Byron remained silent.

"I say all this, not to induce you to change any of your plans for Allegra, nor would Claire consent to Allegra residing with us for any length of time. I say it only to let you know mine and Mary's feelings on the subject."

"There now, you have said it all," Byron answered – 'Nor would Claire consent to Allegra residing with us for any length of time ' – is that a *natural* feeling for a mother with no other child to care about? It's certainly not maternal. No, she will not come and see Allegra as if she was a booby in a holiday fair – to touch and play with and then move on. I would not treat even my dogs in that careless way."

Shelley was getting distressed. The situation was becoming unmanageable at his end. Mary hating Claire and wishing she would stop living with them; Claire still in love with Byron; and Byron detesting Claire like the plague.

Shelley groaned. "I wish I could come into your part of the world in any other character than that of a *mediator* in a dispute. I would wish, for once, to be able to come merely as a friend. In any event, I would like that to happen."

"Then it will," Byron said. "No more talk of women or children. This evening I will have a sumptuous feast prepared for you by Valeriano – a feast of all kinds of delicious Italian vegetables for two ravenous vegetarians – and then we will talk politics and philosophy all night like we used to do – and even *atheism* if you wish."

Shelley grinned. "That all sounds more to my taste."

When the time came for Shelley to leave, Byron was sad his visit had come to an end. Shelley reminded him so much of England, and all his friends there ... and the life he once had there ... until he had met that prim and perfect Miss Milbanke, before she had turned into an perfect witch when she became Lady Byron. And, in truth, Claire Clairmont was as like her as a sister – both self-centred, both false. Thank God he had met Teresa, who was as different to them as chalk was to cheese.

"May I tell Mary you will come and visit us in Pisa?" asked Shelley.

Byron inclined his head negatively.

"Claire may not be there for much longer," Shelley said "Before I left Pisa, she was talking of applying for the post as a governess in Florence."

"Well, if she does, and if she gets the post in Florence, let me know, and then I *will* come to see you and Mary in Pisa."

Byron's nostalgia about his home country of England made him moodily melancholy, and sent him riding alone into the pine forest where, as he rode through the trees, he removed one of the pistols from the brace under his coat, and then took a coin of one *soldo* out of his pocket – throwing it high into the air and shooting at the coin it as it fell, before slowly riding on.

He did this, on and off, for over an hour – his usual method of keeping up his shooting practice; the same method he had been using since a boy. Although now it was usually Tita who threw up the coin for him to hit or miss.

When he had used up all his coins, he sat motionless on his horse for a time, thinking. He loved the smells and the solitude of this beautiful forest of dense pines, where some way beyond, on the forest's shore, crashed the tumultuous waves of the Adriatic Sea.

There is a pleasure in the pathless woods,
There is a rapture on the lonely shore,
There is society, where none intrudes,
By the deep sea, and music in its roar ...

In the silence he suddenly heard a shuffling sound behind him and quickly turned his head, glancing two men standing near a tree before they ducked down out of sight.

From the quick glance, they had looked like peasants, but looks could be deceiving. Were they spies? And if so – whose? Guiccioli's spies, hoping to see him with Teresa? Or Austrian spies, seeking to see if he met with Carbonari?

Whichever, for the men to now be so deep into the forest, they must have been following him everywhere, from the moment he entered the woods

He rode on slowly, and heard the shuffling sounds again. He stopped – and they stopped. And so it continued – the two men following and stopping every time he stopped, until he lost his patience.

Keeping his back to them, he quietly reloaded his pistol, and then swiftly turned the horse around and rode back at speed to where they had ducked down again – pointing the gun at their heads and cocking the trigger as he warned they had better stop following or a bullet would come to at least one of them.

The two men rose to their feet, looking terrified; and then he saw that they *were* peasants, not only from their ragged clothes, but from the skeletal thinness of their bodies and their gaunt faces.

"Why were you following me?" he asked in Italian. *"Ma via!"*

The two men began to gabble together like idiots, but slowly he began to understand what they were saying ... "We know you usually ride in the forest in the two hours before sunset, Mylor', and shoot at the coins, and so we follow and find the coins and pick them up to buy food.

... why waste good money?"

Byron didn't know whether to believe them, until they held out their hands and showed him some of the silver coins they had collected already.

"We always follow. And when you shoot with your friends, after you all leave, we collect many more coins than today."

Byron stared down at the money in their open hands, pleased to note that more than half of the coins were nicked or a had a hole in them.

"And can you *spend* coins with nicks or holes in them?"

"*Si, Mylor' si.*" All money was taken by the baker or grocer, good or bad; although the baker made them pay more for the bread when the coin had a hole in it. But those with only a nick at the edge – their wives said the baker always took those with no fuss.

"You have wives?"

They both nodded. "*E bambini.*"

This gave Byron an idea. He could see the two men were nothing more than they appeared, starving peasants grubbing for pennies in the dirt to feed their families.

"You may collect the fallen coins, but keep some distance behind – and in that way you can act as my bodyguards."

The two men looked at each other, their poor half-starved minds confused. They stared up at him. "*Guardie del corpo?*"

"Yes. While you are collecting the fallen coins, if you see any other men following me, you are to send out a loud whistling of warning."

He took out his wallet and withdrew a handful of notes. "Here is your first month's pay. Don't let me down. Keep watch for more than coins."

The two men took the notes into their hands, too surprised to answer; and on that Byron was off, riding at speed back to the Palazzo Guiccioli; where a trusted messenger handed him a note from Teresa.

They had arranged their first private meeting at the Villa Bacinetti for earlier that evening. It was already near to sunset, and he was more than an hour late.

He dashed off a note back to her – *"I shall be free in twenty minutes xxx "*

"Go! Go! Take this note back to her," he instructed the messenger. "I need time to wash."

Suspecting Guiccioli might be watching him from a window, he rode away from the palazzo at a leisurely pace, as if heading for the town; but some miles later he was galloping at speed in the opposite direction, through the countryside in the direction of the Villa Bacinetti.

Slowing down, his ears always attuned to the sounds of Nature, he heard the first call of the *Lucinia* from somewhere high in the trees – the call to lovers.

By the time he reached the Villa Bacinetti the evening air was filled with the songs of more nightingales, and Teresa was standing alone by the porch door waiting for him; her face sweet and smiling, loving him with her eyes.

She stood trembling with pleasure as he ran his fingers through her long hair and kissed her passionately.

Teresa almost wept with the reckless happiness of it. Ah, delight, delight, the taste of his love again. The magic time had come.

Chapter Twenty-One

~ ~ ~

Count Ruggero Gamba's house at Filetto had been built for coolness; a summer retreat with marble tiles covering all the floors and colourful rugs placed here and there. The furnishings were of old-fashioned splendour with big red and green renaissance armchairs and sofas.

Constantly invited to visit there by Count Gamba, and as Allegra was now settled nearby at the Villa Bacinetti, Byron regularly went to see his daughter at the Villa, and then took her in his carriage over to Filetto, leaving her to be fussed over by the girls while he rode out over the green plains with the two shooting-and-hunting sportsmen, Ruggero and Pietro.

At other times he just lazed on the banks of the river talking with Teresa.

A large and cheerful family, the more Byron saw of the Gambas, the more he liked them. He liked their manners, their physical appearance, and their naturalness, all so easy-going and warm-hearted; and they always seemed excited to see him.

The younger sisters often made as big a fuss of him as they did of Allegra, and in return he played with them affectionately, liking *le beau sang* of the girls, the beautiful blood.

Here, at Filetto, he saw the true charm of family life, and the Gambas always made him feel that he was now a part of theirs.

When Byron was in Ravenna, he and Teresa communicated through daily letters, sometimes two or three a day, keeping their servants very busy; but in an Italian country province where work was seasonal and often scarce to the level of poverty in winter, no servant was complaining about the burden of travelling out to the summer countryside.

And why would they complain? Mylord Byron was always polite and respectful, and he always paid a fair price. He was not miserly and bad-tempered like old Count Guiccioli; and although many of the Count's own servants were given the duty of constantly watching and reporting on Mylord Byron, most now no longer bothered – their loyalty slowly transferring to Mylord and becoming his secret champions.

They were Italians, and Mylord was for the Italians: he had even learned to speak their language – but Guiccioli was for the Austrians – so why should they remain loyal to *him*?

At the Villa Bacinetti, Teresa was a frequent visitor, often going over there in the mornings in her little curricle to see Allegra and play with her; and then sending a note of the child's wonderful progress to Byron; describing her intelligence and the way she loved to sing songs, as well as amusing herself in such a comical way by mimicking the peculiarities of an old servant behind his back.

Byron was not happy to hear this.

What you say about my child comforts me very much, except that tendency to mockery, which may become a habit very amusing and agreeable to others – but which sooner or later brings trouble to those who practice it.

Allegra's new talent for mimicking and mockery had reminded him of her mother, Claire Clairmont. In Switzerland, she, too, had often enjoyed mimicking servants with personal oddities, something that neither Shelley nor Mary would ever do. No wonder Mary Shelley could not stand Claire; they were as different as night to day – Mary, gentle and kind and brilliantly imaginative – and Claire, dark-eyed and violent in her passions ... She was no blood relation to Mary – and yet Mary was forced to allow the girl to keep living with herself and Shelley because Claire was her *step*-sister.

And then, of course, there was Shelley himself, who had always been inclined to see no wrong in Claire and forgive her everything. Although Shelley was the man and ruler of the group, it had always been Claire who ruled *him*, while Mary sulked or frowned or took herself off to write her novel. An odd relationship indeed.

~ ~ ~

At Pisa, Mary Shelley was delighted to see her stepsister preparing to leave for Florence. After seven years of enduring a *ménage à trois* existence because Claire would *not* leave, always putting up one excuse after another – now, at last, freedom was is sight. Now she and Shelley could live the life of a married couple, on their own, and in private.

No longer would she be left to tend the house and take care of the children, while Claire took Shelley off walking to go here, there, and everywhere as Shelley's companion.

Still, what had prompted Claire to finally go. she wondered. Was it because of their constant quarrels? Or was it because their neighbour, Mrs Mason, had pointed out to Claire that as she was twenty-two years old, if she continued to live as one of the family with the Shelleys, it would soon be too late for her to find a husband of her own, or even some kind of career to financially support her. It was not fair that Mr Shelley should have to continually support her in his home, along with his wife and small son. He was not rich, and he had no employment.

Mary had thought it a little impertinent for Mrs Mason to say that, but it was true. Apart from a small yearly allowance from his grandfather's Trust, Shelley's only employment was poetry, which did not sell, and which he usually had to pay to have a few copies privately printed, to be distributed amongst friends. And the fact that his father, Sir Timothy Shelley, was a rich baronet and the owner of Goring Castle, was no help to them at all –because Sir Timothy had disowned Shelley long ago for two reasons ... for being an atheist, and for leaving his pregnant wife, Harriet, and running off for pastures new with Mary Godwin.

In the dark of night, when she could not sleep, Mary often felt miserably guilty about that, especially after Harriet had committed suicide ... but what could two young people do when they were so truly in love? Live the rest of their lives in wretched misery?

After another scandal involving Claire, this time with the son of the Gisbornes at Livorno, resulting in the Gisbornes no longer wanting anything to do with the Shelleys – dear kind Mrs Mason had come up with the plan of sending Claire to stay with her friend, Dr Botji, and his family in Florence, as a governess.

Dr Botji was the personal physician to the Grand Duke Ferdinand. He lived in a magnificent house opposite the Pitti Palace, and had a large family of daughters.

"Also," Mrs Mason had pointed out, "in escorting the girls, it would allow Claire to make her entrance into Florentine society."

Claire eventually agreed to go; but did so with a glance at Shelley and a sigh of misery.

Shelley had personally escorted Claire to Florence, arriving in the evening, and spending the night together at the Fontana Inn, before he delivered her into the household of Dr Botji the following morning.

On taking his departure, Shelley was close to tears. This fact of Claire actually leaving them had rendered him secretly heartbroken.

Mary was his rock – his wife and sister and mother all rolled into one – but Claire was his soul mate, the keeper of all his secrets.

Claire was the one who made him laugh after Mary complained about something or other. Claire was the one who took him off gallivanting while Mary was too tired to do anything but look after the baby. And it had always been so – Mary the wife, and Claire the friend.

He truly loved Mary, but he loved Claire too, and Claire loved him. Her loss and absence would be devastating.

Returning to Pisa, Shelley suffered – unable to do anything due to a painful complaint – "*Nephritis*", he told Mary, "a problem of the kidneys" – not admitting the true cause was the absence of Claire. He worried about her, and missed her company.

A week later, at the post office, he received a letter from Claire, telling him how dreadfully miserable she was.

Finding a space in the corner of the post office, he immediately wrote back to her:

Keep up your spirits, my best girl, until we meet again at Pisa. But for Mrs Mason I should say come back immediately, and give up a plan so inconsistent with your feelings – as it is, I fear you had better endure, at least until you come here. You know, whatever you shall determine on, where you will find one ever affectionate friend, to whom your absence is too painful for your return always to be ever welcome.

I have suffered this week with a violent excess of my disease, with a return of those violent spasms I used to have. As to pain, I care little for it; but the nervous irritability which it leaves is a great and serious evil to me, and which, if not incessantly combated by myself and soothed by others, would leave me nothing but torment in life. I am now much better, conversation is of some use to me, but what would it be to your sweet consolation, my own

Claire.

~ ~ ~

At Filetto, the Gamba family were gathered with some neighbours in a field near the back of the house, all waiting for the big event – an eclipse of the sun – all excited and eager to witness the celestial spectacle soon to take place in the sky.

Ruggero had suggested they make a party of it. Chairs were positioned over the field, optical instruments set up, and trellised-tables holding up gallons of wine and trays of glasses were placed nearby, with snacks and juice for the younger ones.

Knowing that Byron was deeply interested in astronomical studies, deeming them a powerful means for learning more about their universe and improving mankind intellectually, Teresa had made him promise to come ... yet still he had not arrived ... and now the sky was dimming, the eclipse close.

When Byron reached the field, the Gamba family and their guests, all wearing tinted glasses, were observing the heavenly bodies, whose encounter was already beginning to wrap the earth in shadow.

He sat down in their midst, not wishing his arrival to break the silence in which they were all following the progress of the luminaries.

All were engrossed. It was a solemn and almost reverent silence, because while that vanishing light is known to belong to physical order, yet this seeming disturbance in the order of nature, so vital to creation, made an indelible impression, which Byron could see was even shared by the dogs and other animals. Even the birds were in hiding.

As soon as the disc of the sun came back into sight, and the lovely blue of the Italian sky was unveiled from its shadow, speech and movement was restored to the company.

Turning and seeing him, Teresa asked him, "Did you

see it?"

Byron smiled. "I not only saw it, I *felt* it. So did all the dogs and birds."

The nearby river had also felt it. During the eclipse of the sun, the river, which flowed near the manor walls, had greatly swollen, bringing with it a huge shoal of fish – a surprising event – since it was usually not easy to catch fish in that river.

Ruggero was thrilled; suggesting they all take part in netting the fish and feasting on them for supper.

All the other men were agreeable, but although Byron often ate fish, he disliked fishing for the same reason he disliked hunting, and had no wish to be present at the shoal's doom.

Returning to the palazzo in Ravenna, Count Guiccioli greeted him in the hall with a sincere and solemn request:

"I would be most obliged, Mylord, if you would vacate your apartments upstairs as soon as possible."

"Sorry, no," Byron shrugged. "I cannot oblige you."

"Why not?"

"It's inconvenient."

"For you? Inconvenient for *you?*"

"Very," Byron replied good humouredly "Unless ... you can now repay all the money you still owe to me? Can you?"

"No."

"Then I shall not inconvenience myself by leaving here. I shall stay, and continue to deduct my rent from the money you still owe to me."

"But you have other houses where you could live! Your palazzo in Venice. A mansion at La Mira. And now I learn you also have a villa at Este!"

"But they are not in Romagna, are they? I could hardly travel back and forth each day."

Guiccioli was at a loss. "But you *must* leave. The Austrians tell me that you must leave."

"Then you must tell the Austrians to go *shoo,*" Byron

advised, "and preferably back to Austria where they will be entitled to bully and blackguard the people to their heart's content. But in the meantime ..."

Guiccioli watched him go as he sauntered on down the hall, twirling his keys in his hand. Such casual haughtiness! And so typical of the *British.* They were not easy to dominate or threaten.

But what could one do in the face of such arrogance? What could even the *Austrians* do? After all, it was the *British* who had given Italy to the Austrians in the first place, as a prize of war. So the Austrians had to be careful with how they handled one of their British aristocrats.

He hurried after his haughty tenant who was now on the stairs. "Mylord Byron, you must recognize, under the circumstances, that your presence here is a great embarrassment to me, in view of your relationship with my wife."

"Your *third* wife, who is now your *ex*-wife."

"I have witnesses, who can testify to her adultery with you. Eighteen witnesses."

"Eighteen witnesses? My goodness, if they all *witnessed* the said adultery, where did so many of them manage to hide in the room without being noticed? In the wardrobes? Behind the drapes?"

"I intend to put their evidence before the Pope."

"Pray do. I am sure His Holiness will be as boggled-eyed as I now am. *Eighteen* witnesses hiding under the bed! Is a man safe nowhere?"

"You may jest –"

"Yes, I may, but no more than anyone else at hearing such nonsense. Still, I have heard enough, and all I can do now is to wish you a pleasant evening, so *buonasera, e buona notte!*"

~~~

A short time after entering his apartments, while reading the letters that had come for him on the afternoon post, another letter arrived by messenger
~~~

from Teresa:

My only Love – for Ever!
What a fine amusement fishing is, my love, I am
fascinated by it. Today I feel I should like to be a
fisherwoman! Always and only on the condition that
you would agree to be a fisherman. I must have cried
out a hundred times on the river bank: Oh, if only
Byron were here, how much more I would be
enjoying myself.

So the tide came up the river, bringing such a
quantity of fish, and there were all my astronomers
abandoning their smoked glasses, and the marksmen
their guns, to go fishing. You can imagine that our
Savage Pietro gave himself up with ardour to this
new sport – he stood in the water – and I stood on
the bank catching in a net the fish he threw to me –
one fish weighed five pounds! Oh, if you had been
there, I'm sure you <u>would</u> have enjoyed yourself. On
Sunday I shall go to see Allegrina.

Byron wrote back:

My Love xxx Fishing and the Fisherwoman. Always
something new with you. Do you know that the
'Milanese Gazette' says that I have <u>arrived</u> in
England! The London newspapers report this also —
and my friends believe it, saying that for the present
I wish to be "incognito." One friend writes to me that
many of them have been to see him — and went
away still not believing that I had not returned —
among them Lady Caroline Lamb, who went away

unconvinced. All this I found in today's post."

As soon as his letter was taken off to Filetto, Byron then picked up another newspaper cutting which Hobhouse had sent to him. This one from the *Chronicle*.

'We rejoice to learn that Lord Byron yesterday arrived in town from Italy.'

From where had they got such an idiotic idea? Did England think he would ever forgive her for believing such lies about him, and scandalising him in their newspapers? Oh, now they were *rejoicing* to learn that he had returned. *Hypocrites!*

More letters came on the same subject in the week that followed, one from his publisher, John Murray, and one from his sister, Augusta.

He replied first to his publisher, to whom he had sent more new episodes of *Don Juan*.

Dear Mr Murray,

I ask you to dispute with your newspapers. Pray do not let them paragraph me back to England. My sister tells me that you sent her to inquire where I was, believing in my arrival, and telling her that I had been seen "driving a curricle into the Palace Yard to visit the Queen." – Do you think me a coxcomb or a madman to be capable of such an exhibition?"

Glancing up from the page to dip his pen in the ink, he noticed Fletcher quietly wandering around the drawing-room with a hangdog expression on his face.

He watched Fletcher speculatively. There was something wrong with him, but what? In the five years since they had left England, Fletcher had returned at least five times to see his wife, returning after a month always looking as happy as when he had left, but this time, he was misery itself.

Now he was standing by the window, gazing out dolefully as if viewing a wasteland.

"Come, Fletcher, out with it. Your holiday in Nottingham has sent you back with a face as sour as last year's rhubarb, so what is it? Are you unhappy to be back here?"

Fletcher turned and shrugged listlessly, "No, my lord, I am very happy to be back."

"You do know that you can quit my service and return to England whenever you wish?"

"Aye, I do know that, my lord."

"Are you pining for your wife?"

"No, not really, my lord. I see her often enough."

"Then why the gloom?" Byron asked. "Is it guilt at leaving her alone in her cottage at Newstead?"

"Well, no, because she's not alone, is she? She has all the staff at Newstead Abbey for company. She even helps out there, now and again, as a maid. And not only that, she's mixed up with some religious women's group in Newstead village."

"So?"

"So she says my visits always come at the worst of times and stop her from attending her meetings."

"Annie? I find it hard to believe Annie said that."

"Oh, she did, my lord, but not in an unkind way. No, not Annie, she wouldn't know how to be unkind."

"No, not Annie," Byron agreed."

"But then, one night," Fletcher went on, "she sits me down and explains to me that when a husband is away for such a long time ... well, a wife gets used to him not being there, and she makes her own life and her own friends. And then when her husband comes back, it interferes with her customary routine."

Byron could only stare, and after a silence Fletcher continued: "Annie said that one of her special friends at her women's meeting, a woman named Bertha, she said that *her* husband is always away also, in the Merchant Navy, and now she, too, feels the same when he comes back, upsetting her usual routine and making the house untidy with his clothes and shoes thrown everywhere."

Byron hesitated. "So to be loved, a husband must always be present and correct?"

Fletcher nodded. "It would seem so. Annie said that when a husband is away for so long and then comes back, it's like having a stranger in your home, and no one cares much for *strangers*, do they?"

Byron could not answer, knowing that Fletcher, along with all his staff, had so often heard him stating how much he hated *strangers* knocking at his door.

"So I don't think I'll be going back so often now." Fletcher shrugged. "Not as Annie always looks fussed when I arrive, and at ease when I'm departing."

Poor Fletcher. No wonder he was looking so miserable.

Later that evening Byron had a quiet word with Tita Falcieri, advising him to be kind to Fletcher for a while, and not to allow any of the others to play their regular pranks on him.

"No? But Fletcho likes our pranks! He laughs too."

"Not as I have heard – sometimes I have heard him roaring fury at you all because of the damned pranks you play on him."

He then confided to Tita about Fletcher's wife no longer being happy about his constant visits every year. "She says it upsets her 'customary routine'."

Tita stared back at him wide-eyed. "Why so is he not happy then? If his wife says that – now he need not feel so heavy his burden of guilt about Marianne."

"Marianne?"

"His mistress. One of the maids. He brought her with us from Venice."

It took some moments for Byron to take it in. "Fletcher has a *mistress?* And which one of the maids is named Marianne?"

"The one you call Madam."

"That one? The big ugly one that flounces around like a Madam?"

Tita shrugged. "Fletcho thinks she is beautiful."

Byron was furious. "And there was I feeling *sorry* for him! Where is he – that master of hypocrisy – go find him and send him to me."

When Fletcher arrived back in the drawing-room, he wore the same hangdog expression and looked as miserable as before.

"Don't put on your damned act with me, Cicero, because I know the truth."

Fletcher was astonished. "How can you know the truth, my lord? I haven't told you it yet."

"About your mistress, the Madam?"

"Oh that ... that's nothing for you to worry about, my lord. I know she can be a bit uppity, but she has a good heart and she takes good care of me."

"I wouldn't care if she threw you out the window. So what is this *truth* you haven't told me? Something from England?"

"Aye," Fletcher nodded, "but I don't like to tell you, my lord, because it's something you will not be happy to hear."

Byron stiffened. "About my former wife?"

"No, it's not about her ... although with Annie being your former wife's former maid, and knowing all her staff and exchanging letters with them and so on; Annie says that Lady Byron has laid down a new rule banning the mention of your name in front of her daughter – "

"*My* daughter?"

"Aye, and young Ada will not be allowed to see any drawing or portrait of you, not until she has reached the age of twenty-one."

Byron blinked. "Not even my picture?"

"No, and even now she is not allowed to know that Lord Byron is her father, but some distant relative who lives abroad. Young Ada is not allowed to know anything about you, not until and unless you return to England and you and her mother should ever become reconciled."

"That will *never* happen," Byron said angrily. "I would rather be dead than live with that woman again!"

"Cruel," Annie said she is. More cruel than Lucifer. Mind, neither of us liked her, as you know."

Byron was doing his best to contain his anger. "And *still* I don't know this truth which you are so sure will make me unhappy – as if what you have said about Ada isn't enough!"

"It will make you sad, my lord, very sad. On my arrival back on the Newstead estate, when I first heard, I cried my eyes out for a while. Nanny Smith was going to write to you about it, but I said no, it would come easier if I was to tell you in person.

"Easier?" Byron threw down his pen. "Getting to any point with you, Fletcher, is like trying to get some ink out of a loaf of bread!"

"It's old Joe, my lord. Old Joe Murray. He has left Newstead and passed on to a better estate."

Even now, Byron could not be certain of what Fletcher was telling him. "Old Joe would never leave the estate of Newstead Abbey, so do you mean ... he has died?"

Fletcher nodded sadly. "Died and gone straight to Heaven. And Colonel Wildman say that one of the last things Joe said to him was, 'When is my young lord coming home?'"

As soon as Fletcher saw the tears coming into Byron's eyes, he said, "*Now* do you understand why it took me so long to tell you?"

Byron did not answer, standing up and going to the drinks cabinet and taking out a bottle of brandy and two glasses. "We must remember him," he said. "You and I, Fletcher, because we are the only two people in this house who knew Joe."

The spent the rest of the night in two of the armchairs, drinking brandy and fondly remembering Old Joe Murray of Newstead Abbey.

"Fifty years he had been head butler there," Fletcher said, "fifty years."

"And looked after me since I arrived there as a boy of ten," Byron said. "He was always incredibly neat and tidy in his dress, and made me likewise, telling me you could always tell a gentleman by the respectability of his clothes and the cleanliness of his person. And even then, when I was a boy of only ten who had inherited this great gothic mansion in a strange place called Nottingham, it was *Joe* who brought me my first dog so I would have a friend. In every way, and often to my mother's annoyance, Joe always looked after me so well."

"And yet," said Fletcher, "he was the one who kept telling everyone how well *you* had looked after him, giving him a good pension when you left, ... but still he worked on. Colonel Wildman couldn't get him to leave the Abbey, and didn't have the heart to force him."

Byron sighed. "Tom Wildman was always a good lad, one of my best friends at Harrow. I'm glad it was he who bought Newstead. Some other purchaser might not have been so kind to Joe."

"He told me ..." said Fletcher, pouring himself more brandy, "Colonel Wildman ... he told me that he fell in love with Newstead Abbey when he first went there for your twenty-first birthday party. And then he couldn't believe his luck when he came back from the war and saw it was up for sale. He told me a few stories about old Joe that he thought you might like to hear, and asked me to tell you them."

"Tell me," Byron said, closing his eyes and visualising his old friend and quasi-grandfather, "tell me all you know about old Joe after I left England."

Fletcher told him: "Joe approved of Colonel Wildman's wife, a genteel young lady of great kindness; and when her husband began organising some repairs to the mansion, apparently Joe would rejoice that the Abbey would once more echo with the sounds of laughter and hospitality ... He asked the Colonel if he would be inviting *you* to come back and visit when the repairs were done, and the reply he was always given was 'Certainly.'

"But then it all went wrong, because in his eagerness

to hasten the repairs, Joe would get up at the crack of dawn and go round waking up the workmen. And when they complained about the early hour, Joe would say that Time was moving too fast for *him* and so he wanted to see the work done. God blast their carcases if the young lord was to come back and the work not done in time."

Fletcher drank some more brandy, and continued all the tales told to him by Nanny Smith.

"And despite his age, past eighty, Joe would often turn out in the early morning in the cold weather and cut sticks for the lighting of all the fires. Colonel Wildman would always kindly remonstrate with Joe for risking his health, telling him there were others who could do the work for him; but Joe would always say – 'Lord, sir, it's my morning bath of fresh air. It keeps me healthy and I'm all the better for it.'

"Unluckily, though, one morning Joe was cutting the sticks and a splinter flew up and wounded one of his eyes. An inflammation set in, and he lost the sight in that eye, and then in the other. Poor Joe pined and grew melancholy.

"'Come, come, old boy, be of good heart, you will get better,' the colonel would tell him, but Joe would not hear it.

"'Nay, sir," Joe would say, 'I did hope I would live to see what I want to see, including the restoration of our Abbey, but it's all over with me now. I know I shall soon be going home'."

Tears were in Byron's eyes; but Fletcher did not notice, because he was now slightly drunk from all his drinking of the brandy.

"Where is he buried?" Byron asked. "On the Newstead estate?"

Fletcher frowned. "Well now, that's a strange story, because Joe had discussed that with Colonel Wildman, stating that you had told him that you wished him to be buried in the same big marble tomb you that had built for poor Boatswain, and for Joe to lie in there also, until you joined both of them in the tomb at a later date."

"I was jesting!"

"Aye, but Joe mustn't have known that, or forgotten it, because he said to the colonel, 'If I was sure his lordship would come along later, sir, I should like the tomb well enough, but I would not like to lie alone with the dog'.

"So when Joe *did* die, Colonel Wildman did the next best thing, and had him buried in the garden of Hucknall Church, at the closest spot to the wall of the Byron vault which is beneath the alter. He was convinced that Joe would be happy there, but I was not so sure, and I told the colonel my reason – 'Why, sir,' says I, 'that vault is where his lordship's mother now lies, and she and Joe always hated each other."

Byron started laughing, tears and laughter together, because Fletcher's talk had taken him back to all the those days and all those people he used to know ...

"What of Nanny Smith? I hope *she* is still hale and hearty?"

"Hale and hearty and as proud as a peacock living in her cottage now, a lady of leisure. She had me worn out answering all the questions she put to me about you, so I can't remember anything that *she* said."

"Then I'm off," Byron said, standing. "I can feel some nostalgic poetry coming on."

"Oh, wait, I remember something now ... there was one very odd thing that Nanny Smith told me, but then she made me promise not to tell *you* ... so what'll I do?"

"If it's another *truth*, then tell me. I won't snitch on you."

"You won't write to her and let her know I told you?"

Byron sighed tiredly. "Out with it, Fletcher, and no long rigmarole beforehand."

Fletcher took another drink of brandy. "Well, it upset old Joe, that's for sure. And he being the head of the Abbey at the time, with no master in it, so what could he do?"

"About what? Not ... Mary Chaworth?"

"Ah no, poor Mary Chaworth ... she's still a sad and melancholy creature. No, what Nanny Smith told me was about Lady Byron, and indeed it *was* odd."

"Annabella has never been to Nottingham or Newstead Abbey."

"She has now, well, she did *then*, about six months after we left England. Nanny Smith said she turned up one day and they didn't know who she was, until she announced herself. And then she began to look through all your books in the library, and when she had finished, she then went up to do some searching in your bedroom, rummaging through the drawers of your desk and leaving papers scattered everywhere. Old Joe was very annoyed."

And now so was Byron. "She had no right to do that. We were legally separated by then."

"Then she began to question Joe and Nanny Smith about the summer when you and your sister stayed there. 'How did they behave together?' she wanted to know.

"'Like any other brother and sister,' says Nanny Smith. 'Why, his sister loved Newstead Abbey almost as much as his lordship did, with Newstead being *her* ancestral home as well as her brother's'."

Byron's face had turned pale with anger. "How dare she go there to interrogate my servants."

"Aye," Fletcher nodded, "and she kept grilling them until they told her what she wanted to hear – but they did not know *what* she wanted to hear. So the questioning did not stop until Nanny Smith began to cry, and Joe was forced to remonstrate sternly with Lady Byron, telling her she was no lady to upset a genteel woman like Mrs Smith in such a way."

Byron stood silent for some moments, his thoughts swirling. And then it came to him, the *truth* of it.

"So, if this all happened six months after I had left England, and seven months *after* the separation was legally finalised, does this not prove that the jealous allegations she made against poor Augusta, and against *me,* were made without any real basis at all?"

"How d'you mean?"

"Why else – all that time later – would she *still* feel the need to go questioning and searching and rummaging for some kind of evidence to prove the so-called *facts* that she had already alleged against us."

"Seems to me she was searching for some kind of evidence to convince *herself* more-like.

Fletcher was shaking his head. "Still, you're free of her now. And all I can say, my lord – now that I've told you the sad news about Joe – is how glad I am to be back in Italy – the land of pranks, pasta, and polenta."

Byron looked at him dryly. "Some of us might choose to more aptly refer to it as the land of painters, poets, and popes."

"Aye, well, each to his own, I'm happy enough whatever you call it, just as long as I'm kept far away from those screaming Italian opera singers."

Chapter Twenty-Two

~ ~ ~

In London, Byron's publisher, John Murray, was happily preparing to read the latest Cantos of *Don Juan*, filling his pipe with fresh tobacco and pouring himself a glass of good Highland Malt whisky.

Now where were we? ... In the previous cantos, *Don Juan*, the young rascal, after the fiasco with Julia in Spain, followed by a Mediterranean storm and shipwreck onto the golden sands of one of Greek islands, resulting in his love affair with young Haidée, until he is captured by her furious father and put aboard a ship to be sold at a slave market in Turkey.

There, he is bought by a servant of the Sultan, Baba, to be a slave to his master; but on arriving at the palace, the Queen, on seeing *Juan*, decides to save him for herself, and so quickly hides Juan in her husband's harem – and poor *Juan* – under protest – is forced to disguise himself as a female.

Murray paused, thinking it such a shame that the Bishop of London had advised all husbands to forbid their wives and daughters to read such a book. Probably because in other books, *Don Juan* is portrayed as a seducing libertine, but in Byron's portrayal, *Juan* is a naïve young man, who never seduces, but is constantly seduced by women, and all told in a comic way.

Although, in truth, few English ladies would be pleased to read about the young *Juan* wandering nervously around a Sultan's harem in Turkey, wearing veil and robe and disguised as a female named *Juanna*.

Although, if they *did* read it, even sneakily, they might be surprised that, of all the girls lying on their couches, the one whom *Juan* – behind his veil – found the most appealing, was not a slender beauty, so usual in stories these days – but a girl with the babyish name of *Dudù,* who was somewhat on the large size.

No Moon at Midnight

Lolah was dusk as India and as warm;
Katinka was Georgian, white and red,
With great blue eyes, a lovely hand and arm,
And feet so small they scarce seemed made to tread
But rather skim the earth; while Dudù's form
Looked more adapted to be put to bed,
Being somewhat large and languishing and lazy,
Yet of a beauty that would drive you crazy.

A kind of sleepy Venus seemed Dudù,
Yet very fit to murder sleep in those
Who gazed upon her cheek's transcendent hue,
Her Attic forehead and her Phidian nose;
Few angles were there in her form, 'tis true,
Thinner she might have been and yet scarce lose;
Yet, after all, 'twould puzzle to say where
It would not spoil some separate charm 'to pare'.

She was not violently lively, but
Stole on your spirit like a May-day breaking;
Her eyes were not too sparkling, but, half shut,
They put beholders in a tender taking;
She looked (this simile's quite new) just cut
From marble, like Pygmalion's statue waking,
The Marble and the Mortal still at strife,
And timidly expanding into life.

John Murray was smiling at Byron's constant *asides* to
the reader, as if he was writing one of his usual letters to
a friend, and telling all, but in verse. Yet, who knew?
Perhaps, in his own mind, Byron viewed all his readers
as his friends.

She was a soft Landscape of mild Earth,
Where all was harmony and calm and quiet,
Luxuriant, budding; cheerful without mirth,
Which if not happiness, is much more nigh it
Than are your mighty passions and so forth,
Which some call 'the sublime'; I wish they'd try it:
I've seen your stormy seas and stormy women,
And pity lovers rather more than seamen.

And then she gave Juanna a chaste kiss:
Dudù was fond of kissing – which I'm sure
That nobody can ever take amiss,
Because 'tis pleasant, so that it be pure,
And between females means no more than this –

The door flew open – rudely jerking John Murray away from the pleasantness of the sleepy harem – and there stood Lady Caroline Lamb, skinny as a rake and eyes popping – "Is it true you have received more poetry from Don Juan?"

"Well, yes – "

"Is it about me?"

"Err, no –"

"Of course it is! All his poetry is about me. Is he still in love with me?"

As far as John Murray knew, Lord Byron had *never* been in love with Caroline Lamb, but she had always been insane about him. Or maybe – she was just insane. Suspecting such, he always treated her with the greatest delicacy.

"Lady Caroline, may I offer you some tea ?"

"Certainly you may. Does Childe Harold still drink *green* tea?"

"I have no idea."

"So he did *not* come to London after all?"

"No, that was a mistake."

"Is he still in Italy?"

"I believe so."

"What about that witch of a wife of his? Is she still crying foul because she knew he loved me more than her?"

John Murray found all this questioning quite unpleasant. He was merely Lord Byron's publisher, not his best friend. That would be John Hobhouse.

He lifted the bell and rang for his assistant, and ordered tea, while Lady Caroline sat herself down on a chair by his desk, and, as usual, took the opportunity of whipping off her hat and shaking out her short blonde curly hair.

Once this was done, she smiled at him, and looked a different person altogether, younger than her thirty-four years, and faced with that smile it was hard to stay annoyed with her.

"Will you allow me to read his new poetry?" she asked.

"I have not yet read it myself."

"When you have done so?"

"I will publish it. Then you can read it."

"Will you send me the very first copy off the press?"

"Of course I will. I always do." He told everyone their copy was the very first one straight from the printing press. It made life so much easier.

"I have been very ill," Caroline said, her voice softer. "Near to death."

"Oh, my dear, I'm sorry to hear that. But you look very well now."

"I am very well now. Although my heart fails to repair. It is still broken."

John Murray sighed, hoping it was not the same old subject again.

"I am not mad, and never was," Caroline said astutely, "although you may wish to think so."

"Lady Caroline, it would be impossible for me to even consider thinking such a thing."

"No, but others do. Does the Corsair ever ask about

me in his letters?"

"He rarely writes letters these day, just packs off his poetry with a short note."

The tea was brought in, and as Caroline sipped from her cup, a soft mellowness came over her face.

"When I was near death," she said, "or at least when I *hoped* I was dying, so that everyone could feel mean and nasty for saying such dreadful things about me, my little maid Bella said to me, 'Lady Caroline, if you die and go to Heaven, and God asks you who were the three people that you most loved on earth, who would you name?' – and I did not even have to think about it."

She took another sip of her tea.

"I told Bella – as I *would* have told God – that the three people I love best are ... firstly, my mother, then Byron, and then my dear son Augustus."

John Murray stared. "Lady Caroline, are you forgetting – your husband, Lord Melbourne?"

"William?" She pulled a face. "William has a good temper, but an ill nature. Whereas Byron had a bad temper, but a good nature. Now, which of them would *you* prefer?"

John Murray could not answer, wishing only to be allowed to return to the Sultan's harem and the soft landscape of the sleepy-eyed Dudù.

Chapter Twenty-Three

~~~

As the summer moved into Autumn, Count Ruggero Gamba, as always, moved his family out of the countryside of Filetto into his warmer townhouse in Ravenna for the winter.

It was a large mansion with many rooms; and although each daughter had her own bedroom, Teresa was designated her own ground-floor apartment of three rooms, which included her own private sitting-room.

This allowed Byron to visit her more frequently, as a friend of the family, usually most evenings, where he would join the family for dinner, or play billiards with Pietro for an hour or so; and then a few hours to spend with Teresa in the privacy of her apartment.

Allegra had also been brought back to Ravenna, and she, too, was often brought in the afternoons to spend some time with Teresa.

Count Guiccioli, who had given up all efforts to inconvenience Mylord, had now changed his tactics, and became so friendly with his rich British tenant, that Byron eventually found himself wondering if Guiccioli would eventually drive him away into a lunatic asylum.

Many afternoons Guiccioli would call up to his apartment carrying some kind of gift, asking to be allowed in, and then would sit on the sofa drinking wine and airing his opinions on Italian politics for at least an hour, while Byron sat at his desk writing letters and paying little attention to him.

"And still no news about my post as British Consul of Ravenna?"

Byron shook his head. "No, but the civil servants in the Foreign Office are always slow, as is the English postal service."

"The post brings *you* many letters."

"Private letters, from friends."

"It is my only true security against the Austrians if the Carbonari cause trouble," Guiccioli said. "And it will also keep me protected from the Carbonari who suspect everybody of being their enemy. Oh, my friend, my dear Lord Byron, I think you should write again to England. Yes, you must write again. Tell them how urgent it is for the British to have an official Consul here in Ravenna. Tell them I will be excellent as their Italian representative."

"No, I'd rather not write again. Like myself, the British do not like to be *pushed*."

Guiccioli did not get the hint.

After more afternoons of pestering, Byron finally relented and agreed to write another letter – to his publisher, Mr John Murray – whom Guiccioli believed was "the top man" at the foreign office.

'Dear Mr Murray ...'

Guiccioli stood over him, watching the black ink of the pen move across the paper and reading every word as it emerged, even though he did not understand a word of English; yet here and there he recognised his own name ... *L'Conte Alessandro Guiccioli ...*

Seeing Byron sign his name at the end of the letter, Guiccioli asked him to read it aloud in Italian.

Guiccioli listened, and appeared satisfied; but then entertained some doubts.

"Is there a possibility they will say no?"

Byron shrugged. "Every situation has possibilities. But if their answer to appointing you is a negative one, I have a solution, which I know they will *not* refuse."

"How can there be a solution if they do not appoint me?"

"I shall request for *myself* to be appointed as British Consul here in Ravenna, which I am sure they will grant; and then I will appoint *you* as my Vice-Consul and leave you in charge of all meetings and ceremonial duties and so on."

"*Eccellente!*"

Guiccioli was so pleased at having the perfect solution to any rejection of himself, later that afternoon he sent Mylord up a case of his best wine; which Byron ordered Fletcher to open and tip away in some secluded part of the garden.

"Although it is probably safe to drink, as now I think he would prefer to keep me alive."

"He's a mad 'un, I'm certain," Fletcher said. "I would beg you to do your utmost to keep him away from you."

Count Guiccioli had no intention of being kept away. Mylord Byron still had a great deal of money which Alessandro wanted to draw from, and he had come up with a certain way for that to happen, *without* the necessity of another loan.

After all, why should he have to pay alimony when his wife had a rich lover? In fairness, the lover should be paying alimony to *him*, to make up for his loss.

In the following weeks Byron found he had to do battle with Guiccioli in situations that were sometimes grotesque, and all under the guise of Alessandro's new feelings of *friendship*.

It was a friendship, a fondness, which Alessandro claimed to feel so strongly, he was now becoming a permanent fixture on the sofa in Byron's drawing-room.

"We have known each other for so long," Guiccioli said, "I feel now like you are one of my sons."

Byron shrugged at the ridiculousness of it. But at least this was better than always having to be on his guard against Guiccioli wishing to murder him.

"I am my mother's son," Byron replied.

"*Si, si* ... but you could be my son too, if you married my daughter Attilia. She would make you a better wife than Teresa."

"Unfortunately, I cannot marry anyone. I am already married."

Guiccioli did not see that as a problem. "It is good that you are a heretic, an Inglese Protestant, because in

Italy if you have not married in the Catholic Church, you are not married at all. So you *could* marry my daughter Attilia, here in Italy."

Byron was confused. "I was not aware that you had any grown-up daughters."

"*Si,* Attilia is now twelve years and a few months. Old enough to be a wife. And such a beautiful girl. *Oh, e una bellissima femmina!"*

Byron stared. "Your daughter Attilia is only *twelve?"*

"Young and fresh." Guiccioli smiled in his red-whiskered foxy way. "And because she is so – *you* would have to pay the marriage dowry for her. One million lira. Others would pay more."

For the first time Byron got a true insight to the reality of all that Teresa had said about her husband, and how he had attempted to use her.

And also for the first time – he lost his temper with the Count, ordering him to leave and escorting him towards the door. "Know this, for I say it loud. You are a man without scruples, a man without honour."

Guiccioli looked back at him scathingly. "What is this talk of honour? From *you* – a man who takes another's wife?"

"And now the husband of that wife wants me also to take his twelve-year-old daughter – his child – in exchange for money!"

At the open door, the Count's mood and manner changed. Sullen and deeply offended by being shooed out of the room like a cat in a chicken-yard ... yet he was prepared to forgive.

"I have treated you, Mylord, with every consideration this last year, every respect, even though you are a foreigner in my country. But you are young, and so I will not bear you a grudge in return for your disrespect to me. I hope, in the near future, we can renew our friendship, when you have learned better manners."

Byron's bodyguard, Tita Falcieri, who always stood behind the door of the adjoining room when Guiccioli was present, had quickly stepped inside the room as soon as he had heard Mylord's anger.

Now Tita stood looking at Byron with some alarm as he closed the door. "I don't like what he say – at the door – about renewing your friendship later. That means he intends to kill you."

"No." Byron was positive. "He won't try to kill me. Not yet. Not until he has succeeded in getting more money out of me. Of what use would I be to him dead?"

Tita threw up his hands. "You don't understand. You are not Italian."

"And you don't understand avariciousness, the lust for money. It is a mental disease, beyond all normal reasoning, whether in Italy, England, or Turkey."

"And when Guiccioli knows for certain that you will give him no more money?"

"Oh no, I would never let him become certain of that. He must always be allowed to think he has a *chance* of getting some more. On that my safety depends."

Tita was doubtful; until a week or so later when Count Guiccioli came back, eager to show Byron some sketches of an old property he owned.

"Seventeenth century, a home fit for a prince, but in need of some little repairs."

Byron looked over the sketches with interest. "It certainly has possibilities, but it looks like it would need a great deal of repairs."

"Some repairs, only a few, and then with how you like to furnish, Mylord, you would have a beautiful mansion to be happy in. You are interested?"

"I am very interested."

"Interested enough to *buy* it – it is not for rent."

"If I am satisfied with it, of course I will buy it. It is my intention to stay in Ravenna and I would prefer to live in my own house. But I would have to personally walk over the property first."

"*Si!*"

"And I would not pay a high price until all of the repairs were done."

"So when? When will you walk over it?"

"Oh, not for a few weeks. I have too much poetry to write and my publisher is anxiously waiting."

"And then you will look?"

Byron nodded. "Then I will look."

~ ~ ~

Arriving at Count Gamba's house in the evening, Byron discovered that all the family were out at the opera. Only Teresa was at home, waiting for him in her apartment.

To Teresa, and only to Teresa, did Byron vent all his exasperations about Guiccioli.

"He is driving me mad with all his visits and strange proposals to me – wanting me to go to Bologna with him – wanting me to marry his twelve-year-old daughter – and now he wants me to buy his crumbling *Casa Raisi* for a high price. God knows what will be next?"

Teresa understood only too well, and sympathised, but she could not soothe Byron out of his irritable mood.

"And now, this afternoon, in the post – guess who is attempting a little blackmail against me?"

Teresa could not guess. "Why would anyone try to blackmail you?"

"Hinting – mark, only *hinting* – to reveal all she knows about the 'intimacy' of my relationship with you at Venice and La Mira."

"But who would know that ...?" And then Teresa's eyes opened wide as she realised. "Fanny?"

"Yes, Fanny! Suggesting I frank the money to her in Venice – frank to Hell! Let the devil pay her. I'll not be blackmailed by anyone – and especially not by Signora Sylvestrini."

Teresa was shocked. "This must be Fanny's way of having her vengeance against you for not allowing her to be Allegrina's nurse. She wanted the pay, and you denied her. Now she is seeking payment in another way. This is shameful! I will disown her and not reply to any more of her letters."

"And now," said Byron, "I see that I *was* correct in thinking she was not the right nurse for a child like Allegra. Still, for Fanny to do this ..."

He sighed, and then walked over to gaze out on the darkened garden. "Do you know," he said, "that in the Bible, after the Garden of Eden, when Cain killed Abel, an angel came and put a sign across Cain's forehead. And now I think I must also have a sign across *my* forehead. I don't know what my sign says in English, but in Italy it clearly says BANK."

"I will never forgive Fanny for making you feel this way, never."

Byron turned to her, an expression of slight amusement on his face.

"The only thing I regret now, is that if Fanny *had* come to Ravenna, I would have liked – just for a moment – to see her effect on your brother Pietro. I'm sure he would have thrown her out the window on the second day."

"Pierino is too hot-headed and idealistic about everything."

"I don't know if *Lega* has any understanding with Fanny, but I have now reached an understanding with *him* on the subject."

Feeling guiltily responsible for Fanny, and feeling so sorry for him, Teresa moved to hide her face against his chest, and then looked up at him with her blue eyes.

"Would it help you, if I gave you a kiss?"

He answered her with a smile, saying softly, "In poetry, the word 'kiss' rhymes with 'bliss'."

She rose up a little higher, kissed him on the lips, and then she took his hand and led him into her bedroom for "an hour of love and rest."

~~~

Byron left Teresa at eleven o'clock, as he always did.

Stepping out to the dark street, he briefly saluted Tita Falcieri who was sitting on a horse waiting for him,
~~~

wearing his wide belt of daggers and pistols around his waist.

After mounting his own horse, Byron paused for a moment to gaze up at the gleaming illuminations all over the Italian sky.

"A night of a thousand stars," he said.

Tita nodded. "And a silent night. So we must not ride too fast and draw attention to the noise of our horses."

Together they rode on in the darkness at a slow pace, picking up speed only when they were clear of the town – heading in the opposite direction to home and the Palazzo Guiccioli – towards a tavern near to the *Porta San Mamante*.

PART FOUR

Revolution

'Supposing that Italy could be liberated, it is a grand object – the very 'poetry' of politics! Only think – a free Italy !!!'

Byron to John Cam Hobhouse

'Byron told me something about his proceedings in the Romagna – he had regularly joined the Carbonari – was initiated – was head of a Ravenna branch called the *Cacciatiori Americani* (American Hunters) and he used to meet members of the 'Young Italy' party at night at the *Osteria Boracina,* outside the *Porta San Mamante'*.

Diary of John Cam Hobhouse

Chapter Twenty-Four

~ ~ ~

The secret organizations of the *Carboneria* were galvanizing towards one main determination, which contained three separate objectives – to overthrow Austrian rule in North Italy; Papal rule in middle Italy; and Bourbon rule over the Kingdoms of Naples and Sicily in the South.

Naples, with over 40,000 Carbonari members, was the largest and the strongest, and rose up in a sudden explosion of revolutionary warfare that resulted in victory for the Carbonari, and Naples being declared a Republic.

All Italy was in a panic, because no warning had been given. The plan of the Carbonari was for all sections of the country to rise as a whole on a pre-arranged date; but Naples had struck out on its own.

The Carbonari in the North were furious, for now their hand was shown, their ultimate plan revealed, and now the action in Naples had placed them all in great danger.

Pietro Gamba, a member of the organisation known as *Young Italy,* arrived at Byron's apartments in the Palazzo Guiccioli in a state of consternation.

"Where can we hide all the rifles and weapons? The Ravenna Carbonari now have nowhere to hide them. All the main residences are being watched, including our own residence – all houses, we think, except the houses of those who are known to be Austrian spies. What will we do?"

It did not take Byron long to come up with a solution. "I know the perfect place."

The following evening, Count Guiccioli was very surprised to be invited to dinner in Mylord's apartment, where he was served with the very best cuisine that

Luigi and Valeriano could cook for him.

A feast fit for a king, which Alessandro was heartily enjoying – and even more so because Mylord was moving closer to buying his *Casa Raisi* – taking another interested look at the sketches and asking many questions.

"There is no need for you to go and look at the casa if you are too busy. I can answer all your questions, every little thing you need to know."

"No, no, I must walk over the property myself before I decide."

"You should decide quickly, because soon we may have no houses left to sell or buy if those damned Carbonari have their way. Their revolution will spread from Naples to everywhere – even to the Romagna – and then where will we be?"

"From what I have heard, the Neapolitans have merely removed the rule of a Bourbon king."

"*Disonorevole!* And you say *merely?* There is no *merely* in the act of removing a king. How can you say so – or do you hate all kings?"

"I am no champion of kings, but I do not feel anything personal against the man who wears the crown, whoever he may be. Yet on a political level, and in the case of government, I think great efforts should be made to curb the absolutism of the monarch."

"Absolutism?"

"Yes. The king – one man – decides and decrees – and his rule is absolute. Not even the elected government can oppose his absolute rule."

"You talk like a liberal, or a republican, like those revolutionaries in America who threw off their king."

Count Guiccioli's black eyes had narrowed suspiciously ... And yet, you are an English Noble, an aristocrat, a lord ... I think that is strange."

Byron smiled, and leaned forward with voice lowered, saying conspiratorially, "And would you think it strange if you were told in a private confidence that I was a member of the secret society of the *Sanfedisti?*"

"The *Sanfedisti?*" Guiccioli sat back in shock. The *Sanfedisti* were a secret society that was even worse than the Carbonari – named after Cardinal Ruffo's *Army of the Holy Faith*. Counter-revolutionaries and anti-liberals, they were organised and controlled by some of the highest aristocrats in Italy, determined to keep the lower orders in their place.

One of their secret leaflets had once been slipped into Alessandro's hand, and what he had read in the leaflet frightened him so much, he had read it many times in disbelief. He was, after all, a dignified and respected man who thought all murders should be quietly done, and done by an anonymous hand.

But those *Sanfedisti* were a bloodthirsty lot. In that leaflet they had urged — "*the killing of all who are even suspected of sympathy towards that infamous sect of liberalism, without regard to their origins, nation, sex, rank, fortune, and without pity even in the face of the cries of infants and the pleas of the aged ...*"

And now it might be that Mylord Byron was one of them. Ah, now he understood. Now it all made sense! No wonder he was so arrogant. He was not a Carbonaro – he was a *Sanfedisto*.

"Mylord Byron," he said, taking a deep slug of his wine, "I have told you many times how much I hate the *Carbonari*. You, Mylord, know that I am loyal to the Austrians, the Pope, and to all the Cardinals of Rome."

"Are you? So loyal? Then you must know that all the Cardinals of the Ecclesiastical Senate in Rome are hoping not only to defeat liberalism, but also to extend the Vatican States to include Tuscany."

Guiccioli frowned. "Why should that matter to me? Tuscany is the hottest den for those *Carbonari* conspirators who should be wiped out before they take over the whole country. Locked up in prison, every one of them – just like those who were arrested in Milan some months ago. Locked up, hanged, or shot? We agree on that, eh?"

Byron inclined his head non-committingly, a wave of

sorrow sweeping over him. Those good liberal friends of his in Milan who had been imprisoned were suffering horribly under the hands of the Austrians. Ludovico di Breme, only thirty-six-years old, had died from his treatment in the prison. And now this hypocrite Guiccioli was saying the others should be hanged or shot.

Now he was glad that he had found a small way of punishing Guiccioli – not only for his ill-usage of Teresa – but for the punishment he was wishing on those noble men now suffering in Milan.

His eye caught sight of Tita at the door behind Guiccioli, and Tita nodded.

"Alas, I fear I have eaten too much," Byron said to Guiccioli, even though he had eaten very little. "We will have one more glass of wine, to celebrate our business with my potential purchase of your *Casa Raisi!*"

Guiccioli smiled. "*Si,* we must drink to your success in getting a very good bargain from me." He took the glass of wine that Byron handed to him. "Others would pay more, but for *you,* I have dropped the price."

Byron watched as Alessandro greedily drank the rich claret.

"Yes, too much food," Byron said, a hand on his stomach, "so you will forgive me if I now beg to retire?"

"So early? It is not yet midnight."

"No, but we English, you know, we are raised on the motto of early to bed, early to rise ... I do hope, Conte, that you have enjoyed your evening?"

The Count sighed, mellow and affable. "Yes, very good, very pleasant, and now your good food and wine has defeated me also ... food is usually no problem, I am capable of eating a horse, but tonight I think I may have *drank* too much of your French wine. Next time, we will drink only Italian."

Guiccioli laughed as he moved untidily to his feet. "And now you are sending me home! Good, it is where I should go. But next time, Mylord ... let us not speak about worrying political matters. Next time we will speak only about my *Casa Raisi,* and how it will be a very good investment for you."

Byron gave Guiccioli's face a glance of the closest scrutiny, noting that his eyes were slightly hazed. "If you *have* drank too much, then at least you will sleep well tonight?"

"My friend, I always sleep well, no matter what, ... births, marriages, deaths ... still I sleep." He smiled as he patted Byron's arm. *"Grazie, mio amico, grazie, e buona notte."*

Byron had no doubt that Guiccioli would sleep well tonight, for he had slipped the contents of a small vial of laudanum into his last glass of wine.

"Have they come?" he asked Tita.

Tita nodded. "Now they are waiting for the lamps in his bedroom to go out."

Count Guiccioli slept the sleep of the well-fed and the drunkenly drugged; unaware that while he slept Pietro Gamba and other Carbonaros were hiding their weapons inside one of the cellars of Guiccioli's house.

"Your dinner with him took longer than we expected," Pietro said. "Do you think he had any suspicions of your sudden friendliness to him?"

"No suspicions," Byron grinned. "Not now he believes I am a supporter of the *Sanfedisti.*"

Chapter Twenty-Five

~ ~ ~

Ravenna was waiting for Bologna, and Bologna was not ready to move – disputes within their two factions of workers and intellectuals as to what do next were ongoing.

Meanwhile, the Congress of the European Alliance met in Troppau in Austria to discuss ways of suppressing the revolution in Naples. Tsar Alexander I of Russia was present in person, as was King Frederick William of Prussia, and Francis I, Emperor of Germany. Britain and France did not attend, other than to send their ambassadors.

In the congress the *Troppau Protocol* was secretly agreed upon, affirming the right of the collective European Alliance to suppress all internal revolutions:

"States which have undergone a change of government due to revolution, the result of which threatens other States, will cease to be members of the Great European Alliance, and will remain excluded from it until their situation gives guarantees for legal order and stability, or if need be, by the use of arms, to bring back the guilty State into the Great Alliance."

So independent countries had become 'States' of the European Alliance. Britain and France did not approve the general principle of the *Troppau Protocol*, yet remained neutral; allowing Austria to protect her interests in Italy by crushing the Neapolitan revolution.

An army of five thousand Austrian soldiers were the first detachment to be sent to Naples, causing a quivering of nerves amongst the intellectuals and liberals of Bologna, and frustrating the lower orders of determined patriots, until all was in disarray.

The leaders were certain – a concerted action of the whole country on the same day would have succeeded – but the rising of a province here and there – against the might of the Austrian forces – could only lead to defeat.

Byron wrote in disgust to John Hobhouse, who had sent a letter complaining about his failure to return to England for a visit, as promised.

"... Another thing that has kept me here, besides my amica, is that we all expected, and they had actually got on their bandoliers for a rising and all that; in which I, amongst thousands, was to have a part, being urged by my love of liberty in general, and Italy in particular; and also by the good opinion some of the confederates had of me as a coadjutor. But all of a sudden, Bologna withdrew from the league, and wanted to temper and to temporise, and left us in the lurch. And without Bologna, the Romagnole towns can do little. The Huns are on the River Po, and here we are, the principals, liable to arrest every day, "some taken and some left" like the "foolish virgins" or some other parable in the Evangelist.

In the meantime, the affairs of this part of Italy are simplifying; but if the scoundrels of Troppau decide on a massacre (as is probable) the Barbarians will march in by one frontier, and the Neapolitans by the other. They have <u>both</u> asked permission of His Holiness to do so, which is equivalent to asking a man's permission to give him a kick up the arse.

Here in Ravenna all is suspicion and terrorism, bullying, arming and disarming, the guards are doubled, palace shut, the priests scared, the people gloomy. The Cardinal is at his wit's end – it's true he had not far to go.

Added to all that, Fletcher is ill, and has insisted on having three pounds of blood drained from him since yesterday – for a sore throat. In his jacket and handkerchief and foolish face he looks much like Liston, or such a figure as he did in Albania in 1809 during the autumnal rains in his jerkin and umbrella. Oh, the merry days that we have seen!"

As soon as the letter was finished, Byron prepared to go into Ravenna for the evening, not only to see Teresa, but also to see Count Alborghetti, who, as Secretary General of the Lower Romagna and aide to Cardinal Rusconi, was now running a great risk, close to treason, in providing Byron with contents from the Cardinal's mail, as well as about the movements of the Austrians, but also whatever inquiries or information might be asked about himself and Teresa.

"They will not shut her up in a convent – now that she is living respectably with her father," Count Alborghetti had told him. "But the Austrians are still concerned about *you*, and annoyed that you should be so popular with the people."

"Popular? In Italy?" Byron laughed. "Do the Huns not know that only opera singers are *popular* in Italy?"

Before leaving the palazzo he called in on Fletcher, whose face was as white as the pillow behind his head, due to the loss of so much blood.

Speaking in a weak voice, Fletcher looked pleased to see him. "My lord, I'm glad you came ... I don't wish to alarm you, but I fear I might be breathing my last ... aye, I think I'm dying."

"If you are dying, which I doubt, then it's your own fault. All that bloodletting for a sore throat! Why could you not do like everyone else and just gargle your throat with a glass of salty water?"

"I tried that, my lord, but my voice still came out like a frog's croak, and so I thought — "

An eruption of gun shots outside the window silenced Fletcher and sent Byron rushing to the window, peering out into the darkness, and then down onto the lamp-lit path directly in front of the house.

Seconds later he was rushing down the stairs and out the front door, where he found the commandant of police, Luigi Dal Pinto, lying on the ground, badly wounded. Closer inspection showed he had been shot at least three or four times and was in mortal danger.

Servants from the ground floor rushed out to stare at the wounded policeman, and then began to wail and pray, joined by others rushing from the streets who also did nothing but stare and lament.

Tita arrived on the scene and Byron gave vent to his annoyance. "As no one will doing anything to help him, except howl and pray – "

"Because they fear the consequences," Tita said. "They can pray, but dare not get involved."

"Then we must," Byron said, ordering Tita to lift up the commandant and carry him upstairs. "He's not *dead*, which is a miracle, so there is still a chance we can help him."

When the commandant was carried upstairs, Fletcher got out of his bed and even he tried to help as best he could, bringing bandages; but as soon as Byron began to use the bandages on the commandant to stop the bleeding he realised the man had expired.

"It's too late. He's dead."

Tita sighed. "Poor fellow, but he had made himself much disliked by the people."

"I wonder why he was outside this house?"

"Perhaps he was coming to see the Count."

Byron turned to look at the small group of Guiccioli's servants who were gathered by the open door. "Where is Count Guiccioli?"

"*L'opera,*" they told him. The Count had gone out to

the opera.

With nothing else that could be done, Byron sent a servant to inform the police, and despatched Valeriano to inform Cardinal Rusconi of the news of the commandant's death.

Cardinal Rusconi was horrified, but he viewed Lord Byron's behaviour in trying to help the commandant as an act of natural humanity.

Not so the *Carbonari,* who were enraged; unable to understand why Mylord Byron had consorted with one of the hated enemy and had even tried to save his life.

Their rage was vocal and vociferous, but Byron refused to be intimidated.

"In the cause of freedom I am with you, in wisdom and influence, but not at *any* price. My wish is that *both* sides would do their best to avoid *unnecessary* violence and savagery. A murdered policeman lying on the street only serves as justification for the government's brutality. A murdered policeman lying on the street does not free Italy. It only serves to make the iron hand hit you harder."

Count Ruggero Gamba stepped forward and put his hand solidly on Byron's shoulder. "This man has done, what I would have done in the same situation. Friend or foe, we must not lose our humanity or the behaviour of a civilised people. I would not leave even a dog to die alone on the street. So would I, also, be judged as not to be trusted by the Carbonari?"

The meeting calmed; all looking shame-faced, while offering their apologies to Byron. *"Ci scusiamo, Mylord? ... Prega perdonaci?"*

Byron shrugged off their apologies with humour and good grace, but their suspicions about his loyalty to the Carbonari – even for such a short time – had rankled him. So much so, that when he got home, he wrote off his irritation in a couple of random stanzas.

When a man hath no freedom to fight for at home,

Let him combat for that of his neighbours;

Let him think of the glories of Greece and of Rome.
And get knocked on the head for his labours.

To do good to mankind is the chivalrous plan,
And is always as nobly requited;
Then battle for freedom wherever you can,
And if not shot or hanged, you'll get knighted.

"Not that a knighthood would do *you* much good," said Fletcher, coming alongside the desk and reading over his shoulder.

Byron looked up and stared at Fletcher – an apparition like death in his dark dressing-gown and muddy-white face.

"You being a baron and a lord and all," Fletcher went on. "Them's far above a knight."

"And you will end up far *below* ground in a coffin if you don't get back to bed immediately! You look like death at my shoulder!"

"Oh, *now* you believe me – now you've seen the bloodless face of the dead policeman. But don't you worry, my lord, because after seeing *his* dead face, I'm beginning to feel a lot better already."

Chapter Twenty-Six

~ ~ ~

Fletcher was soon back on his feet and on duty, bringing household matters to Byron for discussion.

"My lord, I hate to tell you, but the problems with Allegra are getting worse. Her nurse can no longer handle her, and she is defeating most of the servants.

"Allegra?" Byron was not really surprised to hear it. Although only four years old, the child had a temper that escalated into rages when she did not get whatever she wanted. There were times when even he could not pacify or manage her.

He was reluctant to admit it, but – "Her disposition is perverse to a degree," he said to Fletcher, "and when she behaves like that, she reminds me of Claire."

Fletcher made a face. He had never liked the child's mother, whom he had often thought of as a wilful, wanton hussy who had thrown herself at his lordship; but the child could not be blamed for that.

"And I suppose your own mother, if she was alive, would say that Allegra reminded her of *you* in ways."

"Yes, probably, but my rages were always *silent*. What can I do, Fletcher? I have tried everything, but now I don't know what to do."

"Well, now that you ask – my own opinion is that the child is spoiled by having too many adults around her who give in to her every whim, including yourself. She needs other children to mix with. Playmates of her own age."

Byron could see the sense in that; and spoke of it later to Teresa, who put Allegra's temper down to boredom, and suggested it was time now to begin Allegrina's education.

"Do you want her to grow up to be a well-mannered and educated young lady?"

"Of course I do. So should I bring in a tutor to start the lessons now?"

Teresa did not think that was a good idea. "What difference would a tutor be to her nursemaid? Allegrina would see the tutor as just another one of her servants, and would bully the tutor with tantrums until she got her own way again."

"Then *what* do I do?"

"You could do what most good Italian families do, and send her to a boarding convent to be educated."

Byron shook his head. "I could not send her to a boarding school in England. Her illegitimacy would be known, and the other children and their parents would make life hell for her."

"I was thinking of an *Italian* convent; especially as Allegrina speaks and understands no language but Italian," said Teresa. "Somewhere nearby, where she would be taught and disciplined in the ways of good behaviour, and have other children to play with, and where we could visit her."

Byron was silent, until Teresa added, "It would be no different to my own upbringing, and she could come home in summer and at Christmas."

Byron was thinking of Fanny Sylvestrini, and how she had wanted to look after Allegra solely for the *pay* she would receive. Would others be the same?

He remembered his own nursemaid as a child in Scotland, a woman named May Gray, who would take him out as a treat for a ride in his mother's carriage, stopping off at taverns on the way, where he was made to sit in a corner while she drank gin and caroused with some of the men. He was always sworn to secrecy, and he kept his oath about all the gin-drinking, but he had hated that woman.

"I would not want her to be in the care of anyone vulgar. Governesses who care more, and do the job only for the money they are paid, rather than for the child herself."

"The nuns in the convents look after all the children equally," Teresa assured him. "The convent is paid a fee by parents towards the running of the establishment, but the nuns take no pay for themselves."

It seemed the best solution of all ... and Allegra housed in a convent would, at least, keep her safe from all the undercurrents of revolution and trouble here in Ravenna.

The Convent of *San Giovanni Battista* in Bagnacavallo, twelve miles away from Ravenna, was now housing children from the best families in the region. It had been recommended highly to Byron by his banker, Pellegrino Ghigi, whose daughter also attended San Giovanni's convent.

Pellegrino was also kind enough to arrange for his daughter, a year older than Allegra, to be present when Allegra arrived – when she immediately took hold of Allegra's hand and skipped off with her to play with some of the other children in the garden.

Byron was satisfied; yet he felt a strange sorrow as he watched all the children playing together. It reminded him of his other daughter in England, little Ada, who was now six; but he had not seen her since she was a month old.

Later that day he wrote to Hobhouse in England: *"How is my child? You never name her."*

He did not know that Hobhouse, along with all of his friends, was not allowed to know anything about Ada; nor Ada allowed to know anything about her father; and all the presents he regularly sent to her, were put away in a box without Ada seeing them.

In that aspect alone, in keeping all knowledge of him from Ada, preventing her from loving someone she could not know, Lady Byron claimed the victory. Yet her life held no joy. She had made the mistake of separating from Byron while she was still in love with him; not foreseeing that he would leave the country to go abroad, and probably never return. Still, she secretly clung to the illusion that one day he would return to her, and beg for her forgiveness.

Now those who knew Annabella claimed her appearance had changed dreadfully. Her face, always placid in expression, had now deadened. She was constantly ill with some malady or other; was semi-bedridden, living on a diet of only bread-and-milk; and looking much older than her twenty-eight years.

Annabella, herself, was still incapable, as she had always been, of recognising any fault in herself or in her own conduct. She had been a dutiful wife to a man who had preferred to spend his time with his cronies at the Drury lane Theatre, instead of staying at home with his pregnant wife. A man who had *not* loved her. He had loved his sister more – his *sweet* sister – who was also a Byron and therefore could do no wrong.

And now she saw herself as being the *wronged* woman, and took great comfort indeed from the public's pity for her.

Although, of late, she had noticed, that pity for her seemed to have been declining somewhat. Especially among the *beau monde*. Even Lord Holland and Lady Jersey had stopped replying to her letters. And others, she was sure, were deliberately avoiding her. All Byron worshippers. Well, let them do as they may. She had enough people on her side other than that toffee-nosed lot. So many other *wives* who sympathised and admired her for her stoicism.

Beyond that, she really had only two interests in life; Byron's daughter – whom she was certain would eventually draw him back to England seeking her forgiveness – and Byron's poetry, studying each poetic line carefully, searching for some hidden message to her.

Her marriage and separation from Byron had become the central obsession of her life – the sun from which all emotions, all other pre-occupations came. The light of Byron's fame had reflected on her also, but only when she stood in his glow.

Yet *she* could write poetry too, and *good* poetry it was, very good.

She searched through her poetry file and drew out the poem she had written, some five days after Ada's birth: "*On A Mother Being Told She Was An Unnatural One.*

She shrugged – And people wondered *why* she had quarrelled with him?

Next she pulled out and read the few lines she had written on Ada's first birthday:

To Ada

Thine is the smile, and thine the bloom

When hope might image ripened Charms,

But mine is fraught with memories gloom

Thou are not in a Father's arms.

And *there* I could have loved thee most,

And *there* have felt thou wert so dear,

And though my worldly all was lost –

She shoved the poem aside, unwilling to read any more. As far as she was concerned, Ada was now *fatherless*. And whose fault was that? His fault, of course, *his!*

But those days were now gone, and only the future lay ahead. A bleak future, for which she venomously blamed *him* for ruining her life – even though others claimed it was *she* who had destroyed his – his name, his fame, his reputation.

Were they blind? Had they not seen how he had ignored and neglected her? Even at parties, had he not preferred to talk and joke with the men, rather than stay by her side. Was that love? Was that matrimonial bliss? Or was it the actions of a man who had a heart as cold as ice?

Yet ... despite all, she was prepared to forgive him, once he had recognised and apologised for his careless treatment of her. If God's will was to be done, he would have to repent the sin of not loving her, his wife.

No Moon at Midnight

To Lord Byron

But it must come — thine hour of tears,
When self-adoring pride shall bow —
And thou shalt own "my blighted years,"
The fate that thou inflictest — *thou!*

Thy virtue — but from ruin still
Shall rise a wan and drooping peace,
With pardon for unmeasured ill,
And Pity's tears — if Love's must cease!

PART FIVE

Exodus

'Lord Byron loved Italy, and he wished for her greatness, her dignity, and above all her independence, because he loathed the bondage in which she was held by Austria. He was idolized by the Liberals, received their confidences, often unlooked-for, and took advantage of this to make them see the dangers of their lack of unity. The part he took in the task of regenerating Italy was limited to those counsels of wisdom, and his longing to see Italy sovereign.'

Teresa Guiccioli.

Chapter Twenty-Seven

~ ~ ~

The revolution in Naples was smashed by the Austrian army. The newly-established revolutionary Republican Government of Naples collapsed with the arrest and imprisonment of all its leaders. The Bourbon King was restored to his throne as ruler of the two Kingdoms of Naples and Sicily.

Byron wrote despondently — *"Thus the world goes, and thus the Italians are always lost for lack of union among themselves — and now those who would give their blood for Italy can only give their tears."*

He added wistfully, *"If only Austria would yield up her prey, and let it live in the freedom in its own habitat."*

Austria had no intention of yielding up anything. Backed by the might and consent of the European Alliance, they were already building a bridge over the River Po, and were virtually at the gates of Romagna, determined to crush the Italian national movement, north, south, east and west.

And based on the information given to him by Count Alborghetti from the Cardinal's mail, Byron wrote:–*"As it is, they have fifty or sixty thousand troops."*

The Papal government in Rome, controlled by Austria, was now ready to carry out its revenge. Numerous arrests were made simultaneously in all the Legateships of Romagna.

In Ravenna, the first to feel the grip of the iron hand was Pietro Gamba, who was seized and arrested as he came out of the theatre.

The following morning, officials arrived at the Gamba house to inspect the young Count's apartments and search through his papers. His father, Ruggero, had been warned of the search, and so nothing incriminating was found.

The Austrians had also been warned – to be careful. As one of the highest-ranking families in Ravenna, the Gambas could not be treated like common criminals; so their punishment must be less severe.

The officer in charge addressed Ruggero: "Count Gamba, as you are suspected of being one of the leaders of the Carbonari, you are now prohibited from living in this region. Here are your deportation papers ordering you out of Romagna within twenty-four hours."

"I am to be deported? You say that to an Italian in his own country of Italy – and you a *foreigner*. How dare you!"

The officer remained impassive, but there was a malignant look in his eye. "Due to your rank and family connections, we are being very lenient with you. We are not arresting you, merely requesting you to remove yourself from the States of the Church."

"And my son, Count Pietro?"

"He has been deported. He was driven to the frontier this morning."

Ruggero's hands were clutched into fists at his side. "And the rest of my family? My daughters? My aged father?"

"Your daughters may stay, but your father must leave with you."

"My father – he is over seventy years old!"

"And a supporter of the Carbonari. His deportation papers are included with yours. In twenty-four hours from now, if you have not left Romagna, soldiers will arrive to escort you and your father out of the province.

The officer clicked his heels and walked out of the premises, leaving Ruggero with no other option but to quickly make arrangements for the care and supervision of his daughters. His younger son, Ippolito, had not been included. Maybe, because of his young age, the Austrians did not know of him.

~~~
~~~

Cardinal Rusconi was not happy with many of his orders from Rome. Good men being forced to leave Ravenna ... and now – not an order, but a *request* – that Lord Byron also be asked to leave the province.

Cardinal Rusconi did not like to ask Lord Byron to leave. He was a British Noble, not an Italian, so was there really any need for such drastic action?

Why, only last week, after all other measures had failed, Lord Byron had requested his own doctor to send Cardinal Rusconi some particular medicine which had miraculously eased the red and hot swollen pain in his foot, caused by gout.

And now he was being asked to return Lord Byron's kindness by inviting him to abandon his residence in Ravenna and get out of Romagna?

He called in the Secretary General, Count Alborghetti for his assistance, only to find that Alborghetti was appalled at the very suggestion.

"Your Eminence, Lord Byron is not only a British peer, over which Rome has no authority, but he has also been very good for Ravenna in many ways that you don't know about."

"Indeed? In what ways do I not know about?"

"In ways of which I am sworn to secrecy, Your Eminence."

"Secrecy? Even in the face of a Cardinal of the Holy Church, which you must know is a mortal sin. Pray confess this secrecy and cleanse your soul."

Count Alborghetti hesitated. "One of those ways, Your Eminence, is that he has employed me to act as his agent in paying out a weekly pension to some of the poorest families in Ravenna."

Cardinal Rusconi was astounded. "Oh, is *that* why you have a queue of ragged people outside your house every Saturday morning! I thought they were bringing you their prayer petitions to give to me. You bring me enough of them."

"No, Your Eminence, they come early on Saturdays so they can collect their pensions in time to buy food from the stalls in the morning market."

"You say employed – does Lord Byron *pay* you to be his secret agent?"

"Not in coin, no; but he allows me full use of his opera box, and other small favours. He is a very kind and generous young man, and he has now made Ravenna his home. He would be very unhappy if he was asked to leave."

Cardinal Rusconi fretted and sighed, and then decided to abdicate all responsibility and involvement in the matter.

"We will get the *police* to ask him to leave. In any event, being a Protestant heretic as he is, it will be better coming from them, than from a priest of the Holy Catholic Church."

"He is not a complete heretic, Your Eminence. If he was, he would certainly not have sent his daughter to a Catholic convent."

"My dear Count, I cannot disobey the orders of Rome, or the Austrian government in Rome. Pass my order on to the police."

The police were just as reluctant as Cardinal Rusconi. After all, had not Lord Byron been the only one who had tried to help the poor officer, Luigi De Pinto, when he had been shot on the street? Had he not tried to save his life? Was deportation a good way to repay him?

Later that day, Cardinal Marini, the prelate to Cardinal Rusconi, who had been trying for some time to use Count Guiccioli to get rid of Lord Byron, came up with an idea, which he passed on to Cardinal Rusconi.

"The Italian police will hum and hah for weeks or months before they will do anything, mark my words. But I have a solution that will involve no unpleasantness with the Inglese lord."

"You do? No unpleasantness?" Cardinal Rusconi was eager to hear this solution.

"They say he stays here in Romagna solely due to his relationship with the young Contessa Guiccioli. So, if *she* was to be deported, I'm sure he would soon follow her."

Cardinal Rusconi had never heard anything so ridiculous. "And on what *grounds* would we deport the young lady?"

Cardinal Marini smiled his clever smile. "Well, we would not actually *deport* her. The choice would have to be hers ... You see, one of the conditions set out in the Papal Decree allowing her separation from her husband, was that she would henceforth, either live under father's care, or be confined in a convent."

"Oh yes ..." Cardinal Rusconi now remembered that. "And there are no circumstances under which the conditions of the Papal decree can be broken. So she would have to either leave Romagna to be with her father, or enter a convent."

Count Alborghetti lost no time in slipping away to take the news to Lord Byron.

"I think you must go, Mylord. Although you are loved by all classes of the townsfolk, and they will all look on your leaving as a disaster, on the other hand – I have now learned one hour ago that your life is now threatened by those sectarian and anti-liberal fanatics, the *Sanfedisti* – the henchmen of the Austrians."

It was a fearful threat, but at the same time Byron knew it was not in his nature to allow himself to be bullied.

"So am I to run away like a coward because those blackguards threaten me? No, no," he said stubbornly, "I will stay, but I will make sure I am always well-armed. My servants too."

"But when you go to ride in the forest –"

"Even there I have friends watching out for me. If anyone who even *smells* like a *Sanfedisti* comes near me, I will split his forehead with a bullet."

Chapter Twenty-Eight

~ ~ ~

Teresa could not control her tears as her father and grandfather prepared to enter the carriage to leave Romagna.

She hugged her grandfather, thinking it pitiful that a man of his age should be banished by foreigners from the town where he had been born. "Oh, *nonno,*" she cried, "I cannot bear this."

Ruggero had hastily made arrangements for the care of his family and estate. This he placed into the hands of his brother-in-law, the Marquis Cavalli, of whom they were all very fond. All the family would move back to Filetto, and there they would stay until Ruggero commanded otherwise. Fortunately, all the stewards, workers and servants on the estate could be trusted implicitly. Most had grown up with the Gambas, and were almost as close as family.

Poor *Nonno* had to cope with the tears and hugs of all his granddaughters; but when Teresa moved to say goodbye to her father – for how long she did not know – she was completely overcome, breaking down in sobs of terrible anguish. Ruggero felt such anguish himself, he was unable to speak.

As the carriage rolled away, her sisters helped Teresa to walk back indoors, but she could not be consoled.

Not far outside Ravenna, Count Gamba called at the country house of a relative, to settle some business; and also because he feared some action would be taken against his daughter due to her connection with Lord Byron. For that reason he begged permission to stay in the house overnight before travelling on; and he was sincerely welcomed.

Ruggero then wrote a letter to Teresa, which he sent by messenger.

My Teresa, your agitation is in my mind all the time and causes me even greater pain. I had hoped to find comfort in you, and to give some to you in return, but now your weakness frightens me. Take courage, for your own good and for ours, and try to calm your imagination, which can conjure up nothing but tragedies.

As for me, I can assure you that this free air makes my spirit feel free too – and that I felt <u>prouder</u> once I stood outside those city walls that now enclose no one but slaves. Try to strengthen your spirit with such thoughts and to be of some support to mine. Remember that Pietro is waiting for us – and that his eyes are not flooded with tears.

Embrace your brother and sisters for me. Tell Lord Byron that I hope to see him again soon. Think of a happy future – conquer your imagination in this way. If you have any important news to send me, give it to the coachman, who alone has my orders.

Your affectionate Father

Less than an hour later, Teresa received a deputation from the Cardinal Legate Rusconi, informing her that, in accordance with the Papal decree, she must follow into her father's care, or be removed into a convent.

The shock was so great, Teresa could barely think through her anguish; but then, with the help of her sisters and maid, she wrote to her father, who immediately sent a message back to her saying she must come to him at once. They would wait for her and not set out for Tuscany until four o'clock the following day.

So it was done, it was arranged. She was being forced to leave Ravenna.

She then wrote to Byron, enclosing her father's

letters.

My dear Byron – You will not refuse to be the keeper of my troubles – you who alone can understand me and give me peace. I cannot describe my state to you – it is a continual agony. I have to leave you, my Byron, do you think I will be strong enough? This is the first moment I have felt alive since last night, because I am talking to you – but when I am certain that you don't hear me anymore, when my laments are lost in space, my God, my God, I feel as if I wouldn't be able to go on living. My Byron, give me strength, make me able to fulfil my duties as a daughter – T

P.S: Why do you want to take your little girl out of the convent? Wouldn't it be better to leave her in the safe place where she is?

As soon as he received her letter, Byron went to Teresa and calmed her down. He easily managed to do so, since it was his opinion that she should delay setting out to anywhere.

"Did they give you a time limit for joining your father or entering a convent?"

"No, just the order that I should prepare to go to one or the other."

"Then take your time. They know a woman needs a lot of time to pack all her things. You say your father and grandfather are going to Tuscany?"

"Yes, it is the nearest place outside Romagna, and where Pietro is waiting; but they know no one there."

"So who knows if Tuscany will let them stay, even in a hotel? Or if permission for their residence will be granted? Isn't it dominated by Austria as well? And if Tuscany won't keep them, where will they go and pitch their tents for the time being?"

Teresa did not know.

"In any event," Byron said, "I am sure they will be allowed to return to Ravenna after a short absence. If only because your grandmother is a friend of the Pope and she will appeal to His Holiness. And this counter-measure has already been *agreed* for some other exiles."

"But if I don't go tomorrow, what will I say to my father who is now waiting for me? Will *you* write to him, and say to him why you think I should not leave yet?"

Byron wrote to Count Gamba: —

My dear Ruggero – You are Teresa's master by right, and mine by duty and friendship – But in view of the circumstances I should think it better, also for <u>prudence</u> sake, for her not to leave for a few days. If you insist, she will give way, and so will I – who have not and should not have a voice in the matter. But the passports are equivocal – her presence will not be of any use to prevent them if they want to molest or imprison you – nor would it console you, for you wouldn't want to see a woman left alone in such a situation.

If things go well we shall join you – if things go ill, then we shall join you in any circumstances whatsoever – and I shall consider it my duty to find you, even if you are in prison. But I beg you not to precipitate matters for the present, and particularly to think of all that might happen to Teresa, deprived of you, and of Pietro – and in enemy country.

For my part I have no more to say except that I hope to see you and Pietro very soon – which I will do in one place or another – Keep well, and believe me always

> *Your most affectionate friend*
> *Byron.*

Count Gamba's reply came the next morning, forwarded to Byron by Teresa, as Ruggero had written a reply to both of them

He read Count Gamba's letter first, before reading Teresa's accompanying note.

> *"I breathe again! My father is willing for me to remain – read his enclosed letter. Now I am only left with the pain of uncertainty about my father and brother's fate. But what a compensation to be able to stay here – where you are. This evening we shall see each other again."*

Byron was truly fond of Count Gamba, and to know that he and his aged father had been forced out of their home and town, incensed him; but raging against the Austrians would serve no real purpose.

Instead, he set about contacting every person of influence he knew, including the Duchess of Devonshire, whom he knew to be in Italy, and who was also on friendly terms with Cardinal Consalvi, the Secretary of the State.

The Duchess replied, promising to write to Rome petitioning for both Count Gambas to be sent back to Ravenna.

A letter arrived from Pietro Gamba, who had been joined by his father and grandfather in Florence. And knowing that the Austrians opened all mail, Pietro gave vent to his feelings to Byron in his usual honest and high-minded way.

Pietro made it very clear that, as far as *he* was concerned, he would never consider returning to Ravenna, or living in any States of the Church – lands ruled by the double tyranny of clerics and Austrians. And although he desired his father's recall, he added:

"For my part, I neither ask nor wish to be allowed back. No counsel and no power will induce me, perhaps ever, to return to countries that I despise and detest in their present condition."

Pietro had made his own feelings clear, but he had also made the mistake of revealing to the authorities, who opened and read his letter, that efforts were being made by Lord Byron to have Count Gamba recalled to his estates in Ravenna.

The Prelate, Cardinal Marini, was the most alarmed, visiting his friend Count Guiccioli late at night and telling him what he must do.

"Don't you see, Conte, that as the Contessa is no longer living under her father's care and protection, you have recourse to two actions. Either to compel her to come back to you and live as your wife; or compel her to live in a convent."

Count Guiccioli did not want his wife back. One of his maids was now his regular bed-companion and she was far more suited to his tastes than Teresa.

"Why should I do that – compel her to live in a convent?" Guiccioli responded. "Do you want the entire town of Ravenna to *detest* me?"

Cardinal Marini shrugged. "Why should they detest you? It is not uncommon for young ladies who do not wish to live with their older husbands to prefer the seclusion of a convent."

Count Guiccioli did not like the way this upstart young cardinal had referred to him being an "older husband."

"And surely you understand, Conte," the Cardinal went on, "now that we know efforts are being made for Rome to sanction the return of Count Gamba, the presence of his daughter remaining here, will also be enough to keep Lord Byron residing in Ravenna."

"*Si*, he is planning to buy my property, the *Casa Raisi.* I would not want him to leave my palazzo before he does so."

Cardinal Marini smiled his clever smile. "Oh, my friend, that is a false economy ... a *temporary* way of raising money. On the other hand, if you were to compel your wife to the seclusion of a convent, aided and supported by the conditions of the Papal decree, you could apply to his Holiness for the termination of the payment of all alimony to her."

Count Guiccioli had not thought of that.

Cardinal Marini nodded. "Over time, over the years, would that not save you a greater deal of money than what you would get from the sale of the *Casa Raisi?* I would say so."

Count Guiccioli was adding it all up, and agreed. "She is still so young, I could be paying her that ludicrous amount of alimony until the day I die."

"Indeed. So you must take steps immediately to prevent that, by applying for the order to have her forcibly restricted to a convent, and petition that all orders of alimony payments to her should cease."

"Is it possible? Would the Pope agree to make such an order about the alimony?"

Cardinal Marini nodded. "In view of her family's *political* disgrace, it now gives you every chance of your request being granted."

The following morning, Count Alborghetti – always looking busy, yet always listening – overheard Marini informing Cardinal Rusconi of the decision made by Count Guiccioli.

"It is cruel, I know, but he is determined that the Contessa either follows her father into exile, or submits to life in a convent, in accordance with the Papal decree."

Count Alborghetti did not dare to go near the Palazzo Guiccioli to pass on this urgent information to Lord Byron, and instead called on his trusted friend, Count Rampi; who in turn made a hasty visit to Teresa to warn her.

Terrified by the threats made against her; threats

now aided and abetted by her husband, Teresa immediately wrote a letter which was taken by messenger to Byron.

Only this was left to drive me to despair. Count Rampi has just left me, having been sent by Alborghetti to tell me that I must leave Ravenna before Tuesday, because Guiccioli has applied to Rome to demand that either I should return to him, or be shut up in a convent. Rampi says that answer will come in a few days, and that I must talk about it to no one – but leave at night – for if my plan were known, they might even stop it, and take away my passport.

Byron! I am in despair – suppose I have to leave you here without knowing when I will see you again? But I hardly know what I am saying, or why? Certainly not on account of my own danger, but only on account of <u>your</u> danger from the Sanfedisti. Counts Rampi and Alborghetti will call on you at about three o'clock to tell you all this – T.

When those two gentlemen casually called on Lord Byron, like visiting neighbours, they whispered to him the news that Teresa had just sent to him in her letter.

"Then she must go and join her father," Byron decided. "I will not be the cause of her being locked up in some monastic prison."

"You are right to think so," Count Alborghetti agreed. "And who knows how long before they would let you know to which convent she has been sent to."

Byron was exasperated. "It's like living in the twelfth century! The sooner Italy becomes a Republic the better."

"I fear that a Republic is now a long way off," said

Count Rampi. "Now that the Austrians own the jewel which is Italy, they will not let it go."

Byron sighed with vexation. "And now I must let my own jewel go." He looked at Rampi. "Was she very distressed when you told her?"

Count Rampi shrugged. "She was as you would expect – a young lady having such threats made against her."

Byron nodded. "At least she would be safe from all that with her father. I was wrong, in the beginning, to make her delay her departure."

As soon as the two Counts had gone, Byron's innate matter-of-factness took over. He wrote to Professor Costa in Bologna, a greatly respected man whom he knew to be a friend of Count Gamba's, asking him to help the Countess when she reached Bologna, and even, if need be, to escort her to Florence.

The professor replied by the same messenger, assuring Lord Byron that he would carry out his instructions as requested.

When the time came for their parting, Teresa was almost beyond rational thought, begging him not go riding in the woods, or to put himself in any field of danger.

Due to his English education and upbringing, Byron was very good at mastering himself in a manly way when placed in such situations.

He urged her to have no fears on his account, and smiled as he told her, "Do you know what the motto on my crest of arms is – *'Crede Byron'* – Trust Byron."

Oh, and she *did* trust him, and she did her best to put on a brave face as she stepped into the carriage; but as the carriage moved off she thought the horses were going too fast – because they were now speeding her away from Byron and Ravenna.

~~~

Returning to his apartments in the palazzo, Byron was consumed by silent rage. To witness a decent family like the Gambas being torn apart and tormented by
~~~

foreigners in their own country was a humiliation and an outrage. And for what crime? For wishing for the freedom of Italy to be ruled by Italians and not subjected to a foreign boot on their neck.

As the days passed he could see, and was told, that the entire Romagna region was in an intolerable position. It was governed by Cardinal Legates who carried out and interpreted the orders from the Austrian government in Rome.

The Legate in Ravenna, Cardinal Rusconi, a kind but incompetent man, imitated and let himself be led by Cardinal Sanseverino, the Legate at Forli, a man who was so harsh, and authorised so many arrests and banishments that Cardinal Consalvi in Rome had wrote instructing him to stop, stating "The world will say that *it's the Massacre of the Innocents."*

The details of this letter had been told by Count Alborghetti to Byron, who wrote to his friends in England –

"You have no idea what a state of oppression this country is in – here they have arrested above a thousand of high and low – they have banished some – and confined others – without trial, process, or even accusation! *Everybody says they would have done the same to me if they dared to proceed openly. Meanwhile I have my hands full with tyrants and their victims. There never was such oppression, even in Ireland."*

And yet, although the Carbonari had failed so badly, Byron knew that they were not defeated. Their movement and determination would go on until Italy *was* free. Maybe not this year, or this decade, but it *would* happen one day. It was in the nature of all living creatures to protect their own territory.

Chapter Twenty-Nine

~ ~ ~

Cardinal Rusconi was extremely disturbed by the news brought to him by Count Guiccioli.

"Lord Byron? Are you sure? Perhaps it is one of his servants who is responsible?"

"No, Your Eminence, it is *him*. And now I have a crowd gathering outside my house cheering like ruffians. Is he trying to get *me* arrested? Your Eminence, I swear to you my devout loyalty to the Austrians, and to our Holy Father the Pope."

Cardinal Rusconi had such a personal dislike for Count Guiccioli, and such a fondness for Lord Byron, he was not ready to believe it. No English lord would act in such a reckless and rebellious way.

"Leave it with me, I will deal with it," he said to Guiccioli, dismissing him away with a fluttering wave of his hand.

He then sent a messenger to the palazzo to establish if what Guiccioli had said was true or not, or just another of the Count's continual complaints about everything and everybody.

The messenger returned grim-faced. "It is true, Your Eminence. Lord Byron has the Carbonari flag flying from his balcony."

"The Carbonari flag ..." Cardinal Rusconi was swamped with disappointment. "Surely he must know this is a grave offence and a matter for the police."

It was not the police who called on Lord Byron that afternoon, but a commander of the Austrian troops, requesting him to draw in the flag and remove it.

"Why should I?" Byron asked. "I have as much right to fly the Carbonari flag from my balcony, as you have to fly your Austrian flags all over Italy."

The Austrian was not prepared to become involved in any dispute with a British peer. He said with stiff politeness, "Here are your deportation papers out of the region of Romagna, my lord. You are requested to leave Ravenna as soon as possible."

Byron was unruffled and not surprised. "Oh, I intend to leave Ravenna, but in my own good time."

"The papers stipulate that you must leave Ravenna within forty-eight hours."

"They can stipulate whatever they like, but as I have a very large household, and rooms full of furniture to send on before me, I will not leave until I am good and ready. My passport is British, not Italian. It allows me to travel anywhere within the Alliance."

Cardinal Rusconi was astonished at such defiance when it was reported to him by the officer.

"Strange, but he has always been such an *agreeable* young man. A perfect gentleman in every way ... Well, you have served him with the deportation papers, so he knows he must leave. But, if it takes him longer than the forty-eight hours stated in the papers, we will ignore that stipulation for a week or two."

"A week or two?"

"That is what I said. We cannot shuffle him out like some low-class ruffian."

It was a decision that Cardinal Rusconi found himself regretting in the days following, for as soon as the news spread that Lord Byron had been ordered to leave, some of the poorest people in Ravenna were besieging the Cardinal's residence in Cathedral Square, begging for Mylord Byron to be allowed to stay in Ravenna, claiming that due to Mylord's kindness, they had enjoyed the first full meal they had ever eaten in their lives.

Cardinal Rusconi pondered and fretted on this; until he received a despatch from the Director of Police in Rome, stating that all of Lord Byron's poetry was to be banned in Italy henceforth, as hidden lines of subversion had been found in some of his poems, most particularly in *The Prophecy Of Dante,* using Dante's words to urge all Italians to rise up and take back their land from foreign rule.

It was all too much for the Cardinal who yearned for a peaceful life, not all this turmoil. The arrests of prominent Liberals were continuing every day and so many being imprisoned. Why did these men, young and old, insist on behaving so foolishly? Italy maybe ruled by Vienna, but Vienna supported the Holy Catholic Faith and the Pope in Rome. And was the Pope not the Holy Father of Italy?

Cardinal Rusconi's only relief from the constant turbulence was to preach a diatribe at Mass that evening, warning his congregation about the importance of obedience.

~ ~ ~

Byron was very surprised to receive an impromptu visit from Percy Bysshe Shelley, encouraging him to leave Ravenna and come to live alongside he and Mary under the mountains of Pisa, which had a milder political climate than Romagna.

The very suggestion horrified Byron, until Shelley told him that Claire Clairmont was no longer living with them.

"She now lives with a respectable German family at Florence. They have been very kind to her, and have introduced her into Italian society. It was time for her to spread her wings and leave us."

"Is she employed by this family?"

"Yes, as a live-in governess to the children."

So, with Allegra's mother out of the way, Byron could see no obstacle to moving to Pisa; asking Shelley to find him a suitable house there.

"It would have to be a large house, for wherever I go, my servants always insists on going with me. And I could not abandon my animals; the monkeys would cry for days."

"A palazzo, then? I will look for a palazzo for you."

Byron sighed. "I cannot decide anything definite until

I know what is happening with the Gambas. I now view myself as one of their family, and with that comes responsibility for their welfare. Pietro is young and hot-headed, but his old grandfather did *nothing,* and yet he was deported out of his home too, along with Ruggero."

A few days later Shelley wrote to his wife, Mary, in Pisa:

Lord Byron is greatly improved in every respect – in temper, in muscular strength, in moral thews, in health and happiness. His connection with Madame Teresa Guiccioli has been an inestimable benefit to him. He lives in considerable splendour, but within his income, of which he devotes a fair portion to the purposes of charity. He has had mischievous passions, but these he seems to have subdued, and he is becoming a virtuous man. The interest which he took in the politics of Italy, and the actions he performed in consequence of it, are subjects not to be written, but will delight and surprise you.

We ride out in the evening through the pine forest, which divides the city from the sea. Our way of life is this, and I have accommodated myself to it without difficulty – Lord Byron gets up at two – I get up at twelve to breakfast. We talk, read ... till six – then we ride at eight, and after dinner sit talking till four or five in the morning.

I have read the latest canto of "Don Juan" which is astonishingly fine. It sets him not only above, but far above all the poets of the day. Every word has the stamp of immortality. It fulfils, what I have long preached – of producing something wholly new, and relative to the age, yet surpassingly beautiful. It may be vanity, but I think I see the trace of my previous earnest exhortations to him, to write something wholly new.

The day before Shelley was due to leave, a letter arrived from Teresa, informing Byron that the Austrian authorities in Florence were not being kind to her father, but disruptive and insolent. She was sure they would soon try to arrest and imprison him on some false charge. They were now being forced to live in a miserable inn full of travellers."

She had added a postscript:

My dear Byron, I add these two lines to the letter I had already sealed to tell you that the messenger you have twice sent to me has been banished from Florence and imprisoned for two days, merely for having been despatched as a messenger to us.

Byron's mood of defiance was now replaced by the need for urgency.

"Pray look for *two* houses in Pisa," he told Shelley. "Two separate houses for myself and the Gambas, but as close to each other as you can find."

Shelley was delighted. The lonely life that he and Mary had been living in Pisa would soon be over. Now their old friendship with Byron, which had first been established in Switzerland, would return again ... seeing each other every day; literary discussions over dinner, philosophy, politics ... sailing on the river.

"In Pisa we will form a society of our own class, in intellect, or in feeling," Shelley said. "We will become a close circle of friends again, like we were in Geneva. We will live our own private lives and we will *not* allow the outside world to hurt us."

"Will we not?" Byron's blue eyes were now looking curiously at Shelley, alerted by something hidden in those last few words.

"Has someone in that outside world been trying to hurt *you*?"

Shelley shrugged. "No , no ... I am indifferent to such things. Besides, you have enough of your own problems here in Ravenna."

"My only problem is with the authorities here, and that is being dealt with, so what is it?"

Shelley hesitated, and then took from his jacket pocket a letter which he had brought to show Byron and to hear his opinion. A startling letter, which had wounded Shelley deeply; and one of the reasons he had been so anxious to run away from his hurt feelings and come to see Byron in Ravenna.

"This letter, it's from Robert Southey. Did I tell you I knew him some years ago when I was in Keswick?"

"I don't think you did, probably because you know how much I detest that man."

"I was younger then, and I liked him." Shelley sighed, and then went on, "Mostly because he told me that I showed signs of becoming a great poet one day."

"Well, he was right about that, although he's usually wrong about everything else."

Shelley then explained: "When Mary and I were in Rome, we went for a stroll one day around the Barberini Museum, and the only portrait that caught my imagination was the one of Beatrice Cenci, the girl who had been raped by her tyrannical father, Count Cenci, leading to her decision to murder him. I kept staring at her, at her eyes, imagining how awful her life must have been. Her story consumed me, and then I devoted all my time to writing her life in a tragedy for the stage."

"*The Cenci* – you sent it to me."

"I know I did. But have you read it yet?"

Byron had not yet had the time, due to all the difficulties of the Carbonari and the failed revolution and most of all his time with Teresa.

"It's awful work, this love," he complained. "It prevents all a man's projects. But the tears of a woman who has left her husband for a man, and the weakness of one's own heart – "

"I understand," Shelley said smiling; as gentle and forgiving as always.

"But I think now," Shelley added, "that it might be better if you did *not* read it, and save your good opinion of me."

Byron was confused. "Why not?"

"Because I also sent it to Robert Southey – *he* who had such good hopes for me – and now that Southey has been made England's Poet Laureate, I thought his good recommendations might benefit me."

Shelley handed the letter to Byron. "Here is his reply. He has been generous enough to give not only his opinion of *The Cenci,* but also of me."

Such was his dislike of Southey, Byron hesitated to even touch the letter ... but then he did so, reading through the first preamble until Southey got to the point of Shelley and his poetry:

Let us look to the case. I will state it with no uncharitable spirit & with no unfriendly purpose.

When you were a youth at College, you took up Atheistical opinions. As erroneous as your conduct was, it was still to be expected that your heart would bring you right & that every thing might be hoped for from your genius and virtues.

Such was my opinion of you. What I heard of your subsequent conduct tended always to lower it, except as regarded your talent. At length you forsook your young wife because you were tired of her and found another woman more suited to your taste. It is a matter of public notoriety that your wife destroyed herself by committing suicide. Knowing in what manner she bore your desertion I never attributed this to her sensibility, & I have heard it otherwise explained. I have heard that she followed your example as faithfully as she followed your lessons in low morals by afterwards getting pregnant by another man, and the catastrophe of her suicide was caused by her shame.

Be that as it may, ask your own heart whether you have not been the whole, sole, and direct cause of her destruction? You corrupted her opinions, you robbed her of her moral and religious principles, you debauched her mind. But for you and your lessons, she might have gone through the world innocent and happily.

I will do you justice, Sir. While you were at Keswick you told your bride that you regarded marriage as a mere ceremony & would live with her no longer than you liked her. I daresay you told her so before the ceremony and that there was nothing sacred in the tie. But that she should have considered this to be the condition on which she was married, I do not believe. She trusted to your heart, not your opinions.

You have corrupted in yourself an excellent nature. You have sought for temptation and courted it, & have reasoned yourself into a state of mind so pernicious, that your own character, with your domestic relations, as you term it, with your new woman, might furnish a subject for the drama more instructive and scarcely less painful than your detestable "The Cenci".

You say that your only real crime is the holding of opinions something similar to what I once held respecting the state of society. That Sir, is not your crime – it would only be your error. Your offence is moral as well as political. Nor were my opinions ever similar to yours. You would have found me as strongly opposed in my youth as I am at this time to Atheism and immorality of any kind. The Christianity I recommended to your consideration is to be found in the Scriptures & the Book of Common Prayer. I would ask you to apprehend that there is a judgement after death.

And here Sir, our correspondence must end. It appeared to me to be a duty of taking the opportunity of representing you to yourself as you appear to me, altogether hopeless of producing any good effect.

You must remember me as an earnest monitor whom you cannot suspect of ill-will & whom it is not in your power to despise, however much you may wish to repel my admonitions with contempt.

Believe me,

Your sincere well wisher

Robert Southey.

Even before he had finished reading the foul letter, Robert Southey's words to Shelley had ignited in Byron's mind a theme for a new work of his own. He would pay Southey back for this.

"The man is raving mad," he told Shelley. "It's not Poet Laureate he should be – but in a lunatic asylum. Surely you are not taking his words seriously?"

Shelley shrugged. "What he says of me, is no matter. But when the Poet Laureate describes my new work as 'detestable' – what hope has it of ever succeeding?"

"That I cannot say – but I know my enemies and so I

know Robert Southey. He is a bigot and a liar and one of the worst turncoats who ever lived. He's turned his coat so many times that now he cannot be sure if it's on inside or out. And it was *Robert Southey* who, after travelling through Geneva and picking up all the gossip, went back to England and told everyone that you and I had set up a *Satanic* School of worship in Geneva with two sisters."

Shelley was visibly startled. "It was Southey who spread that nonsense?"

"Yes! My friend John Hobhouse overheard him telling it to Thomas Campbell one night at some party."

"But that is slander, dishonest slander!"

Byron shrugged. "My friend Coleridge could tell you many things about Southey to show what a dishonest and shameless hypocrite he is."

"Coleridge the poet?" Shelley smiled, suddenly not feeling so bad. "What does he say?"

"Southey *was* different in his youth – oh, how *easier* it is to be pious and moral at forty-seven than it is at twenty-seven!" Byron exclaimed derisively, and then went on –

"Coleridge told me how Southey, in his twenties, was an out-and-out radical politically, anti-monarchy, anti-establishment, anti-everything. But when Wordsworth turned Tory, so did Southey. And when Sir Walter Scott declined the offer of becoming Poet Laureate, Southey wrote poem after poem in praise of King George, until the king offered *him* the post of Poet Laureate instead of Scott."

"A turncoat indeed."

"And as for Southey's *morals* in his youth, he has little right to be the judge of yours. Coleridge once told me that in their youth, Southey wanted him and some others to form their own *pantisocracy* society, their own form of Utopia, on the banks of some river in the warm sun of the Americas. Their lives would be simple, their work need not be as much as the slaves of luxuries are forced to endure. They would form a community where everyone's possessions belonged to all. They would read only books on literature and science, and each should take to himself a mild and lovely woman, whose part would be to prepare their food, and tend to the duty of conceiving and creating a hardy and beautiful race."

Shelley was grinning. "It doesn't sound like the same Southey at all."

"It *will* sound like him, when you hear this. According to Coleridge, they were to spend their idle hours reading and writing, but the mild and lovely women would not be allowed to do either, due to Southey's ruling that –'Literature cannot have any business in a woman's life' – so I hope Mary did not send her *Frankenstein* to him?"

"No, but she did send it to Walter Scott, who highly praised it."

Byron nodded. "Now there is a man we can all admire, a good man, and a splendid writer. Have you read his *'Tales from My Landlord'*?"

"No."

"I have read every one, more than twice."

Shelley was still curious. "So what happened to Southey's plan for an Utopian commune somewhere in the Americas?"

"What happened?" Byron grinned. "According to Coleridge, who was originally all for it, he changed his mind when Southey decided that it would be easier and cheaper to stay in Britain and set up their idyllic commune in Wales."

"Wales? It's always freezing cold and *raining* in Wales."

"Exactly. It put a damper on the whole thing until the idea drizzled away. I suspect it was the lost dreams of his youth that made Southey the hard and sour man he is today.

"Hard and sour is too kind," Shelley said, "Will you read the *Cenci?* Your opinion is important to me, especially in view of Southey damning it ... In writing it, my aim was to see how I could describe passions that I have never felt, and to tell the most dreadful story in pure and refined language. The image of Beatrice haunted me after seeing her portrait. The story is well authenticated, and the details are far more horrible than I have painted them."

"I will read it," Byron assured him, "when I go to my room. I will read it this very night. And when I have finished it, I will give you my own honest opinion, good or bad."

Shelley was gratified. Whatever else, which may at times require diplomacy or politeness; yet when it came to their poetic works, he and Byron were always truthfully honest with each other.

In his bedroom, before settling down to read *The Cenci*, a play in five acts, Byron wrote to Teresa in Florence.

My Love – My intention is to take a house in Pisa. This letter will be taken to you by the Englishman who is leaving tomorrow. He will explain to everyone many things difficult to write down and lengthy. When all is decided I will send on a part of the household with the heavier effects, the furniture needed for the house – then I will come with the others – I assure you that I love you as I have always loved you; time will show. Greet Papa and Pietro.

In the light of dawn, sitting at his desk, Byron had read to the last page of the play, *The Cenci*, astonished at the greatness of Shelley's genius, and saddened by the world's lack of recognition of him. Was it simply because he was an avowed atheist? It had to be. Only a dark cloud of bigotry could have shaded the eyes of publishers and critics who continually damned his work – all mediocre mortals themselves – they were incapable of seeing the poetic magnificence behind Shelley's atheism.

He closed the book, and then opened it again, writing his opinion at the top of the title-page; before taking the book and slipping it through the gap under the door of Shelley's room.

Shelley was awake, having slept fitfully on and off for a few hours. He had heard the sliding sound at his door, turned his head to look, and saw the book lying there. He lay back on his pillow, tears coming into his eyes.

So Byron had also found The Cenci *detestable*, just like Southey So much so that he had returned the book under the door, rather than face him in daylight with his honest opinion.

He dragged himself out of bed and morosely lifted the book from the floor, surprised when he opened it and saw Byron's familiar handwriting :

> *'The Cenci' is a work of poetry and power. And perhaps the best Tragedy that modern times have produced.*
>
> *BYRON*

Chapter Thirty

~ ~ ~

On his journey south, as Shelley had to pass Florence to return to Pisa, he considered it no trouble to stop off there and visit the Gambas on Byron's behalf.

The first to greet him was Teresa's brother, Pietro, full of questions, which Shelley readily answered.

Count Ruggero Gamba, was more officious. Although they were lodged at an inn, he insisted that Signor Shelley be hosted with all the benefits that the inn could offer, including a room to sleep in and a good dinner beforehand. After all, he had been travelling all day, and there would be plenty of time to talk in the morning.

Shelley insisted that he was not at all tired, and was eager to pass on Lord Byron's new plans for Pisa.

It was not until they sat down to eat that Shelley finally met Teresa, the "lady fair" who had changed Byron from the careless rogue he had been at Venice.

She was indeed fair, very pretty, and her conversation was intelligent. Her only weakness seemed to be her fear for Byron – certain that some *Sanfedisti* scoundrel would try to assassinate him before he left Ravenna.

Aside from that, Shelley decided that when her fears had been proved groundless, and she had settled in Pisa, Teresa and Mary would get along very well as neighbours.

Over dinner they discussed Byron's plan, and all were agreeable to moving to Pisa.

"Lord Byron's instructions to me," said Shelley, "are that two suitable houses are found and leased in Pisa, one for you and your family, Count Gamba, and another close by for himself and his household. He says that as he is now an honorary member of your family, and hopefully one day will become your legal son-in-law, he insists on being responsible for all the expenses."

This brought tears to Count Gamba's eyes, but he

would not hear of it. "My relation, the Marquis Cavalli, will send to me all the money I may need. But you must thank Lord Byron for me. He has a good heart."

As the men talked, Teresa studied Shelley, whom Byron had once described as "*a remarkable man and a wonderful poet, not yet appreciated for his genius.*"

Indeed, Teresa thought, Shelley was a man like no other. He was an unexampled contrast of mental and physical contrasts and harmonies. As a youth he was said to have been handsome, but he was no longer so. His features were delicate and, although he was tall, his frame was slight. His skin must once have been fine, but due to exposure to sunshine and inclement weather, was now marred by freckles. His hair, which was light brown and plentiful, was now threaded with premature silver. He was as yet only in his late twenties, so what sorrow had caused those silver threads at such a young age?

His clothes were just as extraordinary. His jacket was too short, he did not possess gloves, and his shoes were not polished. But for all that he seemed the most perfect gentleman, for when he spoke his voice was modulated with a charm, a mildness, a refinement that touched the heart.

Lost in her thoughts she sat back and remembered an article she had once read by Sir Walter Scott who declared that Lord Byron's beauty made one ponder, as if he meant that it was all but unearthly. Yet the same could be said of Shelley, because *his* beauty lay within his soul, which wrapped him in an attractive aura. It was the fervour, enthusiasm, the intelligence that lit up his features and made him such a likable being – and above all a certain expression of veneration for anything beautiful, such as the paintings of Michelangelo in Rome, which he and Pietro were now speaking about.

His visit had made them all happy, and Teresa had liked Shelley so much, that a few days later she wrote to him at his address in Pisa. He replied to her by return of post in perfect Italian:

My dear Madame, I have only a moment to answer your letter, and I feel quite incapable of expressing to you my feelings about the confidence with which you have been pleased to honour me. I hope that you will find me worthy of it.

Be assured that I will omit no measure that may hurry the departure of his lordship, for I am certain that his happiness, no less than yours, depends on the nearness of her who has been his good angel, of her who has led him from darkness into light, and deserves not only his gratitude, but that of everyone who loves him.

I have almost settled on your house, and hope to be in time to announce the signing of the contract before the post goes. Forgive the rough phrases of a sincere heart, and do not doubt the profound interest you have awakened in me.

And that I am, and always will be,

Your servant and friend,

Percy B Shelley.

P.S. Please give my greetings to your father and brother.

~ ~ ~

Shelley was true to his words, and less than a week later the Gamba's left the inn in Florence to begin the sixty-mile carriage journey to Pisa.

Arriving late at night at the address Shelley which had sent to them, they found the windows of their new home, the *Villa Finocchietti*, to be aglow with lights. The door opened, and Shelley came down the steps to greet them.

Teresa was smiling. "Did *you* light all those candles in the rooms?"

Shelley grinned. "No, it was Mary. She's inside now preparing a hot supper for you all."

They entered the house to a delicious smell coming from the kitchen. Teresa wandered towards the smell and found Mrs Shelley in the kitchen, stirring a large pot of beef and onions and other delicious vegetables and herbs.

The two young women smiled at each other with instant liking.

"Why do you do all this?" Teresa asked. "We are strangers to you."

"No, you are not strangers," Mary replied quietly. "You are special friends of our dear Albè, and so we wanted to give you a warm welcome."

Teresa wondered if Mrs Shelley had made some mistake, believing they were some other people, and not the Gamba family.

"Albè?"

"Byron," Mary smiled; and then explained to Teresa why Byron would always be *"Albè"* to them. "It is our own secret name for him."

There was something about Mary Shelley that Teresa liked – *all* about her that she liked. They were around the same age, in their early twenties, and when Mary held out a spoon for Teresa to taste the food in the pot to see if it was to her liking, Teresa ignored the spoon and greeted Mary in *the Italian* way, with an embrace and a kiss on both cheeks. "You are as good as your husband," she said.

Mary smiled demurely. "But am I a good cook?" Again she held out the spoon. "I need to know if it tastes good or terrible."

Teresa took the spoon and scooped it into the pot to taste the English beef stew, her eyes widening at the taste. "*Delizioso!* Not too much garlic. But why do *you* not taste it to know if it's good?"

"Shelley and I are vegetarians," Mary said casually.

"But we know all Italians think a meal without meat is not a meal at all."

Only then did Teresa realise what a considerable sacrifice of her own beliefs, had this preparation cost Mary Shelley, and all because the Gambas were special friends of her own dear friend, Albè.

All the Gambas were feeling hungry after their journey, and as they sat down to dinner, the Shelleys left them to it, bidding them farewell.

"Here is our new address," Shelley said, handing a paper to Count Gamba. It is just a few minutes walk away. Pray do not hesitate to call on us if you need anything ... anything at all."

"And you also," said Pietro. "Our home here in Pisa will always be open to welcome you, day or night."

Left alone at the dining table, Count Gamba looked around at his family, emotion on his face.

"Here in Pisa, I think we *can* feel free and relax more," he said. "Here I believe we *can* feel some happiness again, if we try. Already we have been made to feel that we are among friends."

~ ~ ~

Shelley had leased the *Palazzo Lanfranchi* for Byron at the same time he had leased the Villa Finocchietti for the Gambas, but as the weeks passed there was still no sign of him.

Teresa spent a lot of time with Mary, whom she discovered had no other female friend in Pisa, and so they were great company for each other, going out in the Gambas open carriage every afternoon and sharing information. Teresa spoke of her restless worries, wondering why Byron had still not arrived.

"I know he is unharmed," she told Mary, "because every few days I receive silly notes from him that tell me nothing."

She removed the reticule from her wrist and opened it to show Mary some of the notes.

Mary read the first note, and did not think it was silly at all.

My Teresa – we are getting ready – I am in the sweat, dust and blasphemy of the universal packing of all my things, furniture etc – if there is any delay it will be that blessed Lega's fault – whom I will abandon to your reproaches when we arrive. Pray be in good humour. I will come to you as soon as I can.

Teresa handed Mary the next note, in which again Byron was blaming his steward Lega Zambelli for the delay.

Lega continues to delay. I will leave him to your very just indignation and deserved punishment. We will do with him what you will on my arrival.

Mary was beginning to smile when Teresa handed her the third note to read.

I assure you that the slowness and confusion of Lega is something astounding, surpassing even my own slight bad opinion of his qualities.

Then, when Lega had finally set out –

Pray scold him when he arrives. He deserves it. If it were not for my <u>insistence</u> he would not have started even now ...

Mary could not help laughing; this was so typical of Albè.

"In Switzerland," she said, "he used to blame everything on poor Fletcher. When some of the Genovese would invite him to dinner or a party, to which he had no intention of going, he would usually send back a note of apology saying how much he would have like to attend, but his valet, Mr Fletcher, had done this, or not done that – until they must have thought that Lord Byron had the worst manservant in the world."

"But why does Byron not come?" Teresa said, bewildered. "Why does he send us here to Pisa, and then not come himself?"

"He will come." Mary was certain. "But you must remember that it is not so easy for him as it was for you."

"How?" Teresa demanded. "How is it not so easy for him?"

"Because the house Shelley leased for you was fully and beautifully furnished, but Byron specifically requested his house to be *unfurnished,* as he has to remove a whole floor of his own furniture from his present residence – his numerous desks alone would take up one wagon entirely."

Teresa understood all that. "But why is it taking him so *long?* We have been here now for more than a month, and still he does not come. And I don't believe him when he blames Lega."

The truth was four-fold. Firstly, Byron's long delay in Ravenna was a deliberate act of defiance against the Austrians. He had told them he would take as long as he liked, and he meant it. And the Carbonari flag continued to fly from his balcony, no matter how many times they came and confiscated it. Another was always quickly and anonymously delivered to him, and was soon flying again.

The second reason was that he had been spending most of his time, while defying the Austrians in staying put for a while longer, in writing poetry. A new poem, *The Vision Of Judgment,* based on that line Southey had written in his letter to Shelley — "*I would ask you to apprehend there is a judgement after death.*"– giving him the title for his own poem in which he had pulled no punches in lampooning Robert Southey in the style of his own vindictive vitriol, and then had sent it *post express* to his publisher John Murray.

The third reason, was that, of late, he had been having some pangs of conscience about giving his *Memoirs* to Thomas Moore; when, in all fairness, Lady Byron should also be allowed to read them, as they included so much about her.

Fortunately, he had kept a copy, as he did of any manuscript he wrote.

He placed his own copy of the *Memoirs* into a packet, which he sent to Annabella, and which also contained his first letter written directly to her, informing her that the manuscript, which went no further than 1816, contained many things, including a "*long and minute*" account of their marriage and separation:

... I would wish you to see, read – and mark any part or parts that do not appear to coincide with the truth. The truth I have always stated – but there are two ways of looking at it – and your way may not be mine. I have never revised the papers since they were written. You may read them – and mark what you please. You will find nothing to flatter you – nothing to lead to the most remote supposition that we could ever have been – or be happy together. But I do not choose to give to some future generation statements that we cannot rise from the dust to prove or disprove – without letting you see fairly and fully what I look upon you to have been – and what I depict you as being. If seeing this – you can detect what is false – or answer what is charged – do so – your remarks shall not be erased.

You will perhaps say why write my life? Alas, I

say so too, but those who have traduced it and blasted it and branded me, should know. It is no great pleasure to me to live over again the details of our existence together, but it has become a necessity, and even a duty.

If you choose to read this, you may, if you do not, you have at least had the option.

B.

And then, finally, the fourth reason for his not yet having left this region and journeying to Pisa, was that after three years living here, he had come to love Ravenna and its people, and he was sorry to leave.

His heart had found rest here, since his personal feelings had long been in a state where all uncertainty had vanished. He loved Teresa, and she loved him. As for his intellect, it too had been contented in Ravenna. In this ancient city, away from the pressure of tourists and their visits, his peace and concentration on his work had been more unfettered than anywhere else from the time he had achieved fame.

Would he find the same peace in Pisa? He hoped so. For to Pisa his destiny was now taking him.

As he prepared to leave, and was about to enter his carriage, Count Alborghetti came rushing along the path. "Mylord Byron, do you leave without me being able to wish my dear friend a farewell?"

Byron smiled as Alborghetti embraced him with affection and kissed him on each cheek.

"I hate farewells," Byron said, "but if they must be done, they should be as brief as possible."

Count Alborghetti was still holding onto his arms, his portly figure and plump face a sight Byron knew he would always remember.

Alborghetti's eyes were now dark and serious. "My friend, let me tell you ... your arrival in this town was always spoken of as a piece of public good fortune, and now your departure is spoken of as a public calamity. Ravenna will never forget Lord Byron, including the very poor people of Ravenna, who still bless your name every day."

Byron struggled with his thoughts for a moment, and then turned and climbed into his carriage, closing the door behind him, and then holding his hand out to Alborghetti through the open window.

Count Alborghetti took Byron's hand in both of his own, but was unable to speak.

He stood watching as the carriage rolled away, feeling only sorrow and regret. No, indeed, the people of Ravenna would never forget Lord Byron, how could they? He was a foreigner, an Englishman, who had taken their side against the forces of oppression, and especially in these latter weeks, he had not even tried to hide that fact – every day flying the flag of freedom in the face of the oppressors, knowing only he could do it without risk of imprisonment, protected by his Noble rank as a British Peer.

Yet he also must have known that every day he risked a sudden bullet from the hated *Sanfedisti*, and how he had escaped one of their bullets was still a mystery, for he still went riding somewhere in the forest every day with his bodyguard, shooting his coins in target practice.

As Alborghetti turned to walk away, he saw the face of Count Guiccioli peering slyly through one of the open ground-floor windows, and that enraged him. Oh, *now* Guiccioli would relax! *Now* he would come out into the world again.

For almost six weeks Guiccioli had kept himself hidden in his own apartments, never venturing outdoors, not even to attend the theatre – convinced that those of the Carbonari who remained undetected and uncaptured would blame and repay *him* for Lord Byron's deportation.

Everyone now knew that *he* was the one who had

gone running to the Cardinal about the flag and vowing his loyalty to the Austrians.

Before walking on, Alborghetti suddenly swivelled round to put his face near the open window where Guiccioli was hiding and gave a long hiss of furious contempt, *"Traitor! Informatore! Serpente!"*

Chapter Thirty-One

~ ~ ~

In London, in his office in Mayfair, John Murray was in a good mood. But then he was always in a good mood when a new despatch of poetry arrived in the post from Byron. Everyone else was so respectable in their creations, writing such perfectly modulated classic verse in iambic hexameters about all the usual poetic stuff, but Byron never failed to surprise.

He settled himself at his desk to read *The Vision of Judgement*:

Saint Peter sat by the celestial gate,
His keys were rusty, and the lock was dull,
So little trouble had he be given of late;
Not that the place was by any means full.

The angels were all singing out of tune,
And hoarse with having little to do,
Excepting to wind up the sun and moon,
And curb a runaway young star or two.

Innocent enough at the beginning, but then Murray found himself chuckling at comic verses every bit as good as Shakespeare's.

William Gifford, his revered Editor came in and was taken aback a the unusual sight of Murray giggling to himself. "Have you been drinking?"

"No, of course not. I'm reading this high-spirited satire from Byron. It's full of such wit, that I would go so far as to say it is a comedic masterpiece."

"You said that about Don Juan."

"Yes, but that is not finished, is it? And we don't know what will be coming next in Don Juan. One never knows with Byron, do they?"

"And this one?"

"Oh yes, this one is finished. Some may take offence, but it really is very funny. His lordship is no admirer of kings, as you know, and so in this poem he has both King George the Third and Robert Southey standing before Saint Peter, trying to get into Heaven, but Saint Peter won't let either of them in."

"Let me read it!"

"Not yet, not until I have finished it. Here – you can read his preface which is levelled squarely at Southey, although he has written it under one of his ridiculous pseudonyms ... and this one is ...." Murray lifted the preface page and read – "*Quevedo Redivivus.*"

Gifford laughed. "With a name like that, everyone will *know* it is Byron."

"Oh, certainly, and even if they don't, I think the preface itself would give them a clue. But in any event, *we* can say that we have no idea who the man behind the name is, as we were offered the work by his book agent."

"Jolly good." Gifford took the preface pages. "You will let me have the verses as soon as you have finished?"

"Yes, but before you read them, let me know if you consider the preface to be a bit *too* forthright, or does the occasional undertone of banter save it?"

"Banter? Or ridicule?"

Murray shrugged. "A bit of both."

William Gifford was not only John Murray's editor, but also a stringent critic for the *Quarterly Review,* and he, too, was a man who pulled no punches when reviewing the work of writers. Although he had long ago stopped classing Byron as a writer, and simply a poetic genius.

At his desk he put on his spectacles and adjusted them on his nose, ready to read the preface ... Ah, now here was not the poet, but the man himself, talking to the reader.

It has been wisely said, that "*One fool makes many,*" and it hath been poetically observed,

"That fools rush in where angels fear to tread."

If Mr Southey had not rushed in where he had no business, the following poem would not have been written. It is not possible that it may be as good as his own, seeing that it cannot, by any species of stupidity, be *worse.*

The gross flattery, the dull impudence, the intolerance and impious cant by the author of *'Wat Tyler'* are something so stupendous as to form the sublime of himself – containing the quintessence of his own attributes.

So much for his poem – a word on his preface. In his preface it has pleased the magnanimous Laureate to draw a picture of the supposed 'Satanic School,' which he doth recommend to the notice of the legislature. If there exists anywhere, except in his imagination, such a school, is he not sufficiently armed against it by his own intense vanity?

But I have a few questions to ask.

Firstly ⁻ Is not Mr Southey the author of *'Wat Tyler'*?

Secondly – Was he not refused a remedy at law by the highest judge of his beloved England, because it was a blasphemous and seditious publication?

Thirdly – Was he not called by William Smith, in a full Parliament, "a rancorous renegade"?

Putting the preceding items together, with what conscience dare *he* call the attention of the laws to the publications of others, be they what they may?

I say nothing of the cowardice of such a proceeding; its meanness speaks for itself; but I wish to touch upon the *motive,* which is neither more or less than that Mr Southey has been laughed at a little in some recent publication by Lord Byron. Hence all this skimble skamble stuff about 'Satanic Schools' and so forth.

If there is any thing obnoxious to a portion of the

public, in the following poem, they may thank Mr Southey.

QUEVEDO REDIVIVUS

P.S ⁻ It is possible that some readers may object, in these objectionable times, to the freedom in which saints, angels, and spiritual persons, discourse in this 'Vision.' But for precedents upon such points I must refer them to Fielding's *'Journey from this World to the Next',* and to the *Visions* of myself, the said Quevedo, in Spanish, as translated.

In his office, John Murray was feeling somewhat guilty for laughing – after all, King George the Third was only a year or so dead, and yet here he was still getting it rough from Saint Peter and the Archangel Michael for all his warmongering against America and Ireland and France, not to mention the treatment of his own people in England; while Satan also stood by the gate, hoping to claim King George for himself. But lo! another caller arrived at the celestial gate ... Robert Southey.

> Here, Satan said, I know this man of old,
> And have expected him for some time here;
> A sillier fellow you will scarce behold,
> Or more conceited in his petty sphere.
>
> Now the bard, glad to get an audience, which
> By no means often was his case below,
> Began to cough, and hawk, and hem, and pitch
> His voice into that awful note of woe.
>
> He said – (I only give the heads) – he said,
> He meant no harm in scribbling, 'twas his way
> Upon all topics; 'twas, besides, his bread,
> Of which he'd buttered both sides; 'twould delay
>
> Too long the assembly (he was pleased to dread)

And take up rather more time than a day,
To name his works – he would but cite a few –
Wat Tyler – Rhymes on Blenheim – Waterloo.

He had written praises of a regicide,
He had written praises of all kings whatever;
He had written for republics far and wide,
And then against them, bitterer than ever.

For pantisocracy he once had cried
Aloud, a scheme less moral than 'twas clever;
Then grew a hearty anti-Jacobin
He turned his coat – and would have turned his skin.

He had sung against all battles, and again
In their high praise and glory; he had called
Reviewing 'the ungentle craft' and then
Became as base a critic as ever crawled –

Fed, paid, and pampered by the very men
By whom his muse and morals had been mauled:
He had written blank verse, and blanker prose;
And more of both than any body knows.

He had written Wesley's life – here, turning round
To Satan, "Sir, I'm ready to write yours,
In two octavo volumes, nicely bound
With notes and preface —

John Murray had to stop reading due to laughing – but, oh was this too much? Could he really *publish* this?

He would wait for the opinion of William Gifford, he decided. A level-headed man like Gifford took no risky chances.

Gifford came in with the preface and his opinion. "Well," he said, "fair play and all that, but Southey started this war of words with Byron, demanding that *Don Juan* should be banned, and all that other nonsense."

Murray was shaking his head. "A foolish thing to do, start a war of words with Byron."

"A *public* war of words."

"Southey's mouth is too big by half, and he never stops using it. All that pontificating to everyone since he became Laureate. What Byron is saying in this is that Southey would sell his soul to the devil if the price and the prestige was right."

"Let me read it!"

"I haven't finished it. Oh, very well ... you read it now and I will finish it later. Your view of it might be very different to mine."

Gifford took the manuscript and disappeared into his own office, while John Murray sat and waited, musing to himself ... On the other hand, it was Southey's demand that *Don Juan* be banned that had led to it trebling its sales all over the country and even in Europe and America. Byron was even more popular now than he had been in the past.

One other person, though, besides Southey, who would surely hate it, was Lady Byron; and she had taken lately to demanding that the first copy of all Byron's works be sent to her straight from the press; and she was as big a pontificator as Southey – and worse, always threatening to use her *legal team* for the slightest thing. That infernal woman.

Of course, when faced with Lady Byron, he was always as nice and polite as could be, because he was terrified of offending her – the slightest fault in word or action and he might find his name burning in heated whispered gossip throughout the drawing-rooms of London.

Minutes later, he heard hoots of laughter coming from Gifford's office, and could not resist getting up and going in to see which part he had reached.

"I'm at the part where Southey insists upon reading his own perfect *Vision of Judgement* to the angelic gathering," Gifford said, "but on the fifth line Saint

Peter loses patience and knocks Southey down with his keys, sending him falling into the infernal lake below, where –

> *He first sank to the bottom – like his works,*
> *But soon rose to the surface – like himself."*

John Murray was grinning. "Of course, one would have to *know* Southey, as we do, to explain our delight; but what of the general reader? Do we publish it?"

"Of course we do!" Gifford was certain they should publish. "And don't mind all that Quevedo Redivivus nonsense – everyone will know it is Byron, man, *Byron!* It will sell like hot meat pies on a winter's day!"

"What about Lady Byron?"

"Oh, just as long as there is no person resembling herself in it, she will keep quiet. His poetic works are nothing to do with her anyway. I don't know why you allow it!"

PART SIX

Pisa

"The Countess Guiccioli is twenty-three years of age, though she appears no more than seventeen or eighteen. Unlike most of the Italian women, her complexion is delicately fair, her eyes large and languishing, and are shaded by the longest eyelashes in the world. Her hair falls over her shoulders in a profusion of natural ringlets, and she has the most beautiful mouth and teeth imaginable.

It is impossible to see her, without admiring – or to hear her speak without being fascinated. Her amiability and gentleness show themselves in every intonation of her voice. Notwithstanding that she adores Lord Byron, it is evident that the exile of her father sometimes affects her spirits, and throw a shade of melancholy on her face, which adds to the deep interest that this lovely girl creates."

Captain Thomas Medwin.

Chapter Thirty-Two

~ ~ ~

Pisa, famous for being the home of Galileo, and its equally famous leaning Tower.

Byron tilted his head to one side as he stood looking up at the huge tower – magnificent in its structure – but lopsided.

The Tower's oddity amused and delighted him. It reminded him of his own slanted figure when his limp was bad.

On the banks of the River Arno, Shelley had found and rented for Byron the Palazzo Lanfranchi, with its own stone steps down to the river, and a garden and orange grove at the back.

The Shelleys had also moved – from their old lodgings, to apartments on the top floor of the *Tre Palazzi di Chiesa,* and from the windows of their new quarters, they could see Byron's future palazzo on the other side of the river.

It was from one of these windows that Mary Shelley had watched the arrival of eight wagons of Byron's covered furniture, followed by his "brigade" of servants.

"There is scarce employment in Italy," Byron told her later, "so what was I to do – throw them into paupery?"

She later discovered that each and every one of his servants was completely devoted to him, some even willing to die for him, especially his big and black-bearded bodyguard, Tita Falcieri, whom she found so lovable, she hoped there would be no such necessity for such a drastic act on Tita's part.

But the sight that was most amazing, drawing a crowd to stand and stare, was the arrival of the strangest cargo of all – Byron's animals – taking up the space of three wagons.

From her window Mary had watched with the small crowd as the animals disembarked – five dogs; three monkeys; four cats; two cranes and a heron in separate cages; a sleeping squirrel in his cage; a goat with a broken leg; a shuffling badger on a chain – shuffling because one of his feet was damaged – and Mary knew instantly that the cranes, heron, squirrel, goat, badger, and some of the cats and dogs were the latest finds in Byron's addiction to the rescue of injured strays, whom he always hospitalised and cared for in his house and garden, before he sent them on their way, fully recovered.

And no doubt he would soon spy out more poor injured animals in Pisa. No wonder he always needed a large palazzo with a big garden.

Mary's thoughts drifted back to their wonderful summer on the banks of Lake Leman in Geneva, when they had been a close mix of friends and had associated with no others.

But there *were* others – English tourists who felt no compunction about spying on Lord Byron's house night and day with their telescopes and binoculars to try and get a glimpse of him; forcing herself and Shelley to give Byron the nickname of "Albè" so they could talk to each other openly about "Albè" in the Geneva bookshops and other places without anybody knowing to whom they were referring.

It was a nickname which had been conjured up by Shelley, due to all the strange tales which Byron had told them in Geneva about his time in Albania, and his initials of LB.

"*Albè – the dear, capricious, fascinating Albè,*" Mary whispered, full of joy that he was returning to the friendship of herself and Shelley, and this time with no Claire at hand to spoil it all.

Yet no sign of *him*. Wherever he was, he had still not arrived at the district of the Lung' Arno.

In the six weeks they had been in Pisa, the Gamba family had already gathered a circle of Italian friends around them, for Pisa was a place to which many of the uncaptured Carbonari had escaped and fled. Few of them now talked of revolution in Italy, preferring to discuss the revolution that had started across the waters in Greece. The Greek slaves were now rising up against their Turk rulers, unable to tolerate any more of their brutality.

"How can they succeed?" said Count Ruggero. "The Greeks are so poor they have little enough money for food, so how can they afford to buy weapons?"

"We could start a contribution fund from the Italians," Pietro suggested; and many of the Carbonari agreed. If they helped the Greeks now, maybe one day in the future the Greeks could help Italy to gain her own freedom.

Count Gamba did not think it could be done, that Greece was beyond help. "We think the Austrians are bad, but they are more civilised than the Turks with all their slashing and cutting and beheadings."

This talk about the Turks was so horrible to Teresa that she preferred to spend most of her time with Mrs Shelley. Every afternoon she would collect Mary in her carriage and the two would go out driving for hours together, talking like two old friends; and then returning to Mary's apartment where Teresa liked to play with Mary's little son, Percy Florence, before the maid took him away, leaving the two friends to take tea together.

Today, over tea, Teresa finally dared to ask Mary about Allegra's mother.

Mary sighed. "I have no wish to speak ill of my stepsister, but she *did* chase Lord Byron all the way to Switzerland. She told us he had arranged for her to meet him in Geneva, and persuaded us to go with her."

"Persuaded? You did not want to go?"

Mary shrugged. "We were leaving England anyway, with the intention of coming to Italy, so a detour to Switzerland was not that much out of way – but imagine our shock when we finally met his lordship and he seemed not to know Claire at all. In fact, for the first few weeks he treated her like those silly women in London who followed him everywhere, and now one of them had followed him all the way to Switzerland."

Mary still frowned at the memory of it. "There would have been no friendship between us at all, had he and Shelley not got on so well together."

"Ah, Mr Shelley," Teresa smiled. "Anyone would like him."

"And they had so much in common," Mary explained. "Both English in a foreign land, both poets, both from the same class."

Teresa was surprised. "Shelley is an English aristocrat?"

"Of a sort," Mary replied. His father is a Baronet, Sir Timothy Shelley of Goring Castle; and as his oldest son, Shelley is heir to his title and his wealth."

"So one day you will be *Lady* Shelley?"

Mary smiled. "Not that Shelley and I care much for titles and wealth, although a little extra money now and again *would* be a great help."

They might have talked more, if Mary's Italian maid had not rushed into the room in a fizz of excitement. "He is here! The famous Mylord Byron! All windows are open to see him!"

Mary and Teresa rushed to the window and stared across at the Palazzo Lanfranchi where Byron was stepping out of his carriage. Moments later all the people at their open windows began clapping their applause.

"Why are they clapping?" Mary asked her Italian maid, who replied, "It will be very good for the city of Pisa, Signora, to have someone famous living here. It will bring to us many visitors and much money."

"Oh dear, I had not thought of that," said Mary, staring at Teresa.

Teresa was shaking her head. "My Byron will not like that at all. If people stare at him, he will leave. That is why he loved Ravenna so much. They treated him like one of their own. No one stared at him."

"After three years of living there, I should think not," Mary quipped, and then smiled. "Still, let us not be so pessimistic. Shall we go over and welcome him, or would you prefer to go alone?"

"No, we must go together," Teresa replied, her expression very grave now. "Like two ladies on a friendly visit. It will then not be so obvious to the staring people that I am Byron's *donna*."

Shelley was already in the palazzo, insisting to Byron that he had made a wise choice in coming to Pisa.

"Mary and I have never been so happy anywhere else, as we have been here in Pisa. You will like it."

Byron liked the palazzo, but the feature that fascinated him the most was the huge and beautiful marble staircase of the house, which the Lanfranchi owner *insisted* had been designed and sculpted by Michangelo in the sixteenth century.

"Michelangelo?"

The owner nodded, using the name all Italians used for Michelangelo. "*Il Divino*. It was he who carved this staircase."

Byron could not know if that was true or not, but he was more than happy to believe it.

Chapter Thirty-Three

~ ~ ~

Byron had expected that life now in Pisa would be similar to the secluded life that he and the Shelleys had led in Switzerland, a small group of friends, keeping to themselves in their own peaceful world; but it was not to be so.

More friends arrived, one after the other, and all were friends of Shelley.

The first was a cousin of Shelley's, a Captain Thomas Medwin, a British officer aged thirty-three, who was on his way back home after serving seven years in India.

He was accompanied by Edward Williams, a young lieutenant who had also served in the Eighth Dragoons in India, and with him was his wife Jane. The couple leased the ground floor apartment of the *Tre Palazzi di Chiesa,* while Medwin lived with the Shelleys on the top floor.

All loved literature and poetry; and all were eager to meet Lord Byron, and all were very surprised when they did so, for he was quite the opposite of what they had imagined.

Edward Williams was so surprised, he wrote a letter home to his parents:

In the afternoon, Shelley introduced me to Lord Byron, on whom we called. So far from his having a haughtiness of manners, they are those of the most unaffected and gentlemanly ease – and so far from his being (as is generally imagined) wrapt in a melancholy gloom, he is all sunshine and good humour, with which his language and the brilliance of his wit cannot fail to inspire those who are near him. He looks as fresh and vigorous as any man I ever saw.

Byron began to spend a lot of time with these friends; sailing in skiffs on the river in the day, horse-riding in the late afternoons, while Teresa spent a lot of her afternoons with Mary and Jane Williams, and all felt themselves happy.

Due to its mild Mediterranean climate, Pisa was a winter resort for many. There were shows at the theatre, street masquerades, and parties given every night by various individuals.

Lord Byron was always invited to the parties, and he always declined, including those from Grand Duchesses; preferring to spend his time in the private circle of his friends and with Teresa.

Once again, Edward Williams wrote home to his family in England.

Lord Byron is the very spirit of this place – that is, to those few whom, like Mokannah, he has lifted his veil. He sees none of the numerous English who are here, excepting those I have named (Shelley, Medwin, myself, and the Gambas). He declines all invitations to parties.

There is a Mrs Beauclere here, with a litter of seven daughters: She is the gayest lady, and the only one who gives dances, for the young squaws are arriving at that age when, as Lord Byron says, they must waltz for their livelihood.

Last night dined at Lord B's with Shelley and Medwin – met there Count Gamba and his son Pietro. Lord B told us of a letter he had received from some professors at the University of Bologna, calling upon him to lend his name and financial assistance to the project of a machine, with which a man, by the aid of wings, is to elevate himself to any height – in short to fly – the whole is to be worked by steam, and the weight of the engine is not considered to be any impediment.

I have very great doubts if a body much beyond the weight of the largest bird can be thus elevated, but Lord B seems to think it could be possible, and at least worth a try.

Shelley was enjoying his new social life, and he too was writing a letter to England, to his friend Thomas Peacock, voicing his approval of the way Byron had readily entered into friendship with his cousin and two friends, who were now daily callers at the Palazzo Lanfranchi.

Every Wednesday evening he now hosts a dinner for the men, without the women, and never has he displayed himself to more advantage than on these occasions; being at once polite and cordial, full of social hilarity and the most perfect good humour; never diverging into ungraceful merriment, and yet keeping up the spirit of liveliness throughout the evening.

Thomas Medwin was also writing about Byron, but not to anyone in particular – all his written words were kept hidden and seen only by himself. Now that he was out of the army, he needed a new career, and thoughts of a *literary* career had the greatest appeal, and the possibility of making a small fortune.

In the same way that Boswell had used their time together to write his diaries about Samuel Johnson, he would now write about Lord Byron, plain and simple, no fiction.

I never met with a man who shines so much in conversation. He shines the more, perhaps, for not seeking to shine. His ideas flow without effort, without his having occasion to think,. There are no concealments in him, no injunctions to secrecy. He tells everything that he has thought or done without the least reserve, and as if he wished the whole world to know it; and does not throw the slightest gloss over his errors. He gives every one an opportunity of sharing in the conversation. He hates arguments, and never argues for victory, and has the art of turning the subject so that it may bring out the person with whom he is conversing. He never plays the author.

Another friend whom Shelley brought to introduce to Byron was a respectable young Irishman, John Taaffe. He was established in Pisa as a translator, and confessed he was "sentimentally attached" to an amiable Frenchwoman.

Byron could not help liking Taaffe, because he had a first-rate sense of humour; although, as he later discovered, Taaffe was, sadly, a second-rate writer.

Taaffe's ideal of happiness, and a reward on which he continually dreamed, he told Byron, "was to find a publisher for his work in England".

"A matter of the utmost difficulty," Taaffe said.

Byron agreed to read his work, willing to help him in that respect – until he read the said work – a translation of Dante, crushed beneath enough of Taaffe's own ponderous commentary to deter a reader from ever picking up Dante's *Divine Comedy* or having anything to do with anything else that Dante had written.

Nevertheless, Byron decided, if some men believed that humans might one day be able to fly in the sky in machines, then surely it might be an easier task to get this second-rate writer published?

He took the unflagging scholar under his patronage, and pressed John Murray to make an Irishman happy. He did not conceal from Murray that Taaffe's poetry was bad, but he joked about it with grace and benignity:

He really is a good fellow, and I daresay his verse is very good Irish. Now what shall we do for him? He will never rest until he is published and abused, and I see nothing left but to gratify him, so as to have him abused as little as possible; for I think it would kill him. You must write, then, to Jeffrey, to beg him not to review him, and I will do the same to Gifford.

Although his writing was bad, Taaffe's humour was as good and as funny as ever – even better, now that he believed he was going to be published – and published in the only place where it mattered; in England. He even ditched his work on translations to go out riding with Byron and his friends in the afternoons.

When the refusal came from London, Byron did not tell Taaffe, but wrote back to John Murray and persisted once again:

What is to done about poor Taaffe? He will die if he is not published – and he will be damned if he is – but that he don't mind. We must publish him.

As nothing more than a favour, John Murray finally agreed to publish Taaffe's book, a limited number of copies, which he would *not* send out to be reviewed by anyone. He had his own reputation to protect.

When John Taaffe was given the good news, he jumped into the air with delight. "*Published!* I'm going to be *published!* BeGod, I'll be the envy of everyone in Balbriggan. They'll all be doffing their hats to me when I go back. They will and all, so they will!"

Byron was full of praise and congratulations, but could not help laughing at Taaffe's exuberance, saying to Fletcher after Taaffe had gone, "Well, if nothing else, at least I have made *one* person happy today."

Fletcher responded, sour-faced. "And if past experience is anything to go by, when it all goes wrong, *you* will be the one that gets all the blame for it."

Byron shrugged. "Oh well, as the Greeks say about these things – 'maybe so, maybe not' ... And what has caused *you* to be so glum?"

Fletcher hesitated. "I don't like to tell you, my lord, because you won't be happy to hear it – and because I know that *I* will be the one who gets blamed for it."

"Of course you will, whether you are responsible or not – so out with it?"

"The badger has died."

"Georgio?"

"Aye, Tita found him dead this morning. You should have left him to die at his appointed time and in his appointed place – back in Ravenna."

Byron was at a loss. "So was I wrong to try and help him?"

"In Georgio's case, yes. Mr Shelley may talk about wanting to save the world, but you should know it can't be done. If a badger is ready to die, he will die."

Byron's expression was sullen. "Trust you to come along and spoil the day for me."

Fletcher turned away in an egregious huff. "There now – did I not say that *I* would be the one who'd get the blame for it."

Chapter Thirty-Four

~ ~ ~

One evening Byron said to Teresa, "Today I met the real-life personification of my *Corsair,* my pirate – or at least a man who styles himself on my Corsair – he even said he sleeps every night with the poem under his pillow."

"Where did you meet him?"

"Shelley and Williams brought him to me. An Englishman, who is so eccentric that he says ever since he was a lad, he has put my Corsair's life into practice, and that all his doings in the Indian Ocean were aimed at making my Corsair a reality."

"Is he a seaman?"

"Yes, a seaman, and also a liar or a fantasist. He has to be around the same age as myself, yet he says he has been acting out my Corsair since he was a lad – but the *Corsair* was published only six years ago."

"And does he claim to have a lover like Medora as well?"

"He says he leaves one behind in every country he passes through."

Teresa was amused. "I am curious to meet him."

Byron looked at her wryly. "You will *not* like him."

A few days later, on arriving in her carriage to take Mary out for a drive, Mary jumped into the carriage as if she was glad to get away, quickly telling Teresa about the new arrival.

"He is most peculiar, and it's his nature to make himself conspicuous and vainly draw all the attention to himself. His manners are not exactly rude, but they are certainly in keeping with his odd appearance."

"How is it odd?"

"Like a pirate – hair as black as a raven's wing, thick and curly, but cut short like a Moor's – a height of six foot and a build like Hercules – just imagine! And his eyes – dark grey – glaring at you – and shaded by bushy eyebrows – he looks more like an Arab than an Englishman."

"Are you sure he is an Englishman?"

"Oh yes, from Cornwall. His manners are very unpolished, but he's a clever talker. He pretends he knows all about literature – but he can't *spell*. Last night he left me a note about what time to wake him this morning, and it went thus – '*If you deside to rise erly in the morn ...*'" Mary's eyes were swivelling. "He tells strange stories of himself, horrific ones, of his adventures on sea and land."

"Where did he come from?" asked Teresa.

"Medwin and Williams met him in Switzerland on their way here. He was a great talker and they enjoyed his tales about all the battles he had fought, and when they said they were going on to Pisa to see Shelley and Lord Byron, Trelawny asked if he could look them up if he found himself in Italy. And here he is – and the first thing he begged of Williams and Medwin was to be taken to meet his hero, Byron ... so poor Shelley was chosen to do it."

"Will he be staying in Pisa, or will he be going soon?"

Mary did not know. "All I know is that he has moved in with us, and for how long, I have no idea."

Mary frowned. "The problem is, Shelley and the others like him, because of all his strange talk which keeps them amused."

Mary had hardly finished her talk of him, when the man she was describing appeared before Teresa's eyes – outside the Porta alle Piaggia – where she saw Byron and other horsemen off on their ride. Byron smiled and nodded, but kept on riding, yet one of the men riding with the group fitted Mary's description.

"That's him," Mary whispered. "Edward Trelawny."

He was staring at the two women, and when his eyes met Teresa's gaze, she was almost scared of the strange look he gave her.

That evening she repeated to Byron what Mrs Shelley had told her, and voiced her nervousness at Byron associating with such a man.

Byron regarded her fears as childishness. "It's only eccentricity on his part," he assured her, "and as for all his crimes – all imaginary ones, no doubt, because he *cannot tell the truth*. Trelawny *is* an oddity, and that's the truth of it. But in his case, a generous and noble spirit may be bound up behind his desperate need to attract attention to himself. Other than that, I think he is harmless. Also, from his talk of ships and his use of nautical terms, I believe he is a very good sailor."

The following Wednesday evening, Edward Trelawny spruced himself up to attend Lord Byron's masculine dinner party for men only. This, Trelawny believed, would be the first step towards his fortune. He knew that Medwin was secretly writing a book about Byron, always jotting down notes from his lordship's conversation; and if Medwin could write a book about the poet, maybe he could too?

Byron was disappointed to see Trelawny arriving at his palazzo without Shelley.

"Shelley is feeling sick," Trelawny said. "A queasy stomach."

"Oh well..." Byron introduced Trelawny to Count Pietro Gamba."

"A Count?" exclaimed Trelawny, delighted. "My word, I am in high company tonight."

And from then on, sitting around the table, dining and drinking, Edward Trelawny dominated the conversation with more of the fascinating tales about his life.

"In the summer of 1820," he said, "I was in Ouchy, a village on the margin of the Lake of Geneva, and the most intelligent person I could find to talk to was a young bookseller, at Lausanne. He told me he was educated at a German University."

"Then he must know all about Goethe," Byron said,

"and particularly being a bookseller."

"He was familiar with the books of all distinguished writers," said Trelawny, "and he and I became good friends. Then one morning, I saw my bookselling friend sitting under an acacia tree reading a book. He said to me: 'I am trying to sharpen my wits in this pungent air, so that I may fathom this book. Your modern poets, Byron, Scott and Moore, I can read and understand as I walk along, but I have got hold of one now that makes me stop to take a breath and think.'

"It was Shelley's *Queen Mab.*"

All the guests round the table looked at each other smiling.

"*Queen Mab* – in a bookshop in Lausanne?" said Thomas Medwin. "Well I never! We must tell Shelley."

"I asked him how he got the book," Trelawny continued, "and he said – 'Oh, with a lot of new books in English which I exchanged for old French ones. And not knowing the names of the authors, I might not have looked into them, had not a priest come into my bookshop, picked up this book *Queen Mab*, and glanced through it, before exploding in wrath and shouting out, Infidel! Jacobin! Nothing can stop this spread of blasphemy but the stake. The world is returning to accursed heathenism!'

"So my bookselling friend's interest was awakened, and he took up the book. 'It requires a strong stomach to digest it,' he said to me, 'but the writer is an enthusiast and has the spirit of a poet. They say he is but a boy, and this is his first offering. If that be so, we shall hear from him again'."

"And again and again," Medwin said. "Shelley lives for his poetry."

"Some days after this conversation," Trelawny continued, "I walked to Lausanne to breakfast with an old friend from the Navy, Captain Roberts. He was out sketching, but soon came in with two English ladies, who he had met whilst drawing, and brought them to our hotel. The husband of one of them soon followed, and I could see from their garb, and the blotches on their faces, that they were walking tourists, fresh from the snow-covered mountains. The English husband was clearly from the North, his accent hard, self-confident and dogmatic in his speech. I like to talk, or listen to talk, in strange company, and so I listened to them chatter away as they drank their coffee.

"The English husband loudly voiced his disgust at the introduction of carriages into the mountain districts of Switzerland, and the old fogies who used them – although he was not young himself, a man of around fifty. 'It was a disgrace to Nature', he said, 'to cut roads through the Alps.'

"Then the husband, hearing a commotion on the street, sprang up on his feet, looked out the window, and then rang the bell violently.

"'Waiter,' he said, 'is that our carriage? Why did you not tell us? Come, lasses, be stirring if you want to go up the mountains before the freshness of the day has gone. You may rejoice in not having to walk'."

Medwin and Williams were laughing. "Typical English hypocrisy! Complaining about the carriages that he himself was using."

"On their leaving the room to get ready for their journey," Trelawny went on, "my friend Roberts told me the strangers were the poet William Wordsworth, his wife and sister."

At this revelation, Byron lowered his head and smiled.

"Who could have suspected this?" Trelawny continued. "I saw no trace in the hard outer face of the man of the divineness inside the poet. In a few minutes the travellers reappeared. We cordially shook hands, and agreed to meet next in Geneva. But now that I knew who he was, I wasted no time, and asked him what he thought of Shelley as a poet.

"'Nothing,' he replied.

"Seeing my surprise, Wordsworth said, 'A poet who has not produced a good poem before he is twenty-five, we may conclude will never do so'.

"'*The Cenci?'* I pleaded."

"'Won't do,' Wordsworth replied, shaking his head, and then got into his carriage and rolled off."

As the voices around the table babbled their indignation against Wordsworth, Byron kept his head lowered, fiddling with the stem of his wine glass. There were so many holes in Trelawny's story it was almost laughable, and probably no more true than those stories of English tourists telling stories of seeing himself in the Borromean islands and other places, when he was actually in Venice.

Secondly, it was bad form to tell such a story in Shelley's absence, probably because Trelawny mistakenly believed that he and Shelley were rival poets, and sought to put Shelley down for that purpose. Shelley had only a few copies of *The Cenci* privately printed for distribution among his friends, so how could Wordsworth have read it to pass judgment?

And thirdly, the very idea of Wordsworth shaking hands with a common and unkempt stranger in a hotel, and agreeing to meet up with him again in Geneva, was also absurd.

But then, every lie usually had a grain of truth in it, so perhaps Trelawny had been told the story by some other person in Switzerland, and had now appropriated the meeting with Wordsworth to himself.

Thomas Medwin was surprised that Byron was showing no reaction and little interest.

"What say you, Byron? Wordsworth sounds a callous and unkind man, does he not? An elder bard passing such a harsh sentence on a young brother poet?"

Byron's blue eyes looked up, directly at Trelawny. "I'm surprised that Wordsworth should be reported as having said such damning words about Shelley's *The Cenci*, because it is a well-known fact that Wordsworth *never* reads the poetry of any other poets – not unless he is begged to review them – and I doubt he has been begged to review Shelley, who is literally unknown to the critics."

Edward Trelawny was shocked to hear this, and was instantly outraged. "So the scoundrel denounced Shelley without ever having read him!"

A hullabaloo of more indignation against Wordsworth arose around the table, even from Pietro Gamba, who was now such a good friend of Shelley.

Byron ordered more wine to be brought, and succeeded in changing the conversation to a lighter topic.

At midnight, as his guests were leaving, Byron managed to whisper a few words to Medwin and Williams: "Pray don't pass that story about Wordsworth on to Shelley, because not only will it hurt him, he might actually believe it."

The two stared, and Medwin whispered, "Is it not true then?"

Byron shrugged. "Maybe so, maybe not ... but at this moment all we know for sure, is that it came from Trelawny. And how many other *tales* has he told us?"

Chapter Thirty-Five

~ ~ ~

The regular weekly reports on Allegra came from the Reverend Mother of the Santa Giovanni Convent at Bagnacavallo, the boarding school where the child was being educated.

Teresa always read the letters, happy to know that the good nuns were lavishing motherly care on Allegrina, and their reports were always full of praise for the child. They said she was cheerful and full of promise. Little Miss Byron could not be sweeter, and had no equal in all the other young ladies.

"Young ladies," Byron quipped. "She is only five."

A few days later another letter came from the Reverend Mother, informing Lord Byron that Allegra was sick, but there was no danger.

"She has the same vulnerability to fevers as I do," Byron said to Teresa, "but we always fight them off."

Nevertheless, Byron immediately sent a courier to find out the details of Allegra's sickness, and gave him a letter for the Reverend Mother, requesting that Professor Tommasini of Bologna be called in to attend upon Allegra.

More letters came every day from the Reverend Mother bearing good tidings about the child, who was going on well and getting better every day.

Byron was relieved, but it set him thinking about his other child, little Ada, in England. She was not allowed to know anything about him, and he was told precious little about her. Consequently he had got into the habit of referring to Ada in letters to his attorney and others as – "Lady Byron's daughter."

This made Teresa sad. "It is as if you have given up all hope of seeing your Ada again."

"And I never will; not until she has grown up and is allowed to decide for herself if she wishes to see me. In the meantime, even if I went to England, her mother will do her utmost to prevent me from seeing Ada; because the child is the only weapon she has left."

The subject made him irritable, snappish even, as he asked Teresa to write to the Reverend Mother to find out if the courier had arrived, or had he come and gone? And if Professor Tommasini had been called in?

"What is taking the courier so long?"

"Byron, you know it is a long journey from here to Bagnacavallo. In future, we will talk no more of that woman in England, because the subject always makes you *irato*. I will send another letter to the convent by express."

The following morning, before the letter could be posted, the courier arrived back in Pisa and called at the Villa Finocchietti, asking to speak to the Contessa, too nervous to take the news to Mylord himself.

Teresa was devastated, hardly able to believe it; and now she had the terrible task of telling Byron. How could she do it?

"I will go with you," her Papa said. "He will need a man, and one who is a father who has endured the same experience, to console him."

As soon as Byron was told that Allegra's fever had taken a sudden turn for the worse and she had died from malaria ... a mortal paleness came over his face, his strength failed him, and he sank into a chair.

From then on he heard nothing that Count Gamba or Teresa said to him. His look was fixed, and his expression such that Teresa feared for his reason. He remained immovable for over an hour, and no consolation seemed to reach his ears, much less his heart.

Fletcher came to the rescue, deeply sorrowed by the tragic news, but urging them to go. "He will not cry until he is alone."

Later that night, when Byron could shed no more tears, he sat alone at his desk and wrote the poem *Cain,* imagining himself in Cain's place and asking all the questions he used to ask himself as a boy when wondering about the fall of Adam and the curse that fell on his son Cain and upon all of Cain's descendants ... Why was the Tree of Knowledge put in the Garden of Eden in the first place? Why was it placed so near to the two innocents? Why was the apple so tempting, and yet the innocents had been warned by God not to touch it?

So many questions, until the Devil appeared, cool and sophisticated with a silver tongue, answering all of Cain's questions with smooth lies and even hard malice, saying to Cain ... *"You must tell your tyrant of a God that his evil is not good."*

~ ~ ~

In London, although he knew very little about the child, John Murray was deeply saddened by Byron's letter, which also contained instructions, which Byron was entrusting to his kindness to carry out on his behalf.

It is my intention, to send her body to England, for sepulchre in Harrow Church (where I once hoped to have laid my own).

There is a spot in the Churchyard near the footpath, on the brow of the hill, looking towards Windsor, where I would sit for hours and hours when a boy at Harrow. This was my favourite spot – but as I wish to erect a wall-tablet to her memory, she had better be interred in the Church. Near to the door, on the left as you enter, there is a monument with a tablet containing these words –

When Sorrow weeps over Virtue's sacred dust,
Our tears become us, and our Grief is just.

I recollect those words (after seventeen years)

because from my seat in the Gallery, I had generally my eyes turned towards that monument. So as near to it as is convenient I would wish Allegra to be interred – and on the wall a marble tablet placed, and inscribed with these words:

In memory of
Allegra
daughter of G. G. Lord Byron
who died at Bagnacavallo
In Italy, April 20th, 1822
aged five years and three months –
I shall go to Her, but she shall not return to me.

The funeral I wish to be as private as is consistent with decency – and I could hope that my old tutor and friend Henry Drury will perhaps read the service over her.

Sadly, John Murray was shaking his head. Despite being one of Harrow's most famous pupils, had Byron been abroad too long and forgotten the religious laws of England? Or maybe he was truly unaware of the fact that no *illegitimate* child could be interred within a sacred Church. It would be a miracle if they even allowed her to be buried within the churchyard beside other graves. Illegitimate children were usually buried *outside* the gates of a churchyard, or in the hills and fields.

How could he write back to Byron and tell him? And how would he say it? It really would have been better if he had given this difficult task to his friend, John Hobhouse.

And then it occurred to Murray – that's what he could do – speak to Hobhouse. That good and clever man always knew how to handle such delicate situations; and particularly with great eagerness when the situation related to his dearest friend, Lord Byron.

John Hobhouse lost no time in going out to the School of Harrow to see the Reverend Henry Drury.

A tutor of the boy-lord Henry Drury may have been, but in Byron's adult years Drury had occasionally spent evenings enjoying dinner with Lord Byron; and on these occasions they were often joined by John Cam Hobhouse, now a Member of Parliament.

Reading the letter which Lord Byron had sent to John Murray, Henry Drury was inclined to be extremely sympathetic, especially as Byron had particularly named himself as the person he wished to read the service over his daughter.

"I would do anything within my power to oblige Lord Byron," he told Hobhouse, "but this I cannot do. No, I cannot. The school could not break the rules of the Christian Church and allow it. The illegitimacy of a child, born out of wedlock, cannot be sanctioned or approved."

"Now I know why I was an atheist for so long," Hobhouse replied tartly. "The Christian Church, you say? And if this innocent little girl, who lived for only five years, was brought before Christ himself, what do you think *He* would say?"

Reverend Drury knew the answer. "He would say, 'suffer the little children to come unto me'."

"Yes, I recall being taught those words in my own school," Hobhouse said. "So what now, as Christians, can we do for Byron's child?"

Reverend Drury sighed hopelessly. "I will speak to the School Board and do my best. If nothing else, I can at least *try* to get them to make an exception in this case."

Two weeks later, when the ship containing Allegra's embalmed little body arrived in the London docks, John

Hobhouse was the first to go on board and take the small coffin into his care, as Byron had asked him to do. And then he travelled in the carriage with Allegra's coffin to Harrow School.

On the journey, Hobhouse brooded. He had not had the heart to tell Byron the truth ... but at least now he would be able to write and tell him that Allegra *had* been buried at Harrow School, and the Reverend Henry Drury had said the prayers over her.

In years to come, whenever Byron chose to return to England, he would discover the truth. But, by then, the personal wound would not be so hurtful. So why inflict it now?

Allegra's funeral was indeed private, as Byron wished, with only three persons present – John Cam Hobhouse, Reverend Henry Drury, and John Murray.

Solely because George Gordon Lord Byron was one of Harrow's most famous sons, who had gone from Harrow and conquered the world of poetic literature, his illegitimate daughter was allowed to be buried within Harrow's churchyard – but no entry was allowed into the Church, and no place near to Byron's favourite spot as a boy could be allowed for the site of the grave.

Instead, Allegra was prayed over and finally buried beneath a small patch of grass, just *inside* the gate of Harrow's churchyard. No memorial stone of her name, age, or parentage was allowed to be erected.

Chapter Thirty-Six

~ ~ ~

The intensity of Spring is so swift in Italy, and especially in Pisa, that already the May weather was extremely hot.

Yet Byron did not go outside, confining himself to the cool marble palazzo, constantly at his desk writing poetry, and showing no interest in the world outside.

On the cover of his foolscap writing pad he had written the words of a proverb, which served as a reminder to him whenever he sat down to write – *"Those whom the gods love die young."*

Percy and Mary Shelley felt great sympathy for him, for in previous years they had suffered the loss of two of their own children to malaria fever, which was why Mary guarded so carefully her last and only child, Percy Florence.

And now, Mary knew that neither she nor Shelley could even try to comfort Byron in any way, nor offer any words to console him, for being manly in his ways, he detested any *show* of compassion or flaunted sentimentality that people usually indulged in at such times. A sincere sympathetic look, or a plain handshake, was of more value to him.

"Poor Albè," Mary kept saying; while seeking a way to get Byron out of the seclusion of his palazzo. Even his Wednesday evening dinner parties had come to a halt.

And that gave her an idea – "Why don't *we* hold a dinner party here," she said to Shelley, "inviting Albè *and* Teresa – if she wishes to come he will feel duty-bound to escort her. And we will also invite the Williams's and Medwin and John Taaffe ... an evening with plenty of good conversation? That should open the shell on Byron's seclusion, especially if the Contessa begs him to escort her."

Shelley thought it a fine idea; and to make sure the

fish would be as fresh as possible, he would go along one of the small rivers off the Arno and catch the fish himself.

Mary sighed, knowing this was just another excuse for Shelley to go out on the water. He loved being afloat on water, and loved boats so much that when he could not be in one, he often enjoyed himself making little paper boats and sending them off to glide away on the surface of the river.

"When?" Shelley asked. "The dinner for Albè?"

"Tomorrow evening – giving him no time to come up with some excuse or to pretend that he has arranged to spend the evening with the Gambas. And we won't say it is a dinner party for him, but a small and relaxed gathering of our small group of friends."

"Friends, yes."

"And you know what they say ..." Mary smiled. "When gentlefolk are gathered, compliments are paid."

"I hate compliments," Shelley said in his serious way, picking up his book and heading for the door, "because when gentlefolk are gathered, most compliments are false."

Mary was not to be deterred, sending her little maid with a note to Albè at the Palazzo Lanfranchi begging him to come; and then heading off to the market stalls to pick out the best vegetables and fruit.

Fortunately, Teresa called that afternoon in her carriage to ask Mary if she wished to go out for a drive.

Mary did not hesitate, jumping on board and telling Teresa of her plan.

"It is a wonderful idea," Teresa said. "He has maintained his composure, believing that all men should uphold manliness in such situations, but I know he is very sad and blames himself."

"Why, if that is so, then I should blame myself for the death of *my* two poor children," Mary said, and then hesitated. "But of course I *did* blame myself, and sometimes I still do ... asking myself what did I do wrong?"

"With malaria, there is no one to blame but the mosquitoes," Teresa said. "They are one of only two bad things about Italy. The mosquitoes and the Austrians."

Mary felt cheered. "You will make him come tomorrow night?"

Teresa nodded. "*Si*. It will do him much good to be with friends again, because it is such a long time since I have seen my Byron smile."

Mary nodded. "Shelley says the same ... although he's a fine one to talk, because Shelley *never* smiles, always so serious in his mission to try and find out the purpose of life and the mysteries of the universe."

"His is a good soul," Teresa said, and then sat thoughtful as her eyes wandered over the passing scenery.

"No, it is not true, because I *have* seen my Byron smile. Sometimes he smiles at me, and sometimes he smiles when he is at our home and speaking with my father and brother; but every time I *know* he is not happy. I know he feels too guilty to be happy so soon after Allegrina has died."

Mary was curious. "How do you know?"

Teresa turned on her seat to look fully at Mary. "Have you seen, in little children, after they have been crying badly with some grief, and then they become calm, but every so often afterwards, in a tremulous manner, they suddenly draw in a long convulsive breath."

Mary had seen it many times, in her own children, and even now in her beautiful small son.

Teresa nodded. "When I see this, in adult persons, I always know that it comes from sorrow."

Mary said – "Tomorrow night will be a good night. We will talk good conversation and tell good stories and we will *all* smile – even our dear Albè."

~

The following afternoon, Mary and Jane Williams were busy at work – Mary cutting vegetables while Jane worked on the fish. chatting as they prepared the ingredients for dinner.

Shelley was about to disappear, wearing his usual black jacket and with a book in his hand, when Mary stopped him. "Where are you going?"

"To catch some fish."

Mary pointed to the fish which Jane was busily cleaning. "And what if you caught none? I could not rely on that, so I bought the fish this morning."

"Oh well," Shelley shrugged, "then I'll go on the river to read my book."

What book is it?"

"Æschylus."

"Now you won't forget," Mary pleaded, "that we are having dinner earlier tonight – at six, not seven – so pray ensure to get back in time to spruce up and change your clothes."

Shelley nodded and disappeared, and Mary looked archly at Jane Williams. "I'm forced to repeat these things because Shelley is so forgetful, his mind always in the clouds."

Jane laughed. "He is not that bad. Shelley is very clever."

Mary nodded. "An intellectual and philosophical genius, and that's the problem. His mind is too engrossed in metaphysics."

"Will Trelawny be coming tonight?"

Mary chopped into a potato. "He has not been invited, but knowing Trelawny, he will probably turn up anyway. He talks so much, and yet his voice is monotonous."

She looked curiously at Jane. "How and where did you all become friends with Trelawny?"

"In Switzerland," Jane replied. "We were staying at an inn, when this strange pirate-looking man started talking to us, entertaining us with all the fascinating adventures of his life ... and then, well, he has been tagging along with us ever since."

Mary frowned. "And now he's tagging onto Shelley, hoping to get closer to Albè."

Jane chuckled. "Oh, yes indeed. He is always writing to people he knows in England telling them what a *close friend* he is to *'Lord Byron'*. Does he not annoy Shelley at times?"

"No." Mary shook her head. "Shelley pays little heed to him. And when he starts on his tales, Shelley sits reading one of his books."

~

Shelley always managed to find a secluded spot somewhere – on the river or in a park – where he could lose himself in his book or in his thoughts. The everyday chatter of most people was of little interest to him. Only with Byron did he find true intellectual stimulus when the two could talk for hours without tiring.

Today Shelley had found a lonely and secluded little spot on a river, near to the bank, and overhung with the shady branches of drooping trees.

Not possessing a boat of his own, he had hired the skiff from one of the huntsmen who used it to cross the streams that intersect the forest of the Maremma. These little skiffs of the poor huntsmen were not as sturdy as other boats, made only of lathes and pitched canvas, but they served Shelley, whose only wish was to be afloat on water.

And here, in the shade, he had been lying flat on his back in the little skiff for an hour, so short-sighted in his vision that his book was held very close to his eyes.

The humid heat became stifling, causing him to frequently lose his concentration, so he remedied his discomfort by taking off all his clothes, folding them into a bundle beneath his head, and laying back down again naked.

Nakedness was very natural to Shelley, for only when he felt the air bathing his skin and its oxygen filling his brain, and his spirit in harmony with nature, did he feel at peace and capable of great study.

The intensity of his reading engrossed him for hours, so much so that he did not notice a strong breeze building up. When his hair blew in his eyes, he absently brushed it away, never pausing to wonder why it kept happening.

~

Byron was often late, but tonight he arrived only minutes after Medwin and Edward Williams, followed by Trelawny.

Teresa was holding Byron's arm, and both looked happy to see Mary again.

"Is Shelley not joining us?" Byron asked.

"Oh, you know that Shelley never allows himself to be ruled by a clock."

Mary hid her impatience, knowing that Shelley in his forgetfulness might not appear for hours.

"He'll be along soon," she said, "but I don't think we should wait for him."

The dinner was served; and very quickly Trelawny dominated the conversation with the story of a beautiful young Arab girl he had loved so much, he had married her.

Medwin and Williams looked surprised. "So where is she now?"

"Oh," Trelawny said sadly. "She died." He leaned forward and said across the table to Byron. "She was very much like your Medora, in the *Corsair.*"

The little Italian maid who had been carrying dishes to the table, suddenly dropped the dish in her hands and let out an exclamation of shock, "*Mio Dio!*"

The crashing of the dish on the floor caused everyone to look at her, and then to where her eyes were staring ... at Shelley, totally naked, dripping wet and with bits of leaves clinging to his wet hair – attempting to slip silently down the side of the dining room to get to his bedroom without being seen.

"Oh my goodness!" exclaimed Jane Williams, putting a hand up to cover her eyes. Teresa blushed and did the same, but Mary was more forthright. "Shelley! Even for a poet this is not acceptable – and in front of ladies too!"

Shelley innocently claimed that he had not wished to cause anyone pain, but then became indignant with his wife at the unfairness of her accusation, drawing himself up to his full height and saying with the air of someone wrongfully accused –

"How can I help it? The wind turned my skiff over and myself and my clothes into the river. I must get to my room to get dry clothes but there is no way to get there but through this room. At this hour I have always found this place vacant. I have not changed my hours for going on the river, but you have changed yours for dining."

Mary was at a loss for words, unable to argue with him, lowering her head and putting her hand to her face in the same way as the other two women, while Shelley stood staring at her as if unaware that he was as naked as a Greek statue.

"Pray, my love, go and put some clothes on," she said stiffly; whereon Shelley wiped some wet grass from his face before walking on and doing so. He returned within a minute, clothes pulled on, and saying with urgency as he rushed down the side of the room – "I must go and see if I can find my book! There's not another like it in Italy."

As he rushed out again, Mary was still mortified with embarrassment, wondering how to apologise to everyone, until she glanced up and saw Byron in quiet hysterics of laughter.

"Do you think it is funny?"

"Extremely," he replied, still laughing at the funniest scene he had ever witnessed. "By God, I'm glad I came out tonight," he said. "This is the first time I have seen a naked man displaying such dignity while talking to a room full of clothed people!"

And then he was laughing again, and the other men who had also wanted to laugh now let themselves go, all praising Shelley who had stood his ground, no matter what.

This only set Byron laughing again, unable to control

himself, until Shelley reappeared, jubilantly holding up his book – "It's wet, but intact! The clothes are gone, but the book was lodged against the riverbank."

He then sat down in his place at the table as if he had not done anything to offend anyone, and began opening the wet pages of the book till he had found the right page, and bent his head low over the book to continue reading it.

"Shelley!" Mary exclaimed, and Shelley looked up in his boyish way – firstly at her, and then at the people around the table. "Oh, sorry," he said, "but when I'm at home I always read while I eat. This book by Æschylus has filled my head with all sorts of questions. You should read it, Byron."

"Oh no, thank you," Byron was still grinning. "A Greek tragedy is the last thing I wish to read. Although, in the circumstances, a Greek tragedy is very appropriate for *you* to be reading tonight. All you were lacking was the fig leaf."

And that got Shelley talking. "Have you noticed in museums, that the naked statues of the Greeks are always modest; but the more modern statues with fig-leaves on them look indecent, drawing people's attention to the very part they don't want them to see. Even now, in some museums, you see copies of Michelangelo's *David* with some ridiculous leaf stuck on him. What man would get up in the morning and pick up a solitary leaf to dress himself in?"

The laughter of the men continued, while the ladies went on blushing and hiding their smiles behind their hands. Only Teresa carried an Italian fan, and it was constantly going up to cover her face.

But all in all, by the end, Mary realised that her dinner party had been a great success and an enjoyable night for everyone, and all thanks to her beloved, unpredictable Shelley.

~

At three o'clock the following day, Teresa wandered

around the Palazzo Lanfranchi looking for Byron, and then saw him sitting on the shaded balcony writing his poetry. She knew he was working on a new Canto of *Don Juan,* and stood watching him – scribbling so fast that the pen seemed to glide rapidly over the paper on its own.

She sat down in a chair opposite him at the table. "You write so fast," she said, "it almost looks like you are writing down the words of some unseen person giving dictation to you."

"Yes," he answered, "dictation from a mischievous spirit who even makes me put down things that I don't agree with. Look," he went on, "I've just written something against love."

"Then why don't you cross it out?" Teresa said. "If it's contrary to what you think."

"It's done," he said with a smile.. "The stanza would be spoilt."

He laid down his pen, and the lines stayed.

Chapter Thirty-Seven

~~~

The month of June and the onset of summer was becoming so hot, that all the friends discussed, and decided, to remove themselves from the city of Pisa for a few months, and head up the coast to the Gulf of Spezzia to enjoy the cooling sea breezes.

Knowing that Byron would want to take half his household and all of his dogs with him, Trelawny decided to make himself a friend of some value to his lordship, by offering to go on ahead and find a house for him to rent in Spezzia.

Byron was dealing with a visit from a stranger; a nobleman attached to the Court of Tuscany, who was rapturously claiming to be his most ardent admirer – a German, named Baron Lützerode.

Normally Byron would have told Fletcher to tell the caller he was "not at home" but he had hesitated, because a man attached to the Court of Tuscany may be of some influence in pressing for Count Gamba to be allowed to return to his family in Ravenna.

Tired of hearing all his praises being sung by the German, Byron readily agreed to go downstairs when Fletcher quietly came and told him that a Mr Trelawny was at the door ... "on a matter of urgency."

"You will excuse me for a moment, Sir," he said to Baron Lützerode, and then went downstairs to see Trelawny at the front door. "What is it?"

"I'm about to go up the coast," Trelawny said, and then made his offer of searching out a house for Byron in Spezia.

"It's kind of you to offer, but Tita is ready to leave for the same purpose."

"Then, by God, we can travel up together, because I'm going up there now to seek out a house for Shelley."

"Are you? But I will be looking for not one house, but
~~~

two houses, as close together as possible," Byron said. "I'm sure the Gamba family would be as glad to get away from Pisa's heat as I will be."

Tita arrived at the door, ready to depart, and repeated to Byron the instructions he had been given. "Two houses, near to each other, and near to the sea."

Byron nodded. "Exactly."

"And, Mylord," said Tita, "when I find our house, the one for us, may I choose my own bedroom first, and stop Lega from always getting the best one?"

Byron smiled. "No, the best available room after my own, must be saved for Fletcher. He *is* head of the household."

Tita shrugged. "I would not wish to have a room near to Fletcho. He is a nightmare that walks. Do you know he believes there are ghosts here at Lanfranchi?"

Byron was surprised. "Does he – ghosts?"

"*Si*! That is why he keeps moving from one bedroom to another and making me change rooms, and Lega change rooms, but all are no good. He says the ghosts keep following him."

Byron laughed. "Fletcher – I can't believe it. He was not frightened of the ghost in Newstead Abbey. What brought this on?"

"The cellars," said Tita. "When we first came here, and Fletcho went down to inspect the cellars, he found old metal rings and chains on the walls, and then he learned from his gossips that those cellars were once used as dungeons. Many of the locals say that in past centuries the Lanfranchi were cruel people who tortured their prisoners, and those poor prisoners now haunt this palazzo."

Byron frowned. "Have *you* seen any of these ghosts?"

Tita grinned. "No, they haunt only Fletcho – in his *mind*. There are no ghosts."

Byron exhaled a sigh of relief. "I'm glad to hear it ... I did wonder why every time I went looking for Fletcher, he was always in a different room."

Tita laughed. "Now you know! But don't tell him I

told."

Tita was still laughing as he climbed into the carriage.

"I'm to come with you," Trelawny said, climbing into the carriage behind him.

Tita turned and stared at Mylord, who nodded to him. "He will be seeking a residence near to ours for Mr Shelley."

As the carriage rolled off, Byron was unsure as to how Tita would like having Trelawny's talkative company with him in the carriage ... but then, Tita was agreeable to most people. And if he found that he really did not like a person, he simply ignored them, or pretended to fall asleep.

He turned and went back indoors, and up to the German Baron who may be able to use his influence at the Court of Tuscany to help him. He would seek help from this man, in the same way he never stopped seeking help from all influential people he knew, or who called on him ... help in the cause of Count Gamba.

When he returned to the Salon, Baron Lützerode was still in raptures. "Everywhere I look around this room, there is something of interest to see ... your books, your pages there on your desk with your handwriting on ... your bust of Napoleon ..."

Byron smiled unashamedly. "He was my hero."

"As *you* are mine! You know, Lord Byron, you have not influenced alone the literature of England, but also of Germany, of Goethe, of Europe. In fact, I may tell you, that at the present moment, the largest prize at the University in Leipzig this year is for the best translation into German of canto four of your Childe Harold."

Byron was so surprised he almost forgot about the plight of the Gambas.

"And next to me in admiration of you, Lord Byron, is our own famous poet, Johann Wolfgang von Goethe. He has the highest regard for your genius, and he has now advised his countrymen to translate *Don Juan* into German, so they may gain inspiration from a style of poetry at once classic, elegant, and comic – a style which, Goethe says, is sadly wanting in Germany."

Byron could not help smiling. "Well, there are some who say I am given to vanity, and now I think I must be, for I have never felt so vain as I do at hearing this – from *Goethe*."

Now Baron Lützerode was surprised. "You do not know? In the universities of France, Russia, and even in Poland, Norway, and Denmark, translations of your works are being made."

The Baron suddenly looked covetously at the handwritten pages of poetry on the desk ... "If I could possess just *one* of your handwritten pages, Lord Byron, it would be to me, my greatest treasure."

Byron looked at him archly. "Then you may have one of those pages, but only if you will promise to try to use your influence to bring about a return to his home for a dear friend of mine from Ravenna."

~~~

Later that evening, at the Villa Finocchietti, Count Ruggero Gamba greeted Byron with his usual welcoming smile and warm embrace; and then the two went off to sit alone together in the garden.

Count Gamba was very heartened to know that yet another person had been asked to help in his cause.

"Today," he said, "with my Italian friends here in Pisa, they all talked of the revolution in Greece, and how we could help the poor Greeks, but few dare to go there."

He looked at Byron, a sad expression on his face. "I tell them, as much as I would like, I can do nothing to help the Greeks, because I am a man who belongs to his family in Ravenna, and it is for *their* cause I must fight. A family of motherless young daughters and an even younger son, who need their father to come home."

~~~

Travelling along the coast of the Gulf of Spezia, Tita could see no house in which even the most humble of gentlefolk could exist.

Trelawny agreed.

Tita's eyes kept scouring the landscape, without success. The shores and the bay were as beautiful as nature, but only occasional fishing villages were scattered along the line of the bay.

Travelling on, between Terenzo and Lerici, they came across an empty house named the *Villa Magni* which they got out to inspect.

Its ground floor was unpaved, and obviously used for boat-gear and fishing tackle, but above it was a first floor that contained a salon and four whitewashed bedrooms. There was only one chimney for cooking, but who needed more than one in summertime?

The best thing about the house was the veranda facing the sea, and almost over it.

Trelawny stood on the veranda gazing out; imagining himself and the friends sitting here in the evenings full of good talk while drinking wine and eating bread and grapes.

"I think Shelley would love it here," he said.

"If you think so," said Tita, "it is not for me to disagree with you. I am here only to find a casa for Mylord."

They moved on to find the owner, who suggested a very low amount for the rent.

As none of the friends had very much money to pay their share, Trelawny agreed the tenancy in Shelley's name; and made the arrangement for taking the house for six months.

Walking back along the sand, Tita was not so content. "For me to find a casa suitable and large enough for an Inglese Mylord and his household near to Signor Shelley, or even near to the sea, seems to me impossible."

He stood for a long moment staring all around him, and then shook his head. "No, nothing here for Mylord," he said, and strode back to the carriage.

On the return journey, as Trelawny launched into more tales about his heroic life as a sailor and pirate, Tita yawned.

"That is the same as Mylord's story of *Il Corsaro* – I also have read that book," Tita said, and then pulled his cloak over his head and face and went to sleep.

Chapter Thirty-Eight

~ ~ ~

News had come to Pisa – from the *"Buon Governo"* of Tuscany – ordering Count Gamba Senior, Ruggero and Pietro Gamba to attend for interviews in Florence.

This order came just a few days after one of the gentlemen of Pisa, Signor Francesco Dupay, had called on Byron and had recommended to him the renting of his own summer house in Montenero, near Leghorn, the *Villa Rossa*.

Byron looked at the sketch and details of the house, and instantly agreed; not only because it was spacious, and less than twenty miles from Pisa, but also because it was near the sea.

"So," said Tita, "Signor Shelley and his friends go north, but we go south."

It was only one house, yet large enough; so Byron suggested to Count Gamba that they all go to Montenero together and enjoy the sea breezes.

The lure of a more cooling climate near the sea was irresistible to Ruggero and Pietro – until the order from the *Buon Governo* arrived, giving Ruggero hope that he may be allowed to go back to his family in Ravenna.

"Do *I* also have to go to Florence?" Teresa asked.

Count Gamba looked at his daughter's crestfallen expression ... and then he turned to Byron. "I will entrust Teresina into your care at Montenero, and when we return from Florence, even if we are allowed to return to Ravenna, we will first join you by the sea on our return."

Teresa hugged her Papa. Was there ever a better father in this world.

The *Villa Rossa*, at Montenero, a large square villa of a deep salmon colour, was the hottest-looking house Byron had ever seen – and proved to be hot inside – or maybe it just seemed so because the summer heat had become even more intense.

It was not quite on the beach, but down a small path. Still, Byron and Teresa were happy. The villa had fine gardens at the front and rear bursting with flowers in full bloom; roses and Spanish jasmine, heliotrope and tuberoses.

Byron was more enraptured with the great terrace of the villa which faced the sea, and from which he could see the islands of Elba and Corsica

He called Teresa up to the terrace and pointed to the Isle of Elba. "The island of Napoleon's first exile."

Like many Italians, Teresa admired Napoleon, because – "Although the French ruled Italy," she said, "Napoleon *united* Italy as one country, not as it is now, broken up into separate provinces here and there and ruled by various Bourbon or Austrian kings and princes."

Byron's gaze was still fixed on Elba and imaginary visions of Napoleon.

"When I was in Albania ..." he said, and then told Teresa about the ruler, Ali Pasha, who had proudly showed him a snuff-box which had been sent to him by Napoleon, with a miniature portrait of himself under the glass lid.

"The snuff box from Napoleon contained a portrait of Napoleon?"

Byron laughed. "Yes, one egotist sending a gift to another egotist, although at that time Napoleon was the Emperor of France, and the snuff box was all part of the play of politics."

"How?"

"Ali Pasha, from his position in Albania, was able to keep watch on the Ionian Islands for the French; while also doing the same for the British, playing a double-handed game with both. When I was sent to him by the Foreign Office, to seek assurances that he was still Britain's friend and ally, I was given a magnificent sword to present to Ali Pasha as a token of Britain's regard for him; stocking up his palace with even more splendid treasures. Oh, the gifts that Barbarian received from both sides in the war."

"Did you tell your foreign office?"

"I didn't need to tell them, because as it turned out, I was not, as I thought, sent to Albania as an envoy, but as a *decoy,* to keep the Pasha occupied in attendance upon me while the British Navy moved in swiftly and took the Greek Islands from the French."

"And you did not know?"

"No! We thought we were being sent there as British diplomats, nothing more. Hobhouse and I knew nothing about it until we got back to Preveza. If Ali Pasha had got wind of what was going on behind his back, Hobhouse and I would have been killed on the spot."

Teresa shuddered at the thought. "No more talk of war or politics. Let us content ourselves complaining about this heat."

Byron suddenly grinned. "Can you imagine if Fanny Sylvestrini was here with us now? She would complain every hour about the heat, as if Italy was the only country in the world to endure strong sunshine."

"I do sometimes miss her though," Teresa said, and wondered how Fanny was getting on in Venice.

"Or *who* is she is fooling and blackmailing now?" Byron said cynically.

Day after day at Montenero was spent bathing in the cool of the blue sea and its white waves, causing Byron to say that Teresa now looked more like a mermaid, because her golden hair no longer fell in ringlets, but was long and sleek.

Their favourite times were the evenings, when the sun sank beneath the waves and they were able to go up and inhale the cool air under the great awning of the terrace. There, in the glow of the starry sky or the soft moonlight, they spent long hours taking in the Mediterranean breezes, which wafted up the sweet fragrances of the roses and Spanish jasmines and a thousand other scents from the flower beds.

One evening they played a round of draughts on the terrace, until Teresa noticed that Byron was teasingly moving his counter in the wrong direction, in order to lose."

"You are cheating!"

"I'm not a board player," Byron grinned, and Teresa knew that to lose was what he wanted, because the loser's penalty was a kiss from the winner.

"And a proper kiss now," he insisted, "not an Italian peck on the face."

Laughing, she told him that people were right to call him the head of the Romantic school, since he broke every single rule, even in a game.

Byron shrugged, preferring instead to watch the little fishing boats in the bay.

She passed the draughtsboard on to Fletcher and Tita, who began to play non-stop, gambling on each game for a small amount of money.

"Draughts is an *English* game," Fletcher said. "You'll not beat me, Tita. So ask yourself – can you *afford* to play me?"

"I will be brave and dare," Tita replied, and then won all Fletcher's money from him, laughing as he collected the coins, "It is a game we Italians *also* play!"

Fletcher threw in the towel and gave up; and now the game became more serious, because Lega sat in his place – two Italians playing against each other – and this time, for higher stakes.

Some of the other servants began to watch, betting money with each other on who would be the winner, ignoring all their usual duties.

Byron came back to the terrace carrying a bottle of wine and two glasses. "We are truly alone here," he said to Teresa. "They are all so busy gambling they have forgotten we exist."

Teresa was standing by the rail, gazing across the harbour towards the flickering lights of Pisa in the distance.

"Do you think," she said, "that they will allow Papa to go home to Ravenna?"

The following day she received a letter, and the news from her father was frustrating:

I am still in Florence waiting for a judgement. The lawyer Lorenzo Collini is making lively representations for us – but nothing, nothing is happening. My only wish is for your sea-bathing to finish peacefully. But when governments issue decrees, they do not allow for either the situations that private individuals are in, nor their interests, nor their health, nor any of the reasons that private people consider to be important.

These uncertainties have beaten me. Let Fate decide. I'm prepared for anything. I'm staying on in Florence, but without a residence permit. So I am at the government's disposal, and waiting for a decision, and then will settle on a course of action for ourselves.

Poor Teresa, how sorry I should be if you had to interrupt your sea-bathing, which has been such a comfort to you lately.

Poor Byron, how weary he must be of all these uncertainties.

"All this time they have kept them waiting and waiting," she said.

Byron, once again, voiced his idea that the best for all would be to emigrate to a younger world, a world that might be less corrupt than this one.

"Europe is the old world now," he said. "It is fraying at the edges, and all of its kings and rulers care only for their own welfare and not the welfare of their people."

"Papa would not leave," Teresa said. "In all the world, he would live nowhere but Italy; because here is where his children are."

Their conversation was interrupted by a messenger at the door of the villa, bringing a special despatch for Lord Byron, with instructions to await a reply.

Four miles away in Leghorn, an American Squadron of two battleships was currently anchored in the harbour; and the despatch now delivered was from the Commodore of the *Constitution,* written in the most flattering terms, expressing the surprise of himself and his officers on hearing that Lord Byron was also in the area, and inviting him to pay a visit to his squadron.

Astonished, yet delighted, Byron instantly wrote his reply, accepting the invitation, stating he would arrive at noon on the following day.

Teresa was equally surprised. "You intend to go?"

Byron nodded. "You may think me strange, but I would rather have a nod from an American, than a snuff-box from an emperor."

"But is Britain not at war with the Americans?"

"They were in 1812, but that all ended a few years ago, because the Americans won – *again.* I suppose now that they have proved their ships are superior to ours, and Britain has given up trying to seize their ships in the Atlantic, the Americans are now more disposed to be friendly to us."

"But why invite *you*?" Teresa asked.

"I have no idea. There are other English nobles here in Leghorn. Perhaps they have invited us all."

The following day Byron was escorted to the American squadron solely by Tita, who was dressed in his best red velvet sleeveless coat, white shirt with voluminous sleeves, the usual wide belt around his waist containing pistols, dagger and sword – but there was no need for any of those weapons.

On boarding the Constitution, a sovereign could not have been welcomed with greater honour or more ceremony than the reception given to Lord Byron by the Americans. Caught unaware, and extremely moved, Byron could see that their reception of him was spontaneous and sincere.

The few Americans who happened to be in Leghorn had also been allowed to board the ship, after pestering the officers, all asking to be introduced to Lord Byron.

"It is a tribute to your genius," Captain Isaac Chauncey told him, showing Byron an American edition of his poetry, "and because you have always resisted the hypocrisy and cant of the ruling English clique in your own country, and shown yourself to be a friend to America."

Byron knew, that as a British Peer, the newspaper reports of his boarding the *Constitution* would cause a great scandal of reprobation in England, but he cared as little about that as he did for all other rumours and scandals about himself.

Commodore Jacob Jones then appeared, greeted his lordship warmly, and took him on a ceremonious tour of the ship.

"I was received with all kindness – and with more 'ceremony' than I would have wished for."

During his tour, one of the sailors' wives proudly showed Byron her tiny son who had been born aboard the ship. "So," she said smiling, "we have named him 'Constitution Jones'."

"A strong name," Byron smiled, and surprised the young mother by placing a gold sovereign inside the baby's small fist.

The Commodore then took him aboard the neighbouring ship, *Ontario,* where the reception was as friendly and as warm.

Seeing that Lord Byron's manner was easy and cheerful, and not at all the gloomy silent person so often described in articles about him, a young American lady – as Byron was about to take his leave of the ship – suddenly moved forward and asked him for the red rose which he wore in his lapel ... the rose which Teresa had put in his buttonhole that morning.

"For the purpose," said the American beauty, "of sending to America something which you had about you, as a memorial of today."

Byron took the rose from his lapel and gave it to her. "May I ask your name?"

"Mrs Catherine Potter Stith, of Philadelphia."

"Smith?"

"No, *Stith*. Lord Byron our home in is filled with your poetry, and you may visit us whenever you wish. The pleasure would be all ours. Oh yes, indeed!"

She was not given the chance to say anything more, due to some of the other ladies surrounding her and asking for a petal from the rose – and she graciously pulled off two or three petals and gave them to her friends, while many of the officers approached to ask him questions.

Although he appeared calm and cheerful, Byron was very moved, and somewhat over-awed by the friendliness of these American sea-heroes, so that when the Commodore made one last request of him, he was unable to refuse.

"We have an artist on board, a Mr Edward West, and we were thinking it would be a fine thing if you would allow Mr West to paint your portrait for us to take away with us?"

Byron blinked. "But are you not leaving this port in a few days?"

Commodore Jones grinned. "It would be a watercolour, and Mr West knows how to draw and paint quite fast."

Returning to the Villa Rossa in Montenero, Byron was thoughtful.

"Is it not singular," he said to Teresa, "that at the same time as my daughter Ada is prevented from seeing her father's portrait for many years, the individuals of a nation not remarkable for their liking for the English in particular – nor for flattering men in general – request me to sit for my portrait?"

The next afternoon in the Villa Rossa, Lord Byron proved to be even more of a surprise to Edward West, for instead of sitting still and serious as most people did when being painted, Byron chatted away easily, wanting to know everything about America, plying him with questions about Washington Irving, whose *'Knickerbocker's History Of New York'* had delighted him.

The final portrait was a disappointment. "It looks nothing like me," Byron said; and Teresa agreed; but knew the reason why.

"You have painted him from the side, and not full on the face, where the magic is."

Yet, despite all this, the mood remained good-humoured throughout; with Byron telling West that every portrait painted of him, had always been greeted with disapproval by his friends.

The poet and the painter parted a few days later, the best of friends; and upon his return to Kentucky, Edward West wrote of his unforgettable meeting with Lord Byron.

My reverence for Lord Byron's genius made me almost afraid to encounter him. I expected to see a person with a stern countenance and lofty and reserved manners. I was much surprised to find almost the reverse. His manners were almost without ceremony.

On the day appointed, I arrived at the Villa Rossa at two o'clock, and began the picture. I found him a bad sitter. He talked all the time, asking a multitude of questions about America – and how I liked Italy, and what I thought of the Italians, &c. "The young men of Italy," he said, "are in a fair way. They long for liberty; let them secure that, and afterwards study politics and learn how to govern."

Our first sitting terminated, and I returned to Leghorn, scarcely able to persuade myself that this was the haughty misanthrope, whose character had always appeared enveloped in gloom and mystery: for I do not remember ever to have met with manners more gentle and attractive.

The next day I returned – he always kindly sent a carriage to Leghorn to bring me – and we had another sitting. Whilst I was painting, the window from which I received my light became suddenly darkened, and I heard a voice exclaim, "è troppo bello!"

I turned and discovered a beautiful female stooping down to look in, the ground on the outside being on a level with the bottom of the window Her long golden hair hung down about her face and shoulders, her complexion was exquisite, and her smile completed one of the most romantic-looking heads which I had ever beheld, set off as it was by the bright sun behind it.

Lord Byron invited her to come in, and introduced her to me as Countess Teresa Gamba Guiccioli. He seemed very fond of her, and I was glad of her presence, for the playful manner which he assumed towards her made him a much better sitter.

The next day, I was pleased to find that the progress I had made in his likeness gave satisfaction, for, when we were alone, he said that he had a particular favour to request of me – would I grant it? I said I would be happy to oblige him; and he enjoined to me the flattering task of painting her portrait for him. On the following morning I began it, and, after that, they sat alternately. He gave me the whole history of his connection with her, and said that he hoped it would last for ever. At any rate, it would not be his fault if it did not.

I was by this time sufficiently intimate with him to answer his question as to what I thought of him before I had seen him. He laughed much at the idea which I had formed of him, and said, "Well, now you find me like other people, do you not?"

In one of our conversations at the dinner table, at which we always sat by ourselves, he wished to know who was the favourite poet of the Americans. I told him that he himself was, but he seemed to think that I meant to compliment him. So on the following day I brought him from Leghorn an American book by the authoress, Miss Frances Wright – a staunch feminine fighter for the emancipation of slaves. In turning the pages over, shortly afterwards, he came to a passage wherein it was stated, "Lord Byron is the favourite poet of the Americans." He pointed to it, saying with some surprise, "I see you were not flattering me."

He then added more seriously that though an aristocrat by birth and education, he was a firm Republican in principle. But he could never be serious for long, and turned back to his amusement of trying to hear from me some "Americanisms", for which he frequently laid traps. Once or twice he caught the words "I expect" and expressed discontent that he could never make me say, "I guess."

He showed me the fifth and sixth cantos of "Don Juan" in manuscript which he often sat up at night writing. I asked him how he created his ideas for Don

Juan, and he laughed, "It's all gin." Meaning, I presumed, that he drank gin when he wrote it. "Gin and water," he confirmed.

Upon the whole, I left with the impression that he possessed an excellent heart, which had been misconstrued on all hands from little else than a reckless flippancy of manners, in which he took a whimsical pride in opposing to those of other people.

~~~

The letters which Count Gamba sent to Teresa from Florence still failed to cast light on the mystery of why they were still kept waiting there. It seemed to Teresa to be the very shabbiness of human conduct.

Byron, on the other hand, had heard that the Tuscan government was mild in comparison to most, and fairly liberal. The delay, he suspected, was undoubtedly due to the *"Buon Governo"* standing up to Austrian pressure from Rome.

Meanwhile they had their own problems in Montenero – the July heat was becoming unbearable and the flimsy walls of the salmon-coloured Villa absorbed the heat instead of repelling it. It was too hot to go outside in the daytime, and at night they could hardly breathe, resorting to placing wet tree-branches inside and around the open windows to moisten the air.

Now all Byron could think of was the cold thick walls, the cool spacious rooms, and the marble floors of his palazzo in Pisa.

"It's time to go back to Pisa," he said. "It's too hot to stay in this flimsy shell of a place any longer
~~~

Chapter Thirty-Nine

~~~

Further up the coast, near Lerici on the Gulf of Spezia, within the house bearing the ridiculously grand name of *Villa Magni,* Mary Shelley was sitting on the veranda with Jane Williams, and both women were still furious with Edward Trelawny for taking this house in Shelley's name.

Trelawny had said it was just the sort of simple summer place that Shelley and Mary would love – a peaceful paradise away from the noise of the city, placed between two quaint fishing villages.

Mary turned to Jane Williams. "Byron was right, when he said that Trelawny was incapable of *telling the truth* about anything."

Jane agreed; for she too had been constantly miserable here. The house was devoid of every comfort. It was barely habitable, and as solitary and as a wild as a desert island in Oceania.

Although backed by a steep hill, the house hung over the breakers, which battered it night and day when the breakers were raging. There were no roads of any kind that led toward a civilised place, apart from a rough footpath to Lerici. So it was much more like a sorry old boat, than a holiday villa.

"Had we been wrecked on an island in the South Seas," Mary Shelley wrote, *"we could scarcely have found ourselves further from civilization."*

"But no matter, we will manage," Shelley had decided cheerfully, and so they had managed to live like the poorest peasants in a hovel of no comfort.

Only little Percy Florence was enjoying himself, playing on the sands and attempting to build a sand-horse.

In the evenings Shelley would often go off and seek inspiration for his poetry from the secrets of the caves
~~~

that pierced the side of the crags along the bay of La Spezia. And having nothing else to do, Edward Williams usually accompanied him, both men coming back to the veranda, delighted with some of their finds like two excited boys – strange-coloured stones and odd-shaped glittering rocks.

"Perhaps we have found gold," Williams wondered.

Neither of their wives shared their bliss, but not wishing to cast a shadow on their fun, put up with the meagre comfort of the house and beach and their conversations with each other; but their unhappiness was often visible. Both women were counting the days and weeks until they could return to their apartments in Pisa.

To improve the situation and provide some fun for their women as well as themselves, Shelley and Edward Williams came up with the idea of buying a boat, which they would name the *Don Juan*.

"Mary, just imagine it!" Shelley exclaimed. "All of us in our boat speeding over the billows with a swelling sail. We could sail around the Gulf, explore the Italian coastline, and visit the neighbouring areas."

The two men were in raptures at the very idea, while the women pretended likewise – although both agreed that any kind of diversion would be a treat.

So the men had gone down to Leghorn to get the boat, but had not yet returned.

"I'll wager that those two rascals have stopped off to see Byron and show off their boat," Jane Williams said; but Mary's thoughts were dark and anxious. A squall was blowing up, and she feared for Shelley on the rough waters.

"Unlike your Edward," she said to Jane, "my Shelley cannot swim."

When the night of the third day came, and the men had still had not returned, a mysterious voice seemed to be warning Mary that a calamity lay ahead. Everything about this place was strange, even the fisher people seemed to her to be too silent and unfriendly on the rare occasions they had met one of them.

And in this deserted place too, Mary knew that Shelley had not been as happy as he had pretended. Once here, after the first few days, he had started taking laudanum every night to help him sleep.

Mary did not know if it was their life of solemn seclusion, living on land and seeing only the sea, and visited by fleeting but frequent hot squalls, and often immersed in the meditations of his books, that had caused some odd behaviour in Shelley – but no, it was the nightly use of laudanum, she was sure of it.

She remembered one afternoon, Shelley talking and strolling along the veranda with Williams, when he stood stock still, suddenly gripping his friend's arm, while staring at the white foam of the sea as it broke along the seashore.

Seeing him staring in such a transfixed way at the sea, Mary had asked Shelley if he was feeling unwell, but his only answer was, "There she is again! There she is!"

He could not take his eyes away from the foaming waves, as if he was in some ecstatic trance, and only when he was snapped out of it, did Shelley explain what he had seen.

He declared that, as clearly as he was seeing Mary, he had seen little Allegra Byron rising upright over the sea; she was clapping her hands as if in glee, and smiling at him full of joy, inviting him to join her.

"How?" Mary had asked him. "How could a person like you, Shelley, who does not believe in the immortality of the soul, believe you have just seen Allegra?"

Shelley did not know. He could not explain it, even to himself. "I know she is dead, but in the water there, she was alive and full of joy."

The more Mary thought about that strange incident, and the longer the hours passed without the men returning, Mary knew she now needed the comfort and reassurance of only one person – Albè.

"He will know what to do?" she told Jane. "He knows

Shelley as well as any of us. And no one knows how to comfort a sorrowing heart as Albè does. He does not argue, he does not harangue, but you can see in his eyes that he feels true compassion and willingness to help. I must go to him."

She went to rouse their servant who was also the driver of their little carriage.

Jane was not so sure. "Now that you mention Byron – for all we know, Shelley and Edward could have decided to call in on Byron on their way back from Leghorn. It is so near to Pisa. The two of them could be sitting in Byron's drawing-room at this minute, full of talk about their boat."

"We don't know that, we *cannot* know that," Mary said impatiently. "All we know for sure is that the third night has come, and our two voyagers have not."

In the Palazzo Lanfranchi, Byron was back at his desk, writing as rapidly as always. They had all left the Villa Rossa and returned to Pisa three days earlier, and were now enjoying the comfort and coolness of its rooms.

Teresa wandered in and sat down on one of the sofas asking, "Will it bother you if I sit here reading my book?"

He shook his head. "No," he said with a smile, "I usually prefer to be alone, but I believe I can write even better when I see you sitting there before me."

Teresa was soon lost in Madame de Staël's book, *Corinne*, engrossed in the sad romance of it. It was after midnight, but she was not tired, and at such an hour the streets behind her were so silent, that the only sound she could hear was Byron's pen scratching across the paper.

Teresa looked up, thinking she had heard a carriage pulling up at the door of the palazzo. She looked at Byron, but his head was bent over his work as if he had not heard anything.

Moments later there was a loud and repeated knocking on the brass knocker of the front door. Teresa ran to the open window and leaned over to look down into the darkness.

"*Che è?*" – Who is it?

"It's me – it's Mary Shelley," an agitated voice replied. "Do please open up – I need to talk to you."

Teresa turned her head and looked at Byron, who immediately jumped up and rushed out to the landing and the staircase.

Moments later when he brought Mrs Shelley into the room, Teresa was shocked at the sight of her. She looked a wraith, her natural pallor was even paler from the weakness of physical fatigue, her eyes dark with worry. Normally so composed, she was overcome by great tension.

"Where is Shelley?" she asked Byron. "We're looking for him. Do you know where he is?"

Byron was also pale, fearing some misfortune, but he could not give Mary any information. As far as he knew, Shelley was at La Spezia, but he encouraged her to cease fretting, as she was probably worrying for nothing.

"So where is Trelawny?" Byron asked. "Was he not staying with you?"

"Oh, he went off somewhere else after a few days. The last I heard, he was at Leghorn, looking after *your* boat there."

"Looking after *my* boat?" Byron said, surprised. "It is not yet completed and I have never used it. But knowing Trelawny, he is probably *living* in it."

"Perhaps Shelley and Williams are with him?" Mary wondered, and then left the house to go to Leghorn.

Byron escorted her down to the street. "Remember, my boat is named the *Bolivar*," he told her. "When you find it, you will most likely find Shelley and Williams talking and laughing in the cabin with Trelawny."

He assisted Mary into the carriage where Jane Williams awaited her, and together they hastened in the direction of Leghorn to find Trelawny

During the next few days, Edward Trelawny set out to

be a lifesaver, sailing along the coast in Byron's boat, the *Bolivar,* which he insisted was now finished and fit for sail.

Byron often accompanied him in the search, and found Trelawny to be a remarkable and capable sailor, handling the boat like an experienced seaman; and his dedication to trying to find the two friends inspired in Byron a new liking for Trelawny.

"I'll wager," Trelawny said, "that their little boat went adrift in one of the squalls at some deserted place along the coast, and now the two of them are sitting on the rocks waiting for someone to come and rescue them."

Byron sincerely hoped so.

Mary and Jane had returned to the *Villa Magni,* for there young Percy Florence had been left in the care of the nursemaid who was also caring for Jane's two small children..

Mary did her best to take care of her little son; keeping all worries from him, and relieved that his only interest seemed to be in completing the sculpture of his sand-horse.

Yet every day was a day of turmoil and uncertainty for the two wives; and the nights were nights of long hours of fear when the oblivion of sleep would not come to refresh and strengthen the mind and the body.

Mary rose from her bed one night and wrote in her journal:

> *The sea, by its restless moaning, seems to want to inform us of what we do not wish to learn. If ever fate whispered of coming disaster, such inaudible, but not unfelt, prognostics hover around us. The distance from all signs of civilisation – the sea at our feet, its murmurs or its roaring forever in our ears – all these things lead the mind to brood over strange thoughts, and, lifting it from every-day*

life, causes it to be familiar with the unreal. A sort of spell surrounds us; and each day that the voyagers do not return, we grow more restless and disquieted.

After eight long days, the drowned bodies of Percy Bysshe Shelley and Edward Williams were finally found on a deserted stretch of wasteland beyond Lerici, where the sea had finally thrown them up to lay on the sand.

Mary Shelley let out a scream that pierced through the air like a hawk screeching in the sky.

Chapter Forty

~ ~ ~

Due to the fact that both bodies were decomposed and not fully intact, and due to Italy's strict sanitary laws, the bodies were not allowed to be buried, but had to be cremated on the beach where they lay.

And in Italy, as in England, women were prohibited from being present at funerals, in order to protect their delicate hearts and minds.

Yet, standing out of sight, on the brow of a small hill, behind a few curious locals, Mary Shelley stood and watched as her beloved Shelley's body burned on its pyre of flaming wood.

It was a solitary little affair on the beach, with only two Italian soldiers in attendance to ensure the cremation was carried out, and both were now standing some distance from the burning flames.

Mary stood observing the scene as if it was not real, noticing small details that were really not important. The two mourners, Lord Byron and Edward Trelawny, were stood away from the soldiers, nearer to the pyre, and Mary noticed that although Trelawny was dressed in his usual dishevelled clothes, Byron had dressed in a black frock-coat and grey trousers and black polished shoes, looking very respectable indeed – but Mary knew that it was *he* who was showing respect – respect to a fellow gentleman, friend, and brother poet – to Shelley.

Byron had also assisted in the disinterment of Shelley's body which been had been briefly buried overnight in the sand for protection. He had also brought with him all the necessary materials for such events, which Teresa had hurriedly procured for him.

The funeral pyre was sprinkled with incense, wine, oil, and salt, and when more oil had been added, the flames grew stronger and she saw Byron stand in silence in front of the red-hot furnace on the burning sand;

saddened but steadfast, while her own tears flowed.

It takes hours for a body to burn. Byron could feel the heat of the fire as well as the sun burning relentlessly down on his uncovered head, but fought off the nausea from the smells of the incense and burning wood by occupying his mind in reflecting on what had led to this disaster.

Did the boat capsize in a squall, or from faulty seamanship? Did they try to save themselves? Williams probably did, because he was a strong swimmer, and was found with his boots missing. As for Shelley, assuredly *not,* because as a non-swimmer it was neither in his power, nor in his character.

Byron's mind went back to his tour of Lake Leman with Shelley in Switzerland, when their boat had nearly overturned in a storm. A string swimmer, he had whipped off his coat in readiness to swim and try and save them both, but Shelley refused to move, sitting on a locker and gripping both ends with his hands, insisting that if he was to die here, he would do so with courage.

Had Shelley done the same when Williams had whipped off his boots? Did the answer really matter now? Shelley was gone, and gone for ever.

Under the scorching sun, the heat of the fire was now so intense, and the smoke from the burning wood so thick, Byron's vision became tremulous and wavy, and in spite of his determination and strength of will, the sorrow and nausea were now rising up in him so strong, so overwhelming, he suddenly turned and ran into the sea, swimming fully-clothed towards his schooner which was anchored further out. On reaching the small ladder of the *Bolivar* he clung on to it, and then was violently sick.

Later that night, in his bedroom at a small inn on the road to Genoa, Byron took out his writing case and wrote letter after furious letter to John Murray, Hobhouse, and others who had warned him against becoming too friendly with a notorious atheist and half-madman such as Shelley.

"You were all brutally wrong about Shelley, who was, without exception, the <u>best</u>, and the least selfish man I ever knew. You do not know how mild – how tolerant – how good he was in Society – and as perfect a gentleman that ever crossed a drawing-room; – when he liked – and where he liked.

And then, in a calmer but more cynical mood, he wrote to another friend and poet, Thomas Moore:

"Thus, is another man gone, about whom the world was ill-naturedly, ignorantly, and brutally mistaken. Perhaps the world will do him justice <u>now</u> – when he can be no better for it."

~~~

The next morning they returned to the beach at Lerici, for now it was poor Edward Williams' turn to be removed from his cover and cremated; and the same process that had been used for Shelley was now enacted for Williams.

A small hut had been erected at the back of the beach, built of pine-tree stems and wattled with their branches, which served to keep out the sun and rain from the lookout man on duty, who had kept guard over the body through the previous evening and night.

The two soldiers were still in attendance, but Jane Williams, who was not as strong-hearted as Mary Shelley, did not attempt to hide herself on the brow of the hill. Broken-hearted, she could not bear to see what was painful to see, and was unable to face the awfulness of it

Once again the pyre burned, as did the sun above, even hotter than the previous day.

Trelawny stood beside Byron, both silent with heads bowed. Neither man had known Williams as well as they
~~~

had known Shelley, but they had liked him.

Byron suddenly remembered, and asked Trelawny, "Where is Thomas Medwin? Did he not go to Spezia with them?"

Trelawny shook his head. "No, Medwin went off instead to try and see some young lady he had met in Geneva. Poor man ... he probably still doesn't know what has happened to his friends."

After another long silence, Trelawny spoke again. "I know Shelley did not believe in any religion, and neither do I, but I don't know about Williams. Do you suppose we should try and say some prayers over him?"

Byron nodded, but then he remained silent and thoughtful, causing Trelawny to think that his lordship must be leaving the saying of the prayers to him.

A moment later Trelawny raised his arms and launched into a series of long chants and strange sounds that were unintelligible.

When he finally paused to catch his breath, Byron said to him dryly, "I knew you were a Pagan, Trelawny, but not that you were a Pagan priest. You do it very well."

Chapter Forty-One

~ ~ ~

Now back in her apartment at Pisa, Mary Shelley wrote to her friend, Maria Gisborne, in Livorno – "*Lord Byron is very kind to me, and comes with the Countess Guiccioli to see me often.*"

Mary's only wish now was to return to England, but first to go to Rome. Shelley's heart had not burned, and Trelawny had managed to lift it out of the carnage, along with handful of Shelley's ashes which had been placed inside one of the two urns which Lord Byron had brought with him to Lerici, to be handed at the end to the two widows.

Shelley's ashes, Mary intended to bury in Rome, in the same grave as their little son, William, who had died in Rome in 1819 from Typhus fever. But Shelley's heart, she had placed into a small velvet bag, and that heart of her beloved, she would keep cherished until the day she herself died.

Inside the Palazzo Lanfranchi, Byron was facing a new disaster. The Gambas had *not* been given permission by the "*Buon Governo*" of Tuscany to return to Ravenna, but had been given new papers deporting them out of Pisa.

"We have been given four days to vacate," Pietro said. "Four days."

"But why?" Byron asked. "Did they give you a reason?"

Count Gamba sighed tiredly, and then sat back in his armchair." We are told it is a little game the Austrians like to play with suspected members of the Carboneiri," Ruggero said. "They allow them to move to one place, but once they have settled, they like to uproot them and move them on again – that is their torture."

Furious, Byron personally visited the government

offices in Pisa the next day, to remonstrate with the officials about Tuscany's shameful and *inhuman* treatment of the Gambas. If they were forced to leave Pisa, then he would leave also.

He was assured that the Government of Pisa fervently wished to retain Lord Byron in its city, where he had made himself at home ... but the Gambas must go.

"Where? Go *where?* What place can they safely go without being moved on again? The only place I can think of is Ravenna!"

No, they could not return to Ravenna or any part of Romagna, but Lord Byron must be assured and reassured that the government of Pisa would now do its best to help him.

"Not me – the Gamba family!"

Two days later Count Gamba received a Notice allowing him to reside in Lucca, some twenty miles outside the jurisdiction of Pisa's government.

A short distance, but what a place!

"Lucca," Count Gamba told Byron, "is a little state which calls itself independent, but is simply a feudal vassal of Tuscany, and Tuscany is held in fee by Austria. Anything that happens in Tuscany, echoes in Lucca."

"So what are you to do?" asked Byron, who, in the two months from Allegra's death to Shelley's death, had lost a lot of weight and was now looking very pale and quite unwell.

Ruggero and Pietro noticed this, and held back from causing him any more difficulties.

"But we shall go there and make the best of it," Ruggero said.

Pietro agreed. "It will not be hard for us to live in Lucca, if only up to the winter."

"And in the meantime," said Ruggero, "we will continue our requests to be recalled to Ravenna. It could happen – God is good."

These last words from Ruggero, gave Byron an idea. In all of the six weeks he had remained in Ravenna himself, the Austrians had made various attempts to try to hurry him, but the Legate of Ravenna, Cardinal Rusconi, had always interfered to prevent them.

Also, members of the secret *Sanfedisti,* who hated all heretics and revolutionaries and worshipped Rome, had placed numerous notices around the town, offering a financial reward to anyone who succeeded in the assassination of the Inglese Lord Byron. The assassin's identity would be kept secret under oath.

In response, he had taken the precaution of arming all his servants, but his biggest defenders were the *priests* – going around the town and ripping down the notices, as well as threatening "Hell and Damnation" from the pulpit to anyone who dared to commit such a mortal sin.

Cardinal Rusconi had threatened worse – *excommunication* from the Catholic Church – never again to be allowed inside its doors or to receive any of its sacraments. A threat even more fearful than Hell and Damnation, because who could *live* in Italy and not be a Catholic? Not receive Holy Communion? Not to be allowed to have their sisters or daughters married in the church – which meant no marriage at all.

All of this had been told to him by Count Alborghetti. And now he decided that he would no longer write to *people of influence* here, there, and everywhere on behalf of the Gambas, asking for their intercessions, but to the *religious* ruler of Ravenna himself, who – if he remembered correctly – was also a long-standing personal friend of Ruggero.

So why not appeal directly to *his* heart, and *his* power? Or was Ruggero too proud to do so?

Byron and the Cardinal had shook hands and parted as friends, so what harm now, in a little friendly correspondence?

My Dear Most Eminent Cardinal Rusconi ...

~~~

Count Gamba and Pietro moved to Lucca, but Teresa
~~~

was allowed to stay at the Palazzo Lanfranchi to care for Byron, who had now taken to his bed due to illness.

"*You* can't look after him," Fletcher indignantly told Teresa. "That's my job."

"But can I not help?"

"No, because there is nothing to help. I run this household like a Swiss clock, and you would just be the cuckoo popping in and out."

"But if Mylord is ill — "

"He is *not* ill. I know what's wrong with him – underneath those smiles he is melancholy and *depressed,* that's all. He just needs time alone to think himself out of it."

Teresa sat silent, not knowing what to say next. Was Fletcher jealous of her presence here?

Fletcher looked at her, and then seemed to relent, saying more kindly, "You have to understand ... when your daughter and friend are taken from you in a flash by sudden death, it can sink the ground from under you, and make you think about the uncertainty of life.

Teresa knew that was true. She nodded, "My mother and sister died suddenly, one after the other."

"Did they? Oh I'm very sorry to hear that." Fletcher genuinely did look sorry. "So you don't need me snapping at you like an old sour-puss. Will I get a nice cup of tea sent up to you?"

Teresa shook her head, smiling slightly, because now she knew that Fletcher was *not* jealous of her presence, but simply worried about his lordship.

"His lordship received a sharp shock when Allegra died, and an even sharper shock when poor Mr Shelley was taken," Fletcher said. " I know that, because I've known my lord since he was ten years old, and looked after him since when he was sixteen. I know all his ways and his moods, so here's my advice to you, Contessa – don't you go to him – wait till he comes to you. And in the meantime, I will do all the looking after."

As she was in his house, Teresa was obedient to his word – not going to see Byron, but going for walks, or reading books, or simply sitting in the garden lost in her own thoughts.

"Does he ask about me?" she queried Fletcher one night.

Fletcher nodded. "He *always* asks about you, Contessa. So be patient. He seems less weary today, aye, a lot less weary, so he's on the mend."

A letter arrived for Teresa, from her brother Pietro. She took it out to the garden to read:

My dear Teresina — The government in Lucca treats us with the greatest courtesy, and has notified us that we can stay as long as we choose in Lucca, but they will not give us a residence permit. Why make us so many compliments, pay us such honours, and yet not give us residence permits? That is the labyrinth, but I think I have found the thread to guide me through it.

I have already told you that I thought it wasn't us they were afraid of, but Lord Byron. If he did come here, they would not have the courage to turn against him, nor find any excuse for doing so, but they fear his Carbonari connections, his liberal views, and they fear the Austrians. But they dare not go against Lord Byron."

Teresa could not comprehend how anyone could fear Byron, or why. The revolution had failed. Another revolution in Italy would not happen again for a very long time ... although the fire in the blood of those young men of the *Young Italy* movement would never be quenched – not as long as the Austrian boot remained on their necks.

The following day she received another letter from Pietro.

Dear T – Last night Mansi, the Minister, announced

to us in semi-diplomatic terms, that without any question, we shall be able to stay out in the countryside of Lucca. We gathered, however, that that they would be very sorry to make Lord Byron suspect their fears – and would be very sorry if Lord Byron had the same idea about them as they know us to have. Yet it seems to me that they still look uneasy, which must be due to a conflict of attitudes with the Austrians, and some bewilderment of their own about it all.

However, Papa does not wish to give up hope of returning to Pisa or even Ravenna, so he advises you to stay there for the time being.

As much as she loved her brother, Teresa was now feeling very annoyed with Pietro. All this talk – as if their suffering was all due to Lord Byron? Had it not occurred to Pietro, as she was sure it must have occurred to their father, that the only reason that *they* – as proven Carboneiri – were *not* in prison yet, like so many others, was because of their close association with Lord Byron and the *protection* his name and noble rank gave to them? Not with the Austrians, but certainly with the Italians.

No wonder the officials in Lucca would be very sorry if Lord Byron had the same idea as ... Byron was coming across the garden towards her – she quickly turned her back to him, pretending to be inspecting a rose – while pushing Pietro's letter down inside her bodice.

"I have nearly four new cantos of *Don Juan* ready," he said, sitting down in a chair beside her, "and as you are now the strict censor of my morals, I can assure you they are immaculate."

She stared at him. "You were supposed to be ill. Fletcher did not say you have been writing."

"Probably because I have been writing in the middle

of the night, when he is asleep. It's the only peace I get from all his fussing."

"So you have *not* been ill?"

"On the contrary, I have *not* been well."

"So why sit up writing in the night?"

He smiled and shrugged. "It's just my way, I can't help it."

Once that had been settled, they carried on in their normal way, talking of this and that; of life and past experiences, but none of it sad, and Teresa made sure to kept their conversation bright and cheerful.

He was smiling as she told him about some comic scenes that had occurred during her schooling in the convent at Faenza.

"There was a carnival, and several of the young ladies dressed up as young men, using their brothers' costumes. The other girls, who did not know of their disguise, followed them everywhere at the carnival, and refused to dance with anyone but them – and some even fell in love and *kissed* their partners, not knowing they were kissing other girls. Oh, the alarm of the nuns! After that, all masculine disguise was banned."

Byron was still smiling. "You have told me about that before."

"Have I?" Teresa was certain she had not. "Are you sure?"

"Very sure, because I used all that you told me in a canto of *Don Juan,* but I reversed it, and changed the carnival into a harem – added, of course, with some experiences of my own."

"Oh, you *demon!"* Teresa laughed. "Now I will be very careful what I tell you."

Later that afternoon they went horse-riding together, when Teresa proved to be as bad on a horse as she had always been. Fortunately the groom had come along, and she had been rescued from falling on her head more than once.

"Never again!" Byron said to Fletcher when they got back. "She needs to be kept away from horses, if only to prevent the torture and terror she inflicts on the poor animals. One minute she's half falling over the horse's head, and the next she's sliding down his back end."

He pulled off his black cravat. "And the poor groom! He spent more time on his feet than on his horse, trying to catch her before any damage was done."

Teresa, in the following days, took his advice and allowed him to go riding in future with the men only, saying haughtily: "I prefer a horse that has a carriage attached to it. It's so much easier."

"For the horse, yes!"

In a carriage, a few days later, they travelled out to Lucca, only to be dismayed to find that the house which the Gambas were living in was not good nor comfortable, but small and cramped.

"What can we do?" Count Gamba said despairingly. "No one wants to rent to us, because we do not have a residence permit, and the Austrians won't let them give us a permit."

Byron thought it all scandalous as he looked sympathetically at Ruggero ... Here was a man, an Italian nobleman, who had been taught and studied in the highest institutions of education in Rome and Parma, who owned a vast and beautiful estate in Filetto, as well as a neighbouring townhouse in Ravenna – and now, because he had raised his hand and voice in the call for his country's freedom from the tyranny of Austria, he was being treated like a fool, and reduced to the life of a beggar.

Even his bank accounts had been stopped, so that neither he nor his relative, the Marquis Cavalli, could withdraw any funds. The iron hand indeed!

Byron left Teresa to talk with her family while he paced around the small garden, deep in practical thought. His bond to this family was strong – stronger than any bond he may have felt during the short year he had lived with his former wife. Even Pietro now regularly referred to him as his *"cognato"* – the Italian term for a "brother-in-law".

He loved this Gamba family, every one of them, and he was not going to allow this humiliation of their dignity to continue.

Returning to the small and dark parlour, Count Gamba was making it clear to Teresa that it was the intrigues of the Austrians that were making any hope of their return to Pisa impossible.

"May I make a suggestion," Byron said. "Why don't we all abandon Tuscany and move to Genoa where Austria is no longer in control of that province?"

"Genoa?" Ruggero sat up, alert. "No Austrian control, it is true, but they say the government is a despotic one and ruled by the priests."

"*No* government is more despotic than those controlled by Austria, which Genoa is not. It has to be better than Tuscany or anywhere else, outside of Ravenna."

Ruggero was thinking about it. "Well, they say Genoa is very beautiful ... people I know who have been there refer to it as *la Superba* ..." He looked curiously at Byron. "Why do you think of Genoa? You have not spoke of it before. Have you been there?"

"No, but yesterday I received a packet from an old friend of mine, Mr William Hill. I had met him in Venice and dined with him. A fine and solid man. In the packet he sent to me was a copy of *The Corsair,* which he begged me to sign as a gift for his son, and then return to him."

"Ah ..." Ruggero now understood. "So you know somebody in Genoa who may help us?"

"I am sure he *will* help us, and he has the power to do so, because he is not only an Englishman, he is also the British Minister in Genoa."

"*Mio Dio!*" Count Gamba stared. "Why did you not speak of this friend in Genoa before?"

Byron sat down. "I met a lot of people in Venice, most of whom I have forgotten, including Mr William Noel Hill, who, until yesterday, when his packet arrived, I had no reason to remember him."

Pietro said, "Genoa is a rich city. The expense of living there — "

"Would be no problem," Byron said. "Not if you all were to reside with me – as one family."

Ruggero looked at Teresa's delighted expression, and then he looked again in amazement at Byron.

"On separate floors, of course," Byron quickly added, "but within the one palazzo. Allow me to at least write to Mr Hill, and see what he says about our possible reception there? Would we be welcome, or would we not?"

Count Gamba had not expected any of this – Lord Byron readily throwing his destiny in with theirs – but it was a welcome ray of hope that they might be able to live in one place, in peace, without being shuffled on again.

He said: "When you write to Signor Hill, will you tell him of our connection with the Carbonari and the reason for our banishment from Ravenna?"

Byron reflected ..."I think I must tell him. But it is a confidence I shall entrust solely to him, and then allow him to decide. To go there, it would be better to know we would be on sound footing, and not on unstable ground."

The mail-coach between the cities of Pisa and Genoa was quite frequent, and within a week Byron had received a reply from the British Minister in Genoa, and the wording of the letter was as fine and solid as Mr Hill himself.

Byron did not even wait to tell Teresa, who was having a siesta, before riding out to Lucca to read the letter to the Gambas.

"So soon?" Ruggero exclaimed. "You have received a reply so soon?"

Byron explained that Mr Hill had lost no time in inviting him to come and establish himself in Genoa, assuring him that if the family of Lord Byron's friends were willing to place themselves under his protection, then he would be delighted to grant it to them against the tyranny of Turin and Rome, especially if that family were to dwell under the same roof as Lord Byron.

Count Gamba had tears in his eyes as he embraced his friend. "*Grazie,*" he said, "*Grazie.* You are a good friend. And Signor Hill sounds to be, as you say, a fine man."

Teresa's grandfather, old Count Paulo, who never interrupted but always listened when he was present, suddenly spoke up, his sincere words in the softest Italian: "In my youth," he said, "I had not much liking for the Inglese, but now I know my impressions were false. All are not the same. In all nations there are good and bad, but to you, Mylord Byron, I beg your pardon. *Mi perdonerai?*"

"*Ti perdono,*" Byron answered with a smile, because there was really nothing to forgive. If Count Paulo had disliked him because he was English, he had never shown it, but then he was such a quiet and dignified gentleman.

"Now you, Pietro," Byron said, "you must be the one to go up to Genoa and find a suitable casa for us. You know what I like, and what you Gambas like. And pray take the house in my name, as Mr Hill suggested."

It was a task Pietro was very happy to carry out.

But then, on leaving, Byron paused at the door, saying to Pietro, "Don't go up to Genoa immediately, wait a day or two, until I send you a note."

"Why?"

"I have a duty to Shelley's widow. In his will he named me as his executor. I can't leave her alone in Pisa without knowing what she intends to do now."

Mary Shelley knew exactly what she wanted to do. She wanted to take Shelley's ashes to Rome, and then return to England, but she did not have enough money to do so. Yet she refused all Byron's offers of financial aid.

"You know that Shelley would never leech off you,

and neither will I."

Byron was saddened by how *chilly* Mary had become in her manner since Shelley's death. At times it seemed she was almost half dead herself.

"I did not mean that offensively, Albè, only to let you know that I will not need it. I have written to Shelley's father, Sir Timothy, asking him to help me with financial aid to return to England. After all, Shelley was his only son and his heir, and now little Percy is his heir. So surely he will wish to support his fatherless grandchild."

Byron was relieved – the fact that she had used her pet name for him showed that her chilliness was not directed against him. Still, her situation was pitiful. Jane Williams had already taken her children back to England, and Mary was now alone.

"A reply from England could take weeks," he said. "So what will you do in the meantime?"

Mary shrugged. "In the meantime, Albè, what can I do? Except wait for Sir Timothy's reply."

Byron was not so sure. How many times had Shelley told him that his father had irrevocably disowned him. Or maybe now that Shelley was dead ...?

He told her about his intention to move to Genoa with the Gambas, and why. Pietro was being sent to look for a house, he explained, as it would take him weeks to pack up all his furniture and servants and animals.

Mary's body jerked, alarmed. "Oh, my goodness! First Shelley, then Jane, and now you? And I to lose *everyone*?"

"Why not come with us? Sir Timothy's reply can be forwarded to you in Genoa. And if you did come, it would be a great help to me."

"Go with you – to Genoa?" Mary sat thinking about it, feeling tempted and comforted at the same time. Certainly she would prefer to go with Byron and Teresa than to be left here in Pisa on her own.

"But in what way," she asked, "would I be of such a great help to you?"

"I have four new cantos of *Don Juan* ready to send to Murray, but no copyist. You know how he complains about my scrawl and then gets half the words printed wrong, so I need a good copyist. And I would not *leech* off you – I would pay you a fair rate for your work."

Mary knew him too well to be fooled, but she liked the idea of being able to work for her living. Perhaps she could even pay her own rent.

After a silence, she asked, "And if I did go with you to Genoa, would I be expected to live in the same house as you and the Gambas? I don't think that would be very sensible."

It was eventually agreed that Mary and little Percy would go with Pietro to Genoa, and rent a small house or apartment near to whatever house Pietro found for Byron.

Mary Shelley and Pietro Gamba left Pisa for Genoa on September 11th.

A few days later, on September 15th, a fine and sunny afternoon, Byron was sitting in the garden of the Palazzo Lanfranchi, his mind thoughtful, while Teresa softly played on her guitar some of the simple melodies he loved and never grew tired of hearing.

His mood was a blend of serenity and sadness, pondering over his past life, and his situation now in Italy.

"After all," he said, when she paused in her playing, "what could I have done, if I had stayed in England? I would have been forced to take part in politics, which I don't like, because it is usually self-seeking. And if I had stayed in England, I would have found myself deep in political and literary feuds – I wouldn't even have the independence to write what I think now. That world is too artificial, where one can not live to one's self, and is obliged to be too much occupied with what others think, and too little with what we think ourselves. What should I have done there? Well, worst of all, I would not have got to know you, and now I am very pleased to know you."

Teresa smiled and twanged out a few musical cheers on her guitar.

"In all sincerity," he went on, "if I had to live my life over again, I wouldn't want to change that much in it, apart from a few unhappy events – and apart from *two* associations in England. Especially the one with Lady Byron, who is getting more unpleasant every year. Do you know, I sent her a manuscript of my memoirs to read and she sent me an answer with only a remark stating she had *'Declined to Read'* As if I believe that for one second."

He sat thoughtful for a long moment, puzzlement. on his face. "It is an odd fact," he said, "but my recollection of her face is so vague now, I'm not sure if I would know her if I saw her again. Not even if she was walking toward me, or along a street in England – "

He stopped and stared ... as if staring at a ghost ... and then let out a surprised shout of delight at the sight of John Cam Hobhouse coming through the open vestibule door – "

Hobby!"

Hobhouse was now walking across the garden, grinning from ear to ear. "I decided to surprise you, and not forewarn you that I was coming."

Teresa knew that Hobhouse had been Byron's constant companion in his youth, and on all his travels, his best of all friends.

She set aside the guitar and stood to be introduced to him, but Byron was overwhelmed with such joy at seeing his old friend, it nearly robbed him of his power of speech.

"I was just talking about England," he said, tears coming to his eyes. "And here England is."

"I did not expect you to get emotional," Hobhouse quipped, "but it's as good a welcome as any, I suppose."

Byron looked at Teresa. "Do you hear that top-drawer English accent? No one but Hobby speaks like that – not even in England."

Chapter Forty-Two

~ ~ ~

Over dinner, Hobhouse's news was the usual – he always liked to pass on the bad news first. "You heard about the death of Napoleon at St Helena?"

"The whole world has heard about the death of Napoleon at St Helena."

"And the Duke of Wellington killed in a duel?"

"Yes, one of the English here told me about it."

"And Polidori? Did anyone tell you about him?"

"Polidori – what about him?"

"He committed suicide."

"What?" Byron looked at Teresa. "I've told you about John Polidori – the young physician who attended us in Geneva and wanted to shoot poor Shelley?" He looked back at Hobhouse. "Suicide?"

"Made himself a glass of poison and drank it. They say he was only twenty-six. I didn't like to tell you in a letter."

"Ah, poor Polidori ... He was such an inept clod he nearly drove me insane, but to hear this ... "

"I think it was being caught out in his plagiarism of your story about the vampyre that done for him, but others say he was heavily in debt from gambling."

"Do you know," Byron said, "I have lately had a premonition that I would hear of the death of someone I know. They say death comes in threes, and now Polidori is the third."

"Are you not counting Napoleon?"

"I didn't *know* him, only of him."

Once dinner was over, Teresa left the two friends to their conversation, and Hobhouse was glad to see her go; for now he could talk to Byron about Greece.

"The situation in Greece is very bad. So bad now, that everyone in England thinks we should step in and help the Greeks – at least the Liberals do – the Tories are too busy fighting amongst themselves."

"What about our old friend Ali Pasha? Is he still rampaging everywhere?"

"No, he is also dead."

"Dead? But that is *four* – are you sure he is dead?"

Hobhouse sat back, sighing with impatience. "Byron, you will have to get rid of all those silly Scottish superstitions from your mother. Ali Pasha is dead, because the Sultan ordered his death, and Ali's head was delivered to him in Constantinople about a month ago."

"Dear God!"

"Now you know why I could not speak of such things in front of the Contessa. I'm glad Ali Pasha is dead because he was a murdering scoundrel. And now the poor Greeks have to face murdering scoundrels equally as bad amongst the armies of the ruling Turks. What do you think Plato would say about that? Or Sophocles? Or Aristotle?"

Byron was silent for a long moment. "Here in Italy," he said, "the Italians have been speaking about the uprising in Greece ... and every time I hear that word "Greece" I can always feel my heart beating faster. As I often say, if I am a poet it was Greece that made me one. I wrote Childe Harold in Greece."

"You would not be able to write anything in Greece now. The entire country is in turmoil. When *we* were there, the Greeks were slaves under the Turks, but now they are *beaten* slaves."

"Yes, *slaves* in their own country. A thousand times worse than the Italians here," Byron said. "But what can people like us do?"

"I can tell you what *I* have done, and have been *able* to do, now that I am a Member of Parliament," Hobhouse said. "I have established *The Greek Committee,* so that members of the House can come up with suggestions of ways to help the Greeks."

Byron was alarmed. "England can't go in – it would cause a Holy War! The Turks would say it was the Christian Crusades all over again."

"No, no, I did not say anything about a war. I said ways to *help* the Greeks. They need weapons to defend themselves, but they're as poor as beggars and have no money to buy weapons. They also need medicines and bandages for the sick and injured. Oh, a whole host of things. You name it, they need it."

"How do you know all this?"

"Because our Consulate in Athens keeps sending letters to us – begging help for the Greeks – saying it is money and equipment they need. Diplomatically, of course, we cannot be seen to be taking sides by helping them – yet we could do it on the *sly,* by raising funds to send to them secretly by emissaries."

Byron paused in the act of refilling his wine glass. "You know I will help you there. As much as I can."

"What?" Hobhouse was visibly offended. "My dear Byron, I did not come to Italy to get money from you!"

"So why did you come?"

"To see you, of course – my dearest friend. Why else?"

"Then it is fortunate that you came to Pisa now, or *you* would have been the one to get a surprise, because in a few weeks I will be moving to Genoa."

Teresa scarcely saw anything at all of Byron during the next five days. Five days that felt like five centuries.

His friend, Mr Hobhouse, had not come to Pisa alone, but was on a tour of Italy with his eighteen-year-old half-brother Isaac, and his two half-sisters, Amelia and Matilda. All were all staying at a hotel on the Lung' Arno, no more than a short walk away. but these relatives could not be brought to Lord Byron's house because his relationship with her would be considered a scandal by the English.

Even Mr Hobhouse seemed to disapprove; although on that first evening he had made great efforts to hide his disapproval.

So Byron went everywhere with them instead, showing them all the wonderful things to see in Pisa, as was his duty.

Only on the last evening of the family's five days in Pisa, did Mr Hobhouse return alone to have dinner at Lanfranchi with Byron and Teresa, but first they relaxed in the drawing-room.

"On my way here, in a bookseller's shop," Hobhouse said to Byron, "I found the *Liaisons Dangereuses* and the *Nouvelle Héloïse* and both with indecent pictures, which the man had a licence to sell – although every good and decent book I asked for, was prohibited."

So certain was Teresa of Mr Hobhouse's disapproval of her and the morals of all Italians, she pleaded a headache and dined in her room, then went to bed early with a book.

Downstairs, at the dining table, John Hobhouse and Byron were free once more to speak about Greece.

"There are now twenty-six members of the Greek Committee," Hobhouse said. "All are Members of Parliament and all are Whigs – although some are now referring to us as *radicals*."

"Who are they? These radical Whigs?"

"Sir John Bowring. Sir Francis Burdett. Lord John Russell, you would know them all if I named them. All are prepared to contribute money from their own bank accounts to help the Greeks."

"What of the subscriptions? Have you raised much funds from them?"

Hobhouse pulled a face. "Very little. Too many see Greece as a lost cause and doubt the Turks can be defeated. Also, a Scotsman recently came back from Greece and told them of all the horrors he had seen there. How the Turks not only slash and kill the Greeks in battle, but they strip their dead bodies of all their clothes as the final indignity. Shocking, quite shocking."

"Can *no one* help them?"

"*You* could help them, Byron. In a big way. Sir John Bowring thinks the Committee may be able to raise a loan on the London Stock Exchange, and if *you* were to join the Greek Committee and support the cause, your name alone would raise the stakes."

Byron smiled cynically. "If it's only my name you want, you can have it and use it, by all means."

It was one o'clock in the morning when Hobhouse stood to leave and say farewell, and this time it was Hobby who was slightly emotional. From their days at Cambridge he had loved Byron, garnered his heart in all ways for him, and this visit had been too brief.

"Would you not consider leaving Italy and coming back to England?"

Byron hesitated. "In the Spring, perhaps, for a visit."

"You always say that."

"And I always mean it."

"No you don't."

Byron shrugged. "Well, who knows?"

In the hall, near to the front door, Byron stood silent while Hobby delayed looking at the various pictures hanging on the walls, and then picking up odd items here and there, gravely pretending to inspect them.

Byron knew Hobby was feeling upset, not sure when and where they would meet again. It was four years since they had last seen each other in Venice, when Hobby was supposed to stay for a few months, and yet had not left until a year and half later.

And now, during these past five days, even though four years had passed since that time, such was their friendship and ease with each other, it had been as if they had been separated for only a week.

As Hobby delayed even longer to inspect the carvings on the hall table, Byron said quietly: "Hobby, you should not have come ... or you should not go."

Hobhouse looked at him, a shade of grief and also some anger in his eyes.

"I am not like you, Byron. I cannot just walk away from it all and go and live somewhere else. I am a politician now, a man with a duty to the people of England, and now I am trying to help the people of Greece. *You* are the one who should not have abdicated England and everyone in it to come here – and now, yes,

I *should* go."

When the door had closed, Byron saw no point in climbing up the great Michelangelo staircase to go to bed, so he sat down in a chair in the hall to wait.

How long would it be this time? Five minutes? Ten minutes?

Surprisingly, it was almost half an hour before the rapper knocked.

He stood and walked over to the door, opening it to Hobhouse.

"Byron, I'm awfully sorry. Of course I have no right to tell you what you should do with your life. And of course you are free to do as you please."

Byron was not prepared to be lenient. "Abdicated England? You used the word *abdicated*. I am a poet, not a king."

"I know, I know," Hobby said regretfully, "but well, you know ..."

"I know you are still as crabby and disagreeable as always, Hobby. But I forgive you, as a Christian should do, which is that I will not forgive you for as long as I live, and I shall certainly pay you back in kind, *with* interest, at the first opportunity."

Hobby smiled.

"But then," Byron shrugged, "that need break no squares between us, as it has been our custom ever since Cambridge."

"And long may it continue," Hobby grinned, holding out his hand.

Byron took his hand to shake, before the two briefly embraced and Byron slapped Hobhouse on the back. "Go now, Hobby, go on and prosper."

PART SEVEN

Genoa

"A man ought to do more for mankind than write verses."

BYRON

Chapter Forty-Three

~ ~ ~

Casa Saluzzo, a large and square mansion with a four-sided French roof, consisted of three main floors, and sat high on a hill in Albaro, only one mile distant from the centre of Genoa.

Pietro had taken Byron's words of "large house" too literally, for the *Casa Saluzzo* contained at least forty rooms, and so was spacious enough to allow the Gambas to live on a completely separate floor of apartments from Byron's floor; and also allow Fletcher and Tita and Lega Zambelli to dispute over which of all the bedrooms on Byron's floor would be theirs.

As the "*capo della casa*" Fletcher got to choose his room first, leaving Tita and Lega to argue over their choice of rooms, while all the other servants were satisfied with their accommodation on the ground floor.

The house had a large walled-garden at the rear, filled with orange trees; a garden large enough to become the favourite playground of Byron's animals; especially the dogs, who excitedly ran up and down all over the house exploring every room.

It had been after midnight when they had arrived, but now, in the light of day, from the balcony of his high-ceilinged drawing room, Byron was pleased with his magnificent sea view, and also the green lawn adorned with shrubbery and flowers which stretched out beneath his windows.

He was also pleased to discover that the Casa *Saluzzo* was near enough to the much smaller *Casa Negroto* just over half a mile away, where Mary Shelley now lived.

For the Gambas, their delight was of a different kind, for Genoa was not Italian territory. In the Treaty of Paris in 1815, Genoa had been ceded to the Kingdom of Sardinia, so no Austrian rule prevailed here.

The first thing Byron set out to do was to visit the British Minister, Mr Hill, not only to greet him again, but also to obtain his advice on finding himself a good banker.

He was recommended to a Mr Charles Barry, a senior partner in the firm of Messrs Webb & Co., English bankers of Genoa and Leghorn.

Mr Barry had heard of Lord Byron, but not for some years since his time in London – a young man who had been reputed to be England's most famous "bad boy". A young man whom, they said, always had a trail of women following him because he wrote poetry.

Not that *he* had ever read any of Byron's poetry. In the world of business there was no time for such flowery nonsense. So he would take the bad boy's money into his bank, and then send him on his way.

Mr Hill had also said that his lordship was very interested in the Greek cause. More nonsense! Why should anyone care for those unprincipled rebels? They and their revolution were damaging the trade of the Levant, and turning the Ægean Sea into a nest of pirates under the pretence of fighting the Turks.

Why, they had even seized a consignment of goods which the firm of Webb & Co had financed. Robbers! – the lot of them – including the damned Turks. But at least the Greeks did not kill the sailors after seizing the goods, unlike the bloody Turks, which was the only good thing he could say about the Greeks.

The following day, when Lord Byron was announced, Mr Barry decided to be civil, sort out an account for him, and then send him on his bally way. And if this Byron thought his title would carry any sway with *him*, then he was going to be sorely disillusioned. The Italians here in Genoa had so many titles between them, they were almost ten a penny.

Within minutes of his visitor entering his office, Mr Charles Barry found that he was not only losing track, he was also losing ground.

This very handsome young gentleman was indeed a

lord, a very *English* lord, in his manner and in his bearing, and in every word he spoke. Not that his behaviour or manner was in any way top-drawer, but there was a *refinement* about him, a politeness and a courtesy, that was quite disarming in its elegant simplicity.

And there was something else that appealed to Mr Barry's normally hard heart – a "something" which caused Mr Barry to do all kinds of favours that he would not have done for any other client.

"A "something" which caused Mr Barry every day to journey out to Albaro and climb the steep path to the Casa Saluzzo and spend an hour or two in its cool and spacious rooms, drawn by an attraction that he could not "for the life of him" explain.

He was also interested in the young Countess Gamba Guiccioli, who was spending a part of every day trying to learn English. Some of her English she tried out on Mr Barry – whole long sentences at a time – after which she would smile and ask him, "Is good?"

"Is dreadful," he wanted to say, but always merely nodded and told her it was near enough, and with a little more study and practice, it would be perfect, quite perfect.

One afternoon, after his second glass of wine, Mr Barry regretfully told Lord Byron of his former preconceptions about him, and how he had intended to sort out an account for him, and then send him on his way.

Byron smiled. "Pray don't feel guilty, because I shall certainly pay you back in kind, one way or another."

Mr Barry laughed, believing he was joking.

~~~

In the month of November, Byron called in to the Casa Negroto, as he often did, to see Mary Shelley; but this time he was not carrying a manuscript for her to neatly copy out, but holding a letter, which had been forwarded on from Pisa.
~~~

Instead of sending a servant down with the letter, he had chosen to deliver it personally, because he could see from the red crested seal on the back of the cover that it came from Shelley's father, Sir Timothy Shelley.

"At last!" Mary said. "It has taken him long enough to reply."

She pulled the cover open, squaring out the pages, and then began to read, her eyes moving rapidly over each line, before exclaiming a sound of horror, and almost collapsed down into her chair.

"What is it?"

"He says that our boy Percy is *not* his heir, and seeks to remind me that Shelley has two other orphaned children in England from his first marriage, and the son of that marriage, by his birthright, will become his heir on his grandfather's death."

She stared up at Byron, disbelief in her eyes. "He wants nothing to do with us!"

Byron took the letter. "I will write to him. As Shelley's friend and executor perhaps I may be able to soften his rancour, by reminding him that Shelley had no personal fortune of his own to leave, but he *has* left a widow and a three-year-old son with no financial means. And although the boy may not be his heir, he is still his grandson."

Half an hour after Byron had left, Teresa arrived to comfort Mary and share her disappointment.

"He is a man who has forgotten how to be a father," Teresa said indignantly. "A man who claims to be a Christian, and yet – and yet – I cannot imagine such a man!"

"I can," Mary said. "He hated Shelley for being an atheist, and he believes I am the same ..." She then confided to Teresa that since Shelley's death, she had often slipped inside a church and said some prayers for his soul.

"I know he still *has* a soul, because I can often feel him near me, even though I can't see him."

Three days later Byron brought down a new

manuscript for Mary to copy out, entitled *The Island*.

Mary was glad to have some distraction from her own thoughts, *any* distraction – but she looked at Albè with some surprise. "Not Don Juan?"

"No, the young Don is now about to arrive in *England*, when I intend to comically expose all the ridiculous hypocrisies of the upper classes – and all their pious dodges to get out of their own individual responsibilities."

He shrugged. "But then ... I really don't know why, but the other night I was looking down on the great harbour of Genoa, at all the ships in port; and those ships for some reason reminded me of Captain Bligh and the mutiny of Fletcher Christian. No one yet knows to where Christian and the mutineers went, but as they had previously been in Otaheiti, I rather imagine they must have gone to some island near there."

"So this poem is about the mutiny on the Bounty?"

"More or less, but more from the point of view of the sailors. Will you copy it for me?"

Mary was glad to do so, but waited until little Percy was in his bed asleep, before sitting down to read words that took her mind away to a midnight ship that was sailing on the ocean somewhere in the South Seas:

The gallant Chief within his cabin slept,

Secure in those by whom the watch was kept:

His dreams were of old England's welcome shore,

Of toils rewarded, and of dangers o'er;

His name was added to the glorious roll

Of those whom search the snow-surrounded Pole.

The worst was over, and the rest seemed sure,

And why should not his slumber be secure?

Alas! his deck was trod by unwilling feet,

And wilder hands would hold the vessel's sheet;

Young hearts, which languished for some sunny isle.

Where summer years and summer women smile;
Men without country, who, too long estranged,
Had found no native home, or found it changed ...

Sir Timothy Shelley replied to Lord Byron's letter with more speed than he had troubled to answer the woman who "refers to herself as Shelley's wife".

In Sir Timothy's view, his son had already possessed a wife when this Mary Godwin had run away with him to revel in his atheism, bearing him children, out of which only one had survived. And then she had written that disgraceful and monstrous book about a Dr Frankenstein thinking he could create a human with the same powers as God! "May God help the poor boy for having such a woman for a mother."

Byron was both grieved and scandalised as he read Sir Timothy's letter. "This man is inhuman," he said to Teresa. "Telling a mother to give up her son, if she does not wish him to die of hunger."

"Poor Mary!" exclaimed Teresa. "She *lives* only for that boy of hers, and for no other reason. Without her son to care for, she would probably fling herself into the sea. "

Byron could not bring himself to take this hard-hearted letter down to Mary, nor even to send it to her by a servant. It was a reply to his own letter to Sir Timothy, so Mary need not see it.

After a few days, Teresa persuaded him that it was wrong to leave Mary waiting like a fool, and also left in complete ignorance of the truth of her father-in-law's sentiments.

"All she is doing now is waiting to know her destiny. Is she to go back to England with her son, or are they to stay in Italy? And ... my love, she trusts *you* to always be sincere with her. So what will she think if she finds out that you have betrayed her?

"I am not betraying her, I'm trying to *protect* her."

Yet Byron knew that Teresa was right; and so, with extreme reluctance, he took the letter down to Mary, but no amount of delicacy, no amount of tact or sensitivity had any chance of covering up Sir Timothy's proposal when Mary snatched the letter from his hand and read it.

She kept staring at the letter in disbelief. "He wants me to give up my son to him – but from then on, neither will have anything more to do with me?"

Nothing could console her, not until later that night when she wrote in her journal – the journal that had now become a communication in which she spoke to her beloved husband, her darling Shelley.

"Yet it was not the refusal or the insult heaped upon me that stung me to tears –it was their bitter words about our boy – Why I live only to keep him from their hands – How dare they dream that I held him not – far more precious than all save the hope of again seeing you – my lost one.

Visit me in my dreams tonight, my beloved Shelley, – kind – living – excellent as thou wert – & if you do, the event of this day shall be forgotten."

~ ~ ~

Byron was content in his life with Teresa. His relationship with her had been the longest. And although not so *crazily* in love with her as he had been at the beginning; – now, after four years together, he was somewhat astounded that he was still in love with her; telling Mr Barry that – "If we were to marry, or could be *allowed* to marry, I think we would prove to be a perfect example of marital happiness."

It was only himself that he was now dissatisfied with, believing that, as a man, he should be doing more with his life than writing poetry.

His mind was continually drifting back to the land of Greece, as if seeing it from afar, the place which had inspired his poetry to become more serious. and where he had written stanza after stanza.

Yet how he could he now *forget* Greece? When he was receiving despatches from London's Greek Committee every week, first informing him that he had been accepted as a member of the Committee, and then that he had been *elected* as their European representative. And since his election, the Committee's delegates had risen from its original number of 26, to now 80 Members of Parliament.

He had been receiving numerous letters from a Captain Edward Blaquiere, who had spent much time in Greece, and was now in London seeking aid for the Greeks and pleading their cause. And now, in his letters, Blaquiere was begging to know – "Would your lordship be willing to go to Greece, to assess the situation there on behalf of the Committee?"

The very suggestion of Byron going into a war-zone terrified Teresa, so much so that he was forced to assure her that it was merely an inquiry, and nothing more. As always, he managed to placate her fears.

Not so, Mr Barry, the banker, who was not only displeased with Lord Byron, who had settled down very well in Genoa, but on occasions his behaviour was most odd, and not at all regular for a young lord with a high standard of reputation to maintain.

Mr Barry believed that a gentleman – especially an *English* gentleman – must always hold himself regular to the traditions and standards of behaviour, in order for everyone to know their place in this world; and those from high society did not stoop to mix their thoughts or conversation with the ones habited on a lower level. Had no one ever taught Lord Byron that?

Obviously not. And, at times, it was an embarrassment to walk through the town of Genoa with his lordship – a deep embarrassment, which Mr Barry passed on discreetly to the British Minister, Mr William Noel Hill.

"He has a passion for flowers," Mr Barry revealed.

"And he purchases bouquets from the vendors on the road, who have their tables piled with them. He bestows charity on every mendicant who asks for it. The people all seem to know his face, and to like him, and they even dare to keep him standing while they tell him all their private affairs, as if they are certain of his sympathy."

Mr Barry hesitated, frowning prodigiously. "And then there's the *dogs* – he is simply incapable of passing a wandering dog without pausing to have a conversation with it."

Mr Hill laughed. "He is clearly eccentric, as most poets are, but he also has many fine qualities. And you must remember, Mr Barry, that we English are mere transients here in Genoa, and this city belongs to the Genoese people. This is *their* world, not ours. And so surely it cannot do much harm if one of our celebrated Englishmen shows some interest in them?"

Mr Barry was persuaded to agree, not wishing to oppose the British Minister who preached "diplomacy" in all things and on every level.

Mr Barry finally took his leave; unaware that he had merely cemented Mr Hill's opinion that the banker was a perfect specimen of the typical English *merchant,* who traded his currency and his prejudices even in foreign lands.

Chapter Forty-Four

~ ~ ~

On a sunny afternoon in the early spring of 1823, under a mild blue sky, two men stepped off a boat in Genoa, and checked into the hotel *Albergo Della Villa,* where they washed and changed in their separate rooms, and then asked the manager at the desk for directions to the *"Casa Saluzzo".*

A short time later Byron returned from his afternoon ride to be told by Fletcher that two gentlemen were waiting for him in the drawing-room.

"They say they have come all the way from England," Fletcher said, "so I did not like to send them away."

"Are they familiar? Do we know them?"

"No, my lord, they are strangers."

"Poetry fanatics?"

"No, both say they are soldiers, although one of them is a sea captain" ..." Fletcher looked down at the card in his hand, "A Captain Edward Blaquiere."

"Blaquiere?"

Byron entered the drawing-room and finally met the Irishman who had sent him so many letters about Greece.

Both men appeared pleased to see him, shaking his hand with smiles. Byron said curiously, "Blaquiere is not an Irish name, is it?"

"No." Blaquiere explained that he was from a family of French emigrants who had settled in County Londonderry. "Many years ago."

His companion was Greek, Andreas Luriottis, a delegate of the Greek Provisional Government who had gone to London to seek English aid. The two men were now on their way back to Greece, and had stopped to see Lord Byron on the advice of John Cam Hobhouse.

"Mr Hobhouse says you know the terrain of Greece very well."

"Yes, I lived there for two years, but as I now live in Italy, I don't see how that can help you?"

Andrea Luriottis asked: "Do you wish to help us?"

"Of course, in any way I can."

"Then, Lord Byron, let me tell you something you should know. Your name is known all over Greece. We know you to have a great love for Greece. You have written it so in your poetry. But our people are not succeeding in their fight against the Turks and so they are not united. Some have lost heart, and some have gained strength. Some are coming to the battlefield, and some are leaving it. And now all is confusion."

Byron was a little confused himself.

"A lack of unity was the main cause of ruin for the Italian effort for freedom," he said. "They lacked strategy and co-ordination. But as for Greece, I don't see what I could possibly do to help you, apart from financial aid, and that I have already pledged to the Greek Committee in London."

"We have been slaves for too long," said Luriottis, "but if it was known to the Greeks that Lord Byron had personally come to the Levant to support our cause, you would be like a William Wilberforce to us. Those who have lost heart would rise up and return to the battlefield."

They spoke for some hours, after Captain Blaquiere had given Byron a letter from the London Greek Committee, asking if he would consider making a reconnoitring expedition of the Greek Ionian Islands for a few weeks and then to send to them his report on the state of the country.

Byron told them he was willing to go, but there was an objection of a private nature that could prevent him from doing so

"But I shall try to get over it," he said, "and if I fail, then I must do what I can from where I am – but it will always be a source of regret to me – to think that I might perhaps have done more for the Greek cause on the spot."

When the two men had left to return to their hotel, Byron picked up the letter again from the London committee, and saw then that Hobhouse had scrawled a personal note to him at the end:

If you go in," Hobhouse had written "don't stay long."

My dear Hobhouse, – I saw Captain Blaquiere, and the Greek companion of his mission on Saturday. Of course I entered very seriously into the object of their mission, and the Hellenic struggle, and I have now said that I will I go to the Levant in July, if the Greek provisional government think that I could be of any use. It is not that I could pretend to anything in a military capacity; nor is it much that an individual foreigner can do in any other way, but perhaps as a reporter of the actual state of things there. I might be of use; at any rate, I will try.

Also, as you may imagine, my personal concerns are by no means favourable to it. The Contessa is of course, opposed to my quitting her; although only for a few months. And as she had influence enough to prevent my return to England in 1819, she may be successful in detaining me from Greece in 1823.

Her brother, Count Gamba the younger, is of a very different opinion, and wishes to accompany me; or at any rate to go himself, being a thorough Liberty Boy. He says he feels like a caged lion here in Italy. If I do go, I presume the Committee will give me instructions of what they wish to be observed, reported, or done. – B

~~~
~~~

The meeting of the European rulers at the Congress of Verona in 1822 had done a nice job of sorting out Europe by extending boundaries and claiming more territories for themselves. Its aim was to create a new European Order – "in the name of Peace".

Russia extended its powers and was given sovereignty over Poland and Finland. Austria also extended its boundaries; and a new German Confederation was established, on the grounds that France should be surrounded by larger countries to prevent another war, and the rise of another Napoleon.

"How dare they call themselves the Holy Alliance," Byron fumed, "when their object is to indulge in the oppression of entire nations!"

And Greece? he wondered. What of poor Greece? Ignored and forsaken by the great Powers, and left to struggle all alone against their Turkish oppressors.

Had the world forgotten the greatness of the ancient Greeks and every valuable thing that Greece had given to mankind? – Democracy? Philosophy? Science? Medicine – no doctor could practice medicine without first taking the oath of *Hippocrates* ... And the drama of staged theatre, first created in Athens long before Shakespeare. And *Archimedes* and his geometry. *Pythagoras* and his order of Mathematics ...

But that was then, and this was now, and Greece deserved better than to be ignored by the world in her time of peril ... But *how* was he now to tell Teresa that he had finally made his decision to sail to Greece?

"It will be for only a couple of months, no longer," he told her. "A reconnoitring expedition around the Ionian Islands for the Greek Committee in London, nothing more."

Teresa reacted as if he had been given a death sentence. Greece was a place of war and Turks and butchery. She could not allow Byron to go there alone, nor could she be calmed out of her fears and tears, resulting in Byron writing wearily to Hobhouse –

"She wants to go to Greece too! forsooth, a precious place to go at present. Of course the idea is ridiculous, as everything I could do there would be sacrificed to keeping her out of harm's way."

Fletcher was also feeling contrary, not at the suggestion of sailing to Greece, which he had not yet been told about – but his continued annoyance at the impertinence of some of his lordship's animals.

Not the dogs – the dogs were as good as gold – and the five peacocks were very reserved and sedate in their behaviour as they strolled around the garden, as was the Egyptian crane – but the three geese were driving Fletcher mad.

It was not enough for the geese to follow Lord Byron everywhere when he entered the garden, but perchance on finding that the front door into the hall had been left open, they would climb up the staircase, cross the anterooms, and present themselves at the door of Lord Byron's drawing room and walk in. When he came out, they would follow him, and his lordship – not having the heart to shoo them away himself – would call Fletcher to do it. And more than once Fletcher's hand had been sorely pecked.

"If I had my way," Fletcher said to Tita, "I would have those geese taken up for a good roasting, and then for three nights in a row, serve one up as a nice goose for dinner."

PART EIGHT

Indecision

"What a heavy burden is a name that has become too famous."

                              Voltaire.

Chapter Forty-Five

~ ~ ~

Byron did not *want* to leave Teresa, even for a few months; and, at times, he almost changed his mind about going to Greece. But his word had been given, and with it his honour. The die was now cast, and his travel plans were already on their way to being concluded.

A letter had been sent to him by a brother of Prince Mavrocordato in Greece, advising Lord Byron to establish himself at Missolonghi.

> *... my opinion is that on your arrival in the Ionian islands the best place for you to establish yourself would be Missolonghi in Ætolia, a place which would be very well adapted to serve as a base for your purposes, as it is the one point in our dear fatherland which is the most threatened by the enemy, and the weakest and most in need in present circumstances. In this place, your Excellency could get in touch with General Marco Botzaris, captain of the brave Souliots, who, being honoured by your presence and assistance, could with greater facility increase their numbers, and put themselves in a state to take the offensive against Epirus.*

This was followed by a letter from Captain Blaquiere informing Lord Byron that the Greek Government were eagerly expecting him.

Mr Barry, on the other hand, found all this to be most unexpected, and complained with great annoyance to the British Minister, Mr Hill – "A man such as Lord Byron, a man of rank and genius, a man always so *cordial*, so *whimsical*, so *kind* – so why on earth is he going to help those savage rebels in an enterprise that cannot be *profitable* to him in any way?"

Mr Hill had no idea why. It all sounded as foolhardy to him as it did to Mr Barry.

Yet as time moved on, Mr Hill could not help being amused as he watched Mr Barry fluttering around Genoa like a butterfly, endeavouring to procure for Lord Byron all the things he would need for his journey.

Byron was in talks with a ship owner about hiring a vessel to take him to Greece. Mr Barry was outraged at the cost, insisting he could procure a similar vessel for him at *half* that cost. And so he did – a British brig of 120 tons named *Hercules*.

"Now *this* vessel," said Mr Barry, "will not only take you safely to Greece, but will bring you back safely to Genoa again."

Later that evening Teresa saw the two red and gold military uniforms which had been sent to Byron to aid his protection in Greece. As a British officer, if captured, he would be treated far more leniently by the Turks than they would treat a Greek. All knew the power of Great Britain, and all wanted to be Britain's friend. If found in such a situation, Lord Byron must represent himself as a diplomat, nothing more.

Teresa had finally resolved to be strong and brave, for Byron's determination to assist the Greeks with the expenditure of his own financial resources was all in a good cause. She also knew that his desire to help Greece was motivated by the same feelings of injustice he had felt when he had hoped to contribute to the independence of Italy.

And then another shock came a few weeks later when a packet arrived from Cardinal Rusconi of Ravenna, enclosing Count Gamba's passport, and papers allowing him and his family to return home to Ravenna. Their forced exile was over.

Count Gamba wept tears of joy, thanking God that he could now return home to his young family; but Pietro was furious.

"We are to come and go when they say? Like puppets! I meant what I said," Pietro insisted "I will *never* live in Ravenna again, not until it is free of the rule of Austria."

He turned defiantly to Byron. "I will leave Genoa and accompany you to Greece."

Teresa was just as defiant "And I will *stay* in Genoa and wait here for both of you to return."

Count Gamba looked at his daughter with pity in his eyes.

"My Teresa," he said, "you cannot stay in Genoa. When I return to Ravenna, you must come home with me. It is a rule of the Papal decree, that you must live under your father's roof, or else be confined in a convent."

"It is an unfair and *vindictive* decree," Byron said. "And what if something was to happen to you, Ruggero, and you were no longer alive – would she be made *then* to retreat into a convent?"

Ruggero did not know. "Others," he said, "when they have refused to go to a convent, have been forced to return to their husbands."

"*No!*" Teresa screamed. "I will *not* do that – I will *never* go back to Alessandro!"

"Then you must come home with me," said Ruggero. "All this time we have been in Florence, Pisa, Genoa, the authorities believe you have been living with me, under the same roof as your father. But if they were to know something different ..."

"There has to be another way," Byron said, uneasy at the thought of Teresa going back to live in a Papal State where Count Guiccioli lived, fearing that force may be used against her in some way.

"What if she was to stay here in Genoa, under the care of a respectable lady? Would that be allowed?"

Ruggero did not think it would be allowed. "Even so," he said, "I know my Teresa would not be happy in the house of a stranger, so my wish is for her to come home with me ... home to her brother and sisters in Filetto. As my daughter she will have my protection, She need have no fear of Guiccioli."

Byron looked at Teresa who was wiping the tears from her eyes. "It will be for only a few months," he told her again. "And when I come back to Genoa, you can return here. Do you agree to that, Ruggero?"

Count Gamba nodded his agreement. "Here there is no Austrian rule, and if she will be under your care and protection, then I will agree."

He looked sadly at Pietro. "As for you, my beautiful boy, you are a man now, and I can no longer tell you what to do. If you go with Lord Byron to Greece, I will pray for you both."

~~~

Now that her friends were all leaving Genoa, Mary Shelley had been wondering what *she* should do. Almost all her money was gone, and she had been living on the payments she received from Byron for copying another five new cantos of *Don Juan*. How he wrote so fast was still a mystery to her, although she knew he often wrote through the night, as if the darkness of the real world outside was sealed off from him while he wrote.

And now all his writing and her copying was about to end.

Mary reflected back to that awful day when she had learned that Sir Timothy Shelley was not prepared to help her in any way. And on that day Byron had assured her, "I will be your banker, for anything you may need."

Too proud and too dignified to accept charity from anyone, she had refused, preferring to work as a copyist for payment. But now, knowing she must return to England rather than stay alone in Genoa, she had finally agreed to accept the money for her fare to England, but only as "*a loan.*"

> *My Dear Lord Byron, – I am very grateful to you for your kind offers yesterday. In part I must avail myself of them to get to England; but I know too well how many claims you must have on you ..."*
~~~

Despite their good friendship, Byron now decided it was time to hold true to his good-humoured promise to pay back Mr Barry for holding such a bad opinion and ridiculous prejudices against him upon his arrival in Genoa – even though Mr Barry had never met him and knew nothing at all about him, yet still he had criticised and scandalised his name.

Now, of course, Mr Barry knew him well, smiling with delight when he saw Lord Byron's carriage pulling up at his door, and went out to greet him.

"*Buongiorno,* my lord, good morning! I thought you had forgotten me. You have come to say farewell?"

Byron smiled sheepishly. "No, I have come to ask you for yet another favour ... if you would be so kind as to oblige?"

"Of course I will oblige," gushed Mr Barry. "Anything you may ask, and it shall be done."

"While I am away, I will need someone to look after my few orphaned animals, and as you have such a very large walled garden and such an expanse of lawn – "

"Your beautiful dogs? You wish me to take care of them for you until you return? Why, it will be my pleasure, my lord."

"No, not my dogs, I am taking them with me. But perhaps, if you would agree to take care of a few of my smaller animals?"

"Certainly, that would be no problem, no problem at all. And if you will send to me the address of where you will be lodging in Greece, I will send you regular updates on their welfare."

"Thank you, but perhaps you should meet them, before making a judgement?" Byron suggested.

"Oh, send them down without any more ado," Mr Barry declared. "Animals are all dumb are they not? And I'm sure yours are all very well trained."

"And very good-mannered, in their own way," Byron added.

Returning to the Casa Saluzzo full of smiles, Fletcher made it very clear that *he* was not amused, although he knew that no one was more *easily* amused than his lordship.

"This is a terrible prank you are playing on the poor man," Fletcher said. "He'll be cursing us all to hell and back by the time our ship reaches Leghorn."

On the contrary, Mr Barry was rendered speechless when a short time later, a servant opened the door to Mr Fletcher, who came into the drawing-room followed by three fat geese who stood looking curiously around the room as if they were potential owners.

Fletcher had decided to brazen it out as quickly as possible.

"Now this one is the gander, and those two are his wives," Fletcher told him. "They'll give you plenty of eggs, and they won't cost you a penny to feed them, because they live mainly on grass, so your lawn will always be trimmed nice and neat."

Mr Barry was frowning. "Geese – is it true that geese make a lot of noise?"

"Usually only in the early mornings," Fletcher said. "When they start honking to each other, but it's a sound you soon get used to. It's only a problem if you want to sleep in late. Now I'll just go and bring in Jade the cat and Pharaoh the crane, and then I'll be off to finish the packing. Our ship leaves on this evening's tide."

~ ~ ~

In her room, Teresa was engulfed in sadness, knowing that she would be obliged to return to Ravenna, and live for months, and not even know how many months, on tenterhooks, in a state of alarm, because there in Greece Byron would be constantly surrounded by dangers. Following him was neither feasible nor permitted. Would she be able to stand the grief?

After taking his farewell of her father and Count Paulo, Byron came to Teresa's apartment at three o'clock, and stayed until the last minute before five. It was a melancholy two hours for both of them.

"Perhaps I did wrong in agreeing to go," he said, "but

now I must. Set your mind at rest though, because we shall see each other again soon."

At last, she believed him, although her mind was still plagued by forebodings.

"I did not want you to be alone at the time of my departure," he said, "so I have asked Mary Shelley to come at five o'clock to sit with you. She will know how to cheer you."

Mary arrived at the very instant when Byron was leaving, and she saw Teresa's grief. Unquestionably, she assured Byron, she would endeavour to support Teresa in every way, and to give her a little courage.

She saw that he, too, was very sad. And then, with a melancholy smile for both of them, Byron left the Casa Saluzzo, accompanied by Pietro, Fletcher, Tita, and even Lega Zambelli.

"Even you, Lega?" asked Teresa.

Lega nodded. "All of us. If Mylord is going to Greece, so are we. Who else will protect him?"

And then Lega was gone – off with Tita in the caleche following behind Byron's carriage – all off to a new adventure in Greece; and the dogs at the back of the caleche sticking out their heads and barking furiously with delight, sensing they were going to somewhere new.

When they had disappeared from view, Teresa looked tearfully at Mary Shelley who had come to cheer her in her hour of agony. But how could Mary cheer her? She, who was so unhappy herself, a poor withered flower battered by the storm. Hope had fled too far from her soul, to enable Mary Shelley to convincingly offer cheer to anyone. Teresa was losing her lover, and Mary who had lost her beloved husband, was now also losing her friend.

"What a world, my God!" Teresa exclaimed. "Is all happiness to be taken away from us?"

And so, desolate in their sudden loneliness, they went to Teresa's room, where they both sat and cried together.

~ ~ ~

Two red British military uniforms, and a few servants, some luggage, and three dogs were not the only things Byron had loaded onto the ship. Through Doctor Alexander, he had bought chests of enough medical supplies to treat a thousand injured men for a year.

He also carried £9000 in sterling, and a trunk containing 10,000 Spanish dollars, in ready money, and bills of exchange for 40,000 more. If it was money the Greeks needed to help gain their liberty, he intended they should have money. Thousands more was due to him from his poetry sales, due to *Don Juan* now being bought up by everybody, and – according to John Murray – being bought *slyly* by women in their hundreds.

On board the ship, he was surprised to find a letter waiting for him, handed to him by the captain.

Recognising Mr Barry's handwriting, he almost didn't open it – the last thing he needed now was a severe reprimand for his prank on the banker, who, to be fair, had always been such a good and helpful friend to him.

Yet, he did open it, wide-eyed with guilt as he read the words of Mr Barry:

> *You said that I should be glad when you got off, but I hope you don't think so, believe me, My Lord, I am too proud of having known you not to regret most unfeignedly your absence. I cannot cry like the Tailor's boy but I feel the loss as acutely, & most sincerely do I hope that your return to Genoa will not be at a very remote period ..."*

"When was this delivered?" he asked Captain Scott.

"About half an hour before you arrived."

Byron moved over to where Fletcher was watching the three dogs playing on the deck, and showed to him the handwriting on the cover of the letter.

"From Mr Barry," he said guiltily, "delivered only half an hour ago."

Fletcher stared. "Complaining about the animals?"

"No, not a word, just wishing us well. And now," Byron lamented, "I feel like shooting myself for playing such a trick on him."

"It wasn't that bad," Fletcher said. "You've played a lot worse tricks on Mr Hobhouse."

"Yes, but if I had simply and honestly *asked* Mr Barry to look after my animals for a few months, now I believe he would have said yes."

"But you *did* ask him," Fletcher said. "The trick was that you didn't say *which* animals."

"No, but then – *he* didn't ask either."

Fletcher grinned. "I bet he's wishing now that he *had* asked you, because his eyes were fair boggling at the sight of those three white geese walking into his drawing room."

Byron was shaking his head. "Yet not a word of complaint in his letter, not a reference ... Oh, the dear and good man! – I must write a quick note of thanks and apologies to him, and get it delivered before we sail."

Some hours later, from the terrace of the Casa Saluzzo high on the hill, Mary, Teresa, and Count Gamba stood watching as the *Hercules* sailed out of the bay.

Amongst the crew moving back an forth, Teresa thought she saw the lone figure of Pietro standing on the deck, gazing upwards ... but no sign of Byron.

"Painful farewells should always be as brief as possible," he had often said to her. So no, *he* would not be standing and looking up.

A sharp sensation pierced through Teresa's entire being. "I'm dying," she gasped. "I fear I will never see his face again."

Her father hugged and consoled her, while Mary was unable to utter a word, for she too had kissed her beloved farewell, and had never seen his face again, not in this world. So how could she comfort anyone, when she was still unable to comfort herself.

In a few days, though, she too would be on a ship with her precious son, going back to seek shelter under the grey skies of England, grey like her face, her heart, her mood.

She gazed up at the setting sun in the summer sky, tears flowing from her eyes as she remembered those poignant words written one evening by her beloved Shelley ...

How wonderful is sunset, when the glow
Of Heaven descends upon a land like thee,
Thou Paradise of exiles, Italy!

PART NINE

Greece

Awake! (Not Greece – she *is* awake!)

Awake my spirit! think through *whom*

Thy lifeblood tracks its parent lake,

And then strikes home!

BYRON

Chapter Forty-Six

~ ~ ~

In the first few months after her return to Ravenna, Teresa believed she was slowly dying of heartbreak; and her only medicine – the only cure that revived her for a little while – was the letters that came from Greece. And yet the first letter, from Cephalonia, had been such a disappointment, written by Pietro, and so typical a rushed letter from a brother –

Dear T – Just to let you know that nothing happened during our voyage. Lord Byron enjoyed excellent health and was always in good spirits. We were all cheerful. We cast anchor in Argostoli, the principal port of Cephalonia, where General Duffy and Colonel Napier showed Lord Byron every welcome and invited him to dine at the regimental mess – P.

And underneath, a short postscript in English from Byron:

My Dearest Teresa: I cannot write long letters as you know – but you also know or ought to know how much and entirely I am ever your Amico Amante in Eterno – B.

Her friend and lover forever – it was enough to lighten her heart for a little while, and yet the intervals between each letter seemed endless.

~ ~ ~

Despite his reservations about mixing with the English again, not knowing what lies or scandals had been told about him, Byron knew it would be discourteous and a bad beginning to refuse the Eighth Regiment's invitation to dine, and begged Pietro to accompany him.

"Thanks to my not-so-honest wife, I'm told that most English believe I am either bad or mad, so it's going to be very disappointing for them when they meet a sane and rather dull person like myself. As soon as you see the first yawn from them, Pietro, you must nudge me, and we will make our excuses to leave."

And so, on entering the officers' mess with some anxiety, Byron was taken completely by surprise when every officer of the garrison rose to his feet and excitedly applauded him on his entrance.

The senior officers greeted him with true delight, and the younger subalterns were clearly red-faced and overawed at the sight of "*Byron*" in their midst – most moving forward in eagerness to tell him how, from boyhood, they had learned whole stanzas of his poetry by heart; and how *Don Juan* was now considered in the mess to be "the *only* thing worth reading."

A banquet had been prepared in his honour, which caused Pietro some disquiet, knowing that Byron would eat only a portion of vegetables and ignore all the meat.

Yet no one seemed to notice, and Pietro felt great sympathy for Byron, sitting beside Colonel Napier and blinking occasionally, as if somewhat puzzled by their kindness, while all those young and happy boyish faces kept on staring at him.

At the conclusion, all the officers rose to drink Lord Byron's health.

Byron's reply was given in a soft voice that slightly trembled with sincere emotion, as he expressed his pleasure at finding himself again in the society of his countrymen, when he had been so long in the practice of speaking a foreign language. And seeing so many of them together, he could not adequately express his gratitude and obligation to them all.

As he was taking his leave, to row back to the *Hercules,* Colonel Napier offered him the hospitality of the Residency.

Byron politely declined, saying it was his intention live aboard his ship until he eventually reached Missolonghi.

"Then I hope," said Colonel Napier, "that if you are in want of anything you will call on me to assist you. And pray remember that there are two rooms and two beds here in the Residency that will always be at your service and at the service of Count Gamba."

Back on board the ship, in his cabin, and having promised to keep in touch, Byron wrote to Mr Barry in Genoa, telling him about his evening with the Eighth Regiment in Cephalonia.

"Nothing," he wrote, *"can be kinder than the officers have been individually to us. I say this more readily as I neither expected it, nor had cause to expect it."*

He later went up on deck alone and stood in the darkness, looking across at the lights of Argostoli sparkling on the water, bringing back memories of his first journey to Greece in the company of John Hobhouse.

And just as he had so often done on the ship back then, on that first journey, he decided to spend the night on deck, towards the stern of the ship, sitting alone, and leaning against the mizzen shrouds, humming a tune to himself as the stars twinkled above him, while his eyes constantly followed the track of the moon across the sky.

August 11th 1823

My dearest Teresa: – All Well! And doing well. We are on the point of embarking for Ithaca – after a warm ride in the sun from Argostoli. Pietro will have told you the rest. Do not be alarmed, as our present voyage is merely for pleasure in the Islands. – Ever and entirely your A. A. in e. – B.

The following day Colonel Napier came aboard the *Hercules*, and spent some hours with Byron discussing the present condition of Greece.

"The Greeks have unbounded optimism in their hopes of achieving independence," he said, "but they are hampered in every way, by their lack of finances. And also by the refusal of the ship-owners to allow the fleet to put to sea without first being paid. And then, of course, the *Turkish* fleet *are* on the sea, but the Turks are so certain that the Greeks have not the power nor means nor the numbers to defeat them, they have so much confidence, they often don't even bother themselves to prepare to fight the Greeks."

When people of knowledge spoke, Byron always listened without interruption; and then after a few questions here and there, he allowed himself the time to form his own judgements.

Now he was certain that if he was to be of any use at all to the Greeks, he must make his way to Missolonghi, but first he must contact the leaders to be guided by their instructions.

Captain Edward Blaquiere, he was told, had returned to Corfu. And Marcos Botzari, to whom he had been particularly recommended, was at Missolonghi.

Previous to making any step, Byron judged it prudent to despatch two messengers, one to Corfu, and one to Missolonghi, to collect every possible information from the Morea.

Whilst waiting for answers, Byron took a journey across the Island of Cephalonia to Ithaca, leaving most of the servants and everything else on board the ship, save for Pietro and Tita.

The first day they reached St Euphemia, one of the principal ports of the island on the side of Ithaca. And it was here that Pietro first noticed a change in Byron.

Now that he was in Greece, a new vigour seemed to have come into his spirit, more than he had ever displayed in Italy. There was such a force of energy within him, an elasticity in all his physique, and in his morale, as if he was prepared and ready to overcome even the gravest of crises.

An English magistrate who resided at St Euphemia politely offered Lord Byron and his friends the hospitality of his home; but notwithstanding having done a journey of six hours on mules, under a scorching sun, and nearly impassable roads, Byron was appreciative but determined to proceed on to Ithaca to reach there by evening.

Crossing the narrow strait between the two islands in an open four-oared boat, the beautiful views of the surrounding coasts, made Byron smile and say to Pietro, "Now, was it not worth journeying on, just to see this?

Tita was too busy chatting to the boatman, surprised to discover that almost everyone in the Islands spoke Italian almost as good as well as Greek.

"And some of us," said the boatman, "also speak some *Inglese.*"

On land, it was nearing sunset, and the boatman had said the town of *Vathi* was more than six miles distant over hilly roads, with no house, no sign of human habitation to be seen.

"I am tired," Tita said. "My body needs a rest from sitting on the mule."

Pietro said he, too, was feeling very fatigued and needed a rest.

Byron looked around, and then suggested they rest for the night in one of the many caves along the coast.

"Like an adventure!" grinned Pietro; and before long they were refreshing themselves with handfuls of ripe grapes which grew on the hills, before a swim in the water, while Tita sat on guard, still eating grapes.

Under the approaching moonlight, the three sat on the shore of the lake talking of times past, and learning more about each others' personal lives than they would have done in the course of a normal day; before settling down inside a small grotto, wrapped in their cloaks as they slept.

Tita awoke at dawn of the following day, shaking the other two awake.

They journeyed on, reaching Vathi in the afternoon, where – as soon as he heard that it was Lord Byron in the vicinity, a Captain Knox and his amiable lady came rushing out to invite his lordship to visit their home for some hospitality and take a bed for the night.

Byron bowed, and accepted, but did not actually enter the house until they had done some more sightseeing of the area and its magnificent scenery.

Returning to the house, they dined outside on wine, cheese and fruit. It was a cool night, which refreshed them after the heat of the day, and their host, Captain Knox, who valued himself on his learning and scholarship, made them pay a trifle for his hospitality by obliging them to listen for hours to his long and antiquarian dissertations.

Finally, they were allowed to go to their room, which contained only one bed, and a small bed at that, no bigger than a cot.

Tita was furious; Pietro was perplexed; and Byron was laughing.

"Now you know why so many of the Continentals refer to us as the *mad* English!"

"What do we do?" Tita asked. "Not one of us could fit in that small bed."

The only solution was to do as they had done the night before, and slept on the floor wrapped in their cloaks.

A short time later, fast asleep, all three were suddenly awakened by a violent earthquake which shook the house as if it was made of paper.

A door to the room opened to some stairs leading down to the garden, and Byron was the first to run down them as fast as he could, with Tita following him, yet when they reached the ground Pietro was already there.

"How did you do that?" Byron asked in bewilderment. "I was the first to spring up and get out of the room."

Pietro was grinning. "You were both in my way, so I

jumped over the staircase and reached the ground first."

The earthquake was over within minutes, but part of the roof of the house had been shaken off; and yet when Byron went back inside the house to investigate their safety – he discovered the host and his good lady were still fast asleep and snoring in their bed – obviously not having felt or heard a thing.

"My only conclusion," said Byron, as they rode away, "is that earthquakes strong enough to rattle part of a tiled-roof off, must be quite common in this area, and so they pay no heed and sleep on, trusting in God to protect them."

"As all good Christians should," said Tita, making the sign of the Cross over himself, "but me, I prefer to run."

~~~

Returning to the ship at Cephalonia, a letter was waiting for Byron from Mavrocordato in Hydra:

Marco Botzaris is one the bravest of the Greek captains, and if he could secure your illustrious friendship and assistance you would see by the result what advantageous operations he will be capable of.

Byron had no sooner finished reading the letter when he picked up another letter from Marco Botzaris himself, in reply to one Byron had sent to Botzaris five days earlier.

My dear Lord Byron – your letter has filled me with joy. Your Excellency is exactly the person of whom we stand in need. Let nothing prevent you from coming to this part of Greece. The enemy threatens us in great number; but by the help of God and Your Excellency, they shall meet a suitable resistance. I shall have something to do tonight against a corps of six or seven thousand Albanians, encamped close to
~~~

this place. The day after tomorrow I will set out, with a few chosen companions, to meet you. Do not delay. I thank you for the good opinion you have of my fellow-citizens, which God grant you will not find ill-founded, and I thank you still more for the care you have for them.

> *Believe me, etc – Marco Botzaris.*

That very night – Marco Botzaris had attacked the camp of Omer Pasha and had been shot in the head by a Turkish musket ball. His body was recovered and returned to Missolonghi.

Thus, Byron realised, of the two leaders to whom he had been recommended, one had already lost his life and the other was a refugee in Hydra.

The news of Byron's arrival had now spread throughout Greece, and representatives of each of the contending factions flocked to Cephalonia in the hope of securing his assistance and partisanship.

The only ship Captain Scott cared about was his own, and early one morning, hearing loud voices which drew him up on deck, he was horrified to see about forty small boats around his ship and their occupants, a flock of Suoliotes and Greeks, savage in their appearance and wild in their attire, climbing up the rope ladders to board the ship.

The Captain called to his crew to drive them overboard with hand-spikes – until Byron came on deck in exuberant spirits, delighted to see all the Greeks and Suoliotes, and not at all discommoded as they surrounded him.

Few of these warriors had washed in weeks, but who could criticize them, knowing they had come from the dirt and lack of amenities of the various war zones.

All were clamouring around him, all talking at once, and Byron was displaying incredible patience; although every so often, Pietro Gamba noticed, Byron discreetly fiddled with his scented black cravat and momentarily held one end of it close to his nose as he listened.

Finally, all were ordered to back off – except for the leaders, when each, in turn, stated their needs.

Kolocotrones from Salamis invited Lord Byron to a national assembly at Salamis. Another stated that he would be of no use anywhere but at Hydra. The Governor of Missolonghi had sent a note saying that Greece would be ruined unless Lord Byron would come to Missolonghi bringing medical supplies, as well as money to buy food for the starving and more weapons for the war.

Of the Greeks and Suoliotes still crowding the deck and wanting him to join their particular faction, Byron had only one reply for them all –

"I came to Greece not to join a faction, but a nation. As an envoy of the London Greek Committee, any assistance I can give will not be for one party, but for all. And that I will do from the place where the Greek provisional government has instructed me to reside – in Missolonghi."

Nevertheless, before they left the ship, all had the satisfaction of being given sufficient medical supplies and dollars to take away with them in their boats.

Yet the hostility and rivalry between the Greek factions had disturbed Byron so much, he decided to address an open letter to the Greek Government, in which he stated that no loan from himself nor from England would be forthcoming as long as these dissensions amongst the Greeks continued.

I am very uneasy at hearing that the dissensions of Greece still continue, and at a moment when she might triumph over everything in general, as she has already triumphed in part. Greece at present has three choices: either to re-conquer her liberty, or to become dependent on the sovereigns of Europe, or to return to a Turkish province. She has the choice of only these three alternatives. Civil war is but a road which leads to the last two. If she is desirous of the same fate as the Crimea, she may obtain it tomorrow; or if that of Italy, the day after; but if she wishes to become truly Greece, free and independent, she must resolve all today, or she will never again have the opportunity.

In the weeks that followed, copies of Lord Byron's letter were read out in every town, every Greek garrison; and, miraculously, Byron's words had the desired effect. It would not be one faction fighting for itself or against another, but all in unity fighting for Greece.

Byron was reassured, and resolved in his mission; and even more so when he received a letter from John Bowring, chairman of the London Greek Committee:

"We cannot doubt the importance of Your Lordship's presence in Greece — for the sake of the Greeks, for the sake of our Committee, and on every account. The knowledge of your presence there will increase our funds and our influence at home and abroad. People will have a confidence in the cause itself, and in the distribution of whatever funds they shall give to the cause."

Byron folded the letter, realising no more time could be spent in the Islands. It was time to sail to the mainland.

~~~

The town of Missolonghi is fronted by a lagoon which runs parallel to the Gulf of Patras, from which it is separated by approximately three miles.

In his cabin on the ship, Byron finally donned the scarlet uniform which London had ordered him to wear while acting as her representative in any of the war
~~~

zones.

He then descended into the small-boat which had been sent to convey him across the three miles of marshy waters to Missolonghi. The island of Cephalonia was now a distant forty miles away.

In the boat with him were Pietro Gamba, Tita Falceiri, Lega Zambelli, and William Fletcher, and also his three faithful dogs – all ready to share in whatever destiny lay ahead for their master.

The boat landed amid salvos of artillery, the firing of muskets, and the stupendous wild yells of the populace screaming out chants of "*Vyron! Vyron! Vyron!*"

Amidst all the noise he was led to the door of the house which had been allotted to him, where he was received by Alexander Mavrocordato, Colonel Leslie Stanhope, and a crowd of Greek and European officers.

"I cannot," he wrote in his journal, "easily describe the emotions which such a scene excited: I could scarcely refrain from tears: whether moved by the noise and signs of joy and delight, I know not; or whether from gladness that we were now on the mainland and true Grecian soil."

Chapter Forty-Seven

~ ~ ~

In England, the Greek War for Independence had caused little interest amongst the populace; but two things were radically changing that, and speedily removing their indifference.

The first, was their growing resentment against the powers of the European Alliance, and their British indignation against a foreign policy that was being dictated to Britain from Vienna.

How dared those Europeans tell Great Britain what to do? They were sick to the teeth of it. And to side with the Turks against the Greeks was to side with Russia, who backed the Ottoman empire entirely.

And now Russia, Germany and Austria were moving to place themselves as the dominant leaders in the European Alliance, and – some of the leading newspapers believed – could eventually pose a threat to Britain itself.

The second, and most powerful event of all, was the news that one of their own British nobles, Lord Byron, was out in Greece leading the revolution against the Turks, risking his own life and his own fortune in an attempt to aid Greece.

This changed everything. This made the Greek cause *personal* to Britain, and a matter of *national* interest. This made *news* that travelled around the country and cast a new light on it all.

This alone, in country districts and towns, caused all party politics to be cast aside no matter if they supported one side or the other, the Tories or the Whigs, all were now unified in their eagerness to support *Greece.*

And the fact that it was *Lord Byron*, their most famous poet since Shakespeare – as wayward and capricious as he was – gave the whole enterprise a burst of excitement to the men; while the ladies considered Byron's presence to give the Greek Cause a novel touch of *romance*.

Byron's friend, and one of the leaders of the London Greek Committee, John Cam Hobhouse, was not excited at all, but deeply worried and anxious, for now he was certain that Byron was in too deep, and had gone far beyond the remit given to him by the Committee.

The role the Committee had given to Byron was solely to exercising moral influence by his presence; by his encouragements; by the wisdom of his counsel and the prestige of his name; by financial resources, and undoubtedly by a great number of sacrifices contributing to the liberation of Greece, but *not* by risking his life in battle!

Something which Byron continually seemed determined to do, as he was now bent upon removing the Turks from Patras and attacking Lepanto.

"We shall have work this year, for the Turks are coming down in force; and as for me, I must stand by the cause. I shall shortly march (according to orders) against Lepanto, with two thousand men. I have had some narrow escapes from the Turks, but this you will have heard."

Holy God! – would that man *never* do what he was told to do without veering off in whims of his own – without any thought of self-preservation?

And now Byron had added even more to Hobhouse's anxieties with the arrival of another letter from him at Missolonghi, full of good humour and high-spirits – not only because of the fall of Corinth to the Greeks – but because of the many independent volunteers from various countries now arriving in Missolonghi to join him. Some were mercenaries and adventurers for sure, but in Byron's opinion that did not disqualify them if their service could prove useful.

And from his letter, it seemed that *nobody* was to be judged disqualified if they could be useful:

"There is a Greek tailor, who had been in the British service in the Ionian islands, where he had married an Italian woman, but is now in Missolonghi. This lady petitioned me to appoint her husband as master-tailor of the brigade. The suggestion was useful, and her petition was granted. At the same time, she petitioned that she also may be allowed to raise a corps of women, to be placed under her orders, to accompany the regiment. She stipulated for free quarters and rations for them, but rejected all claim for pay. They were to be free of all encumbrances, and were to cook, wash, sew, and otherwise provide for the men. In Greece there are many circumstances which would make their services extremely valuable, and I gave my consent. The tailor's wife has now recruited a number of unencumbered women of all nations, but principally, Greeks, Italians, Maltese and Negresses. Is this not the thing? – the very thing!

So let me see – my corps outdoes Falstaff's: there are English, Irish, French, Maltese, Italians, Transylvanians, Suoliotes, Moreotes, and Western Greeks in front, and, to bring up the rear, the tailor's wife and her troop of women. Glorious Apollo! no general had ever before such an army."

Hobhouse was still fuming as he made his way to visit Byron's half-sister, Augusta Leigh – a woman who fluttered and flapped nervously at the slightest thing.

He had promised to show Augusta every letter he

received from her brother, but was dubious whether he should show her *this* one?

Perhaps he would say he had inadvertently left the letter behind, but that all was well: good health, good weather, good tidings, and all that.

Upon his arrival, it was Augusta who excitedly greeted him with a letter, which she had received from her relative Lord Sidney Osborne, upon his return from Cephalonia, saying that – she read out – "If Byron had never written a line of poetry in his life, he has done enough, during the last six months in Greece, to honour his name. And that anyone not acquainted with the circumstances over there, could have no idea of the difficulties Byron has overcome. He has reconciled the opposing parties, and has given a character of humanity and civilisation to the warfare in which they are engaged, besides contriving to prevent the Greeks and Suoliotes from offending their neighbours in the Ionian Islands."

Augusta's face was beaming. "Are you not *proud* of him, Hobby?"

"Oh, indeed, yes, indeed, very proud," Hobhouse replied, and then sighed as he realised that love for one's dearest friend could be such a *selfish* and worrying thing.

~ ~ ~

The Greek fleet were back out on the sea, all paid and accounted for from Byron's own funds, and now guarding the waterways to Missolonghi; allowing Captain William Parry and his ship to cut through and deliver some field artillery and a few tons of gunpowder to Lord Byron from the London Greek Committee.

William Parry was a hardened seaman who had been sent out to be their fire-master at Missolonghi.

"Not, my lord, to kill anyone wantonly, mind," said Parry, "but in defence of yourself and the Greeks against the Turks."

There was something about Parry, a rough burly

fellow, but no fool, that reminded Byron of some of the men of his own county of Nottinghamshire; down-to-earth, brusque-mannered men, who could be relied upon in difficult situations.

He also found Parry very amusing, often talking to him for hours at the end of the day and enjoying the sheer *Englishness* of him, for Parry had a fund of pot-house stories, and was a great mimic as he told them.

They talked of Parry's time at sea and how he liked everything to be kept in good order and shipshape.

"I have no objection to a glass of grog," Parry said, "but I can't *abide* drunkenness at sea. I am not a temperance man, but I always restrict myself to drinking no more than my preferred daily allowance."

"And how much is that?" Byron asked.

"Why, a good old bottle of Jamaica rum serves me from ten in the morning until ten at night, and I know that can't hurt any man."

Laughing, Byron leaned back and lifted two flasks from the stool beside the Turkish divan and poured the contents of one flask into the other, gave the full flask a good shake, and then poured some of the liquid into Parry's glass.

"Here, try a gin swizzle, and tell me what you think of it."

"A gin swizzle? That's a new one. What is it?"

"Gin mixed with soda water."

Parry tasted it, and tasted it again, but was not overly impressed. "It doesn't have the kick of my good old Jamaica rum, but I daresay it would do if there was no rum about."

"Parry, do you think you would ever want to, or ever be capable of writing a book?"

"Me? Write a book, my lord? Why, I'd as lief throw myself into the mouth of a shark and be done with it, than torture myself to death trying to write a book!"

Byron smiled. "Then, Parry, I believe you and I can be friends."

Chapter Forty-Eight

~~~

In Ravenna, Teresa was almost at the end of her wits, worrying about Byron. He had not returned after "*a few months*" as he had promised. Nor had he returned in time for Christmas. Now the winter was well in, and it had been two months since she had received a letter – until, at last, two letters arrived from him at the same time – the first dated *December 14th 1823.*

Carissima – but I forgot that I must write to you in English by your own request. Well! – here we are still – but how long we may be so, I cannot say. The Greek affairs go on rather better – but I won't bore you with politics.

The climate up to this day, has been quite beautiful. Tuscany is Lapland in comparison – but today we have a high wind and rain – but it is still as warm as your primavera. Pietro and I are occupied all day and every day with Greek business, and our correspondence already amounts to that of Santa Chiara – even when your Eccellenza was in the course of your education there.

Greet Olimpia from me, also Giulia and Laurina, not forgetting Papa. Yesterday I was caught in the rain and I <u>ache,</u> but it is only temporary. Pietro has been ill, but thanks to our little doctor Bruno who is very pedantic, he is quite well again.

For my part me-me-ne etc. – but always very much my dearest T. – your Amico Amante in Eterno.
~~~

The second letter was dated *January 24th, 1824*, and was no more than a few lines:

My dearest Teresa: You will have heard of our adventures from Pietro. We are well I will write soon at greater length – and I hope to see you this Spring and to talk over these and all other matters with you. In the interim Love me – and be assured that you are the most beloved of your – B.

Teresa was devastated. Now his return was not to be until the Spring – so a long and lonely bleak winter to endure until then – and would his time of *Spring* be delayed yet again until Summer?

Surely the "Greek business" did not take up so much of his time as he said. So much time that he could write only very short letters to her every few months?

And yet, if she only knew, Pietro often thought, it *did* take up all of Byron's time – he was now devoted heart and soul to the Greek mission, and determined to see it through to its end.

"And what if Greece falls?" Pietro asked.

"If Greece falls, then I shall bury myself in its ruins!" Byron snapped.

Which made Pietro wonder now about Teresa and her place in Byron's life.

"Pay no heed," William Parry said to Pietro. "I've seen this kind of thing before. When men find themselves in a battle zone, and have a job to do, they cannot allow themselves to dwell on the softer things in life. Plenty of time for that later, when the job is done and the mission completed."

And yet it was all very difficult for Byron, for not one of the regular British officers or soldiers on the nearby Ionian Islands could be applied to for assistance.

In order to prevent aggravation and displeasure to the countries of the European Alliance – Britain had to be seen as being totally *neutral* in the Greek uprising against the Turks – although if independent British citizens set out for the Continent to help the Greeks at their own expense, that was no affair of the British Government.

And the fact that many members of the British Parliament were also members of the Greek Committee and were actively employed in raising funds to help Greece, that was something else the British Government pretended to have no knowledge of. No knowledge whatsoever.

Lord Byron to John Bowring, London.

The Turks are an obstinate race, as all former wars have proved them – and will return to the charge for years to come – even if beaten – as it is hoped that they will be. But in no case can it be said that the labour of the Committee will be in vain – for in the event of the Greeks being subdued, or even dispersed – the funds which can be employed in succouring and gathering together the remnant – so as to alleviate in part their distresses – and enable them to find or make a country (as so many emigrants of other nations have been compelled to do – would bless both those who gave and those who took –) as the bounty both of Justice and Mercy.

With regard to the formation of a proper Brigade, which Mr Hobhouse hints at in his short letter of this day's receipt, I would presume to suggest, but merely an opinion, that the attention of the Committee had better perhaps be directed to the employment of "Officers" of experience, than the enrolment of raw British soldiers – which latter are apt to be unruly and not very serviceable in irregular warfare – by the side of foreigners. A small body of good officers – especially Artillery is most wanted. Officers who have previously served in the Mediterranean would be preferable – as some knowledge of Italian is nearly indispensable as everyone in Greece can speak Italian.

It would also be as well that they should be aware that they are not going "to rough it on a beef steak and a bottle of Port" – but that Greece has never of late years been very plentiful and stocked for a "Mess" – and is at present a country of all kinds of privations.

This comment may seem superfluous – but I have been led to it by observing that many foreign officers – Italian and French also – have gone away in disgust, imagining that they were going up to make a party of pleasure in Greece – or to enjoy full pay – speedy promotion – and a very small degree of duty.

Those Greeks that I have seen strenuously deny the charge of inhospitality – and declare that they have shared their pittance to the last Crumb with their foreign volunteers.

I beg the Committee will command me in any and every way, and I shall endeavour to obey them to the letter – whether conformable to my own private opinion or not.

Yours etc.
G. G. Lord Byron.

~~~

</div>

Another short letter from Pietro went a good way to calming Teresa's fears:
~~~

The winter has come upon us without us being aware of it. I hope you have resigned yourself to wait until the spring. You must applaud our diligence. All this time here! Can you believe in the "monkish virtues" of Byron? They are above all praise.

In Genoa, Mr Charles Barry, was reading a less virtuous letter from Byron:

If these gentlemen (the various Greek factions) discover my weak side, viz. a propensity to be governed, and were to set a pretty woman, or a clever woman, about me, with a turn for political or any other sort of intrigue, – why, they could make a fool of me – no very difficult matter probably. But if I keep my passion, at least that passion, out of the question, then it will be easy for me, as I have left my heart in Italy.

Chapter Forty-Nine

~ ~ ~

At the end of February the rain began to pour non-stop, drenching everything and everyone and turning the streets of Missolonghi into rivers of mud.

Dark clouds hung over the sea, shrouding the Greek ships in mist. All plans for action against Lepanto had been suspended until the weather cleared.

Every afternoon Byron stood by his window gazing out at the dreariness, wondering if this was the day the rain would stop.

Yet the rain persisted, day after day, black and torrential, upon the marshy lagoons of Missolonghi.

He could no longer ride out to check on the troops, as he had been doing every morning, to make sure they had enough water and food; so he set out in a canoe instead, always accompanied by Pietro and Tita, and four Souliote armed guards.

In the dullness of the inactive days, Captain William Parry was employing his time writing long letters to his mates in England; but now, as Lord Byron's friend, he had promoted himself with a new title, signing off his letters as – *Major Parry of Lord Byron's Brigade, Commanding Officer of Artillery and Engineer in the service of the Greeks.*

Yet, unlike others he had known, such as Edward Trelawny and his like, Byron knew that William Parry was no pretentious humbug. He had worked hard every day drilling the soldiers and training them in artillery fire and in cleaning and guarding the arsenal – and only in one respect had Parry failed – insisting that the Greeks "refused to be disciplined".

"See here, Parry," Byron said with puzzlement, holding a sheaf of papers "Over the past two months I have received all of these letters from a Captain Hastings in England, seeking to advise me on how the

Greek war should be fought, but, for the life of me, I don't know who the deuce this Captain Hastings is."

"An armchair expert, I know them all," Parry said dismissively. "They know as much about war as I know about knitting, but a shilling dropped into a war-aid collection box now and again, and they think it has bought them the right to tell the generals what to do. Pay no heed, my lord, pay no heed."

Byron threw down the letters and moved to stare through the window again, saying, "The marshes of Missolonghi have turned into a mud-basket ... the dykes of Holland, when broken down, are like the dryness of the deserts of Arabia in comparison to this."

"And some of the Greeks are saying that the marshes are turning plaguey," Parry said. "Now that's an added worry for us, I daresay. The last thing we need is men falling down sick. If that happens, the plague, we would have to retire to the mountains."

Byron was not so easily fooled. "You forget, Parry, that I am not new to Greece. But what you say makes me think we must have a sly traitor in our camp."

Parry was both confused and alarmed. "What makes you say so?"

"The plague has not been known here or in the Morea or in any part of Western Greece. But when I was over in Patras in 1811, a similar report was spread by agents of the Turks to disperse the disaffected Greeks, and once that report was spread, in less than two hours the town was empty. It's an old trick."

And so it proved – and the traitor who had been spreading a report of the plague – was detected and put into isolated quarantine – "for the good of his own health."

The drilling of the companies was back in progress, so much so that Byron was certain that – "When this weather clears we will be ready to take the field against Lepanto."

Prince Mavrocordato, who was now in Eastern Greece strengthening the foundations of the provisional government, sent a communication, endorsed by General Londo and four other Greek officials, asking if Lord Byron in person would proceed to the seat of the provisional government as a member; or if he would accept the office of Governor-General of Greece?

Byron's response was laughter, showing the letter to Pietro. "Did I not tell them that although my body and mind are here in Greece, my heart remains in Italy, whence I will one day return, and in a time not too far off, I hope!"

The following day, in mid-March, the primates of Missolonghi presented Lord Byron with a document awarding to him the Citizenship of Missolonghi.

Byron could hardly respond, for he had developed a cold and was feeling unwell.

A few days later, as the weather was finer, The Turkish fleet was observed sailing out of the Gulf of Patras.

Preparations were made for the guns to be brought to the front of the fortress, and all the batteries were manned by the troops of the town.

Byron and his guard rode out for three miles, ensuring all the inhabitants had enough supplies and were not alarmed.

The following day, seeing that Missolonghi had prepared for attack, the three Turkish ships that came into view, obviously thought it prudent to get out of the way, and sailed back to Patras.

"This is their game," said one of the primates. "They will try to wear us down with fear and constantly keeping us on our guard, day and night."

Pietro had a worse fear, for during the previous few days Byron had visibly suffered in health, although he kept insisting it was "only a cold."

Then something happened which lightened Byron's spirits immeasurably – a letter from his friend, John Hobhouse, informing him that the Greek fund from the people of England had reached almost two million pounds, and the first instalment of £800,000 of that amount was now on its way to him, sent into the safe care of General Duffy of the King's Eighth Regiment in the Ionian Islands.

"It is your name, Byron, and <u>your name</u> alone, that has enabled us to raise this amount," Hobhouse wrote with glee, making Byron smile – feeling too ill to do much more.

Finally he was forced to take to his bed, diagnosed with a fever.

"Fever," he shrugged. "I've had numerous fevers in my life, and I've always managed to fight them off. Just a day or two of rest, that's all I need."

In the sitting-room outside his bedroom, Pietro was placing all the blame for Byron's decrease in health to the sighting of the Turkish ships and the three mile ride they had made to the outside the town a few days earlier.

"Because the weather was not threatening," Pietro said, "Byron resolved to ride out on horseback, but three miles out we were overtaken by a heavy rain, and we returned to the walls wet through, and he in a violent perspiration. It has always been our practice to dismount at the walls, and return to the house in a boat."

"That is true," said Tita, "that is always true."

"That day though, seeing the state of him, I begged Byron to go back all the way on horseback, as it would be very dangerous, hot and wet as he was, to remain exposed to the rain in a boat for another half an hour. But he would not listen to me, saying to me, 'I should make a pretty soldier, if I were to care for such a trifle'."

"That's always been his way," Fletcher said, "ever since a boy, he will *not* be told! Oh, the stories I could tell you of how he used to throw himself fully-clothed into the lake at Newstead Abbey, just so his dog would jump in after him and learn how to save a drowning man. Reckless, truly reckless."

Chapter Fifty

~ ~ ~

The next morning Byron got up at his usual hour, and transacted business; but he was perpetually shuddering, and did not leave the house. Melancholy and very irritable, he eventually returned to his bed.

Parry came into his room and was full of excitement. A Turkish brig had been sighted, "about the size of one that would be mounting twenty-two guns." It had run ashore and was grounded on the coast about six or seven miles from the city.

"What will I do, my lord, will I go for it?"

Byron was almost as excited. "Yes, take some troops and go for it, Parry. The Turks always make sure their ships are filled with plenty of food supplies – supplies that will be useful here in Missolonghi. Take the brig, Parry, and if necessary take prisoners – but warn your troops – no slaughter or carnage. In that respect, we are more civilised than the Turks."

"Aye, aye, my lord, consider it done!"

Two days passed before Parry returned, and when he did, he greeted Pietro in the yard of the house, fuming with rage.

"Those damned Turks. What did they do? They took off in a small boats after setting the brig on fire, so we couldn't get our hands on it – burning it down into a bundle of sticks – with all the supplies reduced to ashes. Even their artillery had been smashed down."

Pietro didn't care. "Parry," he said, "do not take this news to Lord Byron. He is very ill."

"Ill? Still?"

"Much worse. The doctors have bled him with leeches."

"Bled him with leeches? Why in damnation did they do that? Surely they know that does nobody any good. A drop of my rum would serve him better! In my experience, and if I had my way, all doctors would be thrown out the window."

Still furious about the destruction of the brig, Parry made his way up to Lord Byron's rooms to report.

To his surprise, Byron seemed rather amused at the destruction of the brig. "Look on the bright side, Parry, and think of the loss it has also occasioned to the Turks."

"About twenty thousand dollars worth, I would say, and one small brig of war – a trifling sum to a large empire like Turkey."

"In war, every loss is a loss."

"By God," exclaimed Parry, "I hate those Turks, don't you?"

"No," Byron replied. "With the exception of Robert Southey and Lady Byron, I hate no one."

"Just those two, my lord, no one else?"

"No, just those two?"

Byron lay back on his pillow exhausted. "Those butchers of doctors have bled my head, Parry, because they say the fever has inflamed my brain. And how else could my poor brain react – in one week I have been ill – the troops threatening mutiny – a Turkish brig burned – a drunken man killed in a fight – an earthquake – thunder and lightning and torrents of rain. Such a week. I shall have to put it all into my next Canto of Don Juan. I would do it now, if my head did not *ache* so violently."

"A drop of rum will set you to rights and calm everything down, my lord, or how about one of them gin swizzles of yours?"

"No, just let me rest, there's a good man. Sleep is what I need, but no doubt there'll be another earthquake or some other bloody disaster to prevent me."

"Then you rest, my lord, and I'll leave you be. Is there anything you might need now?"

"Yes," Byron sighed. "If you could get me a long

summer in Italy under the care of gentle hands, I'm sure my health would be very quickly restored. But I cannot, in all decency, abandon the Greeks now."

No sooner had Parry left, when Fletcher came back into the room to fuss over him, causing Byron to snap irritably, "Will you stop your fussing, Fletcher! It is only a common fever which you know I have had a thousand times."

"I am sure, my lord, that you have never before had one of so serious a nature."

After a pause, Byron said more quietly, "No, you are right, I never have."

~~~

On the 17th April Lord Byron was reported by his doctors, Bruno and Millingen, to be alarmingly ill, but they would not allow Parry or anyone else to see him, except Fletcher and Tita Falcieri.

Dr Bruno, in his pedantic way, sought to explain to Parry and others, all anxious, about the seriousness of his predicament.

"I have charged his faithful servant, Battista Falcieri, to repeat to His Excellency the alarm I feel, and the fears which I begin to entertain, if he does not allow me to bleed him again."

"Bleed my arse!" Parry said furiously. "It's probably your earlier bleeding that has made him so weak now! If you keep bleeding him you will eventually kill him!"

Tears bubbling to his eyes, Dr Bruno indignantly expostulated: "I am astonished to hear such words from you, Captain Parry, since you should be made aware of how great was my veneration for him, that I agreed to leave my widowed mother in Italy in order to follow his eminent lordship to Greece. And you should also know that it is only due to my deep conviction of the absolute necessity of bleeding him further, that I propose it."

The following afternoon Parry found Pietro Gamba in tears and questioned him.
~~~

"I fear the worst," Pietro said. "Fletcher told me they bled him with leeches on his head last night, while he was asleep, but now Fletcher thinks they put the leeches too near the main artery, taking out too much blood, and now he looks as pale as a death."

Parry fled up to the room and as soon as he saw Byron, he knew all hope of his recovery was gone. He was sitting up in bed, his back leaning against a pillow, and a white bandage around his head.

Tita was sitting by the bed, holding Byron's hand, and Fletcher on the other side, while Lega Zambelli stood morosely over by the window. ... all three men were silently crying.

"He needs to sleep," Dr Bruno said, "but he won't take this mixture of bark and opium."

"What's the point?" Byron said weakly. "It's like warning a man to beware of his wife, *after* he has married her."

He looked up at Parry. "Parry, they all refuse, but will *you* be good enough to remove this bandage from my head. It's so tight it's causing me great pain."

Parry did not hesitate. He set about loosening the bandages and while this was being done, Byron gritted his teeth, and uttered the Italian exclamation of "*Ah, Christi!*" And after it was loosened he shed tears.

Parry encouraged him to weep, and said, "My Lord, the bandages are loosened now, and I thank God, I hope you will now feel better. Shed as many tears as you can, and it will help you to sleep and find ease."

"Yes, thank you, it feels better ... I remember now, how my mother often used to say to me, 'never let doctors bleed you, promise that you will never let them bleed you.' These doctors, Parry, they seem to be saying that I am dying ... is it true?"

"I would say those two idiots of doctors have helped to kill you," Parry wanted to say – but instead, he silently nodded.

"So, it *is* true?"

"If they say so, my lord. I would not disagree with

them, and I could not in all conscience lie to you."

At that Tita's tears overcame him and he tried to get up to leave the room but Byron was holding his hand too tightly, so he sat down again, and turned his tearful face away.

Byron seemed shocked to know it for certain. "So I *am* dying, Parry? But why then ... why was I not told this sooner? And why did I not go to England first before coming here? ... to see my daughter Ada? Or back to Italy ...?"

His tears began to spill again at the stark realisation of it, and Parry realised that up until that moment, although knowing he was very ill, Byron had possessed no idea whatsoever that he was in fact dying from his illness, and his life would soon be over.

"His little daughter Allegra died from the same malaria fever," Fletcher moaned, and then bit his lip, realising he should not have spoken so.

Pietro entered the room, and then everyone in the room was weeping, except Parry, who was prevented from doing so by the hard thumping of his heart against the block in his throat.

"Come, come, no weakness!" Byron said, as if talking to himself. "Let's be a man to the last."

"But, my lord," Fletcher said despairingly, "only a couple of months ago you turned thirty-six – too young to leave us."

"It is not *my* will, Fletcher, I would have it otherwise. But now let me give you some instructions. You will be provided for – and now hear my last wishes."

Fletcher begged that he might bring pen and paper to take down his words, and at the same time expressed a hope that he might yet live.

"No," replied Byron, "there is no time for pen and paper – I feel time vanishing – and mind you execute my orders. I want you to ... "

His voice faltered and became weaker and almost indistinct, and yet he continued muttering something in a very earnest way for almost twenty minutes, though in such a tone that only a few words could be distinguished ... "Ada" –"Augusta" –"Teresa "– "Hobhouse"

He then took a deep breath and said more clearly, "Now I have told you all."

"My lord," replied Fletcher, "I have not understood a word you have been saying."

Byron looked distressed, "*Not* understood me?"

"Not a word, my lord."

Byron lay back on the pillow. "Then it is too late ... I have not the energy to say it all again."

His eyes caught sight of Pietro – "*Mio caro Pierino,*" he said, and beckoned him to come closer.

Pietro did so, bending low over him, and Byron said something quietly to him in Italian, relating to *"Mia carissima Teresa."*

Pietro nodded, kissed Byron's face, and then, in an agony of grief, had to withdraw from the room.

Fletcher adjusted the pillow under his lordship's head and Byron lapsed into a deep sleep of unconsciousness for almost twenty-four hours without waking, blood constantly trickling down his face. The vein in his head which the inept Dr Bruno had opened, had been opened too wide, and would not close again.

Without ever regaining consciousness, Byron breathed his last breath and died at 6:15 pm on Monday the 19th April, 1824, in Missolonghi, Greece, aged 36.

PART TEN

"It is not one man nor a million, but the spirit of Liberty that must be preserved. The waves which dash upon the shore are, one by one, broken, but the ocean conquers nevertheless. It overwhelms the Armada, it wears out the rock. In like manner, whatever the struggle of individuals, the great cause of Liberty will continue to gather strength."

Lord Byron.

Chapter Fifty-One

~ ~ ~

Missolonghi was stunned into silence at the news of Lord Byron's death. None of the inhabitants would believe their great benefactor had left them; but he had left them, and all too soon the awful news began to sink in.

At daybreak on the 20th April, the silence was broken by thirty-six explosions fired into the air and echoing over the lagoons from the artillery, honouring the thirty-six years of his life.

Hearing the explosions, and understanding the codes of war, the Turkish garrisons at Patras and Lepanto knew that a great and honoured man of thirty-six years had died at Missolonghi – *"Vyron!"*

The Turks replied with their own gunfire of salvo after salvo of rejoicing and delight.

In London, on that same day, John Cam Hobhouse was happily writing a letter to Byron, telling him of the favourable disposition displayed towards him by the Prime Minister, George Canning, and the gratitude of the Greek Committee for all his great exertions on behalf of Greece.

" ... Nothing," Hobhouse wrote to Byron, *"can be more serviceable to the cause than all you have done; everybody is more than pleased and content. As for myself, I can only trust that the great sacrifices which you have made will (I have no doubt they will) contribute to the final success of the great cause of the independence of Greece. This will indeed be something worth living for, and will make your name and character stand far above any contemporary. At the same time, do not, I*

pray, expose yourself to any danger, either by flood or field – Above all take care of your health, and do not go to the feverish marshes of the Morea, where you were once so ill.

Your money matters, Kinnaird will tell you, are going on swimmingly, and with the sale at last of your property and coal mines at Rochdale, you will have – indeed you have – a very handsome fortune; and if you have health, I do not see what earthly advantage you could wish for that you have not got. Your present endeavour is certainly the most glorious. Campbell said to me yesterday that he envied what you are now doing (and you may believe him, for he is a very envious man) even more than all your laurels, blooming as they are. Go on and prosper.

Your devoted friend,
John Cam Hobhouse.

P.S. – All friends here make many inquiries after you, and hope you will take care of yourself in Greece, and will return here after the good fight has been foughten."

Hobhouse posted his letter, not knowing that Byron had died the previous evening at Missolonghi; and did not know of it, until he received a letter on the 5th of May from Pietro Gamba, and almost collapsed with a rush of stabbing pain as he read the opening paragraphs:

Signor Hobhouse, – The misfortune that has befallen us is terrible and irreparable. I scarcely have words to describe it. Lord Byron is dead. Your friend, and my friend and father, the saviour of Greece, is dead. I cannot tell you the inconsolable grief of his friends and of the whole of Greece. In the flower of his prime, and of such – "

Hobhouse could read no more, engulfed in tears of grief and shuddering pain.

Later that day, when he had calmed, Hobby did read the full letter, in which Pietro explained that the primates of Missolonghi had issued a proclamation decreeing that the Easter Festival would be suspended; that all the shops would be closed for three days; that a general mourning for twenty-one days should be observed; and that at sunrise the next morning, thirty-six minute guns would fire the last post.

A surgeon had come over from the Ionian Islands in a fast-sailing boat, *a mystico,* and had embalmed Lord Byron's body, and seemed astonished at the perfect symmetry of it.

Prince Mavrocordato and members of the Greek provisional government wanted to take Byron to be buried in Athens, on the hill of the Acropolis. But the English surgeon, Dr Meyers had said no, that he was an English Peer of the Realm, and so he should be brought back to England.

Lord Byron's coffin containing – *"the immortal poet and soldier of Liberty"* – had now been put aboard a ship, the *Florida,* and was returning to England accompanied by William Fletcher, Tita Falcieri, Lega Zambelli, and a guard of Greek soldiers.

"I am coming to England too," Pietro wrote, *"but on a different ship."* and then explained his reason for this was due to him being a Gamba, and he did not wish to cause any gossip or scandal due to Lord Byron's relationship with his sister Teresa. *"I will go to walk behind his body,"* Pietro wrote, *"but I shall remain a stranger to all but you, Signor Hobhouse."*

Reading the full letter *"tore my heart to pieces, and I*

broke down again," Hobhouse wrote in his diary. *"It showed the boundless and tender attachment of all about him to my dear, dear friend."*

He finally ventured out to call on Sir Francis Burdett and Douglas Kinnaird, who were both almost as badly and sadly affected by such unexpected and distressing news.

"What is most afflicting," said Hobby, "judging by what I read in Count Gamba's letter, is to think that with good care he might have recovered. To fancy that he *might* have been saved, and was not, doubles my regret ... I shall never forget this dreadful day."

Sir Francis Burdett took charge of all further necessary proceedings. "We cannot inform everyone, it would take too long. So I think we should now make our way, gentlemen, to the newspaper office, in time for tomorrow's front page."

"Which newspaper?" Kinnaird asked.

"Oh, *The Times*, of course," Sir Francis replied; and Hobhouse agreed. "It is the main newspaper that is read in *every* household and office. And this is something that the whole country would want to know, and will be shocked to know."

The news of Lord Byron's death at Missolonghi, as published on the front page of *The Times* electrified the people of Britain, and became the only subject of conversation.

All were absorbed in the dreadful sadness of it – as if not one had ever repeated with relish a scandalous tale which Lady Byron had spread about Byron in her whispered confidences to her female friends and legal agents.

And, as she scandalised Byron so terribly during the business of their Separation, not one person now called on her at her home at Kirby Mallory in Leicester to offer their condolences to her. Nor did the usual letters of sympathy, so normal at times like this, fill up her letterbox, which remained empty.

She was even ignored, or openly cut dead, by locals and neighbours she met in the street. She was excluded from the highest circles and ignored. She had happily stirred the scandalous wind which had sent her husband into exile, and now it was time for her to reap the whirlwind that had come gushing back on her.

The reaction against her was so strong, so virulent in its new hatred of the woman who had been the cause of all Byron's unhappiness and early death, by forcing him out of England in the first place, with all her whispered and dramatic scandals, caused Thomas Babbington Macaulay to feel duty-bound to introduce some truth and rationality into the subject of Lord and Lady Byron, in an item in the *Edinburgh Review*, which was also read throughout the country.

"He was the creature of his age; and whenever he had lived, he would have been the creature of his age. Under Charles I. he would have been more quaint than Donne. Under Charles II. the rants of his rhyming plays would have pitted it, boxed it, and galleried it, with those of any Bayes or Bilboa. Under George I. the smoothness of his versification, and the terseness of his expression, would have made Pope himself envious.

But then, Society, capricious in its indignation as it had been capricious in its fondness, flew into a rage with its wayward and petted darling. He had been worshipped with an irrational idolatry. He was persecuted with an irrational fury. Much has been written about those unhappy domestic occurrences, which decided the fate of his life. Yet nothing is, and nothing ever was, positively known to the public, but this, — that he quarrelled with his lady, and that she refused to live with him. There have been hints in abundance, and shrugs and shakings of the head, and "Well, well, we know," and "We could and if we would."

But we are not aware that there is before the world, substantiated by credible, or even by tangible evidence, a single fact indicating that Lord Byron was more to blame than any other man who is on bad terms with his wife.

The professional men whom Lady Byron consulted, were undoubtedly of the opinion that she ought not to live with her husband. But it is to be remembered that they formed that opinion without hearing both sides.

We do not say, we do not mean to insinuate, that Lady Byron was in any respect to blame. We think that those who condemn her on the evidence which is now before the public, are as rash as those who condemned her husband.

We will not pronounce any judgment; we cannot, even in our own minds, form any judgment on a transaction, which is so imperfectly known to us. It would have been well if, at the time of the separation, all those who knew as little about the matter then, as we know about it now, had shown the forbearance, which, under such circumstances, is but common justice.

We know no spectacle so ridiculous as the British public in one of its periodical fits of morality. In general, elopements, divorces, and family quarrels, pass with little notice. We read the scandal, talk about it for a day, and forget it.

But once in six or seven years, our virtue becomes outrageous. We cannot suffer the laws of religion and decency to be violated. We must make a stand against vice. We must teach libertines, that the English people appreciate the importance of domestic ties.

Accordingly, some unfortunate man, in no respect more depraved than hundreds whose offences have been treated with leniency, is singled out as an expiatory sacrifice.

If he has children, they are to be taken from him. If he has a profession, he is to be driven from it. He is cut by the higher orders, and hissed by the lower. He is, in truth, a sort of whipping-boy, by whose agonies, all the other transgressors of the same class are sufficiently chastised.

We reflect very complacently on our own severity, and compare with great pride the high standard of morals established in England, with the Parisian laxity. At length our anger is satiated. Our victim is ruined and heart-broken. And our virtue goes quietly to sleep for seven years more.

The case of Lord Byron was harder. First came the execution, then the investigation, and last of all, or rather not at all, the accusation.

The public, without knowing any thing whatever about the transactions in his family, flew into a violent passion with him, and proceeded to invent stories which might justify its anger. Ten or twenty different accounts of the separation, inconsistent with each other, with themselves, and with common sense, circulated at the same time.

What evidence there might be for any one of these, the virtuous people who repeated them neither knew nor cared. For in fact these stories were not the causes, but the effects of the public indignation. They resembled those loathsome slanders which Goldsmith, and other libellers of the same class, were in the habit of publishing about Bonaparte — how he poisoned a girl with arsenic when he was at the military school — Lord Byron fared in the same way.

His countrymen were in a bad humour with him. He had been guilty of the offence which, of all offences, is punished most severely; he had been over-praised; he had excited too warm an interest; and the public with its usual justice, chastised him for its own folly.

The obloquy which Byron had to endure, was such as might well have shaken a more constant mind. He was excluded from circles where he had lately been the observed of all observers. It is not every day that the savage envy of aspiring dunces is gratified by the agonies of such a spirit, and the degradation of such a famous name.

Two men have died within our recollection, who, at a time of life at which few people have completed their education, had raised themselves, each in his own department, to the height of glory. One of them died at Missolonghi."

PART ELEVEN

Greece's Hero

"Without Byron, there would have been no Navarone, and no Greek Independence."

Alexander Mavrocordato.

Chapter Fifty-Two

~ ~ ~

Other people may talk, and gossip and consider the event – but in her small house in Kentish Town in North London, when Mary Shelley heard of Byron's death, she let out a scream of disbelief and pain —

"Albè -- our dear, capricious, fascinating Albè has left this world! God grant that I may die young! I don't want to live in this empty desert."

Later, she consoled herself in the only way she knew how, by writing in her journal – "Life is the desert and the solitude -- how populous the grave -- and that region now adds the resplendent spirit of Byron, whose departure leaves this dull earth as dark as midnight."

And then, at last, she remembered Italy and Teresa, poor Teresa – that poor girl – still waiting – had anyone told her yet?

The Italian messenger who had been given the task of taking Pietro's message to Teresa in Filetto, was trembling with dread, and whipped off his hat nervously when a maid opened the front door.

He was about to give her the message, which he had been entrusted to give verbally to Teresa, with orders that he should "speak gently" and he attempted to do so – until the young Contessa herself followed the maid to the door, her expression curious.

As soon as the Contessa heard the words that Byron had died in Greece, she swiftly turned her head away to the side, as if not wishing to hear anything more, and the maid, in a fluster, shut the door in his face.

Dark, dark, darkness, all hope gone, all love gone, never to love in such a way again, no consolation, none at all ...

Until Teresa received a kind letter from one who had also suffered as she was suffering now.

My dear Teresa.

How shall I write to you? How shall I express to you the immense grief that is breaking my heart? Poor Teresa! So there we are, already sisters in misfortune! I am afraid that my letter will only double your sorrow, and I am all too aware that I cannot give you any consolation. How can I tell you that peace will come back to your heart once the woe of bereavement has healed – when I have the proof within myself that these wounds are quite beyond curing by time? – because we feel more and more, how worthless the world is, when we have lost the object of our love.

Did not dear Byron himself say, and he knew a woman's heart to its very depths, that the whole of a woman's existence depends on love, and that when you lose the one you love, there is no other refuge than to love again – "to love again, and be again undone ...?"

But, my dear Teresa, we are bereft of that sole refuge. Destiny has given the two of us the leading minds of this age. When they are lost, to have a second love (to love for the second time) is not possible – and our hearts, forever widowed, are (will be) henceforward, no more than memorials testifying to the happiness that lies buried with them.

Alas! so I shall never see the handsomest of men again! – the glorious creature who was the pride of the world. So I shall never hear his voice again, never read any new poetry of his, the daughter of his genius, which was beyond compare (had no equal).

Perhaps I ought not to relieve my feelings in this

way, and to make you shed tears, now that my eyes are sore with weeping. But when I lost the beloved other half of myself, nothing gave me relief but hearing his praises sung. I fed on them. And it seems to me that you too will be glad to hear the echo of your crying in a friend of Byron's who is voicing her distress.

I would like to be at your side, my dear Contessina. We would talk together about Byron, so deeply loved; we would speak of (bring to mind) the time we spent together, our outings, when he came to meet us in the splendour of his beauty; our conversations would be endless.

But have courage, since it appears that Nature has a new law, and will make us all die young – courage, then! because for us the unknown road of death has been trodden by our nearest and dearest; and when we make that same journey, and arrive in a land beyond our ken, those whom we love are there already, and will hasten to bid us welcome. Dying for us will not be a separation from the good things of life, but recovering the treasure that death has seized from us for a while.

Yours, dear Teresa,
Mary Shelley

The letters between the two friends went on continuously, writing to each other almost every day.

Although Teresa was aware that if Byron had been able to read Mary's letters, he would consider her to be a real "*Job's comforter*" – but Teresa did not want anyone telling her to "cheer up" – No, she wanted someone to share in her memories and her grief, and Mary Shelley did that, all too well.

In England, poor old Fletcher could have done with some eloquent help with words from Mary Shelley, for he was constantly being asked by everyone, what were Byron's "last words?"

And as Fletcher had not heard one word of what Byron had actually said at the time; he was now forced to make up whatever words he thought would please the questioner.

To Lady Byron, he responded to her note saying that his lordship's last words had been – "*My wife, my child, my country!*"

To Byron's sister, Augusta Leigh, he told her that his lordship's last words had been, "*My sister! My poor dear sister!*"

And so it went on, with Fletcher making everyone happier to know *they* were last person Byron spoke of in his last moments – all except John Cam Hobhouse, who did not believe a word of it; because he had already heard from Pietro Gamba what Byron's last whispered words to him had been –

"*I am leaving behind me those I love and someone very special. Pray beg her forgiveness, and kiss her eyes for me ... mia carissima Teresa.*"

~ ~ ~

AFTERWARDS

Pietro Gamba – carried all of Byron's personal papers to England and gave them into the care of John Hobhouse, who was Byron's executor. On leaving England, Pietro returned to Missolonghi where he rejoined the fight for Greek Independence, and where two years later he died of typhus fever, at the age of 25.

William Fletcher – gave up his role as a valet after Byron's death, and, in partnership with Lega Zambelli, the two men opened their own small Macaroni factory in London, importing and selling Italian macaroni to the English.

Giovanni Battista Falcieri – (**Tita**) – Also returned to the war in Greece, where he met and was employed by Benjamin Disraeli, a fanatical devotee of Byron the man and Byron the poet; and who later became the Prime Minister of Great Britain. Tita returned with Benjamin Disraeli to Buckinghamshire, where he married the maid of Mrs Isaac Disraeli, and became a cherished member of the household. Tita's portrait still hangs today in the Disraeli home at Hugehendon Manor in Buckinghamshire, which is now owned by the National Trust.

William Parry – left Greece and returned to England a few months later, where he faithfully described the last days and hours of Lord Byron's life in the house at Missolonghi; and then rapidly drank himself to death on Gin Swizzles and Old Jamaica Rum.

Percy Bysshe Shelley – It was not until some eighty years after his death that Shelley's poetry was discovered by students at Oxford University, which led to Shelley's amazing posthumous fame; and he became then – as he still is now – recognised in England as one of the great poets of the Romantic Movement.

Mary Shelley – lived her life devoted to the memory of her husband. She had numerous offers of marriage, but refused them. She earned a meagre living from her writing, on which she brought up her son, Percy Florence Shelley. When Shelley's first son from his first marriage died young, Mary's son, Percy Florence, inherited all of his grandfather's wealth and property, including ownership of Goring Castle, and the title of a baronet.

John Cam Hobhouse – remained devastated by the death of his friend Lord Byron for many years, and devoted his life to "protecting Byron's fame". Yet six months after Byron's funeral, (perhaps due to shock and loneliness) Hobhouse made an offer of marriage to Lady Julia Hay, a young woman he barely knew. They married and had three daughters, but Hobby's "dear Julia" died seven years after their marriage, leaving him to bring up their three young girls on his own.

Hobhouse became a formidable politician in the House of Commons, constantly fighting on behalf of the poor, and the abolishment of child labour. He was later given a knighthood, and then was elevated to the House of Lords and ennobled with the title of *Lord Brougham*.

Teresa Gamba (Guiccioli) – six years after Byron's death, Teresa finally set out on a pilgrimage to England to visit Byron's ancestral home of Newstead Abbey in Nottinghamshire, and then to the church at nearby Hucknall where his coffin had been laid inside the Byron vault, next to that of his mother.

The sexton of the church took Teresa to the side-alter and showed her the large slab of stone of the floor which lay above the exact position of Byron's coffin in the vault beneath.

Unaware of the passion of Italians, Teresa shocked the sexton by silently laying face-down on the stone slab above Byron's coffin, and did not move from there for over an hour. Her memories of her years with Byron became the dominant force of her life.

Greece and Byron – Lord Byron's efforts and death in Greece inspired volunteers from countries all over Europe and even America flocking to Greece to join the fight for freedom, resulting in the victory of Greece's independence from the rule of the Ottoman Empire in 1829.

Although the name of Byron has long been cherished in Greece, with statues and memorials to him still to be seen in various parts of the country, it was not until this century – in 2008 – that the Greek Government decided to honour Byron with "a day of his own" by adding a new feature to the modern Greek calendar, which was ratified by the Greek Parliament – announcing that henceforth, the day of *19th April* in every year – the date on which Lord Byron had died in Greece – would become a National Bank Holiday and known as *"Byron's Day"* in honour of their own fallen hero and soldier of liberty.

Inaugurating 'Byron Day' in Parliament, the Greek government said that the initiative would burnish the memory "of a man who believed deeply in democratic values "

Readings of literature, drama, poetry and school outings were recommended as events on Byron's Day to celebrate the role of the poet.

Newstead Abbey, Nottinghamshire – Lord Byron's former home, before his marriage, is a Grade I Listed building and is a treasure now owned by the Council of Nottingham. It contains many of Lord Byron's personal possessions, and every year it is still visited by thousands of visitors from all corners of the world.

Ada Byron Lovelace (Byron's Daughter) – Ada was not allowed to know anything about her father, or have anything to do with literature or poetry, being educated at home by private tutors when she developed her own love and genius for the magic of mathematics. This later led to her working for some years under the tuition of Charles Babbage, the inventor of the first computer.

Ada had her own ideas and configurations about the possibilities of computers, and sought financial patronage to develop them, but her hypothesis were rejected by all without a glance, simply because she was merely a young female and so was not taken seriously.

Her dreams of great strides in computer science dashed, she married the man she loved, Lord Lovelace, and gave birth to three children.,

Persuaded by her husband, Ada finally travelled with him out to Newstead Abbey, still owned by Byron's schoolfriend, Thomas Wildman, who had collected many of Byron's possessions and letters.

Here, Ada was able to stand in Byron's bedroom, restored to how it had looked when he had lived there as a boy and young man, gazing out on the lake and the peaceful scenery all around.

Here, Ada must have wondered how the poet could have married such a difficult and quarrelsome woman as her mother – a woman who had controlled and dominated her younger life, and to whom she was no longer on speaking terms.

Ada spent a lot of time at Newstead Abbey, reading every word of her father's poetry and his letters to friends and his publisher, and in this way she came to know him, and to love him. – and to form her own opinions on his marriage to her mother.

This drew a letter from Lady Byron, so blatant in its dishonest attempts at self-righteousness and self-justification, even Ada was not swayed by it.

"If the Mythic idea generally entertained of your father affords you satisfaction, do not forget, dearest Ada, how much of it is owing to my own line of conduct ... I was his best friend, not only in feeling, but in fact.

It often occurs to me that my attempts to influence your Children, will be frustrated and turned to mischief if they are allowed to adopt the unfounded popular notion of my having abandoned my husband from want of devotedness and sympathy – But from the whole tenor of my conduct towards you and Lovelace you must be convinced of my repugnance of anything like self-justification."

But the estrangement between Ada and her mother continued, until Ada was diagnosed with cancer, and she died at the same young age as her father – 36.

Her last will and testament left instructions that as she had not been allowed to know her father in life, she would rest with him forever in eternity; and so she was buried inside the Byron Vault at the church at Hucknall in Nottinghamshire, beside her father, George Gordon Lord Byron.

Yet Lord Byron's daughter – Ada Lovelace – is still with us today, every time we open and use our computers.

More than a hundred years after her death, in 1950, when all advances in computer science had come to a standstill, a lock-box of some of Ada's possessions were opened, and inside it were found all her mathematical notebooks containing her concepts and programme for the first-ever computer algorithms which she had written in 1843, and which today forms the grounding of all we do with computers.

So much of what Ada wrote in 1843 resembles the template of writing computer software today. The computer language used by the United States Military and Department of Defense is named ADA in honour of Ada Lovelace, and the Department of Defense's Military standard for the language, MIL-STD-1815 – was given the number of 1815 due to being the year of Ada's birth.

Gretta Curran Browne

To Lord Byron from his Friends

~

What was the charm that bound us all?
    What was the magic of thy spell?
What pleasing traits does time recall
    To make and mourn our fond farewell?

Was it the whirl of fashion's pool
    That drew us in and dragged us down
Companions of each airy fool
    That swims the bubble of the town?

Not so – to us who knew thy soul
    In all the turns of fortune tried,
Still pointing towards the only pole,
    Unvaried by distress or pride –

To us – who more have felt and seen
    Than hate or admiration can –
Who long have stood within the screen
    That veils the poet from the man –

To us whom not one feverish year
    Of fondness closed, alas, in strife –
But all the scenes of youth endear
    With hopes of friendship fixed for life –

To us each feature nobly bold
    Thy pencil drew – each speaking line –
Served but to show our hearts foretold
    That fame which surely would be thine –

And hence though all who love the Muse
    To thee their lingering looks shall bend,
Tis we lament – tis we that lose
    The warm companion and the friend.

We lose that voice of candid praise,
   That feeling sympathy of tone,
And all the courteous winning ways
   That made each heart at once thine own.

We lose that converse keen yet kind
   That polished playfulness and ease
That speaks to every liberal mind
   And please all whom wit can please.

To us thy parting steps announce
   That misery worse than all relief,
Which bids us break the chain at once
   And find our fondness in our grief.

The World's Byron was not the Byron of his friends. They knew he was neither demon nor angel. They saw his fame as something that he and they brushed aside in the ordinary associations of friendship.

They knew his generosity and kindness, his dark moods, his wit and humour. After his death they fought fiercely in his defence against any detractors who tried to raise themselves up by talking him down.

Thomas Moore was always vehement in his defence of Byron, John Hobhouse's slap-downs were lethal. The publishing house of John Murray cherished his name. And all remembered that final line of advice which Byron always gave to his friends – *"Go on and prosper."*

And most did so.

The day will come when democracy will remember all that it owes to Byron. England, too, will, I hope, one day remember the mission which Byron fulfilled on the Continent; the European *rôle* given by him to English literature, and the appreciation and sympathy for England which he awakened amongst us.

Before he came, all that was known of English literature was the French translation of Shakespeare. It is since Byron that we Continentalists have learned to study Shakespeare and many other English writers. From him dates the sympathy of all the true-hearted amongst us for this land of liberty, whose true vocation he so worthily represented amongst the oppressed. He led the genius of Britain on a pilgrimage throughout all Europe.

England will one day feel how ill it is — not for Byron, but for herself — that the foreigner who lands upon her shores should search in vain for that temple which should be her national Pantheon, for the poet beloved and admired by all the nations of Europe, and on news of his death Greece and Italy wept, as if it had been that of the noblest of their own sons.

Giuseppe Mazzini

Thank you

Thank you for reading *'No Moon At Midnight'* the final book in the Lord Byron Series. I hope you enjoyed it.

Please be nice and leave a review.

*

I occasionally send out newsletters with details of new releases, or discount offers, or any other news I may have, although not so regularly to be intrusive, so if you wish to sign up to for my newsletters – go to my Website and click on the "Subscribe" Tab.

*

If you would like to follow me on **BookBub** go to:-
www.bookbub.com/profile/gretta-curran-browne
and click on the "*Follow*" button.

Many thanks,

Gretta

www.grettacurranbrowne.com

Also by Gretta Curran Browne

LORD BYRON SERIES

A STRANGE BEGINNING

A STRANGE WORLD

MAD, BAD, AND DELIGHTFUL TO KNOW

A RUNAWAY STAR

A MAN OF NO COUNTRY

ANOTHER KIND OF LIGHT

NO MOON AT MIDNIGHT

***

LIBERTY TRILOGY

TREAD SOFTLY ON MY DREAMS

FIRE ON THE HILL

A WORLD APART

***

MACQUARIE SERIES

BY EASTERN WINDOWS

THE FAR HORIZON

JARVISFIELD

THE WAYWARD SON

***

ALL BECAUSE OF HER
A Novel
(Originally published as GHOSTS IN SUNLIGHT)

RELATIVE STRANGERS
(Tie-in Novel to TV series)

ORDINARY DECENT CRIMINAL
(Novel of Film starring Oscar-winner, Kevin Spacey)

www.ingramcontent.com/pod-product-compliance
Lightning Source LLC
Chambersburg PA
CBHW072007180726
48291CB00001BA/171